Also by Janet Fitch

White Oleander

Paint It Black

a novel

Janet Fitch

LITTLE, BROWN AND COMPANY

LARGE PRINT

Little, Brown and Company
Hachette Book Group USA
1271 Avenue of the Americas, New York, NY 10020
Visit our Web site at
www.HachetteBookGroupUSA.com

First Large Print Edition: September 2006

This Large Print Edition published in accord with the standards of the N.A.V.H.

ISBN 0-316-01771-X / 978-0-316-01771-8

10   9   8   7   6   5   4   3   2   1

Q-FF

Printed in the United States of America

To Alma

I see a red door and I want it painted black,
No colors anymore I want them to turn
black . . .

"Paint It Black," The Rolling Stones

Paint It Black

1
Echo

Cold numbed the tip of Josie Tyrell's nose and her ass, just outside the reach of the studio space heater. Her leg had fallen asleep. She twisted her slight torso, enough to release tension, but not enough to disturb the painter working across the room in his paint-spotted Mao suit, his hair in a waist-length braid. Henry Ko wasn't painting well today. He had to stop every few minutes to wipe his eyes on the back of his hand, while *Double Fantasy* circled around on the studio stereo. Everyone was playing it now. John Lennon had just been shot in New York, and wherever Josie went, people were playing the same fucking Beatles songs until you wanted to throw up. At least *Double Fantasy* had Yoko Ono.

On the cover that leaned against the dirty couch, John and Yoko pressed together for a kiss they would never finish. People were always trashing Yoko Ono, blaming her for breaking up the Beatles, but Josie knew they were just jealous that John preferred Yoko to some bloated megaband. Nobody ever really loved a lover. Because love was a private party, and nobody got on the guest list. She liked the pictures of Yoko and John in their white bed, their frizzy hippie hair. They'd retreated to the country with two passports only. From the outside it looked like death. People could pound the walls all they wanted, but they'd never find the door. Nobody could guess at the gardens inside.

Out the long windows of Henry Ko's studio, the hills and shacks of Echo Park tumbled toward Sunset Boulevard like a child's bedspread scattered with toys. Bare winter jacarandas broke the view with their angular arms, round pods hanging from their branch wrists like castanets. Henry kept crying about John Lennon. Josie felt worse about Darby Crash. Darby had just killed himself in an act of desperate theater, a gesture swamped by the Beatle's death like a raft in the backwash of a battleship. But at least she'd known him, with his shyness, his broken-toothed smile. She'd hung with him at the Masque, at the Fuckhouse, and on Carondelet. He hadn't been a natural performer, he had to get wasted, cramming anything he could swallow into his mouth, then played shows so intense that they hurt you to watch, made you feel like a creepy voyeur. Darby just needed people to notice him, someone to care. All their friends had gone to the funeral, everybody but her. His death was so horribly unnecessary, such a stupid stunt, acted out by someone so sad and fucked up he would kill himself out of a need to be noticed. Josie thought it was repulsive to treat it like a party. And then the Beatle took it all away anyway.

"But he wanted it that way," Pen said. She'd covered it for *Puke* magazine, saying who'd been there, like it was an afterparty.

At least they'd known him. Whereas look at Henry. Getting all teary-eyed over John Lennon whom he'd never even met. Huge crowds converged last weekend in Griffith Park to mourn the lost Beatle. They didn't go, she and Pen and their friends, you could just tell it was going to be some overaged love-in, hippie beads and "Give Peace a Chance." When anybody could tell, nobody was ever going to give fucking peace a chance. Nobody was going back to Woodstock anytime soon.

But she was sure old Henry'd showed up with the other granolaheads, lit incense and rang finger cymbals and blew some pot, no doubt, in John's memory. *Om rama rama*. Did John Lennon really want all that? Was that what he was about? From what she'd heard, the guy'd had some wit and brains — did he really want to be the dead guy of the hour, like a melting centerpiece?

Finally, the artist stepped away from his easel, sighing. "What say, Jo-say. Pack it in?"

She unfurled her legs, felt the blood rush back, that tingle and burn, stretching fragile shoulders, their delicate bones clearly visible, small breasts with their dark nipples, the black triangle that contrasted with her unlikely bleached hair, the roots coming in dark. She put her clothes back on — a vintage dress she'd traded for a domino bracelet, torn leggings — and worked her feet into spike-heeled pumps from Goodwill. As Henry cleaned his brushes, she touched up her bloodred lipstick, then joined him on the couch, orange velvet edged in brown dirt. He rolled a joint, special dope he called "The Spider" — brown turds of buds his friends in Hawaii sent him. Old hippies got so into their pot. She didn't mind sharing, but you didn't have to make a cult out of it.

As they smoked, Henry went on about John Lennon, how he couldn't believe he was dead, like the guy was some fucking saint. "He'd finally found himself," he kept saying. "That cat had just finally worked it out."

She toked along with him, knee to knee, and thought about the guy who shot Lennon. Shot by *a desperate fan*. On the news, fans were always desperate. Got his signature and then shot him down. The saddest thing about it was that she wasn't more shocked. To Josie, it just seemed part of the way things were heading, Ronald Reagan, greedheads running everything. Killing John Lennon seemed like just mopping up. Thirty thousand people missing in El Salvador, those nuns, and everybody in America was worried about who shot JR.

She and Henry leaned back against the couch. The Spider, she had to admit, was major deluxe. Henry turned his head slowly, keeping it supported on the couch back, looking at her with his small pot-reddened eyes that always smiled, even if he was angry or sad. He smelled of some weird liniment he brewed himself for nursing his tai chi injuries, roots and licorice and some kind of bugs. He put his hand on her knee. "Josay, you still with that guy, that Harvard cat?"

His hand on her knee. Henry Ko was like thirty-five, what was she supposed to do with an old guy like that? "Michael. Yeah, we're still together." At least she hoped they were. Maybe he was back. In fact, he might be home right now, waiting for her. Suddenly, she had to go. She put her child-sized hand on top of the artist's turpentine-dry one. "But I'll let you know if we break up, Henry, I swear."

She drove back to Lemoyne in her rattly Ford Falcon, a powder blue relic with band stickers on the trunk — *X, Germs, Cramps.* It was normally a three-minute drive, but she hit a line of cars with their lights on. Why were they going so slow? Maybe another John Lennon thing. She honked, wove, and passed until she got to the front and saw it was a hearse. Mortified, she turned off onto a side street and stopped, redfaced. How was she supposed to know — a line of cars crawling along with their lights on?

Some days it felt like her sister Luanne had just dropped her off at MacArthur Park day before yesterday.

She drove the rest of the way under the speed limit, parked in front of her house, took the mail from her mailbox, and pulled the noose on the gate. Careful in her high heels, she descended the rickety steps to the little cabin behind. Nothing more than a shack, but they loved it back here, the giant birds-of-paradise netted with morning glories, so private they didn't need curtains. She opened the door, threw her key in the red bowl, and called out, "Hey, Michael?"

Silence. The empty chairs, the paintings, the wooden-bead curtain between the main room and the kitchen. The only sounds came in through the open window, that overlooked the steady traffic on the 2 and the 5. It had been five days since he'd stood there, in the kitchen doorway, beads pushed aside, grinding coffee with his brass Turkish grinder shaped like a tube. Telling her he was going away. She'd been getting dressed for a booking in Northridge. "I'm going up to Meredith's for a few days," he'd said. His mother was gone, off on tour in Uruguay or Paraguay and good fucking riddance.

She'd stopped in the hall, finishing her

lipstick, accurate even without a mirror. "What for?"

"It's a project I've been thinking about," he said, grinding. "I need time to concentrate." Casual, like it was nothing.

And she'd stared, trying to understand what he was really saying. They'd never been separated, not even when they fought. "Since when do I bother you when you're working?"

"I thought you'd be glad that I'm working at all," he said.

She was glad, but why would he think he had to leave?

He kept cranking the brass arm of the mill, standing in the kitchen doorway in his baggy jeans and bare feet with their long Greek toes. "I need the space, Josie. Try to understand."

"But you always painted fine here." It was true, the shack was small. It was hard for him to paint anything even the size of the blind Merediths. And his mother's house was standing there, empty, up on the hill. "What if I come with you?"

He set the grinder down then and put his arms around her, tight. Kissed her. "I'll be working. You know how I get. Trust me, it's better this way." She held on to him, her eyes closed, drinking in his smell, pine and moss and some peculiar chemistry of his own, that she craved the way an addict craved freebase. She could lick him like candy. He held her for the longest time, crushing her to him, his scratchy beard.

She missed him like fire. She threw the mail in the bowl on the orange footlocker where the phone sat silent. She'd called him twice already, but he hadn't answered — he'd never answered a phone as long as she'd known him. But if he didn't come home soon, she was going up there, she didn't care how much he needed his space. Screw that. Three days was one thing, but a week was a separation. She'd barely managed to stay away this long, doing her best to keep busy — book extra sittings, going with Pen to see the Weirdos at the Hong Kong Café, a party on Carondelet. Maybe it looked like she was living it up, but all she was doing was waiting for him. What was he painting that he couldn't paint here? Or was he just dumping her? "Hey, fuck him and his brother too," Pen had said when she'd worried aloud at the Weirdos show. "This is great, just like the old days. Carpe fucking diem."

It felt strange to be alone in the little house, in the tranquillity of the afternoon. This was the first time she'd ever lived alone. She straightened the pillows on the couch, looked through the mail, put on the Clash, *Sandinista!,* sat down and got up. She couldn't settle anywhere. The house seemed so empty, her presence didn't alter its emptiness. At home in Bakersfield, she'd shared a room with Luanne and Corrine, and on Carondelet, she'd lived with Pen and Shirley and Paul. Later in the Fuckhouse, it was half of punk Hollywood. Now she was alone, her only company the paintings and drawings he'd done, furniture they'd salvaged, collections they'd accumulated, toys and hats and flatirons. Without him, it took on the quality of a stage set where the actors hadn't yet come on. She sat on the blue couch and leafed through an art magazine. A man making paintings using smashed plates. They'd seen his show at the county art museum. She'd liked the big, heavy-textured works better than Michael had, their confidence, their bold beauty. "Shtick," he'd said. "Ya gotta have a gimmick." Always so critical, he hated everything artists were doing now. He only liked Francis Bacon and Lucien Freud, who painted like bloodhounds on the scent of human imperfection. And his beloved Schiele.

Why couldn't he sleep here and paint there? Other artists had studios. If it was too small for him, he could at least come home at night. She was afraid it was just an excuse. That he'd decided, finally, he didn't want to be with her anymore. She yearned to call him, but hated the sound of the phone ringing, ringing, knowing that he might be standing right there, not picking up, knowing it was her.

She sat in his chair by the window, overlooking the hills, Echo Park, Silverlake, and beyond: the Hollywood sign, Griffith Park. The observatory's green copper domes stood out perfectly clear against the pale blue winter sky. She loved to sit in this chair with him, her arms around his neck, drinking his smell. She pressed her face to the waffled coarseness of the chair back, trying to smell it, her eyelashes fluttering against the skin of her cheek. Catching then losing it.

Still stoned from the Spider, she shuffled back into the kitchen, drank a glass of milk standing up at the sink, peeled a finger-sized banana. She tried not to look at the wooden breakfast nook with its cutout hearts, where they ate their meals, and the painting that hung there, her at the old stove, light from the kitchen window pouring over her. When he was the one who did all the cooking. She couldn't do more than heat soup from a can.

She went into the bedroom and lay on the bed, the fragrant linens that still smelled of their last lovemaking, their painting of Montmartre on all the four walls. She kicked off her shoes and crawled under the covers, white on white in the colorless light. It was almost Christmas. She needed to finish making his shirt, with the stripes cut horizontally, to make it unusual. Green to match his eyes. Maybe she would find him some sheet music at one of those little places on Hollywood Boulevard, dirty Twenties blues, all *new jelly roll* and *cakewalking babies from home.* She could decorate the house in paper snowflakes, hang them from the ceiling, thick as leaves. How surprised he'd be when he came through the door and saw them. Of course he'd be back. Just another day or two.

She was thinking about snowflakes when the phone rang in the living room. Flinging herself out of bed so fast her head reeled, she got to the phone and grabbed it before the third ring. "Michael, thank God, I —"

"Excuse me, this is Inspector Brooks . . ."

Some government fuckhead.

"I'm from the Los Angeles County Coroner's Office. To whom am I speaking, please?"

Fuck. Luanne. The crank. The last time she'd

seen her sister, she'd been down to ninety pounds. Though it could be Jimmy. Tommy. Any of them. "This is Josephine Tyrell. What happened?"

"Your phone number was found on a motel registration. We're in the process of running fingerprints, but tell me, has there been someone missing?"

"I don't think so," she said.

She heard the shuffling of papers. "White male. Registered as Oscar Wilde."

All she heard was the roar of blood in her ears.

"Miss Tyrell?"

She could barely hold the phone. All the strength had gone out of her arms.

"Do you have any idea who this person might be?" said the voice on the other end, as if nothing had changed.

"Yes," she said. "No." She sat down on the furry couch before she fell. "I don't . . ."

"This person you're thinking of, how old is he?"

She searched for her voice. "Twenty-two."

"Height?"

"About six feet," she whispered.

"Weight?"

She didn't know his weight. They'd never had a scale. "Skinny."

"Eye color?"

"Green." Please, let him say brown.

"Scars or tattoos?"

She thought of his body. She ran her mind over it like fingers. "A scar, on his right hand. Between the thumb and first finger." She rubbed her face, trying not to drop the phone, trying to listen through the roaring static in her head. "A mole, on the right side of his rib cage." An artist's model, her body memory never failed. It worked independently of her mind, which had shut off. It couldn't be. This was a Tyrell call, speed contest, stabbing, shoot-out. An OD at the Fuckhouse.

There was a pause. "Is there someone who can come with you? We'll need to see you downtown."

Josie stood on the sidewalk holding herself together with both arms, as if her guts would spill out onto the concrete if she let go, watching for Pen's red Impala. Her friend slammed to a stop in front of the house, her purple hair a flag in that old convertible. She threw open the side door. "I got here as fast as I could. Oh, Josie, don't think anything yet. It could be anyone."

She was still closing the door as Pen peeled out. It was deep into rush hour. They skipped the freeway and took Riverside Drive, the back way along the river, past the Brewery where she'd just modeled for Tim Delauney the week before last. *Don't think anything. It could be anyone.* She hoped it fucking was. Anyone else.

Macy to Mission, the foot of the concrete mountain that was LA County General. The coroner's office wasn't up at the hospital, it was down at the bottom, with the trucks and light industrial, a boxy two-story government building, the lettering painted right on the side of the building, LOS ANGELES COUNTY DEPART-MENT OF CORONER, MEDICAL EXAMINER, FOREN-SIC LABORATORIES, PUBLIC SERVICES.

Pen left the Impala parked sideways across two spaces and they dashed into the foyer, all brown marble and beige linoleum and patched acoustic ceiling, like the lobby in a building full of cheap dentists. At the counter, a heavy black woman looked them up and down, Pen's purple hair and black lipstick, Josie's punked-out bleach job, her yellow fake fur. Like they were a sideshow act.

"I got a call," Josie said.

The woman just stared.

"From some Inspectorman —" Pen said.

"Brooks —" Josie said.

"Across the breezeway." The woman pointed to the twin building out the smudged glass doors. "I'll tell him you're here."

They waited on cloth chairs in a smaller lobby, Josie's hands crammed deep into the pockets of her coat, her whole being reduced to a pinpoint of fear, like the nucleus of an atom about to be split and blow up the world. She had no mind at all, just the tremor in her right foot that would not stop shaking.

"You're okay," Pen said, stroking her hair, her neck. "You're breathing, you're okay. What's taking this fucking creep so long anyway?" She got up, shook the locked knob, kicked the metal door with her Doc Marten, sat back down next to Josie.

"Light me a ciggie," Josie said, her hands in tight balls in her pockets. She could feel every hair follicle in her scalp.

Pen dug around in Josie's schoolbag purse, found her cigarettes, Gauloises Bleues, lit her one, put it between her lips. Josie forced smoke into her lungs, the cigarette helping her remember how to breathe. She removed a hand from her pocket to take it on exhaling. Her mind was a fist, no thought would enter, except *no no no.* It was the longest five minutes in history.

"You're going to be okay, you're going to get through," Pen said, lighting one of her own Camel straights, and their smoke filled the small waiting room. Outside the winter sky turned to rose. *If I finish this cigarette before the guy comes, it won't be Michael.*

"I hate places like this," Pen said. "I'd like to blow this place up."

They watched the heavy door into the hall, a little caged window. Before she was even halfway done with her cigarette, a black man in a blue blazer opened the door and stepped into the lobby. "Miss Tyrell?"

Josie stood up.

"Can you come with me? Both of you."

They walked down the hall, the fluorescent light bathing them in its weird green glow. Inspector Brooks's office was windowless, small, vomiting books, papers, folders, the walls covered with charts and a list on a blackboard, initials and magnets. They sat in two metal chairs, and he took a seat at his desk. "Are you all right, Miss Tyrell?" he asked.

"No, she's not the fuck all right," Pen said.

"Can't you see she's practically puking? Can we get through this already?"

Josie lifted a shaking hand to her lips, toked on her cigarette. If he didn't like her smoking, he didn't say anything.

"When was the last time you saw your boyfriend, Miss Tyrell?"

She saw the standing ashtray, flicked ash into it, her upper lip stiff and bowed and frozen in its downturned U. "Five days ago. Wednesday."

"And when did you realize he was missing?"

Josie just stared at the lit tip of her cigarette. *How long was he missing?* She hadn't known he was missing at all. She had just let him go. "I didn't. I still don't."

The man pursed his full lips together and pulled out some white cardboard. "I'm going to have you look at some photographs," Inspector Brooks said. "I want to warn you, they're pretty disturbing. But it's important to know, for everyone."

White squares in his hands, the backs of two photographs, as he went on talking, talking, explaining about what she would see, the bullet entered the mouth and exited the back of the head, *effect of the gunshot wound* . . . She nodded, not listening. She wanted to rip those pictures out of his hands. Finally he laid them in front of her on the metal desk.

A face. Black eyes, like they'd been in a terrible fight. Swollen closed, though they weren't completely closed, God, they should have closed the eyes. Whoever's eyes they were. *Not his.* It couldn't be. She could only see a little of the hair, there was a sheet all around the head, and those black eyes, a slight rim of blood around the nostrils, the mouth, no, she didn't recognize him, it wasn't Michael, and yet, how could she be sure? *How could she know? He was alive the last time she saw him.* "I can't tell. I just don't know," she whispered.

The inspector gathered his Polaroids and put them aside with a folder, *John Doe.* "Does he have living parents?" Inspector Brooks asked.

"His father's Calvin Faraday, the writer. He lives in New York." Inspector Brooks wrote it on a legal pad, with the case number at the top, Michael's name and notes from their phone call. "His mother is Meredith Loewy." She spelled it for him. "She's in South America. On tour."

"Well, first let's see if it's him." He dialed his pea green phone. "Yes, we're ready," he said into the receiver, and stood up. Josie crushed her cigarette in the ashtray and they stood and walked back across the breezeway. She clung to Pen, using her like a Seeing Eye dog. All she could see was the image from the Polaroid, the black eyes, she hadn't even thought to look for the little scar on his upper lip. This wasn't real. Michael was alive. He was up at his mother's house, painting in the room off his childhood bedroom. She pictured him painting there in all the detail she could muster. The oaks outside the windows. The brightness of the winter sun. How they would laugh about this later. *Imagine, for a split second I thought you were dead.* If only she could see it clearly enough, it would be true.

Pen never let go of her hand, let her crush the hell out of it. She could smell the leather of Pen's jacket.

"Whatever this is, we'll get you the fuck through it," Pen said. "You hear me?"

Inspector Brooks came across from the other building, and let them through a doorway in the brown marble. They walked down a dirty hall, pinkish beige, the doors all had black kickmarks at the bottom. They came to an elevator, Inspector Brooks held it for them, got in and turned a key in the operating panel, the door shut and the elevator descended. Josie stared down at the streaky linoleum. *Please God. Let this not be happening.*

The doors opened, and right there, against the gray wall, against a busted water fountain, on a gurney, lay a human form under a white sheet. She held Pen's arm, or was Pen holding hers, and the smell was different from anything she had ever smelled before, dirty, like old meat, and Inspector Brooks was saying, "He's not going to look like they do in the funeral home, they've cleaned him up some but he's going to look like the photos, all right? I'm going to lower the sheet now."

He folded back the top of the sheet. The body lay wrapped in another one, a knot like a rose at the chest, the arms folded in, the head covered, there was blood on the sheet, *don't look at that, don't look, only the face.* The bruised eyes, bruised mouth, lips dark as if he'd been drinking ink, the dark stubble, the handsome eyebrows, the eyelashes, *his eyes were not closed.* She slipped hard to her knees. The Inspector and Pen caught her but not in time. "His eyes . . ." The most diabolical thing she had ever seen. She threw up, on her coat, on her knees, on the floor. *A project I've been thinking about. Some time to concentrate.*

They picked her up and helped her into a chair. She sat with her head between her knees. Pen crouched next to her, holding her, vomit all over. *His body.* She was shaking, she couldn't stop. *His body, goddamn him! HIS BODY!* Inspector Brooks was covering him again, she got up and yanked down the sheet and laid her face against his sweet horrible one, then recoiled. It was hard, cold. A thing. He'd turned himself into a thing. A goddamn thing. "MICHAEL, YOU FUCK, YOU STUPID GODDAMN FUCK!" she was screaming into his face, but it didn't change. He didn't wake up. He just lay there with his black eyes and the whites showing, and Inspector Brooks covered him up, his hand dark and alive against the sheet.

"Let's go." Pen threw her arm around Josie's shoulder. Brooks held open the elevator, and a brawny man with a beard brought a mop, and then they were going up again. Through the pink hall.

He indicated the bench in the brown lobby. "Please." And then they were on it, she just sat next to Pen, shaking, her teeth chattering, trying to breathe. "Is there anything you'd like to know, Miss Tyrell?"

How could she make this not be happening? How could she turn this movie off?

"What happens now?" Pen said.

"We'll be notifying the parents, they'll make the arrangements, I'm sure they'll let Miss Tyrell know what they've decided."

Pen snorted. "Oh yeah, sure, they'll be right on the phone. Don't be a dick."

"I'll call then, when I know anything, all right?" he said, crouching, putting his living hand on Josie's. She wanted to kick him. She wanted to punch his fucking face in. She hated him for being warm when Michael was hard as wood, wrapped in a sheet. "Anything I find out, I'll call you, Miss Tyrell, I promise. I'm sure it won't be long."

What won't be long? What was he talking about?

"Where'd you find him?" Pen asked.

"In a motel. Out in Twentynine Palms. Believe me when I say how sorry I am you have to go through this, Miss Tyrell."

Michael, in a motel in Twentynine Palms, a gun in his hands. Not at Meredith's, painting in an explosion of new creation. Not over on Sunset, digging through the record bins, or at Launderland separating the darks and lights. Not at the Chinese market, looking at the fish with their still-bright eyes. Not at the Vista watching an old movie. Not sketching down at Echo Park. He was in a motel room in Twentynine Palms, putting a bullet in his brain.

"Let's go home," Pen said.

He didn't even drive, how could he have gotten out to Twentynine Palms? None of it made any sense. It didn't make sense. *Where did he get a gun?* She didn't want to go home. Where could home be now, with Michael here in the basement, tied into a white sheet that was seeping blood? There was no home, only that body, the lips like black leather, dark smudge of beard shading his jaw, dark circles around his eyes against the drained yellow wax of his skin. Though somewhere in Twentynine Palms was a motel room splattered in the most precious scarlet. Suddenly, she wanted to go there, to be the one to clean it. Unthinkable that a stranger, some poor woman with a bucket, would look at his blood and think, *Christ, that's never coming out.* Having no idea this had been Michael Faraday, no idea just what had died in that stinking motel room, bleeding to death onto the moldy shag.

She drew her knees up inside her coat and lay on the bench, shaking, she couldn't stop. Her head on her red schoolbag purse, she fought the urge to vomit again. She hid her face in the furry collar of her coat. *Registered as Oscar Wilde.* She wanted to wake up like Dorothy and see Michael's face peering over the side of the bed, laughing. *Why, you just hit your head.* But it was no dream and there was no Kansas and he was never coming back.

PAINT IT BLACK 25

2

Pool

She awoke on the blue couch, in a shadow-filled room lit by a single lamp, wrapped in a granny-square afghan. At the other end of the long couch, Pen lay passed out, snoring drily. Josie blinked, trying to remember, why was she sleeping in the living room? And what was Pen doing here? She sat up on one elbow. The lights from the stereo gleamed, and the lamp reflected harshly in the darkness of the uncurtained windows. Iggy was playing on KROQ. Iggy wanted to be her dog. Bow wow wow. She rubbed her face, rubbery, cold, and reached for a ciggie. As she lit it with her father's Ronson, it hit her, real as rain. Pen, sleeping on the end of the couch, the dials, the ashtray, the voddy.

No, that was wrong. He was at his mother's. A bad dream. He was up at Meredith's, painting, he was coming home soon, he said he would be. He would walk right through that door. And she'd tell him, *They thought you were dead* . . .

But he wasn't coming. He wasn't up at his mother's. He'd gone to Twentynine Palms and shot himself in the head.

She closed her eyes, pressed her forearm across them. In her head, a line repeated. *Never and never* . . . A line from some poem. *Never and never in the* something something . . . What was that? Michael would know. Michael would know, but he was dead.

Fuck fuck fuck fuck.

He was just here. He was coming back. But he wasn't. *You asshole. You asshole! You stupid goddamn fuck!*

The clock on the piano read 3:10. The world had changed but she couldn't feel it. He was dead but she just couldn't get it. After a couple of Percocets, she should have been out like road-kill, like Pen, but she was awake in the middle of the night and Michael was never coming through that door again.

She lay on the couch, smoking her Gauloise, the cigarettes he smoked. *The smell of Paris.* They were going to go to Paris . . . But no, they weren't. *You goddamn stupid motherfucker.* What did he think he was doing? What was on his fucking mind? *Here, here's my dark world. You carry it for a change. I'm out.*

She sat up, rubbed her face, gazed out the uncurtained windows, lights glowing in the hills. Cars trickled by on the 5 and the 2. Iggy wanted to be her dog, and Michael was out there lying on a rack cold as meat. She tried not to think about the way his face looked, but her mind kept looping back around to it, like a piece of paper he once showed her that looped around to where you began. *What the hell, Michael? What did you think you were doing?*

Against the wall, his piano waited, keyboard open, for him to come and play it. She could see him sitting right there, playing his Twenties blues, Big Bill Broonzy, Lucille Bogan . . . *Tricks ain't walkin', tricks ain't walkin' no more.* Showing off that rolling blues style. And the way they danced. Sun filtering through the eucalyptus. Naked except for her orange kimono. His hard-on knocking against her. *And I've got to make my livin', don't care where I go . . .*

Her lungs closed around the air hard, like fingers slammed in a car door. *Goddamn you, Michael, goddamn you to hell.* She reached for the Stoli, unscrewed the cap and took a great swallow, set the bottle on the floor so she could reach it easily. Pen was snoring with her mouth open. Josie could see her fillings. *Say, Blaise, are we very far from Montmartre?*

He'd thrown Montmartre away, Blaise and little Jeanne, everything, just like that. As if his life was a drawing that didn't turn out right. *But you can't start again, Michael. There was only that one.*

Suddenly she thought, what if he'd been murdered? What if it wasn't what it seemed?

But she knew it wasn't murder. Knew the second she saw him. He just threw her away. Everything they had been, could have been. *For she is my love, and other women are but big bodies of flame.* Who in the world would have thought of her like that? When was the last time someone thought, *I know what Josie will like. A book. Yeah! A poem, by a dead Frenchman.* Who else in the history of the world? When most people looked at Josie Tyrell, they only saw a certain collection of bones, a selection of forms filling space. But Michael saw past the mouth and the eyes, the architecture of the body, her fleshly masquerade. Other boys were happy enough to enjoy the show, they just wanted to be entertained in the body's shadow theater. But Michael had to come backstage. He went down into the mines, into the dark, and brought up the gold, your new self, a better self. But what good was it if he was just going to leave her behind?

She took another drink from the Stoli, let it burn all the way down. She wanted it to burn more, she wished it was hot wax, boiling oil, gasoline, she could drink it down, let it burn out her guts, then it would feel real. He'd always seen her. The only one. With those eyes the color of aquarium glass seen sideways. That day she'd lingered behind in the Otis drawing studio. The students filtering out, but she'd waited, lighting a cigarette, so he could catch up with her, the boy in the tweed jacket with the glass green eyes. He'd brought her a Danish from Victor Benes. Of all things. Not the usual boyish gifts, a hemp necklace, a seedy joint, a ticket to a free concert. A fancy cheese Danish stuffed with white raisins. Even then, sensing her hunger.

They'd walked out onto the street together, where a silver-gray Jaguar waited across the street, a dark-haired woman at the wheel. A rich lover, she'd assumed. Though it was mostly gay boys who had them. She'd put on her dark glasses, so he wouldn't see how intimidated she felt. And he'd hung back, embarrassed, waiting for her to leave first, so she wouldn't see him get into that car.

Josie gazed at the painting hanging opposite the couch, the one he called *Civilization and Its Discontents.* Blind women climbed the white stairs through a ruined city in moonlight, carrying fruit and lizards in their arms, books and babies and the head of Sigmund Freud. And their faces all were Meredith's. Josie leaned over and dug through Pen's purse to see if she had any more Percocets, but they'd done the last of them.

On the footlocker next to Pen's bag lay the bowl of mail. *Michael Faraday, Michael Faraday, Mr. Michael Faradaz.* Junk mail, an *Art News.* A package from France, special gum erasers, and a kind of pastels he liked that you could only get in a certain shop in Paris. When they'd sent them, he was alive. *Why'd you have to buy these fucking erasers if you were just going to kill yourself, Michael?* Another girl would open it, but not Josie. She never went through his things. It was part of the way she loved him. She let him have his secrets.

You stupid fuck. You ignorant fucking twat.

She let her eyes wander the bowed book-cases, stuffed with paperbacks white with wear, old books of pebbly leather, crumbly calfskin embossed in gold. Books from his mother's house, books that had followed him home like stray dogs. Michael couldn't pass a hippie with three books on a blanket without rescuing one. *Crime and Punishment for twenty-five cents? Can you believe that?* And on the top shelf, the line of black journals, which she had never read.

She could read them now. But what would she find there, except discovering what a bitch she'd been, an idiot, stupid fucking moron? Things she should have known, that could have saved him. *Should have, could have.* She should have read them, should have read them all along.

But that was never the deal. When you started spying on someone, where did you stop? Read his mail, cross-examine him, follow him around? Sleep across the doorstep? She trusted him, trusting that it would all turn out in the end. She had to. He would have hated her if she hadn't, he would have left her long ago.

Through the spongy murk of voddy and the remnants of the pills, dread fattened inside her like a thick black snake. It grew, crowding her guts. She drank down the rest of the voddy to see if she could burn it back. It shrank enough to let her breathe. She stood and stumbled as far as the dining table, where she sat down heavily. She turned on the lamp, the rice-paper shade Michael had decorated with Chinese figures. Harmony. Peace. *Tao. Ming. Ming* meant destiny. It was shaped like hair with a part in the middle, a line for a forehead wrinkle, two square eyes and a nose. *Ming* also meant death. It never occurred to her to ask, what was *ming* doing in there, along with peace and virtue? So many things she hadn't asked when she had the chance. Afraid to. Who was the blind woman here?

She pulled out one of his sketchpads and spread it on the scarred tabletop. *Life Drawing. Michael Faraday.* His mother's address on Via Paloma, the old phone number. She touched the writing. Vertical, regular, the *e*'s like *3*'s. Backward-flipped *d*'s, the *g*'s like *8*'s. Down-crossed *t*'s. *Never and never* . . . No more of that handwriting. No more of the waves in air that made his voice, the sound of his laughter.

Pen moaned in her sleep and turned over, the ass of her tights stretched tight over red panties. "Oh for fuck's sake," she mumbled and then after a moment the snoring started again. *Vista del Mar.* Josie opened the smudged yellow of the sketchpad cover.

Contour drawings. That spontaneous line. It was already there, the liveliness of the forms. The proportions already good, the bodies had weight, the gestures vitality and direction. Just a beginner, but he learned so fast. Everything came so damn easy to him.

Not true.

The hard things came easy. But the easy things he found impossibly hard.

She touched her fingertips to the black charcoal fingermarks on the page. His long fingers nearly twice the length of his palm. Those beautiful hands. Christ. She wished she could feel them right now, on her naked body. It was the only thing that ever made her feel better. He always knew how to make her feel better. When he wanted to. *Fuck you, Michael, you son of a bitch.* On her own now. All alone.

Focusing on the pages, turning them carefully, not to tear the yellowing paper, she watched his

progress through Introduction to Life Drawing. She recognized most of the models — Frank the dwarf, all chunky defiance, his huge cock — Michael had seen him as mythological, menacing as a figure in a dream. Colleen Keen with her long legs and wide hips, like a drip of water. Marguerite's stupid modern-dance poses. Funny. And Pen.

She didn't realize he'd had Pen. She glanced over at her friend, skirt bunched up over her ass, face burrowed into the couch back, breath coming ragged. On the page she was all bristly imperiousness, hand on hip, weight on one foot, impatient. Even her pubic hair looked aggressive. What did it mean, that the two people she loved best in the world hated each other? It was the sides of herself, irreconcilable.

Finally, Josie herself. The curve of her back, the delicately articulated bones. Her somber face over the small shoulder. His poet's lady, his silver lily.

A sudden image gored her, like a vicious animal she'd caught, not knowing how powerful it would be. Michael once told her about his famous father going boar hunting in Hawaii. "They have to weld a brace across the spear, to keep it from mauling you." But she wanted to be mauled. She let it run right up the spear, sink its yellow tusks into her flesh.

A day hot and so smoggy you needed a snorkel. He'd caught up to her after class, asked if she wanted to go swimming. "But we'll have to take the bus," he said. "I don't have a car." He didn't want to be controlled by a machine, he explained, but she just figured he couldn't afford one. So she drove, up Vermont past the auto-body places, the punk shops and cafés. She still could remember, she'd had Patti Smith on the tape deck. The song was "Frederick," and she had thought, *If Patti can be in love, anything's possible.*

A park grew in the center of the street above Los Feliz, planted with enormous magnolias, roots snakily intertwined. Houses big as hotels sitting back on giant lawns. When he'd pointed out the turn, she'd had the strongest impulse to take that long finger in her mouth. But she didn't. She didn't know him that well yet.

The steep road turned and forked, she lost track, *Vistas* and *Coronas* and *Villas,* until he finally told her to park in the shade of an immense wall. Messy pittosporums and orange trees littered the sidewalk, and a fancy iron gate barred the way. He smiled then. That was when she fell in love, right then, as he lifted the chain and opened the gate. Showing her it wasn't really locked, just wound around to look that way. He was a boy who knew things, things that looked one way but proved to be another.

In a lot of ways.

No, she would not think about that. *Now* was too big, like a giant dark planet coming up over the horizon. She wanted *then*. The coolness of the overgrown trees outside the Spanish house, moss mottling its thick walls and painting the red tile roof with chartreuse velvet. How she took his arm not to twist her ankle in her high heels. "Whose house is this?"

"Some people I know." The soft voice that made you want to put your ear to his mouth. The sweet smell of his breath. She followed him around the back of the house, an enormous place, uncared for, unpruned white rambling roses climbing high into the trees, the footing treacherous with slick leaves, thinking, *Rich people should take better care of their homes.*

Here it was, the pool. Stained dark, leaves scattered over the surface and dotting the none-too-clean bottom. Still and silent in the shade of the great trees. Certainly not the pool she'd envisioned — freeform, sparkling aquamarine in the sun. Not wanting to betray her disappointment, she'd unbuttoned her dress, stepped out of her underwear, and dove in like a girl in a movie. The shock of the cold. She came up gasping. He hadn't told her it was unheated.

Was he snickering at her, a real swell joke? But he'd seated himself at a green iron table littered with droppings, unpacking his charcoals, his pad. "Aren't you coming in?" she asked. "The water's *wonderful.*" If you were a polar bear.

"No thanks. I am not *sportif,*" he said.

That made her laugh. Boys always bragged about their sportiness, their prowess at things they couldn't do. They never admitted their deficiencies. "How *sportif* do you have to be to float in a pool?" He shook his head, and she dove under again, revealing a flash of ass — mooning him.

And here on the yellowed paper, her white shape took form under black water, blurry as a half-conscious thought. The uncertainty of the pale flesh rising to specifics of face and small breasts. The layers of darkness around her. That's what he'd seen that day, a brightness with darkness all around.

The snake in her gut coiled, flexed. She had to

stop looking and just breathe. Michael watching her, as if she were glamorous, as if she were a rare and mysterious creature. When all she'd been thinking that day was how quiet it was, after the constant noise and bickering at the Fuckhouse.

And he'd told her about the deaf-mutes. The people who lived there, a woman and her crippled son. Recluses. "She doesn't like him to mix with the world. I tutor him sometimes," he said, working charcoal over the surface of the large page.

"So where are they now?"

"At the hospital. The boy has a heart condition."

And a leaf came spinning out of the trees and landed in his dark cropped curls. Yellow. Why could she remember that, and he couldn't remember their whole life together, couldn't remember one damn thing?

And she'd asked, "What about his father?" Not realizing what caves were burrowed in every lapse.

"Dead," Michael had said. "He was epileptic, subject to rages. One day his brain just burst. The boy found him on the study floor, blood pouring out of his ears." He sketched, his hand

moving boldly across the pad, making these eucalyptuses, these pittosporums.

A sad house. She knew it even then.

"Want to see it? Come on. They won't mind."
He picked up his portfolio, and held out his own
hand. She hesitated, but could not resist, she had
never seen a house like this. He took her hand
and pulled her from the water in one swift
movement. He was so strong. She hadn't imagined that from looking at his tall, lanky, lazy
body. Behind him loomed the silent bulk of the
house, the brooding eyes of its windows. She
dried herself off with her dress before putting it
back on, slipped her feet into her shoes. He
found the key under the mat.

With its old-fashioned hexagonal black and
white tiles the big kitchen was a disappointment, a sink with the built-in washboard and a
faucet that came right out of the wall. Not at all
elegant. China piled up to the ceiling on sagging
shelves inside glass-fronted cabinets. The house
had an odd scent, like floor polish and cedar and
mothballs. In the dining room hung a chandelier, bagged in muslin like a cluster of bees suspended over a vast lake of table. A silver tea
service gathered dust on the sideboard, and she
remembered thinking, *Maybe cleanliness was*

just middle-class. How would she know, she grew up on a tow yard in Bakersfield.

The living room, down three steps. All that fragrant wood under enormous, worn-out Oriental rugs. At the end, a piano gleamed. Black and long as a pickup truck. "Which one plays?"

"They both do," Michael said. "They play music for four hands."

Deaf-mutes playing songs for four hands that neither of them could hear.

Under the sweep of stairs, a room paneled in dark red leather lay hidden. She had never seen anything like that. Like a womb. Against the walls, stretching from floor to ceiling, bookcases bore elegant leather-bound volumes. She pulled one out. It was filled with music, but not the way it was usually written, just single lines down the page — *2 Flöten, 2 Oboen, 2 Klarinetten in B.* Notes in the margins.

"The father's room," Michael said. "He died, right there on the rug."

Someone had died there, but not the father. The house was nothing but *ming,* with its great sweep of staircase, iron railed, floored in stone. She'd run her hand along the strange sponginess of the curved stucco wall, it was as if the house had grown there, like a fungus after rain. He'd opened the door at the head of the stairs, let her in first. "This is his room." The boy's.

It was decorated like the library of a monastery. No rug on the wooden floor, a trestle desk, a narrow iron cot guarded by a primitive painted Madonna and made up with a coarse gray blanket woven with a single red stripe. And books. All the books, tattered and whole, tall leather-bound ones and paperbacks, vertical and horizontal. "Lucky he's deaf and not blind," she'd said, teasing him. After all, how would a crippled boy climb all those stairs? But she understood, even lies could be true, if you knew how to listen.

They moved through the French doors into the crippled boy's studio. Where he was supposed to have been. *I need the space, Josie, try to understand.*

But she didn't understand. She didn't. Maybe it was the voddy and the Percocets and maybe she was just stupid but she didn't. Maybe she was blind and mute and deaf and falling in the darkness, but she didn't. He was finally working again, they were good again, it was good. He'd been so cheerful. He loved her, they were going to give it a chance. It was just going to be a few days.

She could see it so clearly, him in that studio, the windows opening onto trees through their rusty screens. His orderly worktable, cans full of brushes. That smell of turpentine and linseed oil, a canvas on the big easel, as it had been that day, when she'd tried to peek under but he stopped her, smoothing the tarp. "He's an artist too, the deaf boy?"

"He'd like to be," Michael said, turning his back to her. "But he hasn't the confidence. He's afraid he'll never be great."

Try to understand.

"Does it matter so much?"

He straightened the charcoal twigs that were already straight. "It's the only thing he's really suited for." Flicked the tip of a brush in the coffee can, running his thumb over the clean bristles. "If he can't do that, then why exist."

"As long as he likes to do it, what difference does it make? He's just got to do it, and fuck what people think," she said. "Otherwise it'll get all twisted up inside." Brushing her cheeks with a fan-shaped brush, like she was putting on makeup. "We had this neighbor, once. He'd been crippled in Vietnam. He used to get drunk and sit on the porch in his wheelchair and pretend to shoot you."

Michael smiled, looking down at the art supplies, so fastidiously arranged. "I heard you have to have a permit."

And here she'd thought he was someone who could see. She could feel the disappointment in her mouth, it tasted like dirty nickels. "It wasn't funny. He was imagining blowing your head off." That asshole's house, bottles on the porch, the broken panes repaired with newspaper and duct tape. The sound of his laughter when he "got" you. Her brothers threw dogshit on his porch, so it would get in the wheels of his chair and then onto his carpet. "He wanted to kill you, don't you see? He wanted to. If he'd had a gun he would have."

Michael shook off the smile then, dark eyebrows knitting over pale green eyes. Now he was listening, now she knew she could trust him. She picked up a sketchbook, started to open it, but he pulled it away. "Please don't, Josie."

Jo-cee. No one else ever said it like that, they always said Jozee. She let him have the sketchpad when he asked. She might have teased him over it, allowing it to bring them over the line to touching, to kissing, but she'd never been with a boy like Michael before, it made everything different. She'd only gone with boys like her brothers, they'd share some Olde English 800 and cheap reefer with you and tear your clothes, too mean to undo the buttons. Nick Nitro'd been a god by comparison. But this, this was altogether new, and made her unsure. Putting her hand to his cheek, his scratchy beard, she drew his face down to hers. He was trembling. She felt like she was the boy and he was the girl and that gave her courage. She might not have gone to college but she knew about this, how to press against a boy, wake him up.

That kiss. Sewn on her body, stitched into her skin.

"Show me what to do," he whispered. "Show me what you want."

She led him to the narrow iron priest's bed. The way he looked at her as she unbuttoned her dress made her tremble too. She ran her hands under his jacket, over his jeans, he was more than ready.

"Wait," he said. "Come with me." He took her hand and led her down the hall to the last door. The blinds were drawn, stale air suffused with a smoky perfume. He opened the drapes, cranked open the old-fashioned windows. An astonishing room. Luxurious, feminine, all blue and

white, its antique white furniture with bur-
nished gold trim. He turned down the bed to reveal blue sheets with white piping, shed his
clothes, all but the white shapeless underwear,
the kind her mother bought her brothers in
packages of twelve, and slid in. Lying on the
pillows, his bony square shoulders, his cropped
dark hair. The well between his ribs, the line of
hair. The pleasure of his complete attention. If
only there was a drawing of that.

She took his long finger in her mouth, it still
tasted slightly of graphite, and his closed green
eyes flickered like a dog having a dream, and he
moaned. *Oh* . . .

*How could he have killed himself when we
could make love like that? How?*

She stripped off her dress, still damp from the
pool, and guided his hand down her body, between her legs, she could feel herself pulsing
and curling around his fingers. His face, as he
memorized her. "There," she said. "You ever play
a guitar?" His hands so strong, he could do her
all day. Worlds away from everything she had
ever known. His beautiful body, long and slender on the blue sheets.

Not white. Not dead and cold, wrapped in a

sheet with a knot at the chest. On the stereo, under the dark windows, Richard Hell on KROQ sang "Going, Going, Gone."

If only she hadn't been careful that day. If she'd gotten knocked up, at least she'd have something now, some proof he existed. Instead of these lights, and some paintings and the rest of her goddamn life. She never wanted to be alone like this. She'd finally found someone who could give her everything, and then he took it away. Just took it away. *You asshole!* The joy, the delight, where did it go? *What did you do with it?* Her gut ached, as if her love was being dug out of her with a dull knife. She needed him to make her feel good again, right now. *You son of a bitch. You son of a fucking bitch.*

Tears dripping onto the drawings, ruining them. She closed the sketchpad. She wanted to remember him on the blue sheets but all she could see were those blackened eyes, those inky lips. Were they the same lips he kissed her with? What about what he felt like in her arms, and how they danced to Louis Armstrong? That's what she had to remember. The pleasure they had taken in each other. *Couldn't you remember how I loved you?* But he didn't. The story of her life. God gave you everything just to take it away. Just so you knew exactly what you were missing.

The phone rang on the orange footlocker, by Pen's sagging right hand. Pen groaned and turned, her heavy hand dropping to the floor, and crammed the pillow over her head. Josie staggered over, shin banging into the footlocker, and grabbed at the phone. "Yeah."

The sound of hoarse breathing. Then a slurred, deep, woman's voice. "Why are you alive? What is the excuse for Josie Tyrell? I ask you."

She should hang up, there was nothing but grief on the line. As if there wasn't enough here in the house. *We don't need any more, thank you. We gave at the office.* But she couldn't hang up. This woman had known Michael Faraday. She knew what it meant to lose him. They were sharing a respirator on the same airless planet.

"Tell me," the woman mumbled. "I dare you. Say, 'If Michael never met me, he'd be alive today.' This is all your fault. I curse the womb that bore you."

If it was anyone else, she might have admitted it. Of course it was her fault. But she wouldn't admit it, not to *her.* "You don't even know me."

A laugh like a bark, a single note. "Know you? You're an absolute *bill*board. Josie Tyrell." Spitting out the last two syllables with more pure loathing than Bakersfield could ever have assembled. "Why didn't you stay up there in Tuleville where you belonged? You and he should never have shared a sentence. My son didn't love you. He was just slumming."

Slumming. So blind. The blind Merediths climbing the white stairs. He'd been dying up there. *The crippled boy. The deaf-mutes.* Mother and son, in all that decaying luxury. *We fucked in your room, Meredith. We came on your blue sheets.* "I guess he thought it was more real than living with you."

There was silence, some kind of scuffling. Cello music in the background, and the heavy breathing of someone who'd been crying, who'd put away a fifth of something expensive. "I could make a call right now. Within an hour, someone would come and end your miserable life. Five grand, and you'd just disappear. I think it would be worth it."

Josie looked over at Pen, facedown on the furry couch, her skirt all hiked up behind. She had holes in the ass of her tights. "I loved him too, Meredith. You weren't the only one."

But his mother didn't hear her. She just kept talking, like a drunk arguing with ghosts toward closing time. "You thought you were latching onto a good thing. But he slipped from your clutches. You didn't think of that, you little whore —"

"I hope this is making you feel better —"

"I don't want to feel better. I want you to suffer, the way I'm suffering now."

"Then you didn't even have to call," Josie said, hung up the phone.

3
Funeral

At nine forty-five on Friday morning, Josie Tyrell drove through Griffith Park, her rattly Falcon covered with band stickers making the only noise there was. She passed the lawns and old trees of Crystal Springs, the silent merry-go-round with its proud carousel horses, tented for winter. Last weekend, thousands of people had mourned the dead Beatle here. Today there was only the empty sandbox, the vacant swings. She followed the signs around the zoo parking lot to the back of the mountain, the air heavy with eucalyptus and laurel sumac, pitchy and green. And there it was, just as he said it would be, the metropolis of the dead. Forest Lawn, then Mount Sinai. He'd called as he said he would. Inspector Brooks. "It's Sinai," he'd whispered. "Tomorrow morning, ten o'clock. Off the Five at Forest Lawn."

Mount Sinai didn't look like the Bakersfield cemetery. There were no headstones, just acres of open rolling hillside, green closely cropped lawns, plaques flat on the grass. Easier to mow. You could ride right over the graves. It made her sick just to think of it. And Michael had never wanted to be buried anyway, he'd wanted cremation. But it wasn't his choice. He had nothing to say. *You didn't think about that. Nobody gives a crap what the dead want. It's all her show now. Nobody's asking you shit.*

They were parking cars in a big lot before a massive sandstone building, one luxury car behind the next, tight, like concert parking at the Hollywood Bowl. No leaving early. A young man flagged the weak-mufflered Falcon in behind a Cadillac. The colorless light held the mountains in high contrast, blue and pale gold, and the sky was blue and far away. She adjusted her black sunglasses and got out of the car. She probably shouldn't have gotten high on the way, but she didn't know how else she was going to get through this. Everybody was probably doing Valium by the fistful anyway, what the fuck was the difference?

She walked away from the dusty blue Ford, touching her *Germs* sticker — for memory, not luck. The cold air was shockingly fresh. A Rain Bird rhythmically watered the stiff Saint Augustine grass. She knew she shouldn't have worn her yellow fake fur coat, though she'd cleaned it, though it was the only warm one she had. She knew there was something in her, a persistent defiance, that wouldn't let her do things the way she was supposed to. Even now. Even today.

The other people, wearing drab grays and browns, talked quietly in the sun. She tucked a bit more of her hair into her beret and tried to look as sedate as she could as she followed the passengers of the Cadillac, an elderly couple, the man in a business suit and overcoat, the woman in a fur tipped in sunlight, as far as the Hall of Remembrance. But then she couldn't force herself to go through the doors.

She moved to one side and lit a Gauloise, looking through her big square sunglasses at the naked-trunked eucalyptuses glowing white against the dark green chaparral of the park. How often they'd hiked on the other side of this mountain, watched the sun set from Dante's

View. Made love on the picnic table under the weeping eucalyptus.

Old men stood around on the steps, talking in groups of two and three, like they were going to a business lunch. Uncles, friends, music people of Meredith's. She had never met any of his relatives, though she knew him better than any of them. She could tell they had been here before, citizens of this country, Death. They knew its customs, its rites. Yet the men eyed her with the automatic mix of curiosity, lust, and aesthetic judgment they always gave young women, subject to object, the way you'd stare at an animal. She pretended not to notice. To remind them she was a person was too much effort. Objects bore no guilt. She glanced around nervously, watching for Meredith, that proud head of dark hair. How could she bear to invite people to her only son's funeral? How could she stand it?

Josie ground out her cigarette and went into the Hall of Remembrance. Inside, everything was beige and muted and the light came from nowhere at all. There was a box of satin caps, she took one but a man shook his head. "It's not for ladies," he said, plucking it out of her hand.

Instead, she accepted a booklet from a young

man with a rose in his buttonhole, a slender man with a low forehead — why was he looking at her like that? Did she smell of pot, or was it the yellow fake fur? Or did he know who she was, the one who let him slip away. *It's all your fault, Josie Tyrell.*

She sat in the back, against the far wall. Onstage, the closed coffin gleamed like a black piano. She was glad it was closed, that she would not have to see him like that again. Though they would have him all fixed up, wouldn't they? She suddenly had the strangest feeling that Michael was going to open the lid and sit up and sing "Just a Gigolo" in a funny tremolo voice like Bing Crosby on the Twenties record, or recite a speech, like Meet Mr. Lincoln that day at Disneyland. How they'd howled when Lincoln stood up and said the Gettysburg Address. They'd practically pissed their pants. A short squatty attendant had to come over and tell them to leave. "This is America," he'd hissed. "Have some respect."

She shouldn't have smoked that weed. She was fucking losing it. He wasn't going to sit up and sing any song. He was never singing anything, ever again. He was in there and this was for real and he was never coming out. *Never and never.* Had Meredith seen him the way Josie had, at the coroner's? Or had she waited for the funeral home? Had she closed the lid, the way she would close the top of her Steinway? Closing his music inside. If Josie hadn't seen his body in the coroner's basement, she would have felt different about the closed casket, but she'd seen enough. *It's a project I've been thinking about.* And this was the project, his last work of art.

Piped music filtered in from no visible source, muffled, hushed. A group of old women with set hair turned and stared at her. She pushed the sunglasses further on her face. They knew. She pulled the fake fur tighter, glad she had it, garish as it was, it was freezing in here, the smell of cold flowers. What did she care if the coat was wrong, she deserved to be here, she was the only one who knew him, she had fucked him, had held him in her arms in the early hours, had laughed with him, a million little jokes, had sat through his fury, his gloom. She had loved him more than all these people combined. *Go ahead and stare, you bitches.* They thought they knew her. They didn't know a thing.

Josie examined the booklet, candelabra on

the cover, a program. Brahms, and then Psalm 16, Psalm 32, Bach. A prayer, the Mourner's Kaddish, in the flamelike Hebrew, followed by an English pronunciation, a translation. At least she would not clap in the wrong part. She remembered that night at the Dorothy Chandler Pavilion, Michael so handsome in his iridescent thrift-store suit and green silk tie, she in her Lana Turner black lace and spike heels. How they peered down from their seats in the top balcony at the horseshoe of musicians with their stands and instruments. When the music stopped, Michael caught hold of her hand. Lacing his fingers in hers, he tenderly bit her knuckles. She would have been the only one applauding.

In the Hall of Remembrance, the cold air was dense with flowers, easels and stands and baskets, like someone just won the Kentucky Derby. The beige drapes rippled softly, and on the left, a separate side area, the family sat hidden behind gauze curtains. She could hear sobbing under the music. She should be sobbing like that. He deserved someone better, a girl-friend who would run up there and throw herself on the coffin, screaming. Not sitting back here, stoned, unreal, as if this was happening to someone else. Ahead, people talked and shook hands, they all knew each other. She was the outsider. This was his other world, that she had never seen.

A man with a lion's mane of gray hair came in, tanned and blue eyed, wearing a wrinkled trench coat, and you could hear the buzz of conversation, people rising to shake his hand, squeeze his arm, embrace him, it had to be the father, Calvin Faraday. He wouldn't come when Michael was alive, but he could manage to attend the funeral. Big of him. Making a theatrical entrance, all that was missing were the trumpets. He went through a door to the family area behind the gauze curtain and suddenly, they could all hear Meredith's voice, its angry shrillness, screaming at him. A few moments later, he was back, red-faced, raking a hand through his great head of hair. He took a seat among the old people, put the little hat on, his broad shoulders expressive, shrugging, embarrassed, apologetic. His hair was too bushy for the satin cap, it kept falling off, he had to hold it on with one hand.

The crowd wasn't large, plenty of room in the hall, eight or ten empty rows between her and the rest of the mourners. Didn't they know a million people, his famous parents? But maybe they were keeping it quiet. A few old friends, second cousins. Nothing in the *Times* this morning, no obit. Michael would have hated that, it was his favorite part of the paper. Maybe Meredith just couldn't bear calling people — it was too cruel. Someone had to, but how could you have the strength? Flying all the way back from Uruguay or wherever. Michael's father looked hagged out under his tan, he was older than Meredith, must have come straight from the airport. She couldn't help feeling sorry for him, the way Meredith screamed at him, he was old, it couldn't be good for him. Even if he had been a shitty dad.

The canned music stopped and four old men came onstage with their instrument cases. They sat in a half circle of folding chairs, their sheet music already on the slender stands. Black cases opened and beautiful amber instruments emerged into the old hands. They began to play. It was the Brahms. Yes, that was right, Meredith was right to choose the Brahms. Michael had loved this. The little flavors of Bach you could hear from time to time. He'd even put on the Bach so she could hear it.

"Bach believed the world made sense," Michael explained. "He believed in God. Now listen to the Brahms." He put the other back on and folded himself next to her on the furry blue couch. She listened hard, and yes, she could hear it, the same melodious order as the Bach, but then it all fell apart, into stormy wildness. "It's like he'd like to be Bach, but can't keep it together," she said.

Michael was just like that too. He wanted God, but he was too full of moods and doubts. And she had lost that world, where she could sit on the blue couch, listening to music with her face pressed to his chest. She felt the tears coming, but she didn't surrender to them. She didn't know who she would be crying for. For him or for herself.

The quartet ended, but the old men stayed in their places, their instruments laid across their laps like infants. Two rabbis came to the podium, a chubby middle-aged one with glasses on his nose, and the other old and jowly in a silver tie. Both wore white shawls with blue stripes and long fringe. She wondered if they came with the cemetery. She doubted they were Meredith's. The heavy rabbi sang prayers in Hebrew, and people followed from a book in the back of the seats, singing along, rocking forward and back. Sometimes they stood and sometimes they sat, like a concert. She did what the other people did. The jowly old rabbi spoke. His eyebrows were impressive, his voice important in a fake way. "Dearest friends, we are gathered here to bid goodbye to our loved one, Michael Loewy Faraday. A boy of rich promise, a light in the lives of his parents, Meredith Elizabeth Loewy and Calvin Peter Faraday." She could tell he didn't know Michael from a hole in the ground, he was just saying what he thought they wanted to hear. She preferred the Hebrew, songs so old they scraped the bottom of your heart like a burned pan.

"Who can know God's intentions? Who can know His Mind?" She looked at the coffin, lying there like a giant question mark. Like the monolith in *2001*. One big fucking question. But at the end of the day, who needed a God who'd let Michael get so lost that he'd do something like this? What was the point of a Devil if there was a God like that? Maybe there was just the Devil, the real God of this lousy world. Or maybe there was just nothing at all. And everybody was sitting around praying to a great big nothing, like people praying to airplanes, thinking they were gods. The world one big cargo cult.

She was glad when they told everyone to rise for the Mourner's Kaddish. She read along with the others, following the English phonetics: *Yit-gadal v'yit-kadash sh'mey raba b'alma dee-v'ra hirutey* . . . It sounded like a made-up language, the kind kids invent and pretend they're speaking Eskimo. The translation said nothing about death, only God, praising, blessing. Where had God been when Michael was sitting in that room in Twentynine Palms? It reminded her of the Iranian hostages. You ended up taking the side of your captors, it was called the Stockholm syndrome. Well she wasn't going to fucking praise that kidnapper, that terrorist. *Fuck you, God. Fuck you and your brother too.*

The silent box reproached them all. How could he stand it in there? He was so claustrophobic. The pyre on the Ganges, that's what he'd wanted. What he had seen at ten, in India with his mother. "The burning releases the soul," he'd said. "So it can go on into the next life." They'd been sitting in Echo Park, eating strawberries and watching the Latino men fishing where there were no fish, the flowering lotus five feet tall, safe from thieves because nobody could reach them across the water.

"Do you really believe in that?" she asked, sucking the strawberry juice off her stained fingers. "Reincarnation?" Shirley K. was always into that. How you were working off your karma and shit.

He shrugged, watching a yellow swallowtail dip and dive between the pink lotus blooms. "I don't know. But I like the idea of purification in fire. Public cremation. The bones right there in front of everybody. You see it. It was kind of horrible, really, I had bad dreams about it for years. Not everybody gets burned right, some people are too poor, they don't buy enough wood. Then they just dump the bones in the river. But if it's done right? It's really satisfying. I don't want to go into the ground." And all she'd thought was, *He's been to India.* Only now did it occur to her, what the fuck did Meredith think she was showing him? What kind of a mother took a kid to see dead people getting burned up? Was that her idea of a tourist attraction?

Josie shifted in the seat. Her body ached. She hadn't slept more than two hours straight since that first phone call. The old rabbi talked about donations to a fund, and then the old men played the Bach, the sarabande. Two violins soaring together like birds, spiraling into the sky. After the doubt of Brahms, the pure yearning of Bach. She thought of Michael's body on a pyre, smoke swirling up to a God who might care.

Then it was over, and nobody had said a thing about who he'd been, or how he died. Though really, did she think they would? There was nothing to say except that he found life too painful to bear, a fucking empty room, and checked out, an act that spit in the eye of God and on his flawed Creation. But there was still the graveside — maybe they'd do it there. Or would they go? She didn't know, she had never been to a Jewish funeral. She would just stay with everybody, clap in the right place. She could always come back later.

The old men packed up their instruments, while others came forward, and Calvin Faraday. Together, they picked up the coffin on their shoulders and carried it out. She pitied Calvin, carrying his own son to the grave.

She followed along, blending in with the crowd, hoping no one would notice her, guess who she was, know that she was the one who'd failed to save him, that it was her fault. Outside, she watched the bearers load the coffin onto the hearse. Two old men helped Meredith into a black limousine. She wore a black coat and a big veil over a brimmed hat. They practically had to carry her.

Everybody got in their cars and turned on the

engines and lights. Josie ducked below the dashboard and smoked a little of the joint she'd
brought for afterward. She couldn't wait, she
needed it now, she would do her crying at
home. There was lots of time, like the rest of her
life.

The hearse began to move, and they followed
it slowly up the manicured green of the hill, the
rows of brass plaques under the deodars, a neat
carpet of death. They wound up at the high-rent
district — even here, the rich had their exclu-
sive zone, an enclave marked by a low sandstone wall. They parked in the same order at the
leafless curb. The earth smelled damp as she approached the sandstone enclosure. The grave
was presided over by a line of cypresses, like in
Van Gogh, the word LOEWY chiseled into a stone
in the wall.

She took her place behind the other mourners outside the enclosure. She'd heard of a family plot, but hadn't realized what it meant. His
family was all buried here. The grandfather. A
plot for Meredith and one for Michael, and room
for husbands and wives and children. It had always been here. He'd grown up knowing there
was a grave waiting for him. It was part of being
a Loewy. She shuddered in the cold sun. He'd

known where he was going to end up. The pyre was just a fantasy. Whatever he did, he couldn't have escaped this rectangular hole in the ground, this pile of dirt covered by its blanket of Astroturf. If she'd married him, she would be buried in there, and if they'd had a baby, their child too. There was some *ming* for you. There was some fucking destiny.

But there was no marriage, no child. No more Loewys. And she would be shipped back to Bakersfield or God knew what. Never with Michael, never again.

A few folding chairs waited under a canopy. The old men helped Meredith to a seat. The bearers slid the box from the long car and carried it awkwardly, to the stand by the hole. She wondered that such old men could carry something so heavy, but maybe they knew how. Calvin slipped, but he righted himself. Her heart was crushing in. Just when she thought things would turn out right for them. She had loved him, but not enough. Not enough to stop it.

She watched Meredith in her black coat and pearls in the brilliant sunlight, wondering just how far she could see behind that black veil. She hoped not very far. Josie stood behind an old woman in a mink coat, making herself as small as she could. If she could just get through this morning, this hour.

In the distance, the long chain of mountains — Santa Susanas, Verdugos, San Gabriels — gleamed all the way to Baldy. It was so wrong. It should be pissing down rain, they should be cowering under umbrellas, each in his private shelter, every head bowed. Not basking under a brilliant blue sky. The old rabbi stood by the grave and read another prayer. He spoke about *may God give the family strength, let them find comfort in You and our love for them* yadda yadda. Nothing about pity, or despair. They got the coffin on the lift, and lowered the black box into the grave. She felt her heart compressed with each moment of descent, like a car being crushed at the junkyard, the breaking of glass, the popping of metal. Suddenly Meredith ran to the grave, like she was going to jump in. They grabbed her and she crumpled, weeping. They lifted her up, her legs muddy and stained with grass. They tried to hand her a trowel with some dirt to throw in, but she wouldn't touch it.

Then one by one, each of them was given a white rose by a young man holding a bucket, they passed the grave and threw it in. Josie kept her eyes down as she took her rose and walked to the grave, trying to blend in. Then she heard Meredith scream, "Oh Christ, not her!"

Stoned, she pretended she hadn't heard, all she wanted to do was throw in this rose, *I'm so sorry, Michael,* but strong hands turned her. Meredith's face was inches from her own, a huge face, veiled, it blotted out the world, the wild eyes, whites on four sides, the big teeth bared, and she was ripping the rose out of Josie's hand, the woman's gloved fingers around her throat, those pianist's hands, crazy strong. She couldn't breathe. Meredith's eyes were getting bigger and bigger, she shook Josie by the neck the way a dog shakes a rat. "How dare you! Why are you alive? How can you be alive when he's dead?"

If this was India and there was a sandalwood pyre, she would have thrown herself in. And this paper she'd become would have caught fire, and she and Michael could sail away like two birds. Men in suit sleeves pried Meredith off, and then someone hustled Josie away, a man with his arm around her, as Meredith screamed, "How dare she come here, how dare she!"

Josie stumbled on her high heels, over the graves, on the uneven grass, her throat burning where the gloved hands had squeezed. She had no doubt Meredith could have finished her off right there, in front of everyone. And yet, she was right. It was what she deserved. She hadn't saved him, she shouldn't be here.

"Are you all right?" the man asked.

She nodded, crying, barely able to stand, her nose running, her hands shaking as she groped through her purse for a cigarette. She found one and put it in her mouth, but where was the lighter? Suddenly one appeared, a flame, big hands sheltering it.

It was the father, Calvin Faraday.

"Don't blame her," he said. "It's just so damn hard."

She clung to her cigarette with a trembling hand, as the men at the grave shoveled dirt over the most original human being she'd ever know. "I loved him too," she managed to choke out.

"I know you did," Calvin Faraday said. "But I'd skip the house if I were you."

Josie nodded, glad that there was someone who didn't hate her. Calvin Faraday reached into the pocket of his jacket and pulled out a handkerchief. She wiped her nose and her eyes with it, then didn't know whether to hand it back, it was black with mascara.

"Keep it," he said. He pulled out his wallet, and for a second she wondered if he was going to give her some money. But he took out a business card, wrote something on the back with a fat pen. "I'm staying at the Marmont. Give me a call, I'd like to talk."

Calvin Faraday. What would Michael think? She said yes, she would call, that she'd like to talk. How would Michael feel, if he knew the sense of relief that there was a man, a grown-up man, who could protect her from those accusations? He would be furious, but he wasn't here. She could feel the bruises from Meredith's grip on her throat. She got into her car, pulled out of line, and went back down the hill all by herself, like a kid kicked out of class, humiliated and free.

4
Cal

She didn't change when she got home. She just took a Valium Pen had left for her and sat on the porch off the kitchen, drinking voddy from the bottle, watching the hills opposite and the ones beyond that, and the Verdugos to the north all clear as a postcard. Michael was dead and the sun was still shining. She let the smoke from her ciggie rise, hoping he could smell it, and remember. But Paris was gone. There was no Blaise or little Jeanne. They would never live on one of those houseboats, growing papyrus on tire rafts in the Seine. Never sit out on its deck, her head on his shoulder, as the water slapped against the side of the boat, and the lights from the bridges came on.

She didn't remember falling asleep, but woke to find her cigarette burned out in her fingers, her face cold and briny, the shadows grown long. The phone was ringing. She stumbled inside, and grabbed it.

"Hello, Josie? It's Cal."

Cal? Cal Worthington and his dog Spot? It was all she could think of, a used-car salesman who wore a cowboy hat and walked an alligator on a leash. "Who?"

"Cal Faraday. Michael's father."

Cal. Cal Faraday. The Great Man. The GM, as Michael used to call him. How the fuck did he get her number? She pressed her thin fingers to her lips. Of course. It was Michael's number. Of course he knew it. Her fingers felt like someone else's fingers, a child skeleton's. She felt like she was in a Buñuel movie. First you were strangled by a world-famous pianist, and then Calvin Faraday called you up on the phone. What was next, ants crawling out of a Buñuel hand?

"I'm just leaving Meredith's. Gotta be back here at six to sit shivah. Goy boy like me. But I'd like to talk. Mind a visitor?"

"I guess." What did he want to talk about? On

the windowsill, the little pipecleaner circus Michael made last Christmas paraded, the tumbling clowns, the dancing dog.

"So, where are you?" Sounds on the line.

"Echo Park," she said. Something so funereal in that word, she'd never noticed it before. *Echo.* The death of a sound that had nowhere to go but come back.

"Give me ten minutes." A crusty voice, not deep, sandy and western. She kept thinking he was a New Yorker but that was just where he lived. He was from Oregon, some one-horse town on the coast. "Just tell me where."

Josie looked around the shack. It was clean, but it smelled sinister, like fear, like death. "You know Sammy's Lotus Room?" A drunk bar on Sunset, so tacky it was camp, in the bend where Echo Park took a turn toward Chinatown.

"I'll be there," he said, and hung up.

She was slow in getting ready, with the booze and the downer, and also reluctant, she didn't know what she had to say to Calvin Faraday. She changed into leggings and boots, the scarred leather jacket, souvenir of the day she thought was the worst. Though she was learning there was always worse than that. She washed the makeup from her face, she didn't want Calvin

Faraday to think she wanted to impress him, that she gave a damn what he thought. On the way, she parked illegally in front of Gala's Liquors on Echo Park Avenue and ran in for a pack of Gauloises. She'd laughed at Michael when he'd started ordering them. She'd been so sure a crap liquor store would not stock French cigarettes just because you asked. The shock every time she went in, and there they were. She was used to taking the world as it was, she'd never have guessed you could get what you wanted by asking for it.

She drove down Sunset, past the Chinese market to Sammy's, but she didn't get out, just sat in the car and played the Germs, "Going Down," smoked a joint and waited until she saw a rental-looking white Chevy drive past and make the U-turn, park by the curb. It was four in the afternoon, the light already bleeding away. Cal Faraday emerged, wearing the same wrinkled trench coat she had seen in the morning. He took a look at the Lotus Room and untied his necktie, rolled it and stuck it in his pocket.

She gave him another minute, then crossed the street.

Inside it was dark, the few local drunks hunched over dollar well drinks at the bar, looking like they grew out of their stools like mold, watching the news with the sound off. The new Pres, Ronald Reagan, with his plastic-wig hair and idiot's smile, waved to reporters and pretended he couldn't hear their questions. In a booth by the wall, a Chinese couple sat cheek to cheek, giggling, their table full of glasses with umbrellas. The woman wore one in her hair. The jukebox played "Bali Ha'i." A trio of punk rockers conspired in a corner over their breakfast of longneck Buds. There was no waitress this time of day, only Willie Woo, the Chinese bartender.

Calvin Faraday sat at the bar, his head in his hands.

She slid onto the stool next to him. He was drinking something brown on the rocks. Bourbon, she thought. *Jack Daniel's and make it a double.*

"Vodka tonic," she told Willie Woo.

"You got ID?" he said, sharp, like he always did.

She pulled out her fake ID, he squinted at it in the weak bar light, it was no better than it ever was. She would be twenty-one next summer, but it wouldn't mean shit by then. Without Michael, it would just be another empty day that roared like a shell you put up to your ear. Willie poured her drink. She lit a Gauloise and put the blue pack on the bar.

"Nice place," Calvin Faraday said.

"I like it," she said. "It looks as shitty as I feel."

Willie slammed the drink in front of her, spilling some on the bar.

So, the famous father. She could feel him watching her, his eyes astonishingly blue. She could tell he was trying to put her and Michael together in his mind. Maybe in bed. *This is the girl my son chose.* She let him look. Men never judged her as harshly as women did. Her torn jacket, her boots, her silvery hair and dark eyes, her solemn face with its downturned mouth. She knew what he saw.

"It's not your fault. You just walked in on a bad situation," Calvin Faraday said. "Michael had issues you can't begin to imagine."

Bullshit she couldn't. He'd been obsessed with Calvin Faraday, for one thing. The big-deal writer, on the track of guerrillas in Burma and four-toed wombats in the Amazon. She tried her drink. Like all the drinks at the Lotus Room it was cheap and weak and tasted like soap. "What's shivah?" she asked.

He cradled his drink in his weathered hands. His forearms under the rolled sleeves of his blue and white striped shirt looked strong, snaked with veins, and awfully tan for midwinter. "Every night for a week, they get ten men to go pray at the house. Really just sit around and kibitz, but it's not such a bad idea." Calvin Faraday tilted the brown liquid in the tumbler. "Keeps the bereaved occupied."

As if he was not one of the bereaved. As if she was not. But the shivah wasn't helping her at all. "I didn't think Meredith was religious."

"The doctor gave her a shot. She's down for the count." Michael's father glanced up at some mullah glowering over his beard on TV. "It doesn't matter. It happens, she doesn't have to do anything. It's her old man's friends. They've been through this a few times."

Those old men. She liked men, men who knew what to do, who took care of things when bad shit happened. Men like her father, like Calvin Faraday. She never told Michael that, only that once. She hated to admit it, but it was the truth. And it was the one thing he was no good at.

Cal twirled his drink with a stout finger. His father's hands weren't anything like Michael's. Michael had Michelangelo hands, you could cry just to look at them. His father's were wide and strong and crooked, with hair on the backs of the fingers. Hands that could hold a shovel, flatten somebody's nose. She could see Michael in the shape of the forehead and the straight thick eyebrows, but the father's skin was rough — bad acne as a teen — and his gray hair grew wiry, not soft and dark. Still, they both had the same bony hero's face, the square jaw, the stubborn sailor's look.

The father held his glass between his two big hands, as if trying to warm them. "He called me that last day." His head hung limply over his knuckly hands, he looked like he was praying. "I didn't get the message." He pressed his heavy hand to his face.

She couldn't believe Michael had called his father, who never did shit for him. When he hadn't called her. It sliced right through her, like the little egg slicer Gommer Ida used, a wire contraption that cut the white flesh and yellow heart into clean bare rounds. He had called this asshole, whom he hated, and not her? Was that what Cal came here to tell her? That in the end, she just hadn't meant that much to him? Or was it the contrary, to prove he'd still been important. She could see Cal was waiting for her to say something, but she was such a bad actress, she

never said her lines right, it was something perverse in her nature. And what was her line anyway? No, it's not your fault, Cal? You were a
bang-up dad. Always there when he needed you.
That's why he went and shot himself in the
head. Yeah, if only you had been there. *When
were you ever there, asshole? You left him all to
me. All you people. What was I supposed to do,
I'm not one of you. I didn't know about how to
deal with your son.* But he'd called the father he
hated, in Kuala Lumpur. Not her.

"I just got back to my hotel when the call came
from the consulate," Cal said, drinking his bourbon, rattling the ice. "I almost didn't make it in
time, they had to hold the plane in Singapore."

Josie'd never been to Kuala Lumpur, to Singapore or even San Francisco. Why was it supposed to be more tragic if they had to get on a
plane? The way Meredith used to call him from
South Africa or Beijing. The gods landing for a
moment. "So what did you want to talk to me
about, your travel arrangements?"

He looked at her differently then, a narrower
gaze. Revamping his impression. She wasn't
such a nice girl after all. He gazed down into his
drink as if it was a crystal ball. "I just wanted to
talk. You know, get to know each other."

She waited for him to say more. He obviously didn't want to get to know her, there wasn't that much to know. It had to be something else.

"He talked about you, you know," Cal said.

He'd talked about her with Calvin Faraday? "Yeah? When was that?"

"He called me sometimes. Just to shoot the bull."

He'd been talking to his father. Behind her back. What else? He could drive and he was talking to his dad, what the fuck else didn't she know? It's not like she would've minded, but why hide it from her? Or was this all just some kind of mind trip Cal Faraday was cooking up? "He never called you. I paid the bills, I know."

"He called collect. I didn't mind. Hell, I was ecstatic he was talking to me again."

She exhaled deeply, tried to steady herself, sipped her rotten drink. "What'd he talk about?"

"You. A lot about you. Said you were original. Smart. He loved you. I never heard him talk like that about a girl. About anyone for that matter." Cal pressed his cold glass to the middle of his forehead, rolling it from side to side.

If only she could believe it. People who loved you didn't go off and kill themselves and leave you stranded by the side of the road like some junked car. They believed in their love. They believed that even if things didn't go well, even if things looked like crap for a while, you could hang in there, love was worth hanging around for. *Smart. Original.* Who would ever think such a thing about her again? Tyrell, survivor of the end of the world, along with the cockroaches. The only person who could have seen something like that in her was dead.

"I was glad when he said he had a girlfriend, a real girlfriend, not one of his hyperintellectual Harvardettes, sitting around trading Kierkegaard for Nietzsche and raise you one."

What hyperintellectual Harvardettes? She wanted to grab him by the lapels and scream, *What Harvardettes?* He had never told her about a girlfriend at Harvard. *He was a virgin, for Christ's sake.* She thought of the way he trembled . . . *But he had learned so fast.* God. Had it all been an act? Why bother pretending you were a goddamn virgin if you weren't? Was he just having a good laugh at her? What else didn't she know about him?

"You were good for him, Josie, just what he needed."

Good for him? Just what he needed? This was how good she was, HE WAS FUCKING DEAD.

Maybe he should have kept to his fucking Har-vardettes. Though she knew exactly what Cal meant, that crass masculine wisdom. Meaning a girl who put out. Clear up his acne and whatnot.

"You were real," Cal said. "He liked that a lot. Said your dad drives a tow truck."

"Owns a tow operation," Josie mumbled, unsure she could trust her own voice.

"Listen, mine was a fisherman, out of Coos Bay, Oregon. I was no student prince." Josie knew all about him. First in his family to go to college, and to Harvard at that, full scholarship. Fisherman, logger, hunting guide, bouncer in a nightclub yadda yadda, it was all on the jacket copy. The things Michael so envied. Those battered hands said it all. "Michael was so tired of the air up in Meredithville." He nodded to the north, through the wall and up to Los Feliz, the great house on Vista del Mar. "He wanted to live like a man." What his father didn't know about Michael could have filled an encyclopedia. His wet eyes so blue against the reddened whites, like the flag. "Poor bastard just didn't know how." He shook the ice in his glass.

"Why didn't you show him?" Josie said, the bitter smoke curling from her child's fingers into the light of the TV set. "Why didn't you do something?"

Cal hung his great head, the burly shoulders, like a defeated bull. "That talks easier than it plays. He was a competitive son of a bitch. And loyal. To her. You know what they were like." He wiped his mouth with the back of his hand, as if he was about to say something more and then thought better of it.

She did know, but she wasn't going to tell Cal that. She wasn't going to tell him shit. "I only saw them together once. When he told her he was moving in with me. That we'd rented a place together."

Cal Faraday stared at the bottles behind the bar, his blue eyes watering, a smile playing around his worn mouth. "God, I would have loved to see that. The storming of the Bastille. *Vive la Liberté.*" A tear dripped down his cheek, stubble-dotted, he brushed at it absently.

"She was really pissed."

"I can imagine. You don't know how they used to be. Just the two of them, in their own little world. No intruders welcome. Meaning me of course." He coughed and drank, went back to turning the glass in his hands. "Yeah, she taught him all the diva tricks. I tried with him, you don't know. But I didn't hobnob around with Arnold Schoenberg, I'm just a rustic. He thought of me as some kind of clown. My own son." He signaled to Willie Woo, a raised crooked forefinger, for another JD.

Did Cal feel inferior to his son? She was about to argue with him, but he held up his hand.

"Hey, I know what he thought. He despised me, because I couldn't handle his mother. It's devastating to have your mother reject your father for you. Screws up the whole Oedipal chain of command." He watched one of the punks hovering by the jukebox, trying to choose the most appropriate tear-jerking Lotus Room selection for his late beer breakfast. Sammy's hadn't updated its playlist since 1963. The kid put quarters in the slot, and the machine whirred and began to play Julie London torch singing "Blue Moon." Willie Woo sang it under his breath as he put Cal's fresh glass on the bar in front of him.

Nobody was saying shit about what had really gone down. She wasn't going to be drawn into Cal's scenario. She had known Michael too well for that. "So that's why you called him Sissy-Boy? To help him feel close to you?"

"He was still on that?" Cal lifted his drink to

his thin Oregon lips. "That is a misquote. What I said was, 'Don't be a sissy-boy.' He damn well knew what I said. He was quite a dramatist, just like his mother." Her cigarette had gone out, he lit it for her with her own lighter, shielding the flame with his rough hand.

"And the thing with the ball?" The baseball he'd thrown at Michael, that hit him in the head.

"He could've caught it," Cal said, shaking his head. "He just wanted to make a big deal in front of his mother. He could be tricky like that, working the angles. He played handball at Ojai. At Harvard he was a ranked player. I played with him up there, Parents' Weekend. He was fast, and mean. Beat the pants off of me."

I am not sportif. What was Cal talking about? "He didn't play sports."

Cal took out his wallet, removed a photograph. A boy in white clothes, reaching up with a tennis racket to smash a high ball. Red cheeked and dark haired, she knew it was no mistake. No shred of adolescent gawkiness. It was too much to understand. She just wanted to lie down and sleep.

Cal replaced the photo, on top of a picture of two small girls. The most recent set of Faraday half sibs, children of the latest wife, Harmony, whom Michael called Numbah Foah. One on top of another, like the building of civilizations. Michael must have normally been near the bottom, but his suicide had brought him to the top. How Michael resented that about his father, that he could make a mess and then walk away, start over. Move on to the next woman, make new kids, the world always fresh and new. When Michael couldn't walk away from anything.

Well, Cal wasn't walking away now. Michael had finally gotten his father's full attention.

"You know, I was nosing around up at the house. I had a feeling Meredith was holding out on me." Cal pulled out an envelope from the breast of his blue jacket. He opened the brown manila and removed two white envelopes. He took one and slid it down the bar, put the other away.

Josie Tyrell. Written in that familiar vertical hand, the *e*'s like *3*'s, the down-crossed *t*'s. The envelope was spattered with brown. Just a light spatter, like the overspray from an airbrushing. "I found it in the desk, in her old man's study. She locks it, but I know where she keeps the key." Her father's study, Mauritz Loewy's, who shot himself in the head. The red leather study Michael had told her was Cal's. "She doesn't know about limits. It's the way she was raised. Remember that if you run into her again."

She turned the envelope over in her hands. *Josie Tyrell*. This was for her, and she was afraid. The envelope had been opened, a wavy ink line torn blatantly in two. "She read it?"

"That or the coroner."

"Did you?"

He furrowed his brow in an expression of pity and dismay. "No, thanks, I got one of my own."

"What did yours say?"

Cal Faraday heaved a great sigh, blew the air through his mouth. He reached for her cigarettes, glancing at her for objection or permission. She nodded and he lit one, took a sad exhale. "My son was an angry person. I have to take some responsibility there. Not all, though. Not all."

Josie crushed out her cigarette, and opened the torn flap of her letter, feeling sick, but steeling herself, expecting the worst . . . *Josie, you bitch, you Judas cunt, you low-life piece of crap. I curse the day I met you.* "Why did she have them?"

Cal shook his head. "Must have been the coroner. But he wanted her to see them, he was a smart boy, he had to know she'd open them. So read with a grain of salt."

She took out the letter and held it in her hands, forced herself to start at the top. Motel letterhead, *Paradise Inn. Highway 62. Twenty-nine Palms.* Blood spatters had seeped through the envelope, faintly printing the thin off-white paper in an unholy constellation. *Dear Josie,* it said. *We loved each other — .* She stopped, held her breath, read it again. Maybe he didn't blame her, maybe she hadn't done this after all. *We loved each other . . . Didn't we? I can't remember. You'll have to remember for both of us.* Oh God. Oh God oh God oh God. *I hope you find someone who can meet your needs better than I could. I'm just not up to it. See you in the next life. Michael.*

Simple lines across the page, slicing her open, clean and fast, like a cold razor. Then in a less certain hand below, the ink blobbing, the letters mashed together — he must have been drinking — *I'm so sorry. Sorry sorry for everything. I'm so fucking sorry.* She put her hand to her forehead, so Cal wouldn't see the tears dripping down her nose, onto the bar.

Cal reached out to press his hand over hers,

warm and callused, and she let him. "It's not your fault," he said. "It's nobody's fault."

She snatched her hand away, wiped her eyes, and read it again. The last words he ever wrote. "What do you do with something like this? Keep it in the drawer with your underwear? Along with the love letters? Carry it around all your life?"

"I don't know," Cal said. "I'm plumb out of answers today."

5
These Days

Josie lay on her stomach in the stale white bed that still smelled of Michael, though less each day. She wore his green flannel shirt that she'd found in the laundry, it was filthy and dank and only smelled of her now, metallic with grief. She closed her eyes and pressed her face to his pillow, trying to catch his scent, but it eluded her, she could smell it only by accident now, like a glance caught in a crowd, then lost forever. Out in the living room, Louis Armstrong and the Hot Five played "Big Butter and Egg Man," and her heart lay crushed in an eggshell mosaic.

She turned over slightly and let her eyes cross the Siberia of the sheets to drift along the walls, where they'd painted Montmartre. Their café with its little round tables, Blaise and Jeanne, the street in front, the shops, painted it together in their first weeks in the house. Days he didn't remember. That he didn't want anymore. How those walls had once begged for violation, like a snarky virgin. She'd asked him to paint them. "A picture would be so great here," she'd said, embracing the bare surface. "Please?"

"Mae Fong strictly forbid," Michael said. Their landlady, a gritty sixtyish chain-smoking City Hall secretary, admonished them when they moved in not to touch anything, the walls had just been repainted. Navajo white, landlord's delight.

"Come on, she knew we were going to do it the moment she left." She went out and got his drawing things, the charcoal and pencils. "Do us in Montmartre."

The way he looked at her then. He'd been to Harvard, but it had never occurred to him to defy a landlady's orders. "What's she going to do to us, Michael? Nothing."

"This is what I love about you," Michael said, pressing his forehead to hers, his arm around her neck. "You give me permission, you don't even know."

"I'll give you more than permission," she said, rolling her forehead on his, drinking in that smell, pine and moss. "I'll give you the whole enchilada."

He picked up a piece of crayon, and started on the blank closet doors, drawing a café, the bar, and at the tables, circus people, the strong man and the bearded lady, and in the foreground, a little ballerina at a table alone.

"But where's her lover?" she asked him. "You can't let her be there all on her own. Look at her. Look how sad she is."

"He's coming. He's picking her some violets to pin to her coat."

"Well, he better get there, before she leaves with the strong man."

He laughed easily, the flash of those big white teeth. He quickly sketched himself in, an artist in a floppy tie, uncombed hair long in the front, a rumpled jacket, a sketchpad before him on the table, a bottle of wine and a squat glass.

He mixed acrylic paints in Dixie cups, and surprised her by giving her a brush. "Do that with the red," he said, pointing to the area on which he was sketching paintings in frames. "You're in this now."

So they painted side by side, listening to Louis Armstrong, *Le Jazz Hot.* Django Reinhardt playing his jazzy Gypsy guitar. Piaf and her heartbroken streets. Michael painted the hard parts and she did the easy ones: the wall, the basic shapes, silhouettes, bentwood chairs, the underpainting of the figures in the foreground, while he did the faces and clothing, the little pictures with which the artists had paid for their drinks when they were broke. Just a few strokes, and there was a Picasso — a sad clown and his girlfriend huddled over their drinks. The black candle trees of Van Gogh. The Sacré-Coeur. She had seen these pictures before in the art books where she'd searched out new ideas for poses, but now they were *our Picasso, our Van Gogh.* Every day they got up and painted some more, went for walks, made love. Who knew where Montmartre ended and Echo Park began? Each colored the other, like watercolors, bleeding.

How could he not remember? It was like not remembering his name, like forgetting the color of the sky. She remembered everything, everything. How they carried the last of the boxes down from the street and collapsed on the enormous couch that someone had managed to haul down there. The way the light streaked the wide planks of the floor and filled the windows with trees. Michael stretching out his lanky shoulders in his peculiar gesture, wedging his wrist behind the joint and pressing the whole arm forward, first one and then the other, as he surveyed the box-filled room, the rough posts that held up the ceiling. Then he slipped his arm around her waist, pressing his head to hers. She loved that best, even more than fucking. She could never have imagined such a little thing could fill her with such indescribable sweetness, she felt too small to contain it all. She could feel it even now, the hardness of his head, the smell of his sweat, like a liquor, the way the view shimmered in the summer light, the long silvery eucalyptus leaves that blew across the window like a girl's hair. She'd never lived in a place with a view before, like a tree house. She felt like she could finally breathe. As if there had been a big black frog sitting on her chest as long as she could remember, and now it was gone.

Well, it was back now. Squatting there like a sandbag full of buckshot. Out in the living room, the fucking phone was ringing. "Piss off," she told it. There was no one here answering to a name. No more names, no more numbers. But on the bedroom walls, Montmartre was still there. Their room over the café, the cobblestone street that sloped down to the warren of artists' studios at the Bateau-Lavoir. Their greengrocer and the charcuterie man. The shadow theater of M. Rivière. All so clear. And the lovers who lived there, Blaise and little Jeanne, Picasso and Fernande, Toulouse-Lautrec and Suzanne Valadon. How many evenings had they sat up in this bed, drinking wine, her wearing only the black stockings that drove him crazy, as he read poems to her. Valéry in French — *ce toit tranquille, où marchent des colombes, entre les pins palpite, entre les tombes* . . .

The tombs. Among the tombs, Christ, she'd never thought about it.

Out in the living room, the Louis record ended. Silence filled the house. *Ce toit tranquille, entre les tombes* . . . She couldn't take the silence. She stumbled out into the living room, and started the album over again, a music scratchy with yearning. She lay on the blue furry couch, open like a book that had been abandoned, a book she knew by heart, a book with all the pages torn out. She lay on her back with her arm across her eyes, letting the clarinet complain, then joined by Louis's horn, "Lonesome Blues." Imagining Michael was here again. Dancing with her, naked. She had never lived anywhere so private before, that you could do just what you wanted, with the windows wide open. Drinking kirs, the champagne opening with a soft pop, not splurting out of the bottle, just a fizzy smoke, and he'd filled the glasses, the drinks turning pink with cassis. They toasted their new house with one hand as he slid the other up her thigh. The wine sweet and cold, his fingers warm, exploring her as she drank, until they forgot their drinks and made love, and again.

But he wasn't a virgin.

Virgin or no virgin, what did it matter. She wasn't going to let that asshole Cal take it away from her. An afternoon like that, and after, when they just lay on the couch, not talking, not listening to any music, just watching the sun get lower through the open windows, the color of orange sherbet, melting all over the hills. They had that. They had that. She could still feel that breeze, and his fingers, the look on his face, the lines near his eyes, the lashes fluttering against his cheeks as he fucked her with his piano-strong hands, his cock, practiced, unpracticed, what the fuck difference did it make, it was beautiful beyond anything she'd ever imagined. She pretended her fingers were his, holding her breast, touching her, making her sex ripple like a flamenco skirt. She was almost there when the lock rattled in the door and she just had time to stop fingering herself when Pen walked in with a bag of groceries on one hip.

Reluctantly, she pushed Michael's shirt down, put her arm back across her face.

"Is this what you've been doing all day, just lying there jerking off, listening to old records?" Pen said. She went over to the stereo and yanked the needle off the Hot Five. "This is no good. Pull yourself together, Josie. Enough's enough."

The phone rang again and Pen waited for her to answer it, but Josie didn't want to, it was just going to be Meredith breathing and then hanging up on her as she had been doing for days. Pen picked it up, annoyed. "It's for you," she said, passing the phone to Josie. When Josie wouldn't take it, Pen stuck it in front of her nose, and when she still wouldn't touch it, dropped the receiver onto her face. Josie picked it up reluctantly.

"Yeah?" she said. Nothing good ever came over a phone line, hadn't she learned that by now?

"Josie, it's Cal," came the voice over the line, that sandy, western voice. "How you holding up?"

She was glad it was him. This surprised her. But Cal knew what it meant to lose Michael Faraday, that specific being, that unique and miraculous collision of biology and history, spirit and matter.

"I had this dream, Cal. That he was alive. He was in this white city, and he was carrying this goat down to the water." He looked so beautiful, all tanned and naked except for a pair of cutoffs, with a red goat slung around his shoulders, he was holding it by its legs. "I tried calling but he didn't hear me. Then all these women in white came out onto the stairway, and I couldn't get by them." A religious procession, moving so slowly, carrying a plaster saint. "I knew I had to reach him before he got down to the water. There was a boat and if I didn't reach him, he'd be gone forever. But they wouldn't let me get past."

"I know," Cal said. "Mine are about looking for him after a disaster, a crash in the Andes, an earthquake. I slept about three hours last night." He sighed heavily. "Look, I just wanted to call, to say goodbye."

Goodbye? "Where are you going?"

"Home, Josie," Cal said gently. "I'm leaving on the red-eye."

Home. He was going home. He was going back to Numbah Foah and her children in New York. He'd be in bed with her by morning.

Suddenly, she was as jealous of him as if she had been Cal's lover. How dare he have someone to go home to. How dare he have a life. He was already on his way, his thoughts moving ahead to his new family and what he had to do tomorrow, he was *getting on with it*. When she was lying here fucking herself on this couch like a shipwreck stranded in the middle of a currentless sea.

"Listen, here's my number. If you want to talk, call me. Anytime." But she knew she wouldn't call because if she did, he'd be taking tango lessons in Buenos Aires or beating the bush in Kuala Lumpur. Nevertheless, she pawed in the debris on the orange footlocker to find a pencil, the tears in her eyes keeping her from seeing right. She finally found one, wrote down his fucking number.

"We'll go on, Josie," he said. "We have no choice. We'll find a way."

Will we? Will we really, Cal? You dickhead. You *find a way. You fucking find a way.* After she hung up, she just sat for a while, staring at the phone beyond her bare knees. Pen came out with a bowl of Cheetos.

"Get dressed," Pen said. "People are coming over."

"What people?" Josie said. She couldn't imagine there was still anybody left in the world.

"Your friends," Pen said. "Get some fucking clothes on."

Shirley Kamaguchi came over, and Genghiz, her boss at the shop, a self-proclaimed Aztec from Pico Rivera, fourth generation, and Ben Sinister, and David Doll. They brought boxes of sushi and ate at the battered table. "This is a nice place," Ben said, glancing up at the Chinese characters on the lamp. *Tao, ming.* "Did you do those?"

"Michael," Josie said.

"He always seemed nice. I liked him," said Shirley K., her Kabuki red mouth making a sad pout.

Pen didn't say anything. It was the first time Josie had ever seen her hang on to her opinion, leave a thought unvoiced.

It was surreal to have all these people here. No one ever came to their house, it was their kingdom, their province, lair and clubhouse and center of the universe. Now the spell was gone and people were just walking in. It got dark, and Paul Angstrom came from work at Cashbox with a bag of tamales and Mason and PJ came with Stoli and popcorn. Pen must have put a bulletin up at the Hong Kong Café. They were all so sorry, really kind, but not one of them had known him, no one had known the first thing about him. They talked about other friends who died. Pen told them all how Meredith attacked her at the funeral, and Genghiz talked about a friend of his who had killed himself while he was taking hormones for a sex-change operation. "I just think of the last time he called me, I was in a rush, I said I'd get back to him and then I didn't. I just forgot. And then he was dead. Like, what if there was something I could have done? I mean, I'd just had coffee with him. We weren't that close but it was like, I should have been there."

These are my friends, she kept telling herself.

They drank the Stoli, and PJ had some blow, and Genghiz brought poppers from one of the boys' clubs on Santa Monica Boulevard. It wasn't quite the high she wanted, she really could have used some big fat reds, but you took what you got and were goddamn grateful for it. The poppers blasted her head blank for five minutes, it was great not to have one fucking thought. The blow got her blood moving, she even laughed a little. High, she could even imagine Michael was out shopping at the Chinese market, or down at Launderland, any minute he would come back through the door, unshaved and rumpled in his tweed jacket, and wonder why the fuck his house was full of people he'd never liked. Ben Sinister picked up Josie's blue child-sized guitar that Michael had given her last Christmas, and played a few Bowie songs, "Suffragette City," "Spiders from Mars."

Paul sat down at Michael's old battered upright and put his hands on the keys and started to play, softly, something she recognized but couldn't name, and then she could, the slow opening chords to Patti Smith's "Birdland." He sang it all the way through. It was about a boy whose father died, and the spaceships that were going to pick him up, with his father at the controls. *Take me up, Daddy . . . don't leave me here alone . . .*

It was exactly what she wanted to hear. She went and sat in Michael's chair by the window, looking out at that light-spiked view they had so loved they never had curtains. The lights on the side of the glen, Silverlake, Hollywood. She ran her hands over the torn upholstery, where he'd picked at it, staring out the window, late at night, drinking his red wine, brooding. She'd tried to cheer him up. Sitting on the arm of the chair, pressing her face to his, looking out at the same view, these same sparkling lights. "Look, it's beautiful, Michael," she'd say.

"It's like something from Bosch," he'd say.

And it fucking was.

Ben started playing "Satellite of Love" and Paul joined in on the piano, everybody knew the words, but Josie wasn't really in the picture. How could she pretend she hadn't seen it coming? Now she couldn't help but see. Bosch was everywhere. In the Astroturf at Mount Sinai, in Michael's blown-out eyes. In *I hope you find someone who can meet your needs better than I could.* It was here in the living room full of people who clearly cared about her, though God knew why.

The phone rang, and Pen answered it, her Camel Straight dangling from her lip like a dame's in a noir film. "Hello? Well fuck you too." She slammed the receiver back on the cradle. "It was that bitch again," she called over to Josie. "Your ex-future-mother-in-law." Josie watched Pen in the window's reflection, as her friend came over and sat on the torn arm of Michael's chair, held her against her T-shirt, stroking her dirty hair. "Look, Josie. I talked to Maddie this morning." Maddie, the models' booker at Otis. "Phil Baby needs a model Tuesday, a sitting with Callie McClain. I told her you'd do it. No, don't say no. It'll be good for you, believe me."

How like Pen. Just sign her up, without even asking. Josie sat there with her eyes closed, leaning against her friend, the hands stroking her hair. She knew there were reasons to stay home, good reasons. She could barely stand upright, or take a full breath. She had forgotten her name, how to button a button. She was so transparent, they might not even be able to see her.

And yet, when would it end? She would still have to pay rent, and eat. And Michael would still be dead. He was dead everywhere.

6
Otis

Josie drifted down the hall at Otis, paced by her own ghostly image reflected in the display of student work — her clumpy unwashed hair and pale face, her yellow fur coat. She felt like a hyena, ugly, outcast, a disease. Only the familiar smell of the drawing studio soothed her, the charcoal and sweat, the sound of graphite on paper, Phil Baby bent over some girl, pointing out a problem, and she knew Pen was right, it was good to be here, in this grimy studio where she'd posed so many times. This was real. Phil Baby looked up, his eyes round in surprise, though they were always round, it was the little glasses that did it. He hurried to her. "My God, Josie, what are you doing here?" he whispered, taking her hand in his. Pen named him Phil Baby because he looked like a beatnik, the glasses and beret and pointy beard threaded in gray. Sweet Phil Baby. She wished he wouldn't look at her like that, she couldn't stand anybody to be nice to her right now, she was trying so hard to keep it together.

She shrugged. "They said you needed a model."

"Yeah, but not you. Christ, Josie, what are you doing?" Poor Phil. Just the kind of man who would fall in love with an impossible girl like herself.

"Killing time," she said. She didn't know what she'd do with the rest of her life, but for the next three hours, it wouldn't be a problem. Yet Phil Baby wasn't Henry Ko, who viewed her as a glorified bowl of fruit. Phil wanted to hug her, adopt her, give her the key to his soul, his apartment, his checking account. He wanted to save her. "It's okay, Phil. I've got to get used to it." She pulled away from his graphite-dark hand, hitched her bag, and walked back to the screen where the models changed.

Phil Baby returned to his student, a girl in

overalls sitting in the chair where Michael used to sit. The seat closest to the windows. Suddenly, Josie felt a rush of fury. She wanted to go over there and yank that girl out of that chair, turn it over, kick her to the floor. *Do you know whose seat you're sitting in?* But she didn't. And it wasn't his seat anymore. No, he'd given up any and all seats. He'd written himself off the seating chart.

On the modeling stand, flame-haired Callie moved through her gesture poses. She caught Josie's eye over the art students' self-barbered coiffures, not moving her head, but her eyes speaking sympathy. Josie didn't want anybody's pity. Why wouldn't they just let her get on with it, become an inert shape in space? She liked Callie, though, the way her body challenged the students' ideal of beauty, its elongated breasts and the weals of multiple pregnancies. Josie appreciated that courage. At first, she'd thought, if she ever looked like that, she would disappear into the house and never come out, make love with the lights off. How had she ever been so ignorant? How right that the body changed over time, becoming a gallery of scars, a canvas of experience, a testament to life and one's capacity to endure it.

She went behind the screen and removed her clothes, her shoes. Everything seemed suddenly sharp, dangerous, the hooks, the splintered supports with their graffiti — *Yolo '64, Ben + Harriet*. She felt like old people who forgot what shoes were for, each gesture calling meaning into question — unbuttoning a button, breathing. Movement slowed to half speed, quarter speed, as if the air had thickened. She could take nothing for granted, her hand on her shirt, her ability to keep the floor underfoot.

The students were playing Devo, their geeky mania filling the air. Normally she liked Devo fine, but today she wished she was at Phil's place over at the Villa Elaine — he played Coltrane while he painted, Miles Davis. She wrapped herself in her sarong of a flowered tablecloth and came out to watch Callie. Ridiculous to have to cover herself, when she would be naked in front of them in a few minutes, but it was the convention and she hadn't the energy to protest.

As Callie finished her gesture poses, the baby artists sketched furiously. How real their own futures seemed to them. When any of them might be dead tomorrow. She thought of the prayer Michael told her the Jews said on their New

Year: "On Rosh Hashanah it is opened and on Yom Kippur it is closed, who will live and who will die, who by fire and who by water, and who torn apart by wild beasts . . ." She looked at the students, wondering which of them would be mangled in a car wreck, who would die by a stray bullet coming in off the park. The boy in the skinny tie? The girl in the shaved Mohawk? All looking at the model as if they didn't own flesh, as if they couldn't mount the stand themselves. Their eager eyes unlocking the secrets of the human form, but so much like Cal, talking about "the bereaved" as if it didn't apply to him.

She walked behind them, glancing over their work. Some had airbrushed Callie, they were looking right at her and yet something inside their minds couldn't let them see her nursed-out breasts, her belly's record of babies, while others exaggerated her flaws, like brave children facing monsters, turning stretch lines into claw marks. This body. Who could just look at it as it was, without prettying it up or emphasizing its awfulness? This class should be taught by shamans, not art teachers.

Callie's timer went off. She picked up her robe and slid into it, an olive green kimono that made her freckled skin glow. She came off the stand and threw her firm arms around Josie. She smelled of sweat and roses, her wild flame hair of Prell. "I'm so sorry, Josie. I heard. That lovely, lovely boy. I remember him." She traced her fingers across Josie's neck. "What's this?"

A ladder of green bruises, the mother's hands closing. *How dare you.* "Nothing. Forget it."

"Josie, they're bruises." Callie's eyes darkened with concern.

"Let's just get on with it, okay?" Josie said, sounding colder than she liked to sound. Callie blanched, dropped her hand, left her alone. She was sorry to have hurt her, but she wanted them all to leave her alone, let her keep it together. Kindness was the last thing she needed. She had to stay in the icy place, the numb place, and their warmth threatened to melt her just when she needed the cold.

She climbed onto the model's stand, set her timer, shrugged off the tablecloth. The little model's heater hummed. She began her own short gesture poses. Thirty-second poses were her favorites, they let you take chances, go off balance, reach and twist. She was good at this. When there was nothing else, there was the body. She could always make an interesting shape in space, naked and barefoot before a classroom of strangers, even with her bruised neck and her stricken face. It felt good to put herself aside along with her clothes, and just be.

The sun from the dirty skylight fell onto her shoulders and hair. The students studied her like a puzzle that needed to be solved. She had always liked the way their eyes brought her into focus, found beauty in her assemblage of parts, neck and backs of knees, the knobby piano of a spine. She had not been thought beautiful growing up. No one had looked at her twice. One glance and they knew. Just another Tyrell. *They breed like rats. Why doesn't anyone wash their faces? The mother's not all there, you know. She sits in that house, I don't know if she's been out in ten years.* LA gave her a face of her own. It hung glamour around her like a champagne mink. That was what Michael had fallen in love with. Not understanding that nothing was under it.

She moved between poses, concentrating on creating positive and negative space. *What isn't there is as important as what is,* Phil always said. What wasn't there. The girl in Michael's seat drew in big dramatic gestures, her hand making jagged bursts on the paper. A pimply boy dropped his eyes to his work when she met his gaze. She always knew the ones who were in love with her. They were shy once she dressed, or else talked to her in a weird forced normality, as if they hadn't seen her nude, as if they'd met in a supermarket. This body and its freedom gave her the only power she'd ever had.

On a normal day, she would walk around after a session and let them show her their drawings. Some were proud, others nervous. As she looked at their work, it often occurred to her that no one existed in fact. Simply existed, the same for all. You could see it on every easel. Some fixated on the darkness of her bush and the hair in her armpits, in contrast with the wild bleach job. Others preferred the delicacy of her bones, or the attitude of her sober gaze and the unsmiling mouth. Marco, her first boyfriend in LA, called her an exhibitionist, said she should get a job in a strip club if she liked it that much, it paid better. She did like it, but it wasn't what people thought — a sex job. It was the opposite — a statement, personal, frank, without intention to please. *Here I am. This is me. My fact. I can do this, can you?* Callie with her stretch marks, Frank, who was almost a dwarf. Each body held some truth the baby artists needed to see. Even that of a seventeen-year-old dropout from Bakersfield.

How she used to envy them. Someone was shelling out big money for each and every one of those seats — tuition, rent, art supplies. Although she'd gotten herself out of Bakersfield, and created a life she'd always dreamed about, a glamorous life — modeling, acting in student films, knowing the people worth knowing — still, she'd envied them. All this instruction, everything so well thought out, people like Phil Baby unlocking the world step by step. Nobody had ever shown her shit. Only Michael.

But now, she knew something else. That all the education in the world was not enough. It wasn't always what you knew. Michael had gone to Harvard but it hadn't kept him alive. Ignorance was familiar as sunshine, but now she knew it was possible to know too much.

She remembered the poems Michael once showed her, things he'd written as a kid. Beautiful strings of words like music, talking about the true world, the way he could feel the presence of God like a face gleaming behind a curtain. "These are gorgeous," she said. "You've got to write more."

"They're garbage," he said, taking them from her. "Third-rate imitation Eliot. Dash of Dylan Thomas. A little Sexton on top."

She shifted her pose, twisting, extending her arms, a dancer's pose she'd seen in a book about Matisse. Red bodies against blue. She could re-create that pose, and it was still beautiful, even if it had been done before. But to satisfy Michael, everything had to be absolutely original, better than anything ever before, paintings or poems or music. She had always believed that knowledge helped you do things, but Michael's knowing just took away his courage, his freedom.

"My mother always said, *There's no place in the world for a good concert pianist,*" he said. *"There are too many geniuses."*

At least if you were ignorant, you could do what you wanted, you had no idea what had been achieved in the past. You were free, instead of chewed at by bleeding impotence, dissolved away like a pearl in acid.

She looked again at the girl in Michael's seat. Every term, there would be a new student in that chair by the window, someone who hadn't known that Michael Faraday once sat there and fell in love with a model named Josie Tyrell. With whom he should never have shared a sentence.

Her timer went off. She wrapped herself and walked over to the table with the coffee urn, poured herself a bitter cup, wondering what had happened to his jacket. Meredith. She had to have it. She had the notes, of course she had the jacket. Josie blanched, thinking of how the woman had attacked her at the funeral, when she had every right to be there, every right and more. Whatever Meredith thought, Michael didn't belong to her. She might like to think it, but it wasn't true, it hadn't been true since that day in the blue bedroom. She should have told Cal she wanted that jacket, maybe he would have grabbed it for her while Meredith lay passed out on her satin bed. Josie craved its coarse weave, a memory so strong it made her stagger.

Callie was there, arm across her shoulder. "Are you all right?"

She nodded, staring at her bare foot, thin and childlike, she had painted the toenails black two weeks ago, but it was all chipping off. Her foot looked strange to her, a thing, this odd-shaped thing attached to her. She wondered if she even knew how to move it, it was so stupid, it made no sense, this object, she had forgotten what it was for. Michael's feet were elegant as hands, the long toes, she remembered the first time she'd put those toes in her mouth in the bathtub — how astonished he'd been, that she would think to do such a thing, to give him that pleasure. When she would have done anything.

They had been happy. If she forgot everything else in the world, she would remember that. She was the only one who could remember it now.

She and Callie mounted the modeling stand together. A two-model pose challenged the intermediate student, there were so many angles, so much foreshortening. Callie set the timer, and they found a good pose, Callie on the stool, Josie behind her with her hand on the older woman's freckled shoulder. The softness of Callie's flesh under her hand, its warmth. Not like Michael's at the morgue. His living body turned into a thing. Cold, wooden. Intentional.

She felt Callie's shoulder stir slightly. The body. That had been a source of so much joy. But in the end, it was just a hunk of cold chicken, wasn't it? A weird flesh machine, that kept breathing in and out, mindlessly, digesting, shitting, Bosch on two legs. Good enough to carry you around for a few decades before things started to go wrong. No difference between this body and a load of dead animals carted out from the animal shelter. And there would be fifty years more of moving this puppet thing around, creating other puppet things to replace you. The thought was unbearable. She felt bluish white and raw, like an Egon Schiele woman — Michael's favorite artist.

"He makes everyone ugly," she once told him.

"He's just not sentimental," Michael said.

After class, Phil Baby stopped her before she left. "If I can do anything . . . anything at all."

"Sure, Phil, thanks," she said, and got out of there before he made her cry. She hurried into the dank courtyard with its monstrous rubbery plants, stopping to light a cigarette, but nobody was coming up to her with a cheese Danish with white raisins, and his aquarium eyes. She stepped out into the cold winter sun.

Then she saw it. The silver car, parked at the curb. Was it déjà vu? Was Michael going to come out, was it starting all over again? Her hand went unconsciously to her bruised throat. *I could have you killed. I think it would be worth it.* Wasn't it enough that bitch had read his suicide note? That she hadn't even let her say goodbye to Michael in peace? What would it have cost her? Fucking nothing. So what was next on the menu, shooting her outside Otis in the middle of the street? She thought of the school's side entrance on Seventh Street. She knew she could duck in and make a quiet escape, but suddenly she didn't care. Fuck Meredith Loewy. This was her territory — Otis, MacArthur Park, the Elks Club next door where the big punk concerts were, Carondelet. Meredith could go back to Los Feliz and her big moldy house and fuck herself.

She strode out onto the street, extending her arms in her yellow coat, she wasn't normally one to provoke a scene, but she'd had enough. "What the fuck, Meredith? You gonna kill me right here? Run me over?" she yelled out. "Do it, right where everybody can see. Famous pianist murders son's lover. Come on, what are you waiting for, reporters?"

She could feel Meredith watching her from behind those dark glasses as she came closer, walking on the yellow line right down the middle of Park View. A bum with a shopping cart full of cans stopped to watch. "You better do it," she shouted, "'cause I'm gonna kick the shit out of you in about two point five seconds."

She could see Meredith's big hands, gripping the wheel now, her face edited by those sunglasses like a porn star. Josie kept her eyes trained right on those blanked-out ovals, and kept walking. When she was thirty feet away, the silver car started up and came toward her. *Okay. Get it over with.* She stood and waited for the impact, her arms out, but at the last minute Meredith swerved and drove past her. Dirt and trash blew up in her face. Meredith didn't even turn to look at Josie, who stood in the middle of the street, giving her the finger.

7

Club Rat

Deep in the warehouse district, Pen found a parking place under the loading bay of a nut wholesaler. They hurried along in the unlit street, careful not to get their heels caught in the spaces between the paving blocks that dated from the turn of the century. The road stank of garbage from the produce market on San Pedro. They went in an unmarked door. At the tiny cash booth, a hatchet-faced ticket man eyed them foxily — Josie, heavy eyed with exhaustion in her yellow coat, Pen black lipped and assertive in her purple vinyl and handmade Iggy fan shirt. He wanted to see their IDs, then insisted on the

ten bucks cover. Pen pushed in beside Josie, cigarette poised between patent-leather lips. "Don't
be an asshole. I'm with *Puke.* Pen Valadez, I'm
on the list, fuckhead." She smoked her Camel
Straight like a con, half hiding it in her hand. She
blew smoke in his face.

Ticketman looked down the list. "Have your
friend give us a kiss and we'll let you both in
free."

"Fuck yourself, dickhead." Pen burned a hole
in the Formica with her cigarette.

But Josie leaned in and kissed him. She was a
girl with a dead boyfriend, what good were her
kisses now? He was welcome to them, poisoned
as they were.

He stamped their hands with the face of a boy
who'd just eaten the head off an Easter bunny,
let them pass through the black curtain, into the
dark and the noise of Club Rat. It was just the
end of the Weak Nellies set. Fire-limit punkers
flung themselves around in the mosh pit —
more and more skinheads, they were taking over
the scene, even for an art band like Lola Lola.
Somebody already had a bloody nose. The old
floor groaned beneath the weight of the crowd.
Little else had changed. She hadn't been here
since she broke up with Nick Nitro. His band,

the Nitrogenics, played the Rat. She looked around, praying that at least that encounter would be spared her.

The black-painted woodwork and tinsel still yearned for arson, and tiny, sweating waitresses in corsets and heels pushed their way through the mass, trays held high over their tall sculptured hair. The drag bartender glanced at Josie's ID and flicked it back across the battered bar. No scorn like the scorn of an aging queen for a pretty girl with a crap fake DL. Pen bought them tequilas and beer backs, began edging a place for them at the bar, first resting her drink, then an elbow, finally leaning in, turning sideways for Josie. Josie knocked back her tequila and set the glass on the bar, touched her lips to the back of her hand.

It was good to be here tonight. Nothing reminded her of Michael. He wouldn't be caught dead in a place like the Rat. *Not even dead,* she thought, drinking her beer. He'd hated crowds, never liked punk. He couldn't handle the nakedness of the rage — his own was so well camouflaged, so sophisticated and finely tuned, he could never see the similarity between himself and Donnie Draino screaming into a mike.

She shrugged off her coat in the bathhouse

humidity. Her slight shoulders gleamed under a thin tank top, she looked both glamorous and implausible in a child's pleated skirt worn over torn tights and a pair of red rubber cowboy boots. At the edges of her visual field, she could see the shapes of male faces turning toward her. Even now, when she was transparent as wet paper. She was so tired of herself. She felt irritated, restless, wolfish somehow. She remembered the first time she came here, how impressed she'd been, thinking how cool it all was, when it was just sweaty and crowded and deafening. She ordered another tequila.

"Make it two," Pen said.

They held up their shots and grimly touched glasses. Pen's heavily rimmed eyes regarded her briefly, then knew enough to look away. Pen Valadez, the very first person she'd met in LA. Josie had just come down with Luanne to see some guy her sister had met at the stock-car races, when she decided she wasn't going back to Bakersfield. There was nothing for her back there but more of the same. They'd picked a kid up hitching, a rockabilly goth who said he was an art student, it sounded cool. When they dropped him at Otis, Josie grabbed her bag and got out too. Some kids sitting on the steps told her about the house on Carondelet, to look for the rubber tree in the front yard. She'd found it easily, dark shingled, deep porched, the door un-locked, the downstairs stinking of garbage and cats and stale beer. And upstairs, this purple-haired Latina was taking a leak with the bath-room door open, panties around her ankles, brushing her teeth while she peed. "You looking for the room?" It was just an oversized closet, but it was only seventy-five dollars a month, and it wasn't Bakersfield.

Pen started her modeling, took her to the clubs, introduced her around, got her going, clued her in, how to get into student films and make stuff to sell to the rich punk boutiques. She'd always been on Josie's side. Until Josie fell in love with Michael. And yet she'd held her hand at the coroner's, and never said a word, though she'd predicted disaster from the start. She'd kept her company, fed her, slept on the couch in the house to which she'd never been invited. Bullied her, made her live. *He's going to be dead a long time, Josie. You might as well get off the fucking couch.*

Pen leaned against the bar, nodding to the music, the heel of her boot tucked in behind the bar rail, torn fishnets under the little vinyl skirt. "Did you hear, they just got a deal with Rhino."

Josie noticed the backs of Pen's hands. They were already wrinkled. Time streaming through them, all of them, like yarn. Her, and Pen, the bartender, the hatchet-faced man at the door. Life was just a factory of days and weeks and years, and for what, when you knew how the story turned out, what the product was at the end? She wouldn't mind if the whole place went up in flames right this second. All of them immolated together, their ashes mingling in the smoldering aftermath. What if this ceiling fell in exactly two minutes from now, crushing them all like those layered tortas Michael used to make.

She looked around the club, the boys in the mosh pit, the waitresses in their corsets and tutus, Donnie Draino spewing beer from the stage. How right it would be to die, right here, right now, with all these people. Better than alone in a motel room in Twentynine Palms. The boy in the pompadour, the girl in the white plastic trench coat. The ceiling coming in, crushing them all like cockroaches. The screaming, the weight on top of you, too heavy to breathe, and then it would be over. Save her the problem of having to inhale and exhale, thousands of times a day. Every person, every cow, every dying dog, everyone on the planet, breathing this same tired old air. She wanted it all to stop.

Finally, the Nellies took their break, and Josie was surprised that nothing had happened, no earthquake, no fire. She realized she was disappointed.

Paul and Shirley K. were pushing their way through the crowd, Paul so pale he was almost albino, he practically glowed in the dim light of the Rat. Shirley's glossy Japanese hair caught the lights with its intricate geometric wedges edged in blue. They both kissed her, Shirley touching Josie's dank locks with a professional hand, arranging her hairline. Pen was right to have dragged her out, at home she just sank to the bottom. The Rat was loud and crowded and distracting, she could simply be.

"Allo." A boy in a Sex Pistols T-shirt, the sleeves safety-pinned, his teeth bunched in a lopsided smile, pushed in next to her, ordered a pint of Newcastle, and introduced himself as something or other, from Leeds in England. It was good to meet someone new. Someone who didn't know what had happened, someone to whom it was just another Tuesday night. It seemed Leeds was friends with the bass player for Lola Lola. He'd just moved here, worked at a print shop in Hollywood. His accent was so thick she could barely understand him. It was just as well, she didn't really want to understand anybody. It was easier to nod and drink her beer. How well did anybody know anybody anyway? *His hyperintellectual Harvardettes.*

"Bet you're an actress," the boy from Leeds said.

"Waitress." She turned to the bar, signaled for a third tequila. She didn't like people who tried to impress you by fluffing up who they were. When she said actress or model, they got the wrong idea entirely, that she had ambitions, that she thought she was going to end up on a TV show. She didn't care about any of that crap. That was her edge, her secret weapon. She didn't give a shit. If you didn't have anything truly great to offer, something truly amazing, then you should just shut the fuck up. Unless you were Michael Faraday, for instance. She raised the pale liquid in a mock toast, slugged it down.

"You could be a model," the boy said. "You know, I know some people, they're making videos, like of bands. You might could do that."

She might could, but it only paid twenty a day tops, and she made more in two hours at Otis just standing still. But she didn't give him a hard time, he was just trying to be nice. "So what's Leeds like?"

"Like LA without palm trees," he said.

She laughed. It was a surprise, that she still could. She wouldn't have thought she could even rouse the shadow of a chuckle. She liked the way he talked, he said *f* instead of *th. Wifout.* Like a little kid. They watched the roadies set up for Lola Lola, props and instruments, a giant rubber sex doll. "See the bloke wif the green stripe in 'is hair?" Leeds said in her ear, pointing at a skinny boy in black eyeliner, a ruffled shirt. "He follows her everywhere, says she put a spell over 'im. All over the world. They'll be in Japan and that little wanker'll be there."

A desperate fan. Just like John Lennon. Josie wondered if Meredith had fans like that. Followers. If she fucked any of them. Did Meredith Loewy even have a sex life? That cold beauty, a woman like that, she must still get offers, even at her age. She wondered what kind of man Meredith would pick for herself. She pictured a dark man, in a dark suit with a very white shirt, putting a fur coat around her shoulders for her, saying something quiet and witty. But she'd picked Cal, who wasn't anything like that.

The lights went down and the band took the stage, began the opening number, slow and spooky. They were joined by an enigmatic figure in eye makeup like a mask, Raggedy Ann tights and a red yarn wig, dildos strapped to her skirt like tools from a carpenter's belt. Lola Lola had been thrown out of East Germany for obscenity and incorrigibility. Josie shot a grateful look to Pen, who gave her a shove. *Told you so.*

The singer snarled and crooned over the heads of the crowd, weaving her spells, her black-magic curses, pumping the dildo that hung in front of her short puffy skirt, that fabulous growling voice, a whisper, then a huge burst of operatic sound. They were all a body now, the crowd, and Josie was part of it. She had forgotten about this, the narcotic of the crowd. This is why you came to hear music. To stop being yourself, to let that thing that you supposedly were go, and just be part of a mob, synchronized by the heavy beat, mesmerized by a singer with big smeary red lips, her spooky chant.

Michael hated this, it was the worst thing he could imagine, disappearing into the mass — he didn't know how to submerge himself, he was the puzzle piece that fit nowhere. Pen was right, this was the right place for her. To be no one. Nothing. The wanker with the green hair lurched and jerked as if he were being electrocuted.

Lola Lola sang the song "Heard You Laughing," which Josie knew was for Ferdi Obst. They said Lola had been the one to find him, in her dressing room after the show, with the needle still in his arm. Josie wanted to meet her. Lola Lola would understand about Michael, she could tell her things she'd told no one, not even Pen. The stupid things you say in the rain, that can't ever be washed away. Lola would not blame her, Lola would know just how bad it could get, even with someone you loved more than life.

The boy with the green streak in his hair was screaming, trying to jump onstage. Lola Lola kicked him down with her pointy lace-up boot as she patrolled the lip of the stage. Josie wondered what it would be like to be a star like that, arousing strangers in their deepest fantasies, fans trying to scramble onstage just to touch her, how intense it all was, they just wanted to be near, worship her, and the darkness of that. John Lennon had settled down, that was his problem, people knew where to find him. Lola Lola wasn't making that mistake, she'd been touring for years, living nowhere, like those magical birds born with no legs, who flew until they died, sleeping on the wind. It occurred to her that Lola Lola was a lot like Meredith Loewy, only with more drugs and shittier hotels and less practicing.

"There's a party after the show," Leeds yelled. "Why don't you come? Your friends too." That would be good, the party would go all night, she wouldn't have to be home until sunup. It was easier to sleep in the daytime. And she might meet Lola Lola. Maybe the singer would ask Josie to go on the road with her, she could do Lola's laundry, buy her drugs, and never, ever come back.

They piled into Pen's red Impala, Josie and Leeds in back with Shirley and Paul, and in front, Shirley's friend Ikuko and a guy Pen had picked up, a skinny caved-chest guy with a little goatee like Maynard G. Krebs. He worked for Tree People, teaching kids about nature. They stopped to buy some voddy and beer and drove up to Hollywood, past the lit-up pancake stack of

Capitol Records, and off at Cahuenga. "Have you met her?" Ikuko asked from Maynard's lap, her head crouched under the low roof.

"She's fucking insane," Leeds said. "But not totally. Like an act, but under the act it's real. You'll see. That's it, coming up. Start looking for somewhere to park."

It was an old Deco building right on Cahuenga, Josie had never noticed it before. She expected a fleabag, going in, if the rat-eaten lobby and the shuddering elevator were any indication of things to come, but the elevator opened right into the penthouse apartment, elegant in that Sunset Boulevard haunted way. It was pretty trashed out, had obviously seen many such parties — fine in low light, but depressing in daytime, cigarette burns on the furniture, the carpet filthy. But it had once really been something, back in the day. Pillows and bolsters floated like rafts on the big carpet, and empty bottles already crowded the tables. A vase of gargantuan paper roses stood under a pink light. People sat on pillows attacking guitars, doing "Anarchy in the UK." The Hole had caravanned over, there was nobody left at the Hollywood Towers. She knew all these people. They stared at her, but when she looked back, they pretended they were busy talking to somebody or looking into the bottom of their drinks. Of course they all knew by now. Nobody knew what to say. Like she had cancer.

Lola Lola wasn't there yet. In the kitchen, someone had filled the Sparkletts bottle with a Windex blue liquid. Pen and the others filled paper cups, but Josie passed. Whatever they'd put in the Windex blue wouldn't do her any good tonight. What she needed was booze and some downers, the wine and bread of forgetting. They went out onto the rooftop. A spread had been laid, bean dip and crackers and wedges of cheese, little éclairs, the label must have splurged.

"Hey, Josie," she heard behind her, a familiar voice, unwelcome as VD.

Nick Nitro lounged with a bottle of Jack Daniel's in his hand atop the low wall of the rooftop garden. Nausea overwhelmed her at the sight of his nervy body, the stringy blond hair. How had she missed him at the club? Or maybe he had skipped the gig and come straight to the party. "Hey, I heard what happened. That's a drag. A lot of that going around." He took a swig from the JD and screwed the cap back on. You wouldn't want to fall down and spill your booze.

She held up her hand to ward off any attempt at false sympathy. Christ, what did Nick care about Michael? She hated the idea that they'd even lived in the same world. Pen tried not to meet Josie's eyes, but in the end couldn't avoid her, smiled and shrugged, good as confession. You could always count on Pen, if there was anything you wanted to keep private, she'd make sure it was broadcast on the AM band. You could pick it up in Hawaii. Pen had no sense that someone might want to keep her private life private. Privacy wasn't even a concept. She'd never closed a bathroom door in her life.

"You can always crash with us at the Fuckhouse," Nick said. "If ya get lonesome."

If ya get lonesome. To think, she had once been that lonesome. When she'd had Michael, but didn't. She wished someone would just put a pin in her brain and stir it around, like they did to the frogs in her high-school physiology class. She tasted bile in the back of her throat. People were staring again, knowing she and Nick had been an item, hoping for some drama. "I'll never be that lonesome."

"Yeah, I believe that," he said to Ritchie, his keyboardist, handing him the square bottle. "Josie without dick, yeah, what time is it?"

She flew at him then, but he was too fast, he ducked and then grabbed her wrist as she swung again. She struggled to get her hand free, struck him with her left.

"Hey, I said I was sorry he offed himself." He was shouting at her, ducking her blows. "What're ya hitting me for? I didn't do shit but get you off royal. Didn't I? Didn't I?"

"Shut up, just shut the fuck up!" Hitting him until Pen dragged her off.

"Hey, Josie, it's not Nick's fault. Just stop it."

She sat on the wall, crying right in front of everyone. Fuck them. She'd never deserved Michael. She didn't know how to be with someone like that, how to take care of him. *I hope you find someone to meet your needs.* Nick knew who she was, how to treat her. Like the garbage she was.

"No fighting. Unless it's me," a deep, resonant German-accented voice boomed. Lola Lola made her entrance through the glass doors onto the terrace, posing in the doorway like Bette Davis in a long, red feathered coat. "Why is that girl crying?"

Nick shrugged. "Her boyfriend offed himself. Like it's my fault."

Josie twisted in Pen's grip. "I hate your fucking guts."

He grabbed his crotch at her. "Suck my cock, you do it so good."

Lola Lola turned to Josie, her face right up close to Josie's so she couldn't see Nick anymore. Lola was tall, her yarn wig gone, hair sculptured in great red wings, her eyes painted, pupils dark as quarter notes. She took Josie's hand. "What's your name, *schätze?*"

The inside of her head roared with blood. "Josie."

"Come inside, Josie. We've got some wonderful hashish, you like hashish? We bought it in San Francisco. Afghani. With opium. They say drugs are not the answer, but really, what is the question?"

Inside, the people around the hookah moved over so Lola could sit down, and she made room for Josie next to her. She felt tiny next to Lola, even smaller than usual. She was drunk and sad and her eye makeup was all smeared, her nose was running. Someone handed Lola Lola a hose. Josie felt like Alice in Wonderland. She had eaten from half the mushroom, she was shrinking, and a man who looked like Frank Zappa, in pink-rimmed spectacles, added shredded tobacco to the big bowl of the hookah, then tore hunks of hashish from a dark wad with his thumbnail, put it on top. They all bubbled together. Lola had lungs like an Olympic swimmer. They all stopped at the same time, holding their thumbs over the mouthpieces of the various hoses. Then passed to the next person. Lola offered her hose to Josie. Around the pipe sat a girl whose hair had been cropped and dyed like a leopard, a handsome dark boy in a Bags Band T-shirt, another man in a Sonny Bono haircut. They bubbled together, sharing a breath like a chorus. Josie started coming on immediately, like an elevator going up.

Lola took the hose back, toked, and passed it to her guitar player, who had settled on her left. The others around the circle bubbled on their hoses. It sounded like a children's party, straws slurping. Lola removed her coat and sprawled against the pillow, and the stink of her postconcert body was as strong as the hash. Josie bubbled again. Lola spoke quickly, still on a manic high from the gig, the rush of words when someone was done with a performance. "They tried to arrest us in Santa Barbara, you heard this?" she asked Josie. Her eyes were black from the hash or whatever else she was on. "You've been to Santa Barbara? They are oh so proper there. No strip searches in Santa Barbara. When Eddie had it in his ass all the time."

The Zappa guy nodded. "Anything for you, Lola dear."

Josie thought it was odd to be smoking something that had been up this guy's ass. It was not just the idea of it — most drugs came that way, probably, but usually it was the ass of someone you never met, someone in Burma or La Paz. But here was this guy with the pink glasses, tall and skinny. It made her wonder what else he had up his ass. Furniture maybe, antiques, gold-leafed icons. Human smuggling, illegal aliens up his ass. It made her laugh to herself. It was good to finally be high. This was exactly what she had been looking for.

"It lends an extra thrill, don't you think?" Lola said in her raspy German-accented English, gesturing with the hookah hose. "We're very attracted to shit, as a race. All animals are, of course, but the human being is more complex in this. We cannot admit we love it, our mothers will punish us, us nasty children, playing with our own shit, rubbing it on the wall. But tell me, what child doesn't play with his shit? We love it, the smell, the texture," Lola rubbed her hands together, as if mashing some clay. "It is the element of creation, no? But it shames us. So we pretend we hate this, when we adore it. Think of the toilet, the Western toilet, you see?"

Josie lay pulverized by the opiated hash, thinking how bizarre life was, how Fellini. Michael was dead, and she was sitting here talking to Lola Lola about toilets, when she wanted to have a real conversation about how to live. It was as if the world had been knocked off the little stand that kept it on the desk, and now it was rolling around on the floor.

Those red lips, her big singer's gestures, calibrated for the back of the club. She was still performing. "Growing up in the East, of course, we had the Soviet model, absolutely Spartan, no good Communist should be fascinated with the individual product of the asshole. But in the West, the toilet has a viewing platform. For analysis of the health, or so we pretend. When it is a pedestal, for the admiration and worship of shit." Her lips, smeary with old lipstick, rubbery red animals squirming on her face. "Americans insist on the superior shit, consuming acres of bran cereal, the better to have big attractive ones. Did you know that all the best perfume has a little bit of shit in it?"

Josie shook her head. A little turd floating in the Chanel No. 5.

"You don't believe me?" Her black eyes opening wide in their mask of black. "It's well known. Any perfumer will tell you the same. We find perfume missing that little excitement if it hasn't just a touch of shit in it. Only cheap perfume has no shit, which is why it's so boring. The great perfumes all have it, or something that smells like it. We're the only animal that tries not to smell like one, we obliterate our own body's odor and then add an artificial one, the scent of a flower or a plant. And yet, in the end, it doesn't really make it for us unless it smells like shit. I think we'd be better off if we could just sniff each other's asses. Dogs are much more secure, don't you think?"

Josie lay on the pillows. She couldn't keep her head up. She'd never smoked anything as strong as this Afghani hash. She wondered why it wasn't affecting Lola like that. They must have done some coke or speed on the way over. She thought of people sniffing each other's asses, but it led to thoughts of dogs, she did not want to think of dogs. Goddamn them all.

Lola shook Josie roughly by the shoulder. "It's good? I told you it was good. You have any cigarettes?"

"Yeah, but I'm too high to get them. They're in my purse."

Lola dug through Josie's red schoolbag purse. "Ooh, la la," Lola said as she pulled out the pack of Gauloises and lit one with Josie's lighter. Her father's Ronson. That waft of butane. Josie lifted her hand slow as in a dream, and Lola put the lit cigarette between her fingers, fired another herself.

"Tell me about your boyfriend," Lola said, settling back on the pillows. "The one who dies."

How to sum him up. She couldn't begin, she couldn't find words. How to describe him, it would sound like four different people. His genius, his beauty. How maddening he was, how tender. How she never thought she would ever love someone so much, hadn't even known she had it in her. And then how fucked up it got. She was sure, of all people, Lola Lola would understand, the one person who could. "He believed in a true world. A world behind this one, that shines through it, like a candle through a lampshade."

"A true world," Lola said. "That's very beautiful." Her eyes shiny black as a deaf-mute's piano. Coke, Josie guessed. "How is this world?"

She thought about the true world, the times they had seen it — it was like light glinting on the surface of the river, that shimmering quality when you saw it. It wasn't the thing itself. It was your own ability to see it. Like the nights they lay in bed listening to the mockingbirds sing. Or the time they knelt by the river, and the blue heron came walking out of the reeds. The feeling when time stopped, and you could stay there forever. "You see the beauty inside everything. It doesn't last long — it's either gone in a minute, you just caught it, or else maybe it's something so big that you normally can't get your head around it. Like the fog in your head clears out. The world stops being a puppet show and you see the real thing. It's probably like that all the time, but you just can't see it, except for those little glimpses."

"A beautiful man," Lola said, posing with her cigarette like Dietrich. "I wished I could have met."

Josie dragged on her cigarette to ease her aching lungs, wiped at her face with the back of her hand. "But then he forgot how. He stopped being able to see it."

She smelled burning cloth and saw Lola, burning holes in her stockings with the tip of her cigarette, holding the fabric out from the skin and piercing it with the cherry. The cloth stank as it burned. "And you?" she asked. "Do you believe in this true world?"

Josie gazed up at the ceiling with its intricate plasterwork, interlinking motifs of deer and palm fronds around what must have been a chandelier, but now was just a lightbulb in a red paper shade. Did she still believe in a true world? She didn't know what she believed in. She didn't have the energy to believe in very much. "I used to."

"No. You must believe," Lola said, propping herself on one elbow. She surprised Josie with her seriousness, the way she said it, not playing to the balcony, not talking to hear the grandeur of her own voice. "Don't let them take it away. Promise me." Josie could see the strip that held Lola's false eyelashes on, her face was so close to hers. Her breath smelled of vodka.

How could she promise? The true world was

a million light-years gone. She turned her head to exhale, so she wasn't blowing the smoke into Lola's face. "Why?"

Lola traced the design on the dark Deco print of the pillow with a finger, flower connected to flower by a path of vines. "Where I grew up, there was no such thing as a true world. Only the State and what was good for the State. You come to treasure a moment of great beauty, when the world is more . . . than this. It must still be there. It must be." And Josie knew Lola wasn't thinking of Michael, but of her own boyfriend, Ferdi Obst, in her dressing room in Paris.

Now Lola Lola was looking at her with those shining black eyes in the mask of black, like someone peering out from a cave. Josie pressed her head onto her hard knees, her pale legs in the child's plaid skirt, the red cowboy boots. Trying not to remember her legs around Nick as he fucked her against the wall, while Michael sat at home staring at Bosch. She wished she could say she couldn't remember, could blank it all out, but she remembered everything. It was in the body. Her body always remembered. Michael turning away from her. He was all she ever wanted. But if she couldn't have him, she knew someone who would take her, no questions asked. Rolling around in shit, yes, to punish Michael for pushing her away. And to punish herself, for not being good enough for him, smart enough, interesting enough. Yes. She knew her level and could sink to it anytime. Revert to type. She had no right to even speak about the true world. She would stink it up even by thinking about it. There had been a true world, but the candle had gone out, and all she had left was a Chinese lampshade, *hecho en Mexico.*

8
Christmas

She didn't want a Holly Jolly. She didn't want a Very Merry or a *Feliz Navidad*. It was only eight o'clock and she had the whole night to get through. All over the city, people were sitting down to turkey dinners and trimming trees and schlogging eggnog till they puked. She threaded her raw-mufflered Falcon up and down the hills and drops of Echo Park, of Silverlake and Angelino Heights, drinking and avoiding the house behind the house on Lemoyne Street where no one lived anymore, listening to a Germs tape on the tinny car stereo. They were doing "We Must Bleed." She should have gone down to Fullerton with Pen and Shirley and Paul to the Black Flag show, but that scene was getting so ugly. Phil Baby invited her to a party at his place, it sounded like death on a TV tray — a bunch of art teachers in horn-rimmed glasses smoking J's and getting swacked on hot wine with cinnamon sticks. There was nowhere she wanted to be, nothing to do but get blasted and drive around until her gas ran out.

She cruised Sunset, the families strolling along the broad sidewalks, the stores all decorated, windows spray-painted with snow and cartoon Santas, *Feliz Navidad.* She stopped at the Chinese market, the parking lot was jammed, people buying their last-minute fish and sponge cake. She pushed a cart around for a while, banging into people in the fluorescent light, down the long cold rows of vegetables and fruit. She decided to buy a weird huge fruit that looked like a porcupine, it weighed about twenty pounds and smelled like armpits. Michael would do something like that. There was no trace of Holly Jolly in here, God bless the Chinese. Men with huge cleavers hacked up chickens and hunks of pork behind the butcher case without a shred of tinsel or a single Santa hat. Two tiny withered grandmas stood over a metal sink full of little blue crabs scrambling over each other in a hopeless bid for escape. Maybe that was God. Peering over the edge of the sink as you tried to claw your way out, picking off this one and that one.

She carried her purchases out to the car, some of the bean cake Michael liked, and the stinking porcupine fruit, and started driving again, the half-pint of voddy between her knees. She couldn't shake the feeling that any minute she would see him, walking along with his hands in the pockets of his tweed jacket, the collar up, striped knitted scarf around his neck. There by the newsstand. Or there, in front of Señor Reynaldo's Escuela de Baile.

How many times before had she done exactly this, driven the streets until she saw him, walking along, coming home after work, digging the neighborhood, feeling it like music, and pulled over, pretending she was just a girl who'd seen something she liked, offering him a ride, maybe something else if he had a mind to. "Hey," she'd call out. "Hey, baby, wanna date?"

The Pioneer Market lot still bristled with unsold Christmas trees. They had bought their own tree here, exactly twelve months ago. She could see them, walking together, arm in arm, the tall rumple-haired boy in the tweed jacket, collar raised against the cold, the girl in the yellow coat with the bleached hair. Laughing, spying on people, guessing who they could be, making up stories. The only fucking Christmas they would ever have. Driving home with the tree tied to the roof of the Falcon like a dead deer, carrying it down the steep stairs. They sat up all night making decorations for it, Michael twisting up an entire circus from pipe cleaners — horses with bareback riders, seals with balls on their noses, elephants, and dogs in tutus. The little ringmaster with his top hat and whip. Twisted strings of trapeze artists, pyramids of acrobats. And she made angels from Kleenex and sheep from cotton balls, and they drank eggnog with rum and danced to Piaf on the stereo. *La Vie en Rose.* Michael wrapped all around her, his cheek pressed into her hair.

She pulled into the parking lot, parked sloppily, trying to see through tears that stung like bleach. They had been happy, they had been. She got out and pushed her way between the trees, blindly, brushing their sticky needles with her hands, the smell overpowering, clinging to her arms. She wanted him desperately, fiercely. She wanted him back, now, right now, she didn't think she could live one more moment. "Miss?" A pimply-faced box boy was peering at her through the branches. "Miss, are you all right?"

"Do I look all right to you?" she said, clutching at pine branches. Her hands smelling of pitch pine and loss. "Do I fucking look all right?"

She gave up and drove over to the Diazepam bakery, which was doing quite a business tonight, *pan dulce* and Valium. She put some fresh *pan dulce* on the tray and wrapped a twenty in a couple of ones, and the small, blank-faced Salvadoran put a little something extra in her bag.

All along Sunset, telephone poles and boarded-up windows were pasted thick with advertisements for *Club Bahía, Chicho Montoya y Gloria Núñez, Sábado 9 de Diciembre, 8 PM. La Laguna Azul con Brooke Shields.* A stoic young man in a hooded sweatshirt sold oranges on the corner at Alvarado. He would have to sell them all before he could go home, probably just a room hotbedded with three other migrants in Pico-Union. No better *Navidad* than hers. She rolled down her window and held out two bucks, he brought the sack over, a small corpse in his arms, she passed the money through and took the weight from him. She could smell it, saffron over sour green, it smelled better than the stink fruit in the back, she threw it onto the passenger seat, and tore open the bag, peeled one on the steering wheel as she drove. The rind was thick, the orange smaller than it should have been, cold and sour, but she ate it anyway, knowing somewhere there was a place where the oranges would be allowed to ripen all the way. They would fall off the trees before they were picked they were so ripe, the smell was only a promise. That's where they should have moved, somewhere things were allowed to ripen all the way. Oranges there would be sweet as kisses in paradise.

On the side streets, Christmas lights festooned the houses, in the trees and across balconies, around barred windows. Little houses with their little families, getting ready for Christmas. Flickering lights at the rooflines, trees in the window. Why couldn't they have stayed like that, her and Michael, the way they were last year? She tried to look into the windows of the houses. So pretty. So hopeful, that instinct for light in winter, believing, waiting for a miracle. While she was left with just this, a stinking fruit in the backseat, a bed of snow.

That was the frightening part about believing

in things. You could wake up one day and it could all be gone. And you were just left with Bosch, crabs and grandmothers and fake snow, *Feliz Navidad.* And here were these tiny houses made beautiful by their lights. She knew that the true world was there somewhere. But not for her. This is how Michael had felt, when he looked out the windows at Bosch. He'd just passed it on, that son of a bitch.

She stopped at Gala's and bought another half-pint of voddy and two packs of Gauloises, and ran out before Mrs. Ramirez could wish her a Merry Christmas. Two packs of ciggies and a pint of Smirny on Christmas Eve, couldn't you read her life right there? She drove back along Sunset, her fingers sticky from the orange on the wheel of the car, while Darby screamed *no God to fear — no God to hear your cries . . .*

People on foot pushed baby strollers, going into the 99¢ Store and Launderland. She wiped her tears on the back of her hand. How he'd loved that. Folding clothes hot from the dryer, just so. Not just cramming them into the duffel like she would have done, but snapping and folding, speaking Spanish to the ladies waiting for their own loads to be done. "This is real life," he once said. "Not those middle-class assholes with their Whirlpools and all the conveniences of home." When any woman there would have sold her soul for a Whirlpool and all the conveniences of home, not to have to drag her family's weekly wash through the streets, each child carrying a part of it in a garbage bag or a box like a laundry parade. But Michael loved being in there, loved laundry done in public, learning what he could about ordinary lives. Nothing he hated more than a closed door, though he was adamant about his own secrets. Oh yes.

She passed El Tigre, and the little botanica with its herbs and saint candles. She should stop, buy him a candle, say a prayer. But what would she pray now? *Sleep well, asshole. Thanks for leaving me here all alone.* She considered the Valium in the bag with the bread, it would go well with the voddy, she'd have to pace it if it was going to last through the night.

She turned the Germs up to 9, all she wanted to hear was Darby screaming his voice raw, Pat Smear smashing away on his guitar, *fuck all of you assholes.* She passed Burrito King, passed the Guadalajara with its blacklight sombrero bar and the tiki bar by the TV station, where her fake ID was no good. She turned up Vermont, all done for Christmas, tinfoil and ribbons on the light posts in front of the Italian delis and bakeries, there was a crowd at the door of Sarno's, where the waiters sang opera in between serving your lasagne, and sometimes a patron would stand up and sing. She wanted to stop, buy a cannoli or some spongy Italian cake flavored with wine, lean on the bakery counter and listen, just be in that warmth, the smells of the food and that surprising beauty pouring out of just plain people. But she knew she would feel like a hyena, a jackal, some ugly scavenger, and kept driving.

Half of LA crawled along Los Feliz Boulevard, gawking at mansions decked in vast seas of light, sucking up more power than a village could use in a year. Each one trying to outdo its neighbor. It was disgusting. It was not the true world. Not the same as the small houses with the lights. Just waste and arrogance. She opened her windows so they could hear what the Germs thought of them.

She turned up a side street, bore right and climbed. She knew where she was going. The last place she should. It was as if the car was going there of its own accord. Light emanated from the big houses, windows blazing, you could see into them like dollhouses. Why didn't they pull their curtains? If it was up to her, she would install thick velvet drapes, no one would be able to look inside. How supremely confident you'd have to be to show off like that, when there were people in this city who would kill you for a leather jacket. Here was a Christmas tree, it must be fourteen feet high. That one had a fireplace, and lights reflecting in a tall gold-leaf mirror. One was having a party, there was a wreath on the door and people were arriving, their arms laden.

She drove higher, until the lights all disappeared. No more Christmas trees or fireplaces or white living rooms. She turned down the tape, and finally, turned it off. Now the houses retreated behind high walls and hedges. She recognized the gate, the Spanish house at the top of the drive. *Via Paloma.* Only the living-room window was lit, obscured but not completely hidden by the big deodar. Josie pulled over and parked opposite the lacy ironwork gate. Here was the hugeness and the darkness she wanted. The mushroom softness of the old stucco wall and the moldering sadness of the place, its abandonment, its smell of cedar and pittosporum. It was as if she had been circling this house since Michael died, moving in tighter and tighter orbits around this epicenter.

She rolled down the window to the cold, breathed in the night's wintry freshness. There could be a frost, the stars bristled in the sky like white flecks on a black enameled roasting pan. A piano started, then stopped, started again, the same phrase over and over. She peeled another orange, throwing the peel out the window that she left rolled down for the fragrance of the pines and the music. You would not know it was Christmas up here. This house in its dignified mourning was out of reach of all festivity, any hope of salvation. From behind the palms and the spiky yuccas and the funereal cedars, the piano repeated the phrase, like a bad conscience playing in your head.

She took a Valium, washed it down with voddy, it didn't burn anymore. She lit a Gauloise. As she watched the house, the gate, she could see the little boy standing there, looking out from between wrought-iron curlicues, his little hands wrapped around the bars. She had never met anyone as lonely as Michael. Lonely, and despising his own loneliness, disdaining the crowd while hoping for connection. For her, in child-hood, loneliness had been a rumor, a distant country, an alpine place with rugged mountains jagged against the sky, the rarefied air fresh as snow. She would have given anything for such loneliness as a child, no one yelling or talking or taking stuff away from you, fighting or saying mean things about you because you were a Tyrell. Although Michael said loneliness was a terrible thing, she had only been able to imagine the quiet and the order of such a life. The words *only child* rang with overtones of luxury, atten-tion, dreamy solitude.

The piano stopped, and she could see the dark-haired figure rising, leaving the lit arch of the window, moving into the half shade of the next one. A small lamp came on, illuminating Meredith's face as she lifted the phone's re-ceiver, dialed. She waited and held the phone awhile, and Josie could almost hear the phone in her own house in Echo Park, ringing. How this woman despised her. Josie's crime — loving her son, loving him, but not enough to save him.

The monstrosity of the idea, that she could have saved Michael. He tried to save her, she tried to save him, and neither one got their fucking wish. *You're exactly what he needed.* Cal did seem like a clown now, self-serving in his idiocy.

Josie looked up at the two lit windows and wondered what it would have been like to have grown up in a place like that. It had always amazed her that Michael, who had come from all this, thought her life was more authentic than his, when in fact it was thin and paltry, all her glamour just a brave child playing make-believe. The awful precious moment of receiving her first new dress, store-bought, pink and stiff, with net that scratched her skin. She got it for Christmas when she was seven. Her mother was home from the hospital but she didn't have a baby this time. "Your mother's just tired," her father said, when her mother wouldn't come out of the bedroom, week after week. She'd been afraid to even sit down in that dress, wore it only twice before she outgrew it and handed it down to Corinne who got red punch on it that never did come out. She should have worn that dress. She should have worn it like hell, every day, to school and everything. Maybe her life would have turned out different.

Michael had had tutors and hotels in Europe. Maids. Seats in first class. When he was twelve, Meredith sent him to Cotillion, where he learned to dance with girls who would never have spoken to Josie Tyrell. She'd seen girls like that, with their shiny perfect hair and braces on their teeth, new leather shoes. They played tennis at the country club, out in Stockdale. She and Corinne once rode their bikes out there, sat and watched those girls. They hadn't even hated them, they were so far away. The flash of their tanned legs in white skirts and white shoes, the light gleaming on their faces. She and Corinne never talked about it, but it had remained, in the very back of her mind.

She gazed up at the dark house. She loved this house. That was the truth. This somber place, with its graceful, rusted gate and heavy dark trees. Darker than Stockdale, but even more compelling. This was the place he grew up, the place that had made Michael. It was in his blood, like the Loewy plot at the cemetery. *Ming.* Light glowed through the iron canopy and the trees, the leaded window. The piano started playing again, slow, painful.

Josie sectioned another orange, peeling the bitter felt from the pale meat. She could smell the groceries in the backseat, the stinking fruit, the bean cake. *Feliz Navidad.* Last year this time Michael was painting, full of ideas, he was teaching her to dance the Charleston. Last year this time, she thought she'd signed a lease on paradise.

She gazed at the yellow light through the window, imagining Meredith up there, in the living room with its threadbare old rugs smelling of must and floor polish. The last time she had been in that house, it had been fall. A sunny morning in October. The leaves had all been swept, and she'd worn her yellow print dress with the geishas on it. They'd been together almost two months, and she was going to meet his famous mother. Meredith was back from tour and needed to talk to him, right away. She'd just found out that he hadn't gone back to Harvard. The lawyer told her, that rat fink.

"Come with me, Josie," Michael said. "I want you to be there."

So they had gone, right through those gates. She was nervous and excited to finally meet this woman whom her son so hated and admired.

The house had changed, now that its owner had returned. The furniture was dusted, the tall windows cleaned, dark floors gleamed with wax. An elegant woman in green slacks and a crisp white shirt rose to meet them, dark hair framing her strikingly boned face. Sea green eye-shadow made her eyes even more translucent above those decisive cheekbones. Eyes just like his. When she saw Josie, her smile flared and died, like a scrap of paper that burns out in a second.

"Meredith, this is my friend Josie. Josie, my mother, Meredith Loewy."

His friend? Suddenly she was his *friend?* After fucking him senseless the night before, his *friend?* Josie followed him down into the living room, face flaming, across the polished floor, the worn-out rugs, if they were so rich, why did they have such junky old rugs? His mother stood by the couch, tall like her son. She smiled at Josie, a flicker, then turned to Michael, who came to her and kissed her, lightly. "Michael, we need to talk. I hadn't expected . . . company." A quick flicker of green.

"Josie's not company, Meredith," Michael said. "She's my girlfriend."

Soothing, healing waters, cooling her face, her heart. *Girlfriend.* She felt restored, she had a right to be here.

"But we need to talk, darling," Meredith said. "I thought Irv explained to you —"

"There's nothing that you can't say in front of Josie," Michael said.

Now, sitting outside the great dark mushroom wall of the house, Josie understood exactly why Michael had brought her along that day. She had thought he wanted to introduce her to his mother, show her there was going to be a new setup. Announce that they were together. But now she saw he was afraid he would weaken, give in, if she wasn't there to remind him of what he wanted, who he'd become in the months his mother had been away. He had drawn courage from her. She thought of Cal: *Storming of the Bastille, you don't even know.*

"I see," Meredith said. "I'll have Sofía bring us some coffee." She walked up the three steps to the foyer. "Michael, will you help me for a moment?"

"I'll wait here with Josie." They settled on one of the white couches in the room where all the grandfather's friends had gathered to drink and flirt and forget and remember the Europe they'd left behind — brilliant parties that sometimes went from one day to the next. Composers and writers and movie directors. Stravinsky had once sat here, Billy Wilder. Schoenberg, who at the time was making a living giving piano lessons to rich brats in Beverly Hills. The very air seemed permeated with their foreign voices, the energy of their genius. And here was Josie Tyrell from South Union Avenue, Bakersfield, being invited to the party.

His mother returned, folded herself onto the couch opposite, defended by the leather-topped coffee table with its bowl of bronze chrysanthemums. She reached out and plucked a sagging bloom from the bowl, threw it into the empty fireplace. A painfully upright woman with black hair scraped into a chignon came down the steps balancing a tray filled with cups and saucers, the silver coffee set now polished to a satin shine. She carried it the way you'd carry a crown on a cushion, her nose high bridged and aristocratic.

Michael spoke to her in Spanish, Josie could tell the woman was thrilled to see him, though she pretended she wasn't, wouldn't look at him straight on. Josie would never have guessed her to be the maid, she looked more like a scary Spanish teacher in her gray wool dress. She set the coffee things down, and sent Michael a glance full of messages, then turned back to her boss. "You like me to pour, Señora?"

"No, I will, thank you, Sofía," Meredith said. "That will be all."

That was over a year ago and she could even

remember that flashing glance Michael had exchanged with the maid. And how intimidated she'd felt, sitting there, in a room where Marcel Duchamp had once played chess with the grandfather. Even the maid acted like royalty.

"So," Meredith said, crossing her legs, folding her hands over her sea-green knee. "Irv tells me you're not going back to Cambridge." Irv, the fink lawyer.

"That's right," Michael said. "I'm in art school. I've decided to be a painter." He put his arm around Josie.

How Meredith's eyes flicked almost imperceptibly at the sight of it. As if the eyes themselves could not believe what they saw, the arm, the ease with which they were together. "You never painted before. Why this sudden interest?" She poured coffee into the cups, handed Michael one on a saucer, black, poured another. "Cream?" She was talking to Josie.

Josie shook her head. The mother passed her the cup and saucer, white with little blue designs painted on it, the handle like pointy lace.

"I'm enjoying it," Michael said. "I'm not even half-bad."

"I like ice cream. But I don't drop out of Harvard for a double scoop." His mother's knuckles tight on the saucer, Josie could see the white bone. "Think, Michael. How are you going to compete with people who have genuine talent? Who have dedicated themselves, who have drive and self-discipline?"

Josie took the cup, the saucer, she wished Michael would say something, stick up for himself. Why didn't he say something? But he didn't, just turned a little white along the jaw, and his mother kept going.

"And I suppose you expect me to support you in this little venture, you and your little friend."

"It's Josie," Michael pronounced, slowly and clearly. "Tyrell."

"Of course. Miss Tyrell," his mother said, her eyes like green welding torches. "Do you understand that my son has dropped out of Harvard College? That this is his senior year?"

As if it was her fault. As if she had anything to do with Michael's choice. She blushed to her hairline.

"I'm painting, it's going very well. What's the big deal? It's not like I'm going to be a lawyer or anything." His hand was on Josie's neck, stroking the fine hair at the nape. "You're an artist, Cal's an artist —"

"You're not an artist, Michael," his mother

said, like God separating the light from the darkness. "And I can't abide a dilettante. Art history was the perfect choice for you, I don't understand this sudden change of heart."

"I don't want to study what other people paint, I want to do it myself. I've always drawn."

"Fiddled. Diddled. Dabbled." Meredith sighed and sat back in the deep pillows of the couch, her voice low and patient, like a nursery school teacher. The morning light streamed in through the big French windows, softened by giant camellia bushes twelve feet high. She sipped from her blue and white cup. "It's not something you can just pick up. *Oh, I'm going to be an artist now.*"

"Kandinsky was forty."

"He's really very good," Josie interrupted. "You should see what he's doing."

His mother turned her attention to Josie, surprised, as if she hadn't noticed her sitting there before. It was a little frightening, the ferocity of that face, like being two feet away from a leopard. Speaking slowly, as if she wasn't sure Josie spoke English, Meredith said, "And just where did you acquire your knowledge of fine art, Miss . . . Tyrell?" Sipping from her coffee, holding the saucer just so, the porcelain so delicate you could see the design right through.

She knew that tone. She'd heard it all her life. *You're one of those Tyrells, aren't you?* "I model at the art school. I've seen a lot of work and he's wonderful. His teachers think so too."

"A model," Meredith said. Not a question, a statement, as if a piece of the puzzle had fallen into place.

"There's nothing wrong with your hearing, Meredith. What's this all about?" His arm was not around her anymore. He curled his hand around his fist, leaned forward over the chrysanthemums. "This is not about me and Josie."

"Oh God, Michael, don't be stupid," Meredith said. "Of course it is. I see it all quite clearly. We meet the little match girl and out goes Harvard, we've dropped out and suddenly we're playing *La Bohème* down there in Echo Park. Alas, poor Mimì." His mother drained her cup and set it on the leather-topped table, settled back into the pillows of the white couch, edged in antique fringe. She plucked at the fringe. "You know why artists live in garrets, Michael?"

"Fresh air?" he said.

Meredith wasn't smiling. Her tone became

harsher. "It's not *La Bohème* if there's money from home. You understand me? Go back to Harvard. You're almost done, you cannot keep changing your mind. Especially for this . . ."

Meaning her. His mother was threatening to cut him off, because of Josie. She felt a surprising pang of guilt. It had never occurred to her that Michael might have dropped out of Harvard for her. That wasn't what he said. He just wanted to paint.

"I hated Harvard," Michael said. "It's cold and we were reading things I read at nine. I wasn't learning anything that I couldn't have learned just as well at the public library."

"Yes, but you'll need the credential to be anything in the art world. All I'm asking is that you finish your degree. Surely that's not too much to ask." Meredith uncrossed her legs, leaned in toward her son, that electric face, the intelligent leopard eyes. "I know it's late, but you've already read the books, I'm sure you can catch up." She smiled a quick smile. "After that, you can go anywhere. Florence, Paris, I'm sure the Sorbonne has a program. But not this, Michael. Why don't you and . . ." she paused for an instant, catching a slip before it emerged, "*Josie,*" a smile, "discuss it on your way home. Then you can give me a call when you've decided."

Michael reached across the leather-topped coffee table and took Meredith's hand, surprising her. Still looking her in the eye, he said, "I've already decided."

Her eyes flashed green fire. His own were a cloudy sea.

Declaration of Independence, storming of the Bastille. The man he had begun to become, that day when he'd fucked her in Meredith's own bed.

She unscrewed the top of the voddy, took a swig, let it go down, warm, took another, and screwed it back as jarring fistfuls of notes crashed down through the darkness. Meredith must be pounding on the keyboard with her forearms. A shriveled leaf from a sycamore blew onto the windshield, lingered there like a begging hand.

She'd been so proud of him that day, when Michael sat unmoved, unafraid, across from that furious woman, and told her he no longer needed her approval, that she had no hold on him anymore.

Though of course, it was only an act.

When they got home, he collapsed onto the legless blue couch, his long hands drooping between his knees. "Now what the fuck do we do?"

She put her face against his. "Go back to work."

They sat, breathing each other in. He sighed heavily, drew her close. "I'm going to tell you something I've never told anyone. I've never had a job. Pretty fucking useless, huh?"

She stroked the sides of his face with her fingertips. "It's not a big deal. You'll find something."

"Like what?" Running his hands through his rumpled dark hair. "Washing dishes? Walking people's dogs?"

"Sure, you'd be a great dog walker, why not?" And she created a story about the dogs, his charges, how he'd walk them eight at a time, winding around his legs, snapping at each other at the end of eight leashes. Making him laugh a little. It was just work. No big deal.

But his gloom washed in like a red tide. "But realistically, Josie, what can I do? Nothing."

She shrugged. What did people do? "You can wait tables."

He rubbed his cheek against her hair. "Listening to people's bullshit all day? Watching them shovel food in their faces? I'd kill myself."

She struggled to understand him. Sure, waiting tables wasn't easy, all the standing, and you had to hustle, but it paid well, and every job description included fielding people's bullshit. But then again, maybe it wasn't the same for him as it was for her. He was sensitive, and he had such pride. He would be easily insulted, and people could be so funny about their food. Maybe she couldn't really see him with a white apron and an order pad. "How about teaching people's kids, you know, math and things?"

"No car," he said. "And how would I even get a job like that?"

"Put notes up on bulletin boards?"

He kissed her hair. They sat like that for a while. "I'll find something," he said.

And he looked. He circled things in the paper. He even tried a waiter gig. True to his sense of it, it lasted about half a day. Then one day she came home from a sitting and the house was empty. No Michael in the kitchen chopping fish heads with his heavy cleaver on the round cutting board. No Michael painting by the window, barefoot in his splattered white pants and old T-shirt. Five o'clock, six o'clock, seven. She was getting worried, when he marched in the door with a huge bunch of sunflowers, picked her up, crushing the flowers as he twirled her around.

"What happened? I thought you got hit by a car."

"I got a job," he said, putting her down on the blue couch.

"Doing what?"

He didn't say anything, just sat down at the upright piano and started playing some honky-tonkish number, the razzle-dazzle right hand, the bottom holding the rhythm.

"Michael, what did you get?"

"Oh, but I am not Michael. From now on, you may address me as Señor Music." He switched into a simple little waltz. "At Señor Reynaldo's Escuela de Baile. Four afternoons a week, from *tres* to *seis y media*, and Saturdays, *de diez a cuatro*. I may suck royally, but you don't have to be Serkin to play 'I'm a Little Teapot' for a bunch of five-year-olds. Also Señor Reynaldo appreciates Señor Music's rugged good looks."

Señor Reynaldo with his army of little tiny kids, leading them through hula hoops edged in silk flowers. How Michael had loved that job. How proud he was of those checks, written on Reynaldo's lilac check stock. He even started thinking kids weren't so terrible after all. A gang of little goslings dreaming of Swan Lake. Those were good days. Michael working, painting, her modeling and getting student films. In the mornings they made love, and on the weekends they hunted through garage sales and swap meets. At night, under the covers, they read books. *The Pillow Book of Sei Shonagon. The Ballad of Reading Gaol. The Prose of the Transsiberian and Little Jeanne of France.* Michael reading aloud to her, her face against his chest.

Their Thanksgiving, he roasted a duck. And for the first time in her life, she had something to feel fucking grateful for. Their one Christmas, the tree in their living room decked out with homemade decorations, little candles in tin candleholders. Exchanging presents. She gave him a white muslin shirt she'd made up in secret, and a French folding knife with a wooden handle, the blade long enough to cut salami and bread when they traveled to France. He gave her a tiny hand-sewn book, its pages opening to reveal the painted folds of a vagina, entitled *Your Little Book,* and a blue child-sized guitar.

Her little book, from which he'd read every page, sentence by sentence, with the care her aunt Cora gave her Bible. And still he could write: *We loved each other . . . Didn't we?*

She started feeling the Valium kick in. She put the seat back, thinking how beautiful it had been before it all got so fucked up. Until he started staring out the windows at the light-dotted hills, like a mathematician staring at a problem on a blackboard. His brain grinding, grinding, like pepper in a mill. When all she saw were lights suggesting the shape of the hills. She liked to imagine it was a foreign city, like Istanbul or Cairo, the gabble of languages, smells of pepper and spices in markets, baskets piled on the ground, paprika and cumin and cinnamon. Streets where you'd have to pay small boys to take you where you needed to go, you would never find your way on your own. The cypresses were minarets. She imagined it all as she breathed the saltiness of his hair while he unconsciously pulled at the worn fabric on the arms of the chair and drank off the last of the wine in his glass and poured more from the bottle.

The true world disappearing, heavy curtains slowly closing across the face of God.

The music drifted in through the half-open window of the car, less fragmented now, she recognized it, one of the Brahms intermezzos. It was a simple piece, the kind people learned in piano lessons, but she knew it was one of the last things Brahms ever wrote for piano. Michael played it beautifully, but never like this. Mere-

dith played it very slow, slower than even a beginner, but each note had such a well of sadness
in it, more than you'd think it was possible for a
note to bear. It was exactly what Josie wanted to
hear. The opposite of that sink full of crabs.
Meredith played it as if a person could start
over, and make slow patient sense out of the
world, that there could be order and comfort
and safety, for all the sorrow in it. Josie could
stay here all night, listening to Meredith play.
She felt sleepy, she hadn't slept for so long. She
couldn't remember the last time. Always waking
just as she faded down. But here, outside this
house, listening to this music, she knew she
could. She curled up on the seat, and dropped
into nothingness.

9
Meredith

A rap on the car window dredged her from sleep, a bright light shining in her eyes. She squinted, held up her hand, the hot beam from a flashlight pointing at her face. The figure rapped again, mimed a rolling gesture. Behind her, a black-and-white. *Fuck.* Fuck fuck fuck. She crawled to the top of her drug- and alcohol-thick torpor, a long way. She unrolled the window, her heart thudding dully. The cop leaned down. "You got some business here, miss?"

She blinked into the light, pressed her rubbery lips together as if she could squeeze some

176

probable excuse from between them. *Fuck*. "My mother," she said, finally. "We had a fight."

"Your mother." She couldn't see his face behind the beam, only a mustache, but she could hear the smirk in his voice. Smart-ass. "You don't live up here, girly."

Fucking cops. She never met a cop who didn't think he was the funniest thing on two legs. Josie pointed at the lit window. "Right there."

He flashed the flashlight along the bench seat, its beam caught the vodka bottle, then pointed back in her face. "Can I see your driver's license, miss?"

This couldn't be happening. Christ. *Don't show him shit,* she could hear her father saying. *Hell, you weren't driving. He don't need your fuckin license. No crime if you ain't drivin.* "I'm just sitting here," Josie said.

He finally lowered the light. His name tag over his badge said *Ignaciewicz*. She wondered how he pronounced it. He was about thirty, with a black mustache that he fingered, glancing up at the house, back at her, not believing her for a weasel-eyed minute. Knowing she had no business in a place like this, that whatever she was

up to, it wasn't anything a cop was likely to approve of. "Well, why don't you go on up and
make nice. You shouldn't be out here by yourself. All kinds of types lurking around at night."

Meaning her. Christ. "I'm not quite ready. Can't
I just sit awhile?"

The cop nodded, he was enjoying this whole
thing. Asshole. "Well, that's not an option I'm giving you. You've got two, the way I see it. One —"
He grasped his fat forefinger. "You can go on in.
That's what I'd do, if I were you. Or two —" He
added a second to the bundle. "You can start up
that jalopy and clear on out."

In which case he'd pull her over in half a
block and charge her with DUI. Merry fucking
Christmas.

She hated cops with a pure Tyrell hatred.
Coming around, butting in, throwing their
weight around, just because they had a fucking
badge pinned on. She wanted to spit in his face,
but she wasn't that stupid, even fucked up. She
knew what Pen would say, *Kiss my Mexican
ass, motherfucker.* But it wouldn't be her first
DUI, she might go to jail. Fuck. What would she
say if she really was Meredith's daughter? What
would Michael say? "Well, since you put it so
charmingly," she said, and grabbed her purse, got

out of the car. She made sure not to stumble as she made her way across the street to the gate, no, she was sober as a Sunday school teacher, she'd never been more sober in her life. She could feel him behind her, watching her with his greasy eyes, waiting for her to screw up. The cold helped, and the cold hatred, that this fucking cop thought he knew exactly who she was, where she came from, so sure she didn't belong. *You're an absolute* bill*board, Josie Tyrell.* It was the one thing she hated most in the world, being ID'd at a glance. She unhooked the chain on the gate, the chain that was not really locked, *how'd you like that, Officer Law? If this isn't my house, how'd I know a thing like that?* She went through and closed it behind her.

It smelled fresh here, clean. She could just sit under that tree, out of sight, and not bother anyone. But she could feel Officer Dickwad watching, waiting down there. She didn't even have to turn to see him. So she kept walking, careful not to stumble on the uneven bricks laid out in a herringbone, like a tweed. A tweed jacket. The air dense with pittosporum and pine. She walked slowly, deliberately, acting the part. The girl in the movie, going home after a fight with her mother, hesitating to have to give in. She wasn't such a bad actress. Her heart thumped low, her chest like an empty street.

She was at the door, no idea how she had ended up in such a situation. Christ, she could be down in OC, bashing head against head in the Black Flag mosh pit, drinking herself stinko. She wiped her hands on her pants, her blood pounding in her throat, trying to think of what she could possibly say to Meredith, as she knocked with the heavy knocker.

The piano music stopped. There was silence, and the porch light came on. She tried to compose herself, feeling herself being inspected through the spyhole under the little grated window. Then the front door opened, a crack of light escaping from behind the figure in the quilted satin robe. She forced herself to raise her eyes to the visible slice of the woman's face. Meredith looked like a ghost of herself, her face pale and drawn, wide lips with no lipstick on them, dark hair dragged back in a ponytail, her eyes ringed with shadows. Her eyebrows came together in two vertical lines, as if she were nearsighted and could not quite make out Josie's face. "What are you doing here?"

What was she doing here? She sighed and told the truth. "Nowhere else to go."

She waited for Meredith to slam the door in her face, but she didn't. The older woman turned and walked away, leaving the door open behind her, her aqua satin robe trailing behind her on the floor. And she realized, this was where she'd wanted to be all along. From the very first. She gave the cop the finger and closed the door.

Meredith swept across the foyer and, navigating with the aid of the wrought-iron handrail, down the three steps into the living room, where a small fire burned low in the fireplace. The slick floors gleamed like the surface of a dark lake. Loch Ness. Michael said it was a thousand feet deep. She stepped onto the black water, following Meredith trailing along unsteadily in her movie-star bathrobe, looking like a drunken Myrna Loy in some Thin Man movie. The woman grabbed a fat tumbler, then visited the drinks cart, where she sloshed some liquor into the glass. She didn't ask Josie if she'd like a drink, not that Josie really expected her to. "They're all gone. Thank God. All over. Alone at last. Ha." Although Meredith's voice was weaker, it still held that rich, thrilling tone. "So many friends. My good friend what's 'is name. Funny, how things work out." The way she said it, it wasn't funny at all. Josie wasn't sure if she was supposed to be following this or if Meredith was talking to herself, down into the crystal tumbler. "Sorry, we're so sorry. Sorry for your loss. Then they go off and have their teeth cleaned, eat dinner."

"Yeah, I know." Josie came in as far as the top step of the living room, then hovered, not sure whether she should get any closer. Maybe there was a gun among the bottles, drain opener in a drink. But the awareness that she might be in danger was weaker than the strange sensation of comfort. It was good to have someone talking to you, someone who knew what had happened. "I heard you playing."

"Brahms." Meredith put her drink on the end of the keyboard and sat at the piano, began the slow, sad, simple piece Josie had heard from the road. "Whenever Michael had a headache, he had to have his Brahms."

How odd, that there should be someone else who knew something like that about him. Days when he lay in their bedroom, darkened from the felt curtains she'd made for it, drinking Mountain Dew because he thought the caffeine helped, listening to the intermezzos, the piano quintet.

Meredith bent over her piano, playing gently. Even when she was drunk, you could tell Meredith was the real thing. Josie had heard recordings of her room-filling Liszt, the speed of her Chopin, the complicated brokenness of her Schoenberg. But she played the Brahms like thinking. Slow, hovering, considering, then moving ahead, only to turn back and repeat itself. It was private, it reminded Josie of gondolas somehow, those long black boats, like the piano itself, nosing through heavy mists in narrow canals. The splash of the water. Hushed voices, houses rising up on either side. He was going to take her to Venice someday. But it would have to be another life. Next time around.

"My father had them too. Headaches."

Meredith's father, the composer, who shot himself in this house. Came all the way from Vienna to shoot himself in LA. Escaped the Nazis but not himself. Michael had never met him, but talked about him as if he had known him all his life. Meredith bent over the piano keys like she was praying. Her eyes so much like his. Swords in the tarot deck. Even knowing how the woman hated her, Josie felt strangely close to her. Close and yet far away, like the moon watching the earth.

She leaned against the wall on the steps, still not daring to enter the living room proper, resting her heavy head against the cool, patted stucco. The Brahms was like someone massaging your temples, gently, and the base of your neck. Him and Brahms, praying for order, praying for faith.

On the carved mantel over the fireplace, fine objects gleamed in the flickering light. A clock in a glass dome, a porcelain camel, things that should be in a museum, in a glass case. Meredith knew what to do with beautiful things, things Josie would be afraid even to own. It occurred to her that she should have left Michael up here, undisturbed, deaf-mute mother and son. Perhaps Meredith would have found a way to keep him safe, in a box lined in velvet. That's what her phone calls were saying, or was it the voice in her head — *Why couldn't you just have left him alone?*

When it seemed that Meredith had forgotten her, lost in her Brahms, Josie quietly descended the steps into the living room, padded across the old threadbare carpets to the fireplace. She didn't want to sit down, that seemed a bit too chummy, remembering the last time she had been in this room. She began to examine the mantel's array of offerings. A small terra-cotta head of a young woman, or maybe a boy, part of the cheek and nose gone. The gold clock in a glass case, its pendulum shaped like a harp, dead still. Next to that, a carved ivory ball nested on a rosewood stand. Balls carved inside each other, all intricate with flowers, people, houses and roads — a whole world in a sphere the size of a cabbage. She picked it up, daring Meredith to tell her to put it down. But Meredith was ignoring her, the way you ignore a dog that trots into a room, sniffs around, and leaves again.

Josie turned the white sphere in her child's hands, she could tell it was old and valuable.

"I've often wondered. What do you think my son saw in you?" Meredith asked.

She hadn't sensed that she was under scrutiny. Usually, she knew, could feel it, but Meredith was still gazing down at the keyboard, looking at the keys, her hands. Long fingered, exactly like Michael's. How could someone who looked just like Michael hate her so much? Each time she looked at his mother, she kept seeing him.

I've often wondered . . . She felt the reverberation of the insult, but hollowly, as if someone had slapped a doll. She knew how she looked to Meredith, fucked up and unwashed, jacket scarred, her punked-out bleached hair and Tyrell face. Another day she might have even cried, but not today. "I think he thought he could rescue me. Like if he could do that, maybe he could save himself." Let the woman insult her. She had reached some quiet place, like a carved ivory ball down inside five others. The reasons lay one under the other — which ball was the real ball?

"Sir Galahad," Meredith said. "That doesn't surprise me." The touch of her fingers on the keys so different from the bitterness in her voice. "Yes, he *would* think that."

"Yes," Josie said. "He would."

"No one knew him. Only you." His mother said this last with such disappointment.

It was true. Only her. How hard it must be on his mother, for her son to be such a loner. She had grown up with famous people, Billy Wilder and Isherwood, Garbo. And now her son was dead, and she was stuck talking to Josie Tyrell, the only one who knew him. In this, they were a nation of two, she and Meredith Loewy.

Running her fingers over the impossibly intricate designs on the ball, Josie imagined the years it had taken to carve this chunk of elephant tusk, to create something of such unnecessary beauty. Merchants with their big bellies. Princes. Women in long robes and pleated fans, layer inside layer. What was the point in creating something that was so futile and so precious? Everything beautiful was like that. A little bit of the true world. Beauty said there was something more than just one fucking thing after another. Time could rest for a moment, stop all that senseless motion.

Meredith suddenly stopped playing. She closed the keyboard cover with a bang, and rose from the bench, glass in her hand. She went to the white couches, lay down on one, her fat tumbler in one hand resting on her stomach. "Did he ever tell you about his father?"

"Some," Josie said.

"You know what he used to call Michael? Sissy-Boy. 'Hey, Sissy-Boy,' he'd call out, and then throw him something, which he'd inevitably drop." She laughed a laugh that sounded more like a bark, a catch in the throat, the sound a person makes when knifed. "When he was thirteen — did he tell you what his father did?"

"What?" She wanted to hear Meredith tell it, it was a story they all had a piece of.

She took a sip from the tumbler on her stomach, lifting her head just enough not to spill, then dropped back to the tasseled pillow. "I was in New York for a recital, and thought I'd take him to see his father in the Village. Cal had one of those town houses on Bank Street. Between marriages as I recall. Briefly. It never took him long. Anyway, Cal always kept a ball on his desk, signed by all these famous players, Babe Ruth and so on. Fondled it while he wrote, talk about Freudian. Anyway. We were up there, discussing Michael's future, and he got it into his head to throw it at him. "Think fast!" he said. Like a schoolyard bully. And threw it right at his head. Hit him in the forehead. I thought it would knock him out. You know what Michael did?"

Josie did. It was fascinating to hear someone else tell a story she knew so well.

"He picked it up and threw it right out the window. I mean, Babe Ruth. Rolling down the gutter on Bank Street." Meredith laughed. She had a beautiful smile, big straight teeth. When she really laughed, she wrinkled her nose and lines in the corners of her eyes fanned happily over the apples of her cheeks. "It was fantastic." She took a messy sip of her drink, not sitting up, wiped the overflow on the back of her hand. "God, that was one of the best days of my life."

Josie ran her fingertips over the bumpy carvings in the ivory, wondering if she should throw it in the fire, or pitch it through the window over the piano. Babe Ruth, rolling down Bank Street. The fronts of her legs were growing hot. "Why did he wear his jacket, then, if he hated him so much?"

"Primal transference," Meredith said, slurring the syllables. "Like wearing the skin of an animal you're afraid of." She lifted her glass to her lips again, spilled it now on the front of her robe, had to sit up, shake it off her hand and brush it from the silk. "Cal was so jealous of him. Jealous of our relationship. He never wanted to share me with a child. He wanted me all to himself, like a big spoiled baby. Sick, no? He thought I was going to trail around the world after him, bearing his typewriter aloft like it was the Grail." Her thin elegant nostrils flared slightly, like a ripple in silk. She crossed her long legs. They were very white, with fine blue veins.

What chance did he have, Josie thought, with such a father, such a mother?

Meredith set her drink on the table. "You should have seen him, Josie. When he was a child. We've all been bright, but Michael —" Her long hands made a beautiful, double fan in the air. "He was speaking in full sentences at two. He read at three. At five, he taught himself Greek from a book. From a book! He'd leave me notes in Greek. Ancient Greek. Someone at UCLA finally translated them for me. Sweet little poems."

Even now, Josie envied him. Imagine having a mother who would say, *We've all been bright,* without hesitation. Imagine this woman had been her mother, and not poor Janey Tyrell. If this was her house. If she had been lifted up by all this. But she couldn't picture the first thing. The Tyrells weren't stupid, but they kept each other down. If you had a bright idea, everybody made fun of you so viciously, you learned not to have them. It was how they made sure nobody got away. And if Michael had been a Tyrell? They would have drowned him at two, with his first full sentence. He would never have gotten as far as notes in Greek.

"Did he tell you I wouldn't send him to school?" Meredith asked, sticking her finger in the bottom of her glass, licking it off. "That I kept him at home all to myself under lock and key?"

"Something like that," Josie said.

"It wasn't true," Meredith said, tucking her legs up under her on the couch. "He was the one. Begged me not to send him. It was only later that he changed the story, and I became the villain. He was like that, you know. Blaming me for things he was afraid to do."

She shook the ball, making it turn, ball within ball, flowers and roads and ladies. But deep inside, the central ball was carved in horrors. Dead people in a pile. A horseman, riding down a peasant in a field. Hidden deep inside where the patron would never notice. The swarming murderousness, the almost erotic cruelty, like watching fish feed. She quickly put it back on its rosewood stand. She could imagine the artist, laughing with his secret.

"Josie?" Meredith was holding out her empty glass. *"Per favore?"*

Josie stared at the hand, the glass. Did she think Josie was going to wait on her? Because she was trash? But she suddenly understood that Meredith would have asked such a thing of Michael. She was asking her in Michael's stead. And she knew he wouldn't have hesitated, so she didn't either. She took the heavy cut tumbler and went to the drinks cart.

"The one with the thistle," Meredith said.

Josie poured the chunky glass half-full of amber liquid, it smelled like the day after a fire. "Ice?"

"Nein, Fräulein."

Uninvited, Josie poured a tumbler for herself, the Stoli that smelled like nothing at all. She handed Meredith her drink and sat down on the other couch, not worrying about her pants dirtying the white damask. The woman's son was dead, what did she care about her couch?

"He had a marvelous education. I took him everywhere," Meredith said, lying down again with her big drink, one arm under her head. She took a careful sip and set the glass on the coffee table. "You have no idea how bloody uncomfortable a camel can be after the third day." She rubbed her nose briskly with the palm of her hand. "Ruins were his passion. And I never said no to that child. Never. Did you know the Phoenicians had child sacrifice? At Carthage, they found children buried in the walls. That's what I remember about it — Dido, and that they invented the color purple, and children in the walls." She pulled out a Kleenex from her pocket and blew her nose. "They deserved to become extinct."

Children in the walls. Grandfathers on the rug.

"His Greek period. I had a year's residence in London. Michael practically lived at the British Museum. Red figure, black figure, the so-and-so painter." She shifted her long figure on the couch, let one arm drape back over the end of the sofa. She glanced over at Josie to see if she was following. "Pots. He and the pottery man were inseparable, what was his name? David. Davis. Something. God. A real British academic. Mouth breather, corduroys all baggy in the rear. Even asked me for a date." She laughed a little, completely drunk, letting herself forget for a moment that Michael was dead. "I thanked God when he entered the Renaissance. At nine, he could tell all those tellos and dellos apart, who built the Duomo and who cast the doors and how they did it and in whose honor." She sat up on her elbow to reach her glass. "He read the *Inferno* in Italian. Miles beyond anything a school could have offered." She took a drink. "He had no call to resent that. You couldn't send a boy like that to school. His father never understood that. 'He needs to be with boys his own age, Meredith.'" Imitating Cal, pretty well, too. "For an insane half minute, I let him have his way. Allowed him to be sent off like a prize calf to the abattoir. Michael sent me notes like a prisoner, smuggled out by some janitor, the school censored all their mail. Some boys locked him in the boiler room for a day and a half, and nobody told me about it. Well, that was the end of *that* experiment, I'll tell you."

Michael had recalled that scene to her, portraying himself as a flannel-coated, long-lashed schoolyard victim, the master who caned, the cold, the sadistic gym teacher. And Meredith, sweeping in in a fur coat to rescue him like some kind of mythological bear mother. It was not hard to imagine Meredith whisking Michael out of there in his pajamas in the hired limo, trailing the scent of her strange perfume in the snowy air.

But now Meredith was deflated, looking down into her drink. "Do you think I made a mistake, Josie? Do you think I should have made him stay?" Then she lifted her green gaze to Josie, in a gesture that was so like Michael it sent chills through her. "That he would have come out stronger on the other side? His father said all boys go through that. Bullying and tormenting each other."

It was the last thing Josie would have expected, Meredith asking her if she thought it was her fault. Josie drank the colorless Stoli, hoping it would heat the winter in her veins. She could strike a blow now, tell her this was all her doing, the mess, her fault. But she found she could not bring herself to make the woman feel worse. Even if Meredith had threatened her, tried to run her over, strangled her at Michael's funeral. Michael was dead. What good could it do to make his mother any more unhappy?

"It would have been insane to leave him there," Josie said. "Only a sadist would have done it."

The silence brimmed between them as they drank and the fire burned lower. Maybe that was the only real truth about the world, that there was no answer, that wisdom and experience were no better than a flat-out roll of the dice.

"Put another chunk on the fire, would you? It's going out," Meredith said.

Josie found a hairy piece of wood in the metal carrier and opened the fire screen, threw it in. It landed crooked, so she had to shove it with the poker. The little hairs caught on fire, smoldered, and the underside crackled as the bark heated up, smoking, and then soon trickled with orange flame. "Let's do another," Meredith said. "I'm freezing."

Josie threw a second log in, and the fire went out. Smoke streamed into the room, stinging her eyes.

"Push them back, they're too far forward," Meredith said.

Josie wiped her eyes and shoved both logs to the back.

"Now open a space between them, about an inch, to draw."

She did as instructed, opened the hole between. The smoke rose, though this time it stayed in the fireplace, and then flames began their tattered ascent. She stared in at the licking tongues of yellow and orange. Like Michael, his mother was so precise. *Like Michael.* The thought sent those yellow tongues licking in her. No, not at all like Michael. Not at all. His mother was a devil, she couldn't be trusted. All Josie needed was to succumb to the comfort, the familiarity. She had enough problems. Josie took a big swig of her Stoli and threw the rest in the fire. It went up in a whoosh, like when her father put lighter fluid on the barbecue. "I better go."

"Don't go," Meredith said, quickly. "Stay here. You can sleep —" Then she caught herself. "Anywhere."

And Josie realized she was going to say, "You can sleep in Michael's room." The way you'd invite someone to sleep in a spare bedroom, when the occupant was gone. She looked at Meredith, struggling to prop herself up on the pillow. And she thought of the dead bodies inside the ivory sphere. This house full of ghosts. This poor cursed place. She didn't belong to this. Suddenly, she found herself standing. She had to go. She couldn't pass out here, people died here, they went crazy. Just like this crazy bitch.

"Don't, really, Josie. You'll kill someone on the way home," Meredith said. "Ruin their Christmas."

"Ho ho ho," Josie said. She was very drunk, but she could still leave, she should go while she still could. She made her way across the room, holding on to the furniture, station by station, hand over hand, an easy chair, a standing lamp.

"Don't be like that. Please, Josie, don't go."

"On Donder, on Blitzen." Staggering across the empty spaces, grabbing the rail of the steps up into the foyer, she had to go, it was like those fairy tales where you spend one night and you're trapped forever.

"God, you're as impossible as he was."

Josie stumbled up the stairs and across the foyer, out the front door. In the dark, the cold smell of plants, the rough brickwork drive, she felt like she was waking up from a dream. She realized how warm it had been inside, the fireplace, the gleam of light off the walls, the woodwork. Out here it was just cold and dark, there weren't even any streetlights. She stumbled on the brickwork, fell heavily onto her hands, sat down. Not hard, but just crumpled. It was cold, lying there on the bricks, but it was more of a thought than a sensation. She looked at her hands, slightly lighter than the darkness around them, but she could not tell if she had skinned them or not in her fall. Her body seemed very much like someone else's. She felt around for her purse, but couldn't find it, and it felt like too much trouble to crawl around looking for it, so she curled up on the brick and put her face on her leather sleeve and passed out.

10
After

Her head lay on needlepoint. She could feel the hard threads against her cheek. There was blanket on her, some kind of fuzzy wool. A leather couch, buttons. She opened her eyes. Puffy slits admitted diffuse light that seeped from the sides and bottoms of heavy drapes. Geometric figures on the floor. Oriental rug. Her boots stood neatly together. Something reeked. She peered over the edge of the couch — gently, her head a seismic device — and saw the wastebasket alongside the sofa. Slowly, she sat up, gagging, picked it up and carried it as far as the window, where she groped under the drape, releasing a knife blade of light, to find the metal window crank, felt for the hole, turned until she could breathe fresh air. She slid back onto the couch the way a child slides into first. What time was it? She recalled leaving, but not coming back. *Rolling down the gutter on Bank Street. Do you think I did the right thing, Josie?* Children buried in the walls.

The door opened. She could hear the piano out in the living room. Meredith was up. The maid came in with a tray, set it down, opened the drapes, her straight-backed figure disappearing into glare like a nuclear flash. The woman picked up the wastebasket with an impassive glance, didn't even look at Josie as she took it away. "Sorry," Josie croaked, through her parched lips. The woman closed the door without a sound.

She felt like a lowlife but was glad the wastebasket was gone, and that whatever the woman brought didn't smell. Her brain spun when she closed her eyes, but hurt when she opened them. *You've got two options.* Clean little sounds came through the open window. A sprinkler, Rain Bird–style, *shhhttt sht sht sht sht sht shhhttttt,* the beeping of a backing truck. But what time was it? Her lips were cracked and her tongue was bitter. She groped her way to the desk, squinting down at the offerings. Glass of ice, can of Seven Up, a dish with aspirin. Some round crackers. Toast sticking up like records in a record rack. All on a lace-edged napkin.

She stared at the tray, trying to understand. Michael was dead. And there was this china. And a small vase full of tiny flowers. She started to cry. How could there be something so beautiful when he was dead?

She opened the Seven Up, the angry hiss, drank from the can. Her stomach lurched and plunged. She nibbled a cracker. The maid sure knew what to bring. Must have done this before. She swallowed a couple of aspirin, waited to see if they would stay down. She wondered if Meredith was in the habit of tying one on. A spot just above her eyebrow throbbed, like some tiny monster was about to pop out of her forehead. Like those paintings Michael painted, things crawling out of his face.

How furious Michael would be if he knew she had come here. Spying on him. Letting Meredith tell her version of his life. Alternatives to old favorites. Tearing at the fabric of his image in her mind. Like the one where Meredith hadn't let him go to school. *She doesn't like him to mix with the world.* She pressed the cold can to her eyebrow, the throbbing little devil boring its way out. Though it was possible Meredith was the one who was lying. Very possible. *Do you think I made a mistake, Josie?* But even if she was lying, who could blame her? Her son was dead. No one wanted to think of himself as the bad guy.

And in the end, she would never know the truth. It was hidden between them. If Michael were right here, they'd each stick to their version, pass the blame between them like a football. *He was like that, you know. Blaming me for things he was afraid to do.* Yes, that was true. He could believe something passionately, then later, deny what he had said. Even hand his position to you, while he argued the exact opposite point of view.

She tried the dry toast, thick, home sliced, took two more aspirin, ate a bit more of the toast. Eating in the enemy's lair. She remembered a story Michael told her, about a kidnapped girl who ate six pomegranate seeds in the underworld, so she had to stay and be the queen of the dead. Josie put the toast down. Then she felt stupid and picked it up again. She was a girl who would eat from a tray on a lace napkin when her lover had killed himself. Deep down, she was glad something still worked.

She drank most of the can, waited for the relieving belch, buttered a slice of toast and slowly ate it. Over the mantel, an elongated thoroughbred eyed her with its buggy green eyes. "What the fuck are you looking at?" Her mouth tasted like the gutter after a parade. She found her purse, lit a cigarette, using an enameled ashtray with a gold *ML* interlaced in the bottom. *Mauritz Loewy.* His desk. All the rows of inlaid drawers, like secrets in people's minds. She tried one of the little knobs, but it wouldn't slide out. *It was locked, but I know where she keeps the key.* Meredith had had this twice, her son and her father. No wonder she hadn't wanted Josie to leave her alone.

Josie opened the bloodred leather door. Music billowed out from the living room, she could see just the end of the giant piano. The sun filtered in through the window, more gold than white, it must be later than she'd thought. You had to admire the woman. Her son was dead, but instead of lying in bed on a morphine drip, she could turn to her music. Josie wished she had something like that. Michael had had painting, though in the end he didn't trust it, it was a source of pain and no solace. But Josie had nothing, a book with appointments, a makeup case, her own bony self.

She had to go to the bathroom. There was one in Michael's old room, the monastery library. She padded up the stone risers. The cut-glass knob felt cold in her hand, and she hesitated, listening, but Meredith just kept playing, the maid was nowhere in sight. She quickly went in. That resinous smell — linseed oil, turpentine, pine, mothball — made her catch her breath. That wonderful smell. It was all just the same. The gray blanket stretched tight across the narrow iron bed, the Virgin, crude and painted on a wooden panel with a curved top — what did a Jewish boy need a Virgin for? There were gaps in the sagging bookcase where he'd taken books to their house on Lemoyne.

She felt an odd disembodied resistance, as if the room itself resented her intrusion. She could almost hear the motes of dust settling. *Michael, I'm sorry. Please believe me.* But there was no answer here. Only the sad smile of his Mexican Virgin. Josie used the bathroom, washed, dried her face on the stale towel. Not a terry-cloth towel, but a linen one, like a napkin but bigger. Left over from the last time he was here, a year and a half ago. Meredith had not changed the towel. Once she might have thought that was crazy, to leave a towel dirty so long, but now it seemed perfectly reasonable. Josie hadn't touched his laundry, either, could not sleep in their bed. Maybe a year would go by, who knew how long it might take.

His old toothbrush stood in its holder over the sink. Her teeth needed brushing but she could not bring herself to use his toothbrush. He was gone but these things were still his. Instead, she shook some tooth powder into her hand, scrubbed her teeth with a finger. Its pallid mint taste so recalled Michael, as did the scrap of shaving soap in a cup on the lip of the sink, that pine smell, Lightfoot's soap, he had it sent to him all the way from England. *A fine monk you would have made.* But no one loved old-fashioned things the way he did. Tooth powder, nightshirts, shoe trees, handkerchiefs. He shaved every morning with that soap and a badger-hair brush, a straight razor with its tortoiseshell handle. Tilting his head to one side, shaving under the jaw, a razor sharp enough to cut your throat. She remembered watching her own father shave. Glenn Tyrell did it fast and angrily, as if he could not allow himself the possibility of enjoying it. Tough guy. Where Michael shaved slowly, luxuriously, his long fingers making an art of it. His neatness displayed everywhere. Pinching his nose and shaving the lather off his upper lip, stretching his neck long and drawing the blade gently along the knots and sinews. How terrifying it had been to watch him shave, knowing how easily that razor could cut those sinews. And yet that was not what he had chosen at all.

She caught a glimpse of her tired face in his small bathroom mirror, her dirty blond hair all stuck together from her night on the couch, what was left of her eye makeup a sooty blur. She turned off the light and went back to his room, the Virgin over the bed watching so lovingly. She imagined him lying there, in the unforgiving bed, praying to be relieved of his blessings. The deaf-mute, the crippled boy, who played the piano and tennis. She touched the stretched-tight blanket of the bed, the heaviness of his death sitting on her heart like an old-fashioned iron, the kind Gommer Ida still used, that you set on the stove.

She didn't want to be like this, sneaking, spying. But there had been so many secrets, and she was hungry for more of him, anything. In the top drawer of the dresser, silky socks nested, and neckties in careful rolls, like flowers. She trailed her fingers through the air just above them, not wanting to disturb their perfection. A box of cuff links and round little buttons with earring backs, thin little pieces of white plastic, she had no idea what they were for. She opened the door to his closet, paused from the shock.

It was big as the room she shared with her sisters in Bakersfield. Along the walls, suits and crisp long-sleeved shirts hung in perfect formation. The cedar and mothball smell was intoxicating. She ran her hand gently down the sleeves of the shirts, as if stroking the strings of a harp. She couldn't believe how many clothes he had. She had only seen him in denim work shirts, and his one silk shirt from Goodwill, olive green. Here were suits — pin-striped, black, pale gray, even a seersucker and a tuxedo with a shiny collar, blue jackets with gold buttons on the sleeves, a white silk one, a leather jacket. He'd worn only one jacket as long as she'd known him, the one that had belonged to his father, who called him Sissy-Boy. She couldn't imagine the Michael who had worn these clothes. Her Michael so loved his thrift stores and garage sales, a three-dollar suit from the Salvation Army. But no tweed jacket. Meredith probably wore it when she was alone,

Josie would have. She wondered if Meredith knew there was a sprig of yellow mustard in the pocket, from when they went hiking up at Dante's View.

The shoes of the dead were the emptiest of all, the saddest shoes in the world. Polished shoes, black ones with thin soles and laces, businessman ones with those little holes. She couldn't imagine him wearing something like that. *Who were you, Michael? Didn't I know you at all?* In a corner, rackets and sticks leaned against a golf bag, and three pairs of skis, and a fishing pole. But *La Bohème* didn't have skiing. There were no fish in Echo Park lake.

Which had been his real life, this one, with its patent leather shoes and jackets with gold buttons on the sleeves? Or the life they'd made up together, Montmartre in their shack on the hillside?

"Josie." That sharp, half-whispered voice, the way you call a dog, to get it out of a room, fast, but she heard it. Christ. She turned off the closet light, came out into the room, and there was Meredith, standing in the doorway.

Josie wished she could disappear. Just vanish. Meredith looked better than last night, her hair had been washed, but she wore no makeup, and her beige sweater was unflattering. Her mouth was in a straight line, white with rage. "What were you doing in his closet? You shouldn't be in here. No one gave you permission."

"I-I had to use the bathroom." It sounded lame even to her. The closet was nowhere near the bathroom. She felt her face flush hot, like being caught with purple nail polish in your pocket in the Woolworth's beauty section.

"There's a bathroom downstairs." Meredith turned sideways, an invitation to pass her, but Josie realized that Meredith would not, could not enter the room herself.

"Sorry," she said. "I didn't know." Liar, she knew exactly.

"You don't just go wandering in other people's houses," Meredith said. "It's considered very ill-mannered."

In case you don't know it, Daisy Mae. Josie stood in Michael's room, exhausted, headachy, disgraced.

"You can see your way out, can't you?" Meredith said crisply, her nose sharp as her tone. "I have an appointment at two." And she swept away down the hall like a Thirties actress, Norma Shearer or Joan Crawford, leaving a perfume trail in her dark, smoky wake.

11
Cemetery

Cold air rushed in from the mist-filled hills, lush again after the November rains. She was wiped after the five-hour sculpture class in Pasadena, but her nerves twanged like a cheap guitar. Thank God for the clouds, for the absence of light. On the car radio, the B-52's bounced out "Planet Claire": *She drove a Plymouth Satellite, faster than the speed of light.* She usually loved this band, but today their cheerfulness made her want to crash the car. She punched in a tape, Debussy études. The fluid string of shimmering notes soothed her with its asymmetrical dreaminess. No matter that it was a Meredith Loewy tape. These days, she clung to each last shred of beauty. People thought beauty was bullshit, just a Band-Aid slapped over the abyss, but they couldn't be more wrong. It was like Lola Lola had said, beauty mattered, it was the only thing that fed you when everything else turned to shit.

She shouldn't have gone creepy crawling in Meredith's house, what the fuck was she thinking? She should have gone in and said good morning. She could have done the right thing, for once. What did she think she'd find in Michael's room anyway? A dead boy's neckties. It wasn't the point. It wasn't the point at all. What had she learned in his room, except that everything she'd thought about him was a lie. And the one person who knew him now thought Josie was exactly what she'd first assumed — stupid white trash who threw up in wastebaskets and passed out on driveways. Who wandered through people's houses uninvited. *You should never have even shared a sentence.* Where the night before, she'd held out her hand in friendship, or at least mutual need. *You can show yourself out.* It still smarted.

She looked up and found herself already on the back side of Griffith Park, the green hills rising into the five o'clock mist. She'd missed her exit, and driven into the metropolis of the dead. Christ. *Forest Lawn,* here was the sign. *Mount Sinai.* She hadn't been back once since the funeral. As if not seeing where he lay would negate the reality. Why hadn't she come? What difference did it make what fucking Meredith Loewy thought or didn't think, why did she care? Michael was lying up there, victim of *ming.* She cut across two lanes of traffic and shot down the exit ramp at Forest Lawn Drive. Through the gates at Sinai and past the long building where they'd said the prayers, and Cal had been kicked out of the family box. She wound her way up the road to the Court of Freedom. What was it exactly that court judged? Was it a merciful venue, or a just one?

Once she parked her weak-mufflered car, silence sealed itself over the park again. Her heels sank in the overwatered grass as she hiked through the checkerboard of brass plaques to the sandstone enclosure, the white Loewy tombstone. The heavy-branched trees mourned stoically, her only company, dark pines and deodars.

His grave. It wasn't a dream, not her imagining. He was still here. Though there was no marker yet, just the family one. The seams on the sod were already growing together, the fingers of grass twined and blurred the edges. In another few weeks, it would all blend into the rest. In a vase punched into the grass, big grayish mauve roses bloomed, sad and Victorian looking. So perfect and dejected, just right for a dead boy. Meredith must have brought them. Who else would know about roses like that? She leaned over and sniffed, surprised at the intensity of the scent, not a rose smell at all, but spicy, like mulled wine.

The land of the dead, with its sad roses, its five o'clock in the afternoon, a new country. There was a children's book they used to read together, about the evil Duke who stopped all the clocks in his castle with his cold, cold hand. It never occurred to her that that was death. But now she understood, the land of the dead never changed, you were just left with its rituals, kirs at sundown, a certain picnic table at Dante's View, *The Prose of the Transsiberian,* Louis Armstrong and the Hot Five.

She sat on the bench, lit a cigarette for him, so he could smell it, wherever he was. She wasn't going to cry, but she couldn't help it. She couldn't believe that a human being could physically weep so much. These days everything made her cry. If she couldn't find the address of her sitting. Seeing a pigeon living in a red-light cylinder at Alvarado and Beverly, or a high-heeled shoe left on top of a mailbox.

Shirley K. said the dead understood everything once they crossed over, that they didn't hold grudges. She hoped it was true, but forgiveness had never exactly been a part of Michael's repertoire. He could never put himself in the other person's shoes. He never forgave anyone anything, least of all himself.

"You don't believe in me, in my work," he'd said to her. To her, of all people. Who was working three jobs, once he quit Reynaldo? But she didn't believe in him. "You're undermining me."

As he lay on the couch while she went out on the third job of the day. After he told her Señor Music had had enough of screaming brats and playing "Row, Row, Row Your Boat" and being groped by Señor Reynaldo. Which left her to support them both, the rent and paint and gas and canvas. If that didn't show her faith in him, what did? But he tested her, the way you tested a tooth that had a cavity, seeing if you could make it hurt. He could not forgive her for supporting him, though he needed her to. And she didn't mind, but why did he have to be so mean about it? He stopped reaching for her, he flinched if she touched him. What had she done that was so terribly wrong, that she had to be punished like that?

She stood over his grave. The earth smelled damp as it had the day of the funeral, the day she stood over the open hole with her rose, looking down into the dark. She could still feel where Meredith had wrapped her fingers around Josie's throat. All around her, in the tightly squeezed graves marked by plaques on the ground, the dead muttered in their hollows. All in some way misinterpreted, misunderstood, gradually forgotten, and the memories of their lives altered to fit some more palatable version of reality. The complicated, difficult woman suddenly became the good wife and mother. The furious, bitter man was transformed into a gentle husband. She hated stories that were rewritten, films that were remade. Michael said history existed only in the human mind, subject to endless revision.

You'll have to remember for both of us.

Who said she had to? Who said? Maybe she would check out too and there wouldn't be one goddamn person in the world who would remember.

He never even told her the real story. For

instance, about the hyperintellectual Harvardettes he'd fucked when he was supposed to be a virgin. Or Meredith not letting him go to school when it was him all the time. Or about being *très sportif,* a ranked player, with golf clubs and three pairs of skis. What was she supposed to remember, when he had held out so much of himself, had changed the story? There were all these new pieces, how was she ever going to understand him? He hadn't wanted her to, not really. But then she couldn't help him. *Each man kills the thing he loves.* That's what Oscar Wilde said.

"Why does each man kill the thing he loves?" she'd asked him that day at Dante's View. Hot and smoggy, the sunset coming a little earlier each day, heady with the scent of laurel sumac, the bright pungent green that was the smell of California, merging with the smell of water in the little oasis. They lay on their picnic tables, shaded with eucalyptuses, guarded by giant agaves twelve feet across, fleshy and blue-gray and edged with thorns. Prehistoric. Her soft dress floating around her thighs as he drew her. Reading *The Ballad of Reading Gaol,* a small book, an owl embossed on its cover, the pages thin as onion skins. It was about a man on his way to be executed. That line kept coming up. "I don't get it. Why would you kill the thing you loved?"

The softness of his voice. Even now, under the deodars in the Court of Freedom, her feet in the grass over his silent body, she could hear his voice, clear but soft, you had to stop whatever you were doing, and lean close to hear it. And he had replied so quietly it took a few seconds for it to register. "You kill it before it kills you."

But he was wrong. Wrong wrong wrong. Sitting here on a bench in the Loewy family plot, she knew you killed it by accident. Thinking you were doing something else. It was a cherished vase that broke while you were cleaning it. The phone rang and you dropped it. Shattering, when all you wanted was to keep it safe.

She held herself around her thin waist, her stomach brutally empty, she couldn't stand to eat now, couldn't stand the heaviness in her own body. *She has no body, she's too poor . . .* She wished that was true. She was tired of hauling her body around. The clocks had all stopped, except the clock in the body. She had killed the thing she loved, and she was still here, needing to eat and sleep and pay the rent. She didn't know what she was now, if she was real or just someone Michael had dreamed up.

She watched an old man struggling up the hill, he was overweight and breathed heavily. He stopped at a grave in the Court of Freedom, she could hear him wheeze. He had no flowers and his empty hands looked unnaturally large. He picked a leaf off a grave and absently fingered it as he gazed down. She thought he had said something to her.

"Pardon?"

"Stinks," he said.

"What?" She wasn't sure she had understood him.

"Life stinks." He pulled a handkerchief from the pocket of his Windbreaker and hawked into it, folded it, and put it back in his pocket. "It's rigged, and the house always wins. Remember that. They talk about Nature, how great it is and all that. Believe me, Nature's no walk in the park. This is my wife here. Fifty-three years. Cancer of the pancreas."

She nodded. A month ago she would have been embarrassed at the confidence. Now she felt a surprising kinship. She was a citizen of the new land, a country she had never before visited, only a rumor, this vast unseen tract, its boundary exactly that of the whole world, taking up the space and shape of the world but completely unlike it. It had a different atmosphere, hard to breathe, and how heavy you were here, it pulled you down like the gravity on Jupiter. At the observatory, there was a room with scales, showing what you'd weigh on the different planets. On Jupiter she'd weigh three hundred pounds. You would hardly be able to walk, or even stand up. The new world was just like that.

She looked at the old man in the growing darkness, gazing down at his wife's grave. Fifty-three years with one person. "That's a long time," she said.

"I shouldn't speak this way to a young person," he said. His eyes were owlish in round glasses, under a plaid cap. "But it's a rigged crap game. I spit on it." And he actually spit on the smooth groomed grass.

She shivered, pulling her yellow coat tighter around her, the shawl collar framing her small face looking down at the silvery roses. "My boyfriend killed himself."

The words hung in the air, untouched by wind or water. The old man scratched the back of his head, making his cap fall forward onto his brow. "That's tough," he said. "I got no answers." He scuffed his brown, rubber-soled shoe in the grass. "You know, when my wife was going into the hospital, she made me a month's worth of food and put it in the freezer. Labels on each one. *Thursday. Saturday.*" He took out that same handkerchief and wiped his eyes underneath his glasses. "I can't eat them. I go get Burger King instead."

"That's not good for you," Josie said, imagining him having a heart attack one night because he wouldn't eat his dead wife's cooking. That was probably what the woman worried about, so much that even with cancer of the pancreas, she went into the kitchen and managed to cook those meals for him before she went.

"I can't sleep at night," he said. "I go down to Gardena and play pan until the sun comes up. Then I go home and sleep. The house is just too damn quiet."

The land where the clocks stopped ticking. All night, that relentless absence. "I never played pan."

"It takes up a lotta time, that's what I like about it. They got those other games, too, those Chinese games. It's a Chinese place. They really go crazy. But I always play pan."

She couldn't help but think how Michael would have loved this old man. He loved when people talked to him like this, just regular people. It made him feel human, connected, if someone was comfortable talking to him, saw him as an ordinary man, perhaps he wasn't as estranged from the world as he felt himself to be.

"We liked to go to Vegas, me and Dotty. We usually go to Caesar's. What a brunch they've got there." He smiled, hitched his corduroys around his stout middle. "Telephones in every room, even the can. She liked to call the kids and say, 'Guess where I'm calling from.'"

Josie smiled, imagining her father doing the same thing. Calling from the toilet in a fancy hotel, saying, "Guess where I'm calling from." "My parents got married in Las Vegas."

"Yeah, they got those parlors. 'Feeling lucky today?' Goyim." He laughed, shook his head, as if only crazy people would get married there. "No offense. Dotty, she liked blackjack. Always lost, but did she love to play. Said it made her feel like James Bond. Every day she'd set a limit, how much she was going to lose, a C-note or two. But boy did she have a good time losing, more than most people have winning."

Was that the secret? Even if the house always won — you could still feel like James Bond, have a good time losing your two hundred bucks. Instead of sitting in a window, staring out at Bosch, thinking how you had to beat the house.

The old man gazed down at the green blanket under which his wife lay. "You know, she came to me once. I mean, after she died. You're going to think I'm crazy, but I saw her. She was in the bedroom, at the foot of the bed. She looked like she did when we first got married, in Chicago. Her father drove a truck for a bootlegger. She was wearing this blue dress she used to have, and her hair was dark again. She was so beautiful. And she said, 'Morty, Morty, I saw my mother, and Artie Cohen' — he was a neighborhood kid who got hit by a streetcar." He shook his head. "I hadn't thought of Artie for sixty years."

It occurred to her that old people probably knew more dead people than living ones. To have to go through this over and over again, until everyone you knew was gone. She thought of the old men at Michael's funeral, how familiar they seemed with the place, the men who Cal Faraday said sat for a week every night at Meredith's house. How could people stand it? "Did they do the thing where they came to your house for a week?"

"Shivah. Sure, they came."

"Did it help?"

He shrugged. "Gets you through the week. But then you've got the rest of your life."

His life was only going to be a few years, though. Hers had no end, it was like when you set up the mirrors in the dressing room, so they reflected each other in a long row, getting smaller and smaller but just more of the same. She was having trouble breathing. Years like this. But she didn't have to. Michael had showed her. Cal said they had no choice, but they did. There was always a choice.

It frightened her to even think it.

It was getting cold now, it felt like rain. The light was fading fast. "Would you like to get a drink or something?" Josie asked.

"No, sweetheart, but I'm flattered as hell. I'm going to my daughter's for dinner," the old man said, zipping up his Windbreaker. "Later I'll be at the Four Queens, on Normandie. If you can't sleep, I'm down there every night after ten."

She watched him edge sideways down the hill, picking his way gingerly through the graves, careful not to trip. She wanted to call him back, to stay with her, but he had somewhere to go. She wished she did.

She missed old men, like her own grandfather, Daddy Jack, with his Brylcreem and his Old Spice, Paul Harvey in the morning, Dodgers in summertime, *live from Chavez Ravine.* Daddy Jack didn't know she lived right around the corner from there, though she had never been to see the team play. She hoped he was all right, him and Gommer Ida. She didn't know any old people here. It made LA seem glamorous, but unstable. She wished Michael had had a grandfather like this guy Morty, someone to tell him, "It's a rotten deal, the house always wins. Just sit at the table and play for all you're worth." Instead of one who showed him how to die.

12
Jeremy

The neon signs of Little Tokyo were just coming on when Josie arrived at the Atomic Café. It was really a terrible place, a tiny punk joint on the bad end of First Street. The food sucked and the service was worse, but it was near the China-town clubs and had the best jukebox in LA. She paused in the doorway, looking for Jeremy. She spotted him, at the third table by the window, like an army dug in, papers and notes and books colonizing the tabletop. He posed, tall and blond and famously distracted, forelock in his face, coat around his shoulders like a cape. In his mind, she knew, he saw himself seated before an audience in an immense theater filled with rapt young filmmakers, plying him with questions about how he got his start, his early films, how he became so successful. He woke up in the morning to the sound of his own applause. On the jukebox, Tom Verlaine sang "See No Evil." They said Patti Smith learned to sing from him, the same nasal croon, the odd breaths.

He half stood when he saw her, then sank back into his chair. "Jesus, Josie. What happened to you?"

She knew what he was thinking — was she using, or was she having a breakdown? She lit a Gauloise, watched the tiny Japanese waitress in a towering hairdo shuffle aimlessly behind the counter, looking for something she had already forgotten. There was the Atomic Café in a nutshell.

Jeremy smiled, too wide, too white. "Josie. I don't mean to say you don't look great, you always look great, but my God, eat something, get some sleep." *Your fake Englishman,* Michael used to call him. Jeremy's mother was Danish, his father American, he'd been sent to boarding school in England, where he'd picked up that accent, so it wasn't entirely fake, though he laid it on a bit thick. "You're not a vegetarian, are you?

Get a steak, take some vitamin C. B. You can get shots, I know someone —"

"Is this it?" She reached for the stack of pages, bound with brass fasteners through the holes. *Glasshouse.* She flipped through the pages the way she'd look at a magazine. Jeremy's movies were all variations on a theme, there was no need to read it. She was the Girl in an unnamed city. Walking night streets wetted down with a hose to reflect the neon signs, wearing high heels and black leather, or silver lamé. It didn't really matter what was in the script, Jeremy always threw out the script anyway. He said it was because he didn't like to be hemmed in, but it was just that he didn't really know what he wanted to shoot until he shot it. Which was fine with her, she was good at making things up. She knew just how it would look, what her part would be. *The Girl looks. The Girl walks.* The Girl was mysterious, fatally alluring, always moving, and ended up dead. She would do a lot of running, looking back, and casting smoldering glances.

"It's a thriller. Psychological. Very stylish. Sort of Antonioni meets Buñuel."

A phrase that would have sent Michael into ecstasies of loathing. *Sort of Einstein meets*

Jayne Mansfield . . . Hitler meets Roy Rogers. She remembered the first time Michael met Jeremy, in the lobby of the Vagabond. She and Michael had just seen a Fellini double bill. She'd cried in *La Strada,* the strong man and the little clown. *She has no body, she is too poor . . .* Jeremy spotted them in the lobby and descended like a big gangly bird, interposing himself between her and Michael. Going on about the Fellini, he called it "awesome."

"Was it really?" Michael said, taking her hand. "Did you sink to your knees, did you soil yourself in terror?"

Jeremy stopped talking just for an instant, like a skip in a record, and then continued as if he hadn't heard him, or perhaps he hadn't, he didn't listen well, he only heard himself, and Michael was so soft-spoken, all the more so when he was angry.

"We're taking *Angel Baby* to Toronto." *We,* he already spoke of himself as if he were an entire production company. It was his second-year project at USC, a twelve-minute short they'd shot at Union Station and a skid-row hotel near Wall. He had his leather jacket hooked over his shoulder with one finger, a gesture stagy as a false beard, and tossed his hair out of his face.

"Well, it's not in contention, but we have a screening off campus, so to speak."

"That's great, Jeremy," she said, taking Michael's arm, trying to steer him to the exit before he started a fight. "Let me know how it goes." It was so hard, the way Michael disliked all her friends, and he had a special loathing for grandiose young men who didn't question the meaning of life, who had a plan for everyone and everyone in the plan.

"I'm shooting a band next month, I'm dying for you to be in it," Jeremy called after her. "They're paying. Twenty a day. How about it?"

"Twenty-five," she said. "I'll call you."

How angry Michael had been as they walked back to the car, she could hardly keep up with him. All because Jeremy had kissed her. She hadn't thought a thing of it. Film students always kissed, they were baby operators. She was used to it but Michael fell into a black sulk. "How can you suck up to a phony like that?"

"He's not so bad." Sure, Jeremy was stagy, but he wasn't totally phony, he did make his films, he was already directing commercially and he wasn't even out of film school yet. Lots of people wanted to do things, but Jeremy did them. Maybe he wasn't the genius Michael was, but did you have to be a genius to do something in this world? The important thing was, Jeremy liked using her in his films, he kept asking her, said she looked like a punk Jeanne Moreau, his fetish heartthrob. And he always made her look good. It was fun. It was not that she wanted to have some big acting career, she just liked being someone different.

As she leafed through *Glasshouse,* she was relieved at the thought of being the Girl in Jeremy's film, a girl who didn't have to think for herself, who could run glamorously in high heels and mouth someone else's words and let the ending come as it may. Car crash this time, it looked like. Fine. She wanted to work, keep busy, and never have to go home. A Jeremy film would take up all her time for a while.

Out the window, an old Japanese woman and a young one, both in Western hair but wearing kimonos, walked by. The old woman was about three feet tall, and a hundred years old, and she was laughing, her hand over her mouth, hanging on to the young one's arm with the other hand. Josie stared after them, wondering what an old woman like that could possibly find to laugh about. Tottering along, all hunched over and twisted and wrinkled as wet crepe. How could old people bear it, all the things that life could do to you?

She found some quarters in her purse and went over to the jukebox, punched in Richard Hell and the Voidoids doing "Going Going Gone" and "Lost Boys Love Dead Girls" by Lola Lola, a song about Edie Sedgwick. Lola Lola came on first, her operatic voice going down to gravel, then talk-singing like Dietrich. Sprechgesang. God, she even knew what it was called. *He kiss her picture in the tattered magazine*, came the familiar voice, and their waitress sang along, imitating Lola's threatening growl. Ferdi and Edie and Darby, John Lennon. It was a year of loving dead people.

The petite waitress finally brought their orders, or at least something on a plate, though it was all wrong, a cheese-and-mushroom omelet instead of her udon soup, Jeremy's burger, but cold, and with salad instead of fries, but they ate them without complaint. That was how it was at the Atomic. You placed your order and then you ate what the waitress or the cook or Fate served up. You never got what you wanted but sometimes what you got was edible. Just like life. The old guy from Mount Sinai would approve. She'd never taken Michael to the Atomic, he was too fussy about getting exactly what he wanted.

She kept thinking about it as Jeremy talked about his Concept for the movie, the locations, some house off Sunset Plaza he pronounced "total Sixties, it'll blow your mind." She imagined walking into the house and blowing her head off.

"Someone should tell that moron that language has meaning," Michael had fumed the night of *La Strada,* walking back to the car. "How can you stand him, Josie, how could you possibly take him seriously?" But he meant let him kiss her.

"You think I'm attracted to him?"

Michael said nothing, which meant of course that he did think so.

"This is going to be so fabulous, Josie," Jeremy said over his cold burger, shaking the hair out of his wide-set blue eyes. As he talked about the movie, some kind of cheesy psychological thriller, she just watched him. It was like watching TV with the sound off. Of all the people for Michael to have been jealous of. Jeremy Scott, a being absolutely free of interior life. Ambition was the only emotion he registered. Planning, plotting, big dreams. How absurd people were in all their wanting. Big everything, Technicolor. When the only meaning she could see anymore was a fingerprint left on a yellow sketchbook cover, a piece of pine shaving soap, the last trace of a kiss.

Jeremy wanted to make her a star. It drove him crazy when she said, "I am a star, Jeremy." LA was full of Jeremys — film students and art students, writers and photographers and rock musicians, models and actresses. The armies of the ambitious. For them, the future was like a giant oxygen mask, as if there was nothing to breathe in the present. When the present was all there was ever going to be.

She remembered how she'd taken Michael to one of the shoots, for a goth band, Silent Scream, they shot it in someone's garage in Eagle Rock. His tolerance for boredom was used up in the first half hour, and the repetition of song phrases drove him mad. "Why is it taking so long?" he asked after having watched Josie walk back and forth through the Mole fog twenty times, its stinking oily smoke that was cheaper than dry ice. *Eat your head, eat your head . . .* They could hear Silent Scream in their sleep for a month.

"You're not listening to me. Josie, this is serious."

Jeremy staring at her with his goggly blue eyes. "I'm listening, Jeremy. Of course I am."

Everything about filmmaking was serious to Jeremy Scott. He once sat her down and outlined her whole career for her. Address of an acting school. Some agents to talk to. More polished head shots. *You've got to get serious, Josie.* She hated auditions. It was embarrassing, selling yourself like you were a sweater. At least art modeling was personal, you knew someone and they hired you. What was wrong with not wanting to get anywhere? Was it a crime? Anti-American?

Yet the truth was, she would have liked to be someone. To have some real talent, something to offer. It was her secret. That she would have given anything to have been Michael. With those gifts. It was so tedious to have ambition, to want to be thought special when you were flat-out ordinary. Though Michael thought she was better than that. He couldn't see how ordinary she was. It was just when she was around him, she was smarter, original. He was like those magnets that changed the shape of the filings, made them stand up like hair. But now, she was back on her own.

"So, you still with that guy, what's his name?"

He knew damn well what his name was. "No, we're not together anymore," she said. She heard herself say it. And it was the truth, he had passed her back, had said, *Thanks but no thanks.* Not even thanks for the memories. No memories. She decided not to tell Jeremy about Michael's death. It was easier without the sympathy and a pat on the back. What would Jeremy say anyway? This was better, she could just get on with being the Girl.

He wrote an address on the script. It was a Topanga address, she knew it from Charlie Peacock's drawing class. "We're starting on the fourteenth, can you make it? We have the two cars for the day, it has to be then."

She looked in her book. She had Gloria Reyes in Long Beach, but she could give it to Pen. January 14. It seemed impossible that she would live through another week, and another, into February, and March, the whole calendar was an absurdity, its empty pages a thin strip of blacktop across five thousand miles of desert.

Yet she thought of that old woman, laughing.

How could she laugh like that, when the game was rigged, when you couldn't win, when it was all *ming?* A woman that old, she had probably lost more people than everybody on this whole block put together. Internment camps, Hiroshima, who knows what she'd been through? And yet there she was, like some fucking miracle, one foot in the grave, laughing.

13
Helms

Josie parked halfway down the block-long de-funct bakery in Culver City, with its enormous Thirties sign, HELMS, OLYMPIC BREAD, its stars-and-stripes shield. Nick told her they used to take field trips at Helms Bakery when he was a kid, they got tiny loaves of bread at the end. "Beat the shit out of the Star-Kist tuna plant," he said. Even now, the place smelled of yeast and caramelized sugar. David Doll's band played here on New Year's Eve, in a failed electric-car factory leased by a hippie guy named Merlin, a laser artist who put on light shows and let bands play for free. She still had the hangover — Paul

237

Angstrom had found her passed out in the can, wrapped around a bottle of voddy.

She'd never worked for this photographer before. It was an ad for skateboards, she was the boarder's girlfriend. When she'd asked over the phone what she should wear, the photographer just said to wear what she wore to the casting. Her yellow coat, some patent-leather knee-high boots with stacked heels, the plaid schoolgirl skirt she'd bought at Goodwill, a child's T-shirt, her outrageous hair braided into two tiny pigtails. She normally avoided her modeling agency like leprosy, a cheeseball place in Hollywood, but work was work, and she needed it now.

It took her a while to find the photographer's suite in the warren of workshops and studios. As she walked into the studio, "Heart of Glass" played on the stereo. No wonder he liked her look. A Blondie guy. The photographer stood at the chest-high counter, looking at some film on the light box. Old, maybe forty, with a trim build and curly dark hair, Josie could tell he worked out — he wore a tight black T-shirt to show off his precision-cut muscles. What was his name? Walker, or Parker, something like that. She came over and saw he was actually chopping some coke on the light-box glass. With a quick glance to his assistant, a smart-looking, heavy-featured girl in Elvis Costello horn-rimmed glasses, he laid out lines, did two of them, and handed Josie the rolled-up bill. She did hers up quick. He unrolled the hundred, wiped the last of the grains from the green and ran his finger over his gums, put the bill back in his pocket. Then he looked at her, impersonally, and she could tell he'd forgotten her name too, more interested in her skin. "You have some powder? You're shiny."

She powdered down at a mirror nailed to the wall by the phone, while the assistant adjusted the lights. The coke turned up the volume, a nice sparkly buzz. She checked the mirror to see if there was a rim around her nostrils, and wondered what the assistant was getting paid an hour. She looked smart, probably an art-school grad, and what was she making, ten, maybe twelve? When she, the imitation human, was getting a hundred dollars and free blow for standing still for an hour. What a freaky world. There was no point in looking for meaning. Life was a fucking stretch of surf, and you rode your board, it was all you could do. In the mirror, a face out of Picasso stared back, some cubist nightmare. If her cheekbones weren't there to stretch it out, her face would fold in on itself like wet tissue. *You can get some shots, I know someone . . .*

The photographer directed her to join the other model, a skateboard kid shifting nervously on the white paper drawn down from a big roll on the wall, like the paper that covered the doctor's bed when you went for a crotch exam. "Stand behind him, cop some 'tude," the photographer said. *Cop some 'tude?* She could hear Michael. But she knew what Parker meant. It was no different from life drawing, you made an interesting composition in space. She imagined the tangible shape of herself and the skateboard boy, then let it go negative, where the space was the solid and they were the absence.

"This is a bogus board," the kid told Josie, as the photographer's assistant adjusted the reflecting umbrellas, the lights.

She didn't respond, just let the coke shimmer in her body, finally feeling good for the first time in so long.

"I never did this before." The kid popped his knuckles, nervous as a third grader taking a test. Normally she would have felt sorry for him, but today she saw him the way the photographer did. A shape in space.

"Don't worry, he'll tell you what to do," Josie

said. There was always someone to tell you what to do. It was only when you tried on your own that you got into trouble.

After the lights had been adjusted and readjusted, the reflectors tilted and moved and tilted again, the assistant gave the photographer his Polaroid, and he shot off a few frames, moving around, dancing to Blondie, getting into the whole *American Gigolo* vibe. Photographers had one advantage over artists, they could easily change their own perspective. Some shots he took practically from the ground, angling up at the kid and herself looming behind him. "Yeah," he said as he watched the Polaroid develop in his hand. "Like that."

He showed it to Josie and the kid craned to see. They came off as cool and threatening, towering over the observer, with the graffiti-style logo of the skateboard company showing on the bottom of the board.

"The board should be all shredded," the kid said. "This is bullshit."

The photographer wasn't the least bit concerned. He and Josie were both tuned in to the same station, they'd entered the Blondie world, its cosmopolitan slickness, bright and stylized movie versions of themselves. But the photographer thought it was him, where Josie knew it was just the coke. She ran her tongue over her teeth.

"Like I'm supposed to be this cool hip shredder, with this bogus board," the boy complained over his shoulder to Josie.

"Try getting a real job," Josie said. What she wouldn't give for a ciggie.

"Black-and-white," the photographer said to his assistant.

The assistant handed the photographer his 35 millimeter, took the Polaroid from him, and slid Josie a conspiratorial smile. *I know he's a jackass, but I gotta work here.* Assistants didn't get any coke.

"I thought you were supposed to be my girlfriend," the kid pouted.

"I am," Josie said. "Your dom girlfriend." She nudged him in the ass with her boot.

"Love that," said the photographer, squatting down, lower than the kid. "Hold it." He started shooting the roll. Three from one position, two lower, and the final four lying down, the camera propped on a sandbag. Josie had to admire his limber, compact form, tanned and intricate with muscle. Kind of grotesquely fascinating, like watching a snake, close up.

"My legs hurt," the kid said. "Can I stand up now?"

"No." The photographer shot a couple more, then let the kid up. Josie was glad of the coat, the studio was freezing. The kid towered over her, awkward and simple with his bogus board, a junior from Venice High the photographer had found on the boardwalk. He did a funny little dance, to get the circulation back in his legs. "I hate that prickly thing, you know? I can't feel my feet."

They waited for him to finish, then the assistant put a chair on the paper roll, handed the photographer the camera loaded with color. They did a couple of shots with her leaning over to kiss him, a cutesy Fifties pose, her ass sticking out, and then one of her walking across him and off to the right, him looking after her. Then finished up outside on a bus bench, the two of them waiting for the bus, the board in the middle. "That's the one," the photographer said as they went back into the bakery. "That's the ad. I knew it would be that all along."

"Then why shoot the other ones?" Josie asked.

"So the client has a choice." He didn't pay Josie, but wrote out a check for the kid. The modeling agency would pay her after they'd taken their cut. "The choice I want them to make. Can you stay? I've got some more marching powder. Joanne, don't forget, the shoot starts at nine at the pier. Stop and pick Danny up, yeah?" The assistant already had her coat on. She gave him the *heil Hitler* salute and took off.

Josie put her purse over her shoulder, took out her cigarettes, lit one. Yeah. Yeah, she could use a little more marching powder. It felt good. It felt damn good.

"Don't smoke in here," he said. "I quit last week."

He turned and she gave him the finger behind his back. She went outside. Could she really stay for some more flake with Parker or Walker? Let him take her in his tight workout arms? It was so tempting, just to surf that wave. He'd bark out instructions, maybe put her in costume and fuck her in the ass, something to make her abasement complete.

Then she noticed the kid, sitting on the curb as if he was waiting for someone. Probably his mother. He had his real skateboard with him, that was worn to the wood right through the sandpaper, the ends blunted with repeated impact. "Hey," he said. And she realized that he had been waiting for someone. Her.

She sat down next to him, tucking her skirt around her thighs so she wouldn't expose herself to every passing car. The speed as they whizzed by. Her heart pounded, arrhythmic, a limping gallop. Her lame horse of a heart. She inhaled on her Gauloise. What if she just got up and walked out into traffic? Just a few steps, that's all it would take, someone would hit her for sure. Take her right out. *Do it.*

No. What was she thinking? It frightened her, the clarity of it. Mangled underneath some car wheel. That's what she wanted? She had to think of something else.

The boy was smiling at her. His eyelashes were curly and he was getting a zit right in the middle of his forehead.

"Look, I didn't mean to be such a bitch," she said, flicking her cigarette. "A friend of mine just died."

"Wow," he said. "I never knew anybody who died." He was so young. So sweet. She suddenly wanted to run her hands through his spiky hair, she wanted to kiss him, go down on him, something he would remember the rest of his life. "What'd he die of?"

She sighed and blew out a series of smoke rings. "Death."

The boy spun the wheels of his old skateboard. "Are you really a model? I mean, I thought they were supposed to be tall."

We're all small . . . "I don't get much print work. I do some stupid stuff like the Penney catalog. They make me wear a wig."

"I think your hair rocks."

The whirr of the ball bearings in the wheel as he spun it, like a prayer. Michael once told her about the prayer wheels of Nepal. A huge one they had in Katmandu. That they inscribed prayers on the wheel and as you spun it, the prayers went out into the universe, it was a sacred machine. She liked the idea, something praying for her, even if she couldn't do it for herself. She didn't believe in anything, not anymore. "Give me your board."

He handed it to her. She took out a black pen from her bag, thought about what she should write. She didn't know any prayers. *Help,* she wrote on one wheel. *Please God,* on another. *Sorry,* on the third. And then there was just one left, and on it she wrote the prayer that was too late to pray.

"You're not going to fuck that guy, are you?"

the kid said anxiously, gesturing back to the studio. "He's an asshole. He reminds me of my dad."

She wrapped her arms around her knees. Sitting here with this kid on the curb made her feel old. She had been planning to stay, but now she saw she couldn't. "No, I'm not going to fuck him. I'm not fucking anybody these days. Look, can I give you a lift somewhere?"

She gave the kid a ride out to the Marina, where his mother lived in the Marina City Club, the circular beehive towers housing the old coffee-tea-or-me crowd from the Swinging Seventies, grown slightly older and staler, more comb-overs, more crow's-feet under the Farrah hairdos. She parked sideways across two spaces.

"Want to come up?" the boy asked. "I've got some weed. My mom won't be home until nine."

The ultimate high-school come-on. Shitweed nursed and carried like a condom in a kid's back pocket. She stroked his face, the skin was soft as her own. He was maybe, what, fifteen? She leaned over and kissed him. His lips thin and chapped, his mouth soft, surprised. "Be good," she said, and reached across him, opened the door on his side. The cold, damp sea air rushed in.

"Come on, it's cool, really," he said. "I swear. There's a Jacuzzi and everything."

She sat quietly until he collected his pack and board and got out.

"Can I have your phone number at least, just to, you know, call you?"

Call her. She had never been a girl boys called up, made a date with. She was the kind of girl someone drove by and honked the horn, a girl you asked to stay for a beer or some ludes and fucked and sent home. Walker or Parker knew who she was. Who she used to be. Now she didn't know who she was. Michael saw something else in her, but then he stopped seeing it. She found a piece of paper on the floor of the car, the agency's directions to the shoot, and wrote Pen's number on the back. "Pray for me," she said. She reached out and spun a wheel of his board, the last one, the one that said *True World*.

She drove by the house, but didn't stop. There was nothing inside but the paintings he'd given up on and the books he'd stopped reading, a bed they would never make love in, journals whispering in the dark. Instead, she bought a half-pint of voddy at Gala's, and drove down to the river, a dead-end street where there was a tear in the chain link. She pulled it apart and climbed through. Walking along the top of the embankment in her cracked patent boots, she watched the water flow through ryegrass and cottonwoods. This was better. A flight of ducks rose, and winged in unison off toward their roost at the Silverlake Reservoir. Nature was always there, no matter what. Up above, on the bridge, traffic inched its way along Fletcher Street. Thousands of people passed by here every day and not one noticed the water tumbling on the rocks, the miniature forest that sprouted up through the concrete river bottom. Real water from mountains, that no one had invented, it would be here long after they scraped the city from the face of the earth. The sooner the better.

This was where they had seen the heron that shining morning. A giant blue bird, three feet high, standing in the water, poking through the reeds at the edge of the little island. And time just stopped. The true world glowed in the morning light, the bird and the water, sparkling. They'd held hands, they both saw it, it was right there, the true world. She didn't know how long they stood there because there was no time, it only started again when, eventually, the bird flew off, under the arch of the bridge. They watched it fly upriver, and knew the moment had passed, but they had seen it. The world was an open door. He'd built a little stack of stones to commemorate it. A duck, it was called. "It's how you mark trail in rough country," he said. "Then travelers can look for the next duck, and know they're on the right path."

But the rock pile was gone now, and in the lowering light that stained the water with sad mauve, the world was a closed book. They'd gone hopelessly off trail, and there weren't going to be any other markers, not for a thousand miles.

She sat down on the embankment, watching the river flow in the cold pink afternoon, cracked the bottle of Smirny. The coke had left her wired, her teeth gritting. She drank, her ass growing cold on the cement. Downriver on the other side, some people had dragged a raggedy mattress onto the embankment. She could see, they were fucking on it. Right out in the open. A man and a woman, you could see the rise and fall of his twin-moon ass. She watched, lighting a Gauloise, letting the smoke curl in the still air. It wasn't very sexy, more like watching ants empty the sugar bowl. Something that once had meant so much, sex, now seemed no more interesting than an oil-field pump jack.

Then after a while, it occurred to her, maybe it was something else. Maybe the woman was struggling, maybe the man holding her down. The peace she had felt before, that tiny moment, was gone. She should do something, but what? If she called the cops and they were just home-less people having a fuck, she'd get everybody in trouble.

Anyway, they were so far away. And really, you couldn't tell.

Wasn't that the way it always was? You didn't know, you couldn't tell, you just let it happen.

When they separated and the man rolled over, she still couldn't tell. The woman pulled her dress down and the man stood, zipping his fly, and he was saying something to her, where she still lay on the ripped mattress, and even then Josie could not decide if they knew each other, whether they were joined by love or violence. Then the man walked away, down the embankment, and the woman sat up and looked at the water, her arms around her legs, and Josie knew she would never know. Perhaps they didn't know themselves. Sometimes the line was very fine.

Yes. She thought of the time Tommy had taken her for a ride out in the country in a stolen GTO. Her oldest brother, the one that coroner's call should have been about. Tommy Tyrell, the one they were all judged by. She was still in junior high then, and he'd just gotten out of the youth camp, had only been back a few weeks. He'd picked her up after school, in somebody's red go-fast, and she was flattered that people knew who he was, her badass brother, it was a certain celebrity. "Where'd you get the car?" she'd asked him, running her finger down the glossy red hood.

He shrugged. "Borrowed it." His handsome face, with the same downturned mouth they all had.

They'd gone out into the flatlands past Pumpkin Center, parked by a ditch under an old pepper tree. He had a quart of Olde English 800 he shared with her, they smoked a Sherm. It was a woozy, junk high, and he told her stories about youth camp, the fights, the things he had learned, dirty tricks, how to make a knife from a bedspring, you kept it in your sock. Listening to Aerosmith on KUZZ. His profile as he stared out at the dry fields was just like her father's except for the brown eyes. "You were always the good-looking one," he said. He smelled like motor oil. "How old are you now?" His face was her face, they all looked the same, the same pointed nose, their shiny brown hair the same, though his eyes were hard and full of pain.

"Thirteen," she said.

"Awful small for thirteen, aren't you?"

"We're all small," she said.

And his face darkened as he turned to look at her straight on, and suddenly she saw what everyone saw when they looked at the Tyrells, the sullen anger at having been cheated of everything worth having before they were born, the hunger to get some of it back. He pulled a knife from his jeans, flicked it open. "Take off your clothes," he whispered. "Do it." He held the point to her neck. It was a little sting, not even a bee. She was not afraid, not really. She understood. He just didn't want to be small anymore. So she did what he asked. It wasn't that she was afraid he would hurt her, it was knowing exactly how he felt. It was just a body, what difference did it make? It was what it was, just one more sad thing.

She had never told anybody but Michael. But she knew he would understand, how things could happen to a person, and it was hard to find the names for them, there were things that came in between this and that, that were both A and Z. And he did understand. They had lain in bed, smoking in Montmartre, talking about bodies and what they endured. And he told her that during his last year at his swank private school in Ojai, he was sent to a sanitarium called Meadowlands. "The place was a total fraud," he said, lacing his fingers in hers. "But it looked nice, flowers and fountains sparkling in the sunshine. That's all Meredith cared about. I wasn't nuts, just really sad, they put me on Thorazine and God knows what else. But my freako roommate could not resist the opportunities afforded by my helplessness. All I remember was thinking, how pathetic human life is."

Yes it was. Just like that. Pathetic, vulnerable and senseless. She watched the sun drop to the horizon, a sad wash of red over blue. There were no ducks, no herons now, only the traffic on the bridge and the water, still flowing, for no reason she could understand. Even the raped woman was gone, all that was left was that ragged mattress. She sat alone in the blue twilight, too cold for frogs, as the early sunset bled into the water, the shine of the river lighter than the land.

14
Dining Car

She paused outside Otis to light a cigarette in the noon haze after Melina Varga's head-study class. The best thing about head study was that she didn't need to take her clothes off. She wore layers of clothes, bag lady–style, pants and dress and jacket and hat. She was always so cold these days. The light hurt her eyes, though it wasn't that bright, not through the square sunglasses she wore everywhere now. Students called to her but she pretended she hadn't heard. The park across the street lay under a light mist. Fountains shot water out of the old lake, aerating its obstinate greenness. A bum wheeled his

shivery shopping cart along like a giant tam-
bourine, piled high with bottles and cans, past
the silver-gray Jaguar parked at the curb. Fuck.

The smooth continuous motion of the electric window, lowering. That proud head, the rich
dark hair. "Josie? Josie, it's me."

She would know it at the bottom of the sea.
What did that bitch want now? She'd shown
herself out for Christ's sake, did she look like
she'd missed the exit? She'd been so wrong to
go to Meredith's that night. To try for comfort
like that. As if grief could be shared. They could
only struggle over it, like ladies fighting over a
shirt at a year-end sale at May Company. It was
hard enough just to sit with the things she'd already gotten wrong, ways in which she'd failed
him all on her own. Today was not a day for a con-
frontation. This time she turned around and
walked back toward Seventh Street, knowing
Meredith wouldn't suffer the indignity of running after her.

She was mistaken. She heard the footsteps on
the sidewalk, felt Meredith grab her shoulder.
"Please, Josie, wait."

Meredith was not dressed for running — she
looked like she was going to court, in a black
coat with gold buttons, nylons, black shoes with

high heels. The coat alone probably cost five hundred dollars, an antique stickpin glittered in the dull afternoon light.

"Josie, please. I just wanted to apologize." A car passing by showered them both with street grit. Meredith glanced back at her Jag, making sure it was still there, Josie guessed. *Just walk away.* She knew she should, but something made her hesitate. The tone of the woman's voice, the urgency, the remorse. She looked into Meredith's sunglasses, saw her own masked self reflected there, and Meredith, and her in her own dark glasses, on and on, like the man on the Cream of Wheat box, holding another box with another man on it holding the box. "The way I spoke to you that morning. It wasn't right." She smiled, awkward, unsure. A woman like Meredith, worried about what Josie Tyrell thought. "Let me do something for you. Buy you lunch, I know a place. It's not far at all."

Josie took a drag on the cigarette. "Slumming?"

The older woman took off her sunglasses. The fragile skin around her eyes was stained dark, as if someone had rested a tea bag on them too long. "Josie, you won't hold that against me. I'm really not like that. I'm not myself these days."

"Who are you then?" Josie asked. A woman who needed something from her, somehow. A famous pianist standing on a street corner at MacArthur Park, begging her son's trashy girl-friend to have lunch with her in some swanky place. A woman who wouldn't have been seen in the same room as her when he was alive. The irony, as Michael used to say, was excruciating.

"I don't know," Meredith said, putting the glasses back on. "I used to be someone, but now I can't remember. Come on, let me buy you a de-cent meal."

Josie wasn't sure what it would mean if she went. Yet she was flattered. Yes, flattered. That Meredith had taken the trouble to find her, wanted to take her to lunch, a woman who never thought of her at all except to wish her dead. How Michael would have hated the idea of his mother and Josie, going to lunch. She gazed at this woman in her coat with the stick-pin, her shoes with gold buckles. *What does she want with your pissant self?* She could hear her father warning, *She don't like you. She wants somethin. Watch yourself.* But there was also herself. What she wanted.

The Jaguar smelled of Meredith's perfume, smoky and lingering, and the leather seats, and a whiff of the house in Los Feliz, the cedar and mothballs, and underneath it all, just a hint of Michael. She had to restrain the impulse to bury her nose in Meredith's coat sleeve. What she wouldn't give to have that smell forever.

"Josie, I'm sorry about that morning," Meredith said, steering the big car from the curb. "Really. I was so glad you were there. I needed the company in the worst way. That's the truth."

She had to admit, she was thrilled that Meredith wanted to spend time with her. She knew she was betraying Michael again. Going behind his back. He never wanted her to have anything to do with the Meredith life, that was the whole point, they were as far apart as could be. The buckles on Meredith's shoes were gold and square, like a Pilgrim's. She was curious where Meredith would take her, dressed like Ashcan Sally. In truth, she wanted to know this woman. She wanted to know where Meredith ate, what she ordered, how she held a fork.

The Pacific Dining Car sat on the corner of Sixth Street and Whitmer, in the shadow of downtown. A diner in an old train car, it brimmed with businessmen at this hour, devouring steaks the size of baseball mitts. Meredith quietly checked her reservation with the maître d. Josie could tell he knew, he avoided meeting Meredith's eye for all but the shortest period of time, as if she were terribly burned or disfigured in some brutal way. It struck her — Meredith already had a reservation. She had known Josie would say yes. Meredith turned and waited, and the man helped her off with her coat. The way she did it reminded Josie exactly of Michael's way of assuming people would do things for him. Josie wanted to see if he would do it for her, so she pulled one arm slightly out of the sleeve of her torn leather jacket, and there he was, helping her off with it, he had no choice.

The businessmen watched them go past, she was sure they were guessing how the two of them went together, the bag girl and Miss Symphony Hall. Parole officer and juvenile offender? Rock star and agent? She liked Rock Star, pretended she was slightly embarrassed to be caught dead in a stiff joint like this. She and Michael — they were artists, the true aristocracy.

The chairs were low and leathery, the menus fat, with plump leather covers and gold tassels. She was afraid the dishes would be in French and she would have to fake it, but no, the list was in plain English. Meredith glanced at the menu briefly, as if it was a catalog and she wasn't buying anything. She put it aside. She already knew what she wanted.

The waiter came to take their drinks order. He confirmed that Meredith wanted "the usual," but when Josie ordered a Stoli on the rocks, he gave her a skeptical look, assuming her underage status. She got ready to show her ID, but instead of carding her, he just glanced at Meredith, who raised her eyebrows and gave a small nod. He shrugged, wrote down her order. Josie wanted to remember every detail, the sequence of these tiny gestures. Here was exactly the difference between the rich and the poor, in that one near-invisible interchange. There was a secret code, after all. It was the conspiracy her father always talked about, the line which the poor could not cross because they didn't know the handshake. There was only a glimpse, you had to look fast, but there it was. You could sell information like that. It was the way the world really ran, in little signs and signals.

She studied Meredith from behind her leather menu. The older woman was dressed very simply in a white shirt and black pullover sweater, a straight black skirt, but such implicit richness in that shirt and that sweater, she knew clothes like that didn't come from the Penney catalog.

What she might have learned from a woman like Meredith. The Hindus called it *maya,* the false and distracting detail of life's surface — the very opposite of the true world. But Josie wasn't so sure that it wasn't a kind of true world of its own. She wondered if Meredith enjoyed this knowledge, or if she even thought about it. "A fish has no concept of water," Michael once said. She noticed a strand of pearls around Meredith's neck, inside the collar of her shirt. They showed pinky beige against her skin, each pearl big as Josie's thumbnail. Imagine having pearls like that and wearing them inside your shirt so only a few at the neck would show. *Elegant things.*

The waiter brought their drinks, and Meredith raised a chunky glass. "Here's to — nothing," she said.

Josie clinked her tumbler to Meredith's and drank. She was drinking too much lately, though she rarely started so early. She knew it was a bad idea but these days there seemed to be no good reason not to pursue every bad idea that came along. Meredith ordered a salad with duck. Josie ordered the thing on the menu that sounded the most repulsive, calf's brains. She was pleased at the waiter's surprise, she guessed he expected her to order the cheeseburger.

Old-fashioned framed prints of locomotives lined the walls of the plush red dining car. "Did you ever bring Michael here?"

"When he was a little boy, he loved it. The train. But later, he couldn't bear it. Too many fat cats." She gestured with her drink at their fellow diners. "He'd rather brave botulism at the Burrito Baron."

Josie was surprised that Meredith understood Michael's terror of men like these, men with ties and ruddy aftershaved faces. Meredith smiled, as if she could read Josie's thoughts. "Of course. It was what he feared most. A life with a suit and briefcase and a cigar. Being part of any club. He'd rather die —" Her face paled, and she took a slug of her drink.

"I know. I do it too," Josie said.

The way she looked at her then, over the rim of her glass, gave Josie a jolt, it was so like Michael. The green eyes, their huge startled expression, the length and curl of the lashes, the slow flick of wide eyelid. The ache of loss, profound as if someone had gone into her bones and scooped out the marrow.

"He wanted to be one with the people, but he was such a snob in his way." Meredith played with the saltshaker, unaware of the impact her similarity to her son was having, her gestures, these familiar expressions. "I bet he never once took you to a decent restaurant."

The emphatic curve of the brow, the length of the indent between nose and mouth. Josie didn't know if she could stand it. "We ate at home," Josie said, swilling the enormous Stoli, watching the melting ice swirl with the heavier alcohol. "He was a great cook."

Now Meredith was the one to be surprised. "Michael couldn't boil water."

Josie smiled. Something Meredith didn't know about him. How about that? "He went to all these little markets, and if he didn't know what something was, he'd buy it and find out how to cook it. He has all these cookbooks, *Auntie Ono Cooks Hawaiian. Food of the Gods.*" Moussaka, and tamales that took a whole day to make. The dark fragrant moles he spent hours on, buying spices at Grand Central, then grating and grinding and roasting chiles and chocolate, everything from scratch. "Once he cooked a whole fish from the Chinese market. The head and tail still on. We even ate the eyes. And the cheeks, that's the delicacy."

Meredith listened, her chin resting on her balled-up fist — that fist, it was so Michael. Watching her was like falling on a stake. "Do you think it's awful, that I didn't know my own son any better?"

"Nobody knows everything about someone," Josie said, wishing it wasn't quite so true.

Just then, a man came over to their table, an older man, handsome and slender, with neatly cut gray hair. He said he had seen Meredith at a recital in San Francisco that spring, sorry to learn of her son, he was a huge fan, blah blah blah. *Desperate fan.* Meredith just smiled and listened politely, like a queen. So sure she deserved every word of it. Josie wondered for a moment whether she would give him her hand to kiss. The man was no pimply-faced kid, though, he was nice looking for an old guy, he had cuff links that peeped out from under the sleeve of his jacket, and the contrast of his gray hair and his youngish face might have been appealing to an older woman like Meredith. He was sorry for her loss but by God if he didn't ask for an autograph on the back of a business card. He kept turning to stare at her as he went back to his table.

"Did you always want to be famous?" she asked Meredith.

Meredith gazed at her, luminous green eyes in

the pale face, considering. Again that gesture, the hand cupping the chin, the forefinger half covering the mouth, long thumb under the jaw. Their hands could cover their entire faces, both of them. "I wanted to be esteemed by the cognoscenti."

Josie heard her father in her head, *See, I told you. She's laughin at you.* "Sorry for being so ignorant, but is that a yes or a no?"

The dreamy look in Meredith's eyes dissolved, and the focused intelligence, self-conscious, returned. "By a special few. Those in the know. *Cogno* meaning recognition — *cogitato,* to think." And though it smarted, she understood that Meredith wasn't just trying to fuck with her head. She was like Michael that way, she assumed you were intelligent, gave you a chance to catch up. Josie appreciated that.

The meals came, and Josie was surprised that the calf's brains weren't repulsive at all. They were soft and velvety, grainless, more like liver, but not so strong, and they'd been cooked in a buttery sauce, served with sweet onion and mashed potatoes. *Take some vitamins, eat a steak.* She wondered about brains. If you ate the brains, would you learn what the animal knew?

Though what did a calf know that she didn't? Better to eat Meredith.

Meredith ate the same knife-and-fork way Michael did. Josie had begun to eat that way too, it was so elegant, but she didn't do it now, she didn't want Meredith to think she was just doing it to impress her, and she wasn't that good at it anyway. Not like Meredith, the miraculous deftness with which the woman folded the lettuce leaves with the tines of her fork, and got it all into her mouth in one neat package. Josie would have it all over her face.

"So you're still modeling," Meredith said.

Yes, Meredith, I get naked in front of strangers. Still. Even now. "Among other things."

"And you pay the rent with that?"

"I manage," Josie said.

Meredith signaled the waiter by lifting a single finger and then pointing to her Scotch, which had disappeared. Josie marveled that the waiter watched her so carefully, he could catch a gesture so small. Imagine having the confidence to believe that someone paid that much attention to you. It reminded her of the movies when people went to an auction, and accidentally sneezed and ended up with some huge ugly vase they couldn't afford. "Josie, I've been thinking about this. I should have asked you before. If you need any help, just call me. You have to understand, I was just so angry at Michael, I thought if he didn't have any money he'd come home."

"I know," Josie said. Like Michael, she'd rather slit her wrists than take money from Meredith.

The waiter brought the new drink, took away Meredith's empty glass. She was clearly planning on getting plowed. Now the salad was abandoned in favor of the second drink. Whatever Meredith had brought her here for, she had to get good and plastered to say it. Was this it? Regret at cutting Michael off? Regret at the way she'd treated Josie that morning in Los Feliz? Josie was feeling a little woozy from the Stoli herself.

"The guy with the gray hair keeps looking at you," Josie said.

Meredith glanced at the music fan and his businessman friends without much interest, over the rim of her glass.

"Do you date?" Josie asked. "I don't mean now. In general." To hear Michael tell it, it had always been just him and his mother. There was never another man in the stories he told of their travels.

"Dating," Meredith said, holding her glass in two hands, looking down into it, as if a message was going to print out at the bottom. "It sounds a bit juvenile, don't you think? 'Let's go down to the malt shop, Goober.' "

"So you don't?"

"I have male friends. I'm not celibate."

"Michael thought you were."

Now a slow smile spread across her face. A real smile, wrinkling her nose, the lines fanning out from her eyes. "Well, I didn't wave my relationships under his nose. I once had an affair with a Czech violinist, and Michael was just impossible. Did everything he could to break it up." Meredith stirred her drink with the little plastic stick, watched the ice twirl. "You think I was so wrong? Should I have forced my sex life on him? Would that have been less Oedipal? Or more? I don't know. I was all he had, that was the thing I kept thinking."

But she had set it up that way. He could have had his father, if she'd let him. Or maybe not. It was hard to know whom to believe.

Now, Meredith crossed her arms and placed them on the edge of the table, leaned forward. Her pearls fell out from inside her shirt collar. They soaked in all the light, warmly, they glowed. "I'd like to ask a favor of you, Josie." She held one huge hand inside the other, and she lowered her eyes onto Josie like a lioness. "I want to see where Michael lived."

They've always got somethin up their sleeve, she heard her father say. *There's always a catch. They don't do nothin without a payoff.* And this was it. Meredith didn't want to get to know her, take back preconceived notions of Michael's trashy girlfriend, and so understand a part of him which had escaped her. No. She just wanted to see the place where Michael had finally escaped to. This lunch had nothing to do with getting acquainted, giving her a chance. Her eyes stung with the humiliation. What a fool she was, still. The enticing glimpse of this glamorous world, the Meredith world. Michael's world. Only to have the door slammed in her face.

"Why? You never wanted to when he was alive." Never wanted to see their place, have dinner with them, be with them as a couple.

"Please, Josie." She was practically whispering now. "He's gone. I just want to see . . . his home."

Josie drank from her voddy, though there wasn't much left, just watery ice flavored with vodka. She had some nerve, after what happened at the funeral, and stealing her note. Threatening to have her killed, throwing her out of Michael's room like a thief.

She could see the older woman struggling with her emotions, wanting to reach out and strangle her again — her enormous hands, she wore no rings, the nails were clipped short, un-painted, buffed to a dull sheen. They were like hands in a painting. Meredith gazed at her im-ploringly, her face composed into a trembling smile.

"I thought you wanted to take out a hit on me. Don't you remember that? Calling me and threatening to have me murdered?"

Meredith shrugged apologetically "Josie. People say things when they're upset."

"And now I'm supposed to take you on a tour of my private life."

"You remind me so much of Michael," Mere-dith said, pressing her fingers to her forehead, as if to still a violent headache. "So pigheaded. I'm just asking to see it, for Christ's sake, I'm not ask-ing to move in."

Josie struggled to hold herself firm, but could feel herself sliding toward Meredith, as if the floor itself had tilted. The woman overwhelmed her, her will, her beauty, her likeness to Michael.

She'd never come when he was alive, never wanted to see him living with a girl, as a man. And now she wanted to visit the ruins. Like a tourist arriving after a hurricane.

"Please, Josie. You've been to my house, you saw his room, everything." She lowered her voice, though it was already low. "I've tried to imagine his house, but there's just nothing. I miss him so much. Just a small thing. Please."

Josie could feel herself slipping, scrambling, like a dog on a polished floor. The low hypnotic voice, soothing her, shaping her into a new form, fragile and passive. She knew it would be wrong to let Meredith into the place where Michael had tried to have a life of his own. His only existence separate from his mother. She owed it to Michael to respect his wishes, didn't she?

Meredith waited for an answer. She looked wild, desperate, even in her pearls and cashmere sweater. Her mane of sable hair, her living eyes — alive, and Michael was dead dead dead dead. He was the one who'd left her alone. He was the one who'd broken his promises.

"All right," Josie said. "But I'll drive."

15
Tour

Meredith left the Jag in the parking lot at Bullock's Wilshire. Josie picked her up in the Falcon, at the portico behind the venerable store, supremely aware of how much noise its weak muffler made. She and Pen had once gone inside just to see what it was like, all Deco mirrors and frosted glass, but they couldn't afford to buy anything. Pen kyped a tester of Lanvin. She imagined Meredith had credit here, *Hello, Miss Loewy, Nice to see you, Miss Loewy.* They would remember her sizes, the colors she liked. Josie quickly pitched all the junk into the back as Meredith got in, the black coat gathered tightly around her to minimize contact with the seat. Her pinched face reminded Josie of the time she and Laurie Smart came in from playing at the impound yard, among the towed cars, to find Laurie's mother sitting next to Janey Tyrell on a couch piled with laundry, both women wishing they were anywhere else, Janey, trying to be a good hostess, offering this rare guest a few Oreos on a plate.

Josie punched in a tape of Meredith playing the *Pierrot Lunaire.* The angular phrases, the German woman sprechgesanging. When she heard the music, Meredith's head snapped around, staring at the tape deck. She must have imagined Josie would blast her with Fear. Though really, the Schoenberg was weirder. "Good God," Meredith said, sitting back in her seat, her hands in her coat pockets. "That woman could never get the phrasing right. Singers."

They drove up soot-darkened Alvarado, past the taquerias and travel agencies, onto Sunset. Shoppers wore unaccustomed parkas and scarves over shorts and flip-flops, the LA winter uniform. Vendors lined up along the wide sidewalks selling everything from their mishmash of carts and coolers — coconut and yuca, chicharrones and tamales and carne asada, shaved ice cones, bags of pot. Discount stores operated under elaborate rooftop neon signs advertising businesses extinct since the Twenties: *Jensen's Recreation, Foster Brothers, Lux Vacuums.* Proof as to how completely everything changed, and left just a trace. Meredith flipped up the collar of her coat, as if it had grown ten degrees colder, but her jade eyes had the attentive intelligence of the kids who sat in the front of the class.

"There's our *panadería,*" Josie said. The Diazepam bakery, people standing in line for *Tres Reyes* bread and Valium. And Launderland. "He did our laundry there." A woman was holding the door open for her kids, a big basket of laundry on one hip, steam escaping into the cold. And again Josie had the strongest feeling that Michael was going to come out, their blue and red duffel over his shoulder. She felt the catch in her throat. "He'd always ask the ladies' opinions about detergent or what they were reading in the tabs."

Meredith flicked her long eyes to the small establishment, her head deep in her collar like a turtle, as if someone might recognize her. "Giving up Harvard to do Josie Tyrell's laundry. Talk about fabric softener with underprivileged hausfraus." Her wide ironic mouth, like his in his bitter moods. "He was terrified of people of his own class. Thought he could lose himself among the poor. San Miguel de Echo Park."

Josie gauged the width of the road, to see if she could make a U-turn. She whipped a screaming 180, they were almost hit by a white van coming around the corner.

"Jesus. Are you crazy?" Meredith clung to the dashboard. "We might have been killed."

"The world might be better off."

Meredith leaned her head against the rest, closed her eyes. The choppy twelve-tone modernity of Schoenberg had fallen mysteriously into sync with the ranchero music playing in the car behind them. Josie glanced out of the window at a man driving with a Chihuahua on his lap. It stood up, its little paws on the wheel.

Michael had tried to warn her. Meredith wasn't to be trusted, she was a performer who saved the best of herself for the box with the black and white keys, the upturned faces of the public. She had no right to see their private world, *La Bohème*, the train compartment of Blaise and Jeanne. It was like allowing her into their bed, letting her watch them make love. She turned off *Pierrot Lunaire.*

Meredith put her gloved hand on Josie's coat sleeve. "Josie, please. It's nothing you don't know. He had his fantasies about so-called real life, admit it."

"Is your life so real? Not that I heard." They passed the rancid grease of a fast-food shop, *Chinese and American Food/Donuts.*

"Forgive me. I want to understand. Please don't." The voice dropped to a whisper, urgent, secret. Desperate. "Please, Josie. I do want to understand. I'm so sorry, I can be such a bitch and I don't even mean to. No one is sorrier than I am, you can bank on that."

And Josie began to slow down. There was something in her voice. She thought of Cal. *It's nobody's fault.* At least Meredith wasn't feeding her that cheesy line. They passed the newsstand, where old men read the Spanish-language magazines, smoking, kidding one another, and a young man and a girl were strolling along, arms around each other's shoulders, whispering, casting amused glances at the old people, for whom love was just history. Last year that had been her and Michael. Walking arm in arm. It seemed that love was a crop, and her season had come and gone.

"If I bring you," Josie said, "you can't say anything. Think what you want, but just don't talk, all right?"

"I promise. Thank you," Meredith said.

Josie turned off Sunset, climbing the hill, past the elementary school which was closed, the play yard occupied by older boys who had climbed the chain-link fence for gleeful games of basketball, to skateboard or ride their little brothers' bicycles in stolen freedom. As they ascended, the streets narrowed, she had to pull over for downhill traffic. An old woman with her gray hair scraped into a bun watered her small garden in bedroom slippers and white socks. A little boy in diapers ran up the sidewalk, laughing, naughty, teasing his young mother. Three men bent over the engine of a banged-up Toyota truck, the regular afternoon auto-repair club. Meredith kept her head tucked in like a spy or a cop, registering everything. Tropical plants grew lush in unkempt yards. Spectacular views opened and closed to the left and right, Hollywood, the hills, Elysian Park, the Russian church with its gold domes. Maybe she was memorizing the way they came in case Josie abandoned her.

There was an idea. Let her find her own way home, the globe-trotting pianist in her pearls.

"How do you know I'm not going to take you somewhere and just dump you?"

Meredith appeared unruffled at the thought. "Well, it's good to know that little something about your fantasy life."

The street split and joined again, to accommodate the steepness of the slope, the earth in between filled with jade plants and leggy geraniums. Josie slowed and then parked. The front house, César and Veronica's, was a ramshackle bungalow painted a peeling blue, half-hidden behind a giant bird-of-paradise higher than the roof, its black beaks and pale green crests nesting in the banana-like leaves. It looked pretty to her, but she knew, to Meredith, it might seem tatty and pathetic. She was glad she had forbidden Meredith to speak. She led her to the gate on the side of the house, pulling the noose that opened the latch. Meredith had to go slowly down the steep wooden stairs, clutching the metal-pipe railing. They stopped on the rickety landing at the little back house, shady and private, and Josie opened the door. She could feel Meredith standing behind her, tall, rigid, her long fingers washing each other in nervousness.

Josie put the keys in the bowl on the little table they had painted red, with green mermaids, relieved she'd cleaned a bit, last night, when she couldn't sleep. Meredith remained at the door, motionless, as if she had walked in on a holdup, someone pointing a gun at her, Josie half expected her to raise her hands in surrender. Long eyes unblinking, taking in the room, dense with Michael's presence. Walls covered with his paintings and drawings. Their collection of strange hats and hideous neckties and funny props, their arrangements on tabletops and windowsills. The legless couch Josie had upholstered in blue fake fur. And the view, the observatory on the crest of the hill like a king on a throne. The Hollywood sign like a joke in the flat winter light.

"You can take your coat off," Josie said.

But Meredith didn't seem to even hear her. She walked toward the windows, slowly, as if she was sleepwalking and was afraid of awakening, afraid all this would disappear. She put her hand on the back of the armchair, noticed the pipe-cleaner circus on the windowsill. She picked up Balthazar, the elephant, turned it gingerly against the light. She went to the bookcase, she was touching the books, the journals.

She opened a book of poems, Valéry, Josie wanted to grab it out of her hands. She hadn't realized how she would feel, Meredith in her house. That violation, seeing their life, touching it, it felt somehow that she was erasing it as she went. The house seemed to be bracing itself against her scrutiny. They had had so little company here. It had been heaven after the chaos of the Fuckhouse, though she had to admit, she had grown tired of their privacy. Trapped here with his moodiness, the way he had taken to testing her, pushing her. The tests she failed, that made her cheat and sneak around, like a kid and not a woman of twenty who could do what she wanted without apology.

She left Meredith to fill her senses with the life she had never wanted to know, went into the kitchen to make some tea. She filled the kettle, put it on the stove, lit it with a kitchen match.

"I love this." Meredith came back through the beaded curtain to the kitchen, holding a painting, a self-portrait of Michael as the Magician in the tarot deck. Her Magician. The four emblems on the table before him, cup, sword, wand, and coin. "Could I have it?"

The water boiled in the speckled enamel tea

kettle Michael liked because it did not whistle. She turned off the gas, and pushed past Meredith and her prize. "It's not a shopping trip." She went outside, down into the garden, plucked some mint he'd planted in a stack of tires he'd found down there. That fresh, menthol smell. How small it had been then, just a fifty-cent plant, he'd put it right under the hose bib. They'd planted everything here themselves, this small dark garden. How lovely it had been, to buy plants at the nursery and then plant them in their own yard. Josie had never planted so much as a pansy. Their jungle was going to be like the Garden of Eden. The mint was knee high and two feet wide now. How bitterly ironic, that the mint was thriving so vigorously, but the boy who planted it was not. She tucked leaves from the plant into her sweater front like a pouch.

Everything in the place called his name. The angel-wing begonia, the calla lilies, the morning glories that had grown up into the trees. She went back up to the house, where Meredith was going through the books, looking for something. Let it go. Let it go. She began making tea, thinking, what didn't bear the imprint of his personality. The jars and tins of exotic spices stacked against the painted tiles, from Thai groceries, Indian shops, Korean, Turkish, Salva-doran, Ethiopian. Their battered pots hung from a bicycle wheel over the stove. She couldn't get away from him. They could have the mint tea that they always drank, or Earl Grey, which he hated, but even his hating it made it his. She was beginning to understand why people gave away all their possessions and left town, just moved into a motel off a highway in Bishop. Maybe she should give everything to Meredith and leave with nothing but the clothes on her back. She put the mint into the celadon teapot they'd bought at a student sale at Otis, the color of duck eggs. *Elegant things.* Their game, from a book of his, *The Pillow Book of Sei Shonagon.* "Duck eggs? That's elegant?" she'd asked.

"They're a particular color of green," he said. "Very beautiful. But you should know that, you're from the country." He had no idea, a tow yard in Bakersfield was about as far from the country as Los Feliz. She poured boiling water into the crackle green pot, releasing the fresh brightness into the air. A moment later Josie heard, "Oh God."

Something in the sharpness of the cry made her wipe her hands on a towel and run into the living room, where Meredith crumpled onto the low couch like she was folding herself into an envelope, a tight package of shock, hand over her mouth. She had finally noticed the big painting, *Civilization and Its Discontents.* On her face was the same blinkless horror that Michael got the day they saw the dog hit by the car. The way it writhed in the gutter and he couldn't do anything, staring with exactly that same helplessness. Caught through the eyes, unable to respond or help or turn away.

There on the wall, Meredith finally saw herself, climbing the stairs in her son's nightmares, bearing the world's strange cargo in her arms. Every woman with her face, blind and ascending in a trance. Their idealized faces lacked the ravages his death had ground onto the genuine one. Meredith sat perfectly still, but even so, something inside was making panicked circles, just like the dog.

There was nothing she could have said to make it better. She poured tea into the tiny celadon cups, beautifully glazed. They had once done a real tea ceremony with this set. The tea was powdery and bitter, he whisked it up with a tiny broom. Everything so slow and beautiful, it lifted time away, and you were in that eternal space, it made where you were the true world.

Though Meredith wouldn't have noticed, she gave the cup a half turn before she offered it to her. You always turned the cup.

But Meredith didn't take it, she could not turn her head from the picture. It was like having Michael here, in that mood when she couldn't talk to him, but moved quietly around the place so he'd know he wasn't alone.

That's how it was with his death. There were still more punishments in store for them. Every day there was something new. As if one death was not enough, it spread out, a feast of loss with ever more courses, surprising and painful in ways you could never anticipate. "How can you live here?" Meredith whispered. "I can't even go into his room."

"Sometimes I pretend he's not really gone," Josie said, sitting down next to her, finally handing Meredith her teacup. "I tell myself he's just gone to the store, or he's down at the library, he's coming back anytime. And sometimes, I talk to him, like he's here, I just can't see him."

The older woman put her long hands to her face, the heels of the palms cupped into the sockets of her eyes, the fingers wrapped around the top of her head. "I can't take much more."

That's what Michael used to say, and she

would argue with him, reminding him that these moods passed, that there were good times and they would happen again, if he could just stop making himself miserable, get out of the house, maybe go back to work, start painting again. Why didn't she listen? Why didn't she hear? She was starting to think there might be such a thing as karma — that repetition — maybe you lived through the same thing over and over until you stopped caring. Maybe eventually it got less intense, until it was just nothing. But it only seemed to be getting worse. Through the window in the front door, two, three hummingbirds fought in short vicious jabs over the red blooms of the hibiscus. "Have some tea before it gets cold," Josie said, and sipped her own, the fresh clean scent. Meredith raised her tea to her lips and drank mechanically. She was still caught in the painting. All those blind Merediths, climbing the white stairs. Blind. It wasn't just Meredith, not by a long shot. "We grow the mint ourselves."

"There's no we," Meredith said dully. "It's just you."

Everywhere she turned, a reminder, every tiny sentence a trap and an endless revision. Better to stop speaking altogether.

"I think this was a mistake," Meredith said, putting the cup down, getting ready to rise.

And now Josie was the one who didn't want her to go. "I thought you wanted to see it."

Meredith's sable hair hung before her face as she looked down at two books in her lap, pulled from the case. "These are mine," she said, in a voice both weary and commanding. One was *The Poems of Paul Valéry.* It was in French. She opened the embossed black cover to the inside leaf, where her name appeared in a strong triangular script. The other was green leather with gold letters: *Heart of Darkness.* She opened it to its marbled endpapers, showed Josie the bookplate, a white square printed in blue with a music stand and a baton and Thirties-style moderne script saying *From the library of Mauritz Loewy.* The *L* shaped like a swan. A very short book about a man who goes up a river in Africa, to bring back this other fellow who'd made kind of a cannibal kingdom for himself way back in the jungle. It was the story Coppola made into *Apocalypse Now,* which they'd gone to see at the Vagabond. The journey to capture the white man gone mad, freaky death everywhere, a haunted, vicious place way up the river, which was the place all your fears became real.

Michael said everyone had a Kurtz in them, and Josie had argued with him, heatedly, as if by disagreeing she could push away the darkness that she could already feel deep down in him.

Meredith shut the book with a clap, like slamming a door. "What difference does it make?" she said, throwing it onto the sofa beside her. "When am I going to read Conrad? Never. Sell it. You can get something for it, it's a first edition." She looked around the room again, out at the view. "Was Cal paying for this? I always wondered. Frankly, how did you have a pot to piss in?"

"We worked." Josie stirred honey into a second cup of tea.

"You worked, you mean." Meredith's wide mouth twisted sardonically. That mouth.

"He had a job too." Josie sipped the tea, the freshness reviving her.

"Michael?" The older woman turned to stare at her, as if she were speaking in tongues. She had seen that once, at a tent revival Gommer Ida took her to, the spirit coming in, people writhing around on the ground. It struck Josie as funny. She didn't think there was going to be anything funny about this afternoon, but you never knew. Meredith thought she knew all about Michael, but she didn't know everything.

"He played piano for kiddie dance classes," Josie said. "They called him Señor Music."

Now Meredith laughed, she threw back her head and laughed with her mouth wide open, you could see all her big square teeth, just like his. She kept laughing, wild and desperate, and then tears began to slide from the ends of her long eyes, into her dark hair. "*Señor Music?* But he abhorred children. Even when he was young. The Little Barbarians, he always called them." She wiped at her temples with the back of her hand.

"He didn't hate children. We talked about having a baby."

The laugher faded and Meredith's face recomposed its tragic contours. "Well thank God for small mercies."

Josie's hands were trembling, she wanted to hit this woman, suffering as she was, watching her blind self climbing the stairs.

"Don't look at me that way. Can you imagine, your father killing himself before you were born? Then being raised by some ignorant Okie?"

Okie. She hadn't heard that in a while. It was what her father's people had been. They came out to California to pick cotton, to pick oranges.

Gommer Ida and Daddy Jack hadn't wanted their daughter to marry that Okie, Glenn Tyrell. Okie. That was what she was. After all those years. Just as they looked at Meredith and thought *Jew.* No matter how well she played that fucking piano. She stood and moved away from the woman on the couch. It was probably Meredith's first thought, the very day they met, the fear that a Tyrell would worm her way into the Loewy family with a pregnancy. It was only the oldest movie in the world.

But if she had had a baby, they both would have had something of Michael's. He would have gone on. Now he was gone forever, without a trace. "You're a real bitch, aren't you?" Josie said, picking up the tea tray. "I think you should go now."

She took the tray into the kitchen, set it on the rough wooden counter, dumped the contents of the pot into the sink, wiped the mint out of the pot with her fingers. She put the leaves in the compost can, though why, she didn't know. *She* didn't compost, that was Michael's thing. Composting was important to him, you put the nutrients back into the soil. As if there was a future. Why shouldn't the earth be as raped and sterile as everything else?

Meredith pushed through the wooden beads, stopped at the refrigerator. "I'm sorry, Josie. Forgive me. The things I worried about, they don't even make sense now."

"You wouldn't have even wanted your own grandchild. Michael's child, because it would also be mine." She took a Gauloise from the ashtray on the windowsill over the sink, lit the butt. "You're really a piece of work."

"Look, tell me more about Señor Music."

"No."

His mother ran the beads through her fingers, like she was combing long hair. "Josie. This has just been so much harder than I thought it was going to be. That painting." She whispered this last. "Please tell me. Tell me about him being Señor Music."

Josie rinsed out the pot, looking out at the blue mountains to the north, a line of snow on the ridges. "He liked it because he didn't have to be a genius, he just had to show up. He found out he was good enough, and that's all he had to be." She was not used to being cruel, but Michael had taught her how. Everything she knew she'd learned from him. "It was a relief for him. He was sick of having to be the best at everything."

Meredith stared down at the worn streaked linoleum, dark eyelashes resting against her cheeks just as Michael's did, like pulling down a shade. It was torture to see those expressions again — she felt like she was going crazy.

His mother pressed long fingers to the flat place on her forehead above her eyebrows as if she'd like to stick them through her brain. "You think I pushed him too hard."

Out the window over the breakfast nook, a V of ducks crossed the pale winter sky, heading for evening roost at the river, long necks outstretched. She remembered her father and uncles shooting ducks on the Kern River in the evening, her uncle Dave had a black Lab named Teddy who would fetch their dead bodies. Michael taught her to recognize all the silhouettes from this window — hawk, crow, egret, gull. She liked the ducks' neat formation, but Michael loved the hawks best, redtails with their broad chunky wings. *The hawk on fire hangs still* . . . "What do you care what I think?"

"So what happened? Was he fired?" Meredith asked, then dropped her voice. "Was it drugs? Really, I want to know. He always denied he was on drugs, but I could never be sure."

Josie laughed, once. Jesus, who wasn't on

drugs? Michael told her once Meredith hadn't slept a night without pills since she was nineteen. "That wasn't it. He was tired of working for Reynaldo. He quit."

"He was always quitting," Meredith said. "He would have done the same with the painting, eventually, you know."

Should she disagree? Or just get Meredith out of the house without a fight? "The dance teacher was in love with him. It made him uncomfortable."

"He should have been flattered," Meredith said in her husky voice, her light-filled eyes full of knowledge of the world. Except that there was something she didn't know, something Josie could say that would wipe the smirk off Meredith's face. Michael would kill her, but he was gone.

"No, it scared him. You know, after the rape in Meadowlands."

Meredith had been reaching out to look at an old calendar that they'd put on the side of the refrigerator, but then the gesture faded away. Blink. Blink blink.

Josie washed out the teacups.

"What rape?" Meredith's glazed expression, unfocused, unsure. "You're making this up."

"That would make it easy, wouldn't it?" The clean feeling of the washrag inside the cups — Michael didn't like sponges. The water didn't heat up very fast, so she washed the dishes in cold, not bothering to catch the cold water in a dishpan to save for the plants. She didn't care now if the plants died or not.

"What rape?"

"His roommate. But you knew that."

His mother slid down the doorjamb, until she was sitting on the floor in her straight black skirt, her cashmere and pearls, her legs out at angles on the warped linoleum, like a doll on a shelf. She had her hand up to her throat, as if someone had offered to cut it. "The one with the pimples." She pressed her forehead, and tears came down. "Why didn't he tell me?" A flash of anger burst through the grief. "I would have crucified them!"

Josie tipped the water from the dishes, put them neatly in the drainer. "He wanted it to be over. You've never been raped, you can't understand."

Meredith ground her clenched fist into her forehead. "Oh God. Oh Christ."

Josie gazed out at the hills to the north and the west, it was Bosch in all directions.

"Why didn't he tell me?" Meredith said, and said it again, though she should know the answer. "I should have known. How could I have not known, my own son?"

And Josie suddenly felt she had done a wrong thing, to want to hurt Meredith this way, revenge herself for the Okie crack. Meredith was no Calvin Faraday, she was willing to blame herself and everybody else, which was far more appropriate. Josie stood there a long time, looking out at the view, the shadows lengthening in the short winter afternoon. How could she not have known, how could they not have known? The blind Merediths, the blind Josies. Nobody knew anyone else's private world. In the end, they were all alone as inmates on death row, side by side. Sometimes you could get a look at one another with a little pocket mirror, cell to cell, but that was all.

She heard the scramble of shoes and the slamming of the bathroom door. She heard the water running, and then the deep seal-barking sound of Meredith's sobs. In the spice cabinet, she found her little stash, went out onto the porch in the flat light of January, and smoked the skunky pot she had gotten from Pen, looking out at the tiny houses on the hillsides, listening to the grinding of trains up at Taylor Yards. She peeled paint off the rail that they had painted turquoise when they moved in, but now it was blistered from the western sun, exposing the chalky white underneath. One of the hawks had landed in its favorite eucalyptus, on a bare branch about level with the porch where she sat. *The hawk on fire hangs still. Dilly dilly, calls the loft hawk, come and be killed.*

16
Stripped

Rain yesterday, rain the day before. All the voices of the rain, on the roof, down the gutters. She wanted to curl up and be very small, very silent. But Jeremy called, nattering on about his film in his cheerful, fake-English, cliché-ridden way. He didn't know Michael was dead, and somehow that made it possible to imagine that there was an alternate universe in which Michael was still alive.

"As soon as this rain lets up, we're set to go," Jeremy said. "So you meet with Wardrobe, no? Laura's got these fabulous ideas, absolutely brill."

Wardrobe. Jeremy talked about his films as if he were already Francis Ford Coppola. *My Producer. My Editor.* Already seeing himself accepting an award from AFI. She knew who Wardrobe would be. A certain kind of capable girl desperately in love with Sergio, the sloe-eyed Cuban boy from San Diego who shot all Jeremy's films, *My Cinematographer.* Sometimes she wondered whether Jeremy picked Sergio for his camerawork or for his female camp followers who would do just about anything to be near the sullen, handsome Cuban — drive, move lights, get food. They were a regular mafia.

She didn't want to go out, she'd rather sit here and imagine dancing with Michael as Ethel Waters sang "Sweet Georgia Brown." But in the end, she got dressed and drove out to the Fairfax district, where the storm drains backed up and water eddied above curbs calf deep every time it rained. The worn wipers of the Falcon just smeared water around the windshield, their scraping metronome synchronized elegantly with the Joan Jett tape. She loved Joan, thought of her as a lot like Luanne, a big sister who'd kick ass for you. Though at ninety pounds, Luanne wasn't kicking ass for anybody anymore. Josie spotted a panel van pulling out of a space and snagged it just ahead of a Mercury Cougar, the driver giving her the finger, she could see it, misty, through the passenger window. She pulled up the hood of her black plastic slicker and waded out into the flood, water three-quarters of the way up her red rubber cowboy boots, and dashed down the street to the girl's building, a nice courtyard complex paved in shiny Spanish tile, its empty fountain full of petunias.

When Laura answered the bell, Josie knew her immediately, a Roman-nosed girl with hair so pink you could hear it. Josie had seen her around at the clubs, she worked at Fiorucci in Beverly Hills, a boutique that sold rich kids punk clothing. Josie sold some of her bottle-cap chandelier earrings there, and bracelets and pins she made from dominoes. "Hey," Laura said, letting her in, letting her drip all over the hardwood floors. "Great boots. You must be Elena."

Elena, her character in the movie. Jeremy's characters all had names like Elena and Chloe and Regine, Marie Claire, the kind of girl you'd never meet in your life. Josie thought to correct her, but decided against it.

Laura took Josie's dripping slicker and hung it on a coat tree by the little telephone nook, brought her down into the living room. Josie admired the place, a real Joan Crawford apartment with a beamed ceiling, hardwood floors, wrought-iron chandelier, and little balconies off the French doors. Michael would have loved this. Maybe if there had been no hillside, no Bosch to stare out at, if they'd had something more solid than a cliffside shack, things might have seemed more real for him, less precarious.

The two girls sat together on the cat-hair-covered red-velvet couch. Dresses and petticoats festooned the walls like paintings. A gray Persian prowled amid stacks of fashion magazines. Laura poured champagne. "They do this at *Vogue,*" she said. They drank and Josie shared her cigarettes, and Laura showed her brill ideas for Elena's character. She worked at Fiorucci but she was costuming student films and ninety-nine-seat Equity-waiver theater, getting credits under her belt — not the run-of-the-mill camp follower. "I loved the script, don't you think it's fabulous?"

Josie hadn't even read the script until two days ago. Where Antonioni was supposed to be meeting Buñuel in this thing was anybody's guess. Probably in shots taken from weird angles, and some sort of heavy-handed symbology.

And of course, Elena dies in the end. They always died in the end.

"In a car accident, Josie. Don't you see? It's Fate . . . like, Destiny," Jeremy had said. But just what the hell did Jeremy Scott know about destiny? A grandfather who blew his brains out in the house your mother still lived in, that was some fucking destiny. Not some ridiculous story about a filmmaker and a Girl and the Girl's ex-boyfriend she thought she had killed, dreamed up one night between bong hits, bits and pieces of other people's genius tacked together with chewing gum.

Out the casement windows, the rain sighed, beaded, rattled in the downspouts. It was cold in Laura's apartment. Josie shivered, pulled the sleeves of her turtleneck sweater down over her hands, as the pink-haired girl turned the pages of her old *Vogue*s. "I had something like this in mind," Laura said, pointing at a bony-hipped model in a white cutaway dress with clear plastic inserts. "That's Courrèges. Elena's a slick person, slick surfaces. That's how I see her, don't you?"

The slick heiress, glamorously haunted. Well, she could be Elena now. There was certainly nothing slick about Josie, she was just paper, like brown paper bags in the rain. Water beaded up on Elena, it shed right off, like those old sixties clear-plastic umbrellas. She was happy to sit talking about Elena's wardrobe for this ridiculous movie, grateful Jeremy had made her come. She and Laura got smashed on Spanish champagne, and talked about the mod era, Laura knew a lot about it. She knew about Edie Sedgwick and Andy Warhol's Factory — all that Mylar and tinfoil, false eyelashes and vitamin shots with speed. The Velvet Underground played there, Lou Reed and Nico. It was the center of everything cool. Laura showed her a Nehru jacket that once belonged to Ray Davies, a yellow brocade.

Josie liked the simplicity of Laura's mind. Laura wasn't thinking about God or the true world or whether each man killed the thing he loved. She wasn't thinking about the absurd or what the soul did after it died. She was thinking about clothing, about accessories, about shoes and earrings and hair. The subtle difference between Yves Saint Laurent and Mary Quant. It was good, Josie thought, finishing the champagne, to spend time with strangers. They had no well-meaning advice, what she should do, how she should cope, no one examining her to see how she was holding up. Soothing not to have to think of anything besides eyelashes — two sets, spiky like Veruschka — and trying on a black-plastic halter dress, a bubble hat à la Courrèges, a patent-leather hatbox purse. And talking about whether she was going to touch up her roots, whether she would recut her hair.

If she could only stay right here, wearing Laura's huge plastic disc earrings, a feather top and a Mylar miniskirt, drunk and warm and light on the surface of the world. She remembered Shirley K. telling her once about the light masters of China, who could walk across a sheet of rice paper stretched between two chairs. She felt that was worth working toward. Laura put her in a blue-green fringed go-go dress that had nothing to do with Elena, and they danced to the soundtrack from *To Sir, with Love* and Laura worked the topic around to Sergio, how long had Josie known him, what kind of girls did he like? She heard he had a friend with a place in Rosarito Beach, right on the water, maybe they would all go when the movie was over.

Josie was feeling good when she opened the side gate to the house on Lemoyne, carrying a takeout bag from Canton Express inside her slicker, drunk, splashing in her red cowboy boots. Feeling like she just might get through this, an aspiring light master. Edging down the stairs in the dark, the roughness of the wood, the wet railing, she put her key in the door. It was unlocked. She was surprised to find it open, though these days, she was always forgetting things, leaving her keys in the lock, her purse in the john. She came in and threw the key in the red bowl, turned on the light.

She stood in her own living room, but it was all gone. Blank walls, the empty picture hooks. The piano was gone, the bookcase bare. The toys on the tables, the old flatirons. The pipe-cleaner circus. All his books and journals, his sketchpads. Their records. Everything. She leaned against one of the rough wood four-by-sixes that held up the wooden ceiling of the shack, feeling like a section of her torso had been removed, like one of Laura's cutout dresses. She could not believe this was happening. She moved into the bedroom. The closet was open, empty hangers. The dresser they had painted, gone. Her clothes in piles on the bed. *This, and this . . . and oh, the dresser, that's his.* She'd had a crew, had just come in and taken it all.

She could call the cops, but she hated cops

and anyway, what would she say? *I've just been robbed by my ex-future-mother-in-law.* That would be something to laugh about over donuts at Winchells. *Yeah, and what would a world-famous pianist be doing with a hundred dollars' worth of your old crap?* But she could not get over the idea, somehow that woman had walked into her house and taken everything. She had to do something. She would do something. But what?

Josie went into the bathroom. The medicine-cabinet door was hanging open. Michael's badger-hair shaving brush, the Lightfoot's shaving soap in its white mug, his grandfather's razor. Even his tooth powder. It was too much to take in all at once. With the empty walls, the place seemed smaller. Not one painting left. Not the one of her at the piano, or as little Jeanne of France. No *Civilization and Its Discontents.* Even the ones she hated were gone, the ugly ones, the crazy ones, but she'd grown used to them, they were part of her life, they were special windows in the walls. And now there were walls with no windows, only nubs of nails and picture hooks. She had even taken the music, all the records and tapes, not just Michael's but the ones that were hers, and theirs together.

She stood in the center of the raped room, letting the slow stunned jumble of feelings roll down inside her, sorting themselves out like fruit falling into holes on a sizing board in a co-op warehouse. It was not enough that Michael was dead. Now all the things that would help her remember were gone too. *You'll have to remember for both of us.* She ran her hands on the shelf of the empty bookcase. She should have read those journals when she'd had the chance. What was she doing, protecting a dead boy's privacy? Now she would never get another chance. She tried to breathe, but air would not fill her lungs. It was like trying to breathe on the moon.

Josie sat heavily on the fuzzy blue couch. Her stomach growled but now the Chinese food smelled disgusting. She shivered with cold and sudden nausea. The woman had seemed so resigned, so quiet during the ride back to her Jaguar. Josie thought that would be the last they would ever see of one another. While Meredith was probably planning this already. She had never felt so stupid, so naive.

She didn't want to go back out into the rain, but she couldn't stand the look of the bare walls and anyway, she was down to her last three cigarettes, they would never last until morning. So she climbed the wet stairs and drove over to Gala's, bought two packs of Gauloises and a bottle of Smirny. When she returned she stopped at the door, picturing herself opening it and it was all just a dream. She often did this, focusing on a vision of Michael sitting on the blue couch reading a book, he was just inside, when she opened the door, there he would be.

She opened the door slowly, but nothing had changed, there were the empty picture hooks, the gaping bookcase. She sat in Michael's chair and cracked the Smirny, drank a little, and then a little more. She had a sudden, gut-sinking thought and dashed back to the bedroom, pawed through the pile of clothes — her clothes — on the bed, through the underwear, which was where she kept it. Even the blood-spattered note was gone. Everything, everything.

She stormed back into the living room, grabbed the phone. That bitch. That fucking bitch. She dialed the number she knew by heart, the only thing she did know anymore, and the phone in Los Feliz rang and rang but nobody answered it, not even the sour-faced Spanish maid. She slammed the receiver down, and picked it up and slammed it down again, over and over.

But even in her rage, she knew she was part-
way to blame. Cruel, stupid, greedy. She had
wanted to keep everything. She should have
given Meredith the painting she'd asked for,
given up some of the books. And deep down,
she knew she had done wrong to tell her about
what happened at Meadowlands, out of sheer
spite. It was a long time ago, and what could
Meredith do about it now?

Out the kitchen door, she stood breathing in
the night air, the cold and the rain, the chairs
dripping against the warped wood of the deck,
the lights muted and hazy. There was no end to
the Bosch. She raised the voddy to her lips,
spilled most of it down her chin. Served her
right for having a good day, she had gone almost
a whole afternoon without thinking of him
every moment. Thinking she was doing well,
making progress. There was never going to be
an end to this. Whenever she thought she could
not feel more alone, the universe peeled back
another layer of darkness.

She watched a single car, its blurry headlights,
threading its way up the hill across the glen.
How precarious life seemed. You were only teth-
ered to it by a hair, and all these people sawing
away at it. She thought of Cal Faraday, his energy

to go on, to start over. How did he find the heart to do it again, again and again? She missed her father, she wanted someone to take care of her, someone who knew what to do.

She lay on the blue couch in the cold, wrapped the granny afghan around her, and listened to the voices of the rain. Where once she might have imagined them speaking to her, or for her, now they were mocking, full of derision and laughter. Even the rain was Bosch. She should go down to Gardena, find that old guy, Morty, play pan until the sun came up. Get Pen to go with her. But she didn't want to play pan. She wanted to talk to someone who could understand what had happened, who knew all the players. She dialed the New York number Cal had given her.

"Hello?" Numbah Foah. She had a high, girlish voice, she sounded about Josie's age.

"This is Josie Tyrell. Michael's girlfriend?"

"Oh!" Mrs. Cal took a short breath. "Of course. How are you doing? You all right? I'm just so sorry, what a terrible thing. I would have come out for the funeral, but Becky had a fever. . . . We just loved him so much —"

She knew it wasn't true. Numbah Foah saw Michael as a threat to her little ones, the leftover child. In the days of kings, Michael said, the elder children would poison the younger ones, not to have the competition for the throne. "Is Cal in?"

Cal's wife paused, as if trying to be sure it was worth bothering him. Josie knew she sounded drunk and depressed. "Well, you know it's very late, Josie," Harmony said in her high, funny voice, she sounded like a cartoon character.

"He said to call whenever I needed to."

Then there was no sound at all, she must have caught them in bed, she pictured the wife's hand over the receiver. "Josie." Calvin sounded hearty, as if she had not awakened him, or caught him in some stage of lovemaking. "How's it going, kiddo?"

Josie told him everything, the break-in, that Meredith took everything she thought was Michael's, including things he had given to her. Even the suicide note. Leaving out the part about her not letting Meredith have the painting, leaving out the part about Michael in Meadowlands and how she told Meredith as payback. The partial truth and nothing but. Just as she left out every other thing she had done to deserve this. She struggled not to cry, but the booze, instead of numbing her, which was what it was supposed to do, just made her feel more lost. She hated weepy drunks, and here she was, being exactly that.

"She's obviously lost it," Calvin said. "Jesus. Well, this kind of thing brings out the worst in people."

Where'd he read that, in a magazine in the globe-trotter lounge of British Airways? Cal Faraday, spiritual adviser. He probably couldn't remember the names of all his children, their ages, what grade they were in at school. "She can't just walk into my house, Cal."

"Listen, honey. I know it's outrageous, but, look what she's been through. Did you lose anything important?"

"His books, his art, all kinds of things. The fucking note, Cal."

Josie heard Numbah Foah say something to Calvin, probably to get that drunk off the phone. She pictured them in bed, a bedroom set that all matched, fairly new because they hadn't been married that long, just a few years, done in Mrs. Cal's style, because after all those marriages, Cal was probably used to the idea it would end up belonging to her anyway, and he was gone most

of the time at that. She imagined he wore pajamas, as she thought East Coast people would,
slippers and robes.

"Maybe I should call the cops."

"Christ, don't do that," he said quickly. More
muffled talk between him and Mrs. Cal, she
guessed he had his hand over the receiver but
not tight enough. "Listen, you're not going to
like what I'm about to say, but listen, Josie, you
ask me, really? It might be the best thing that
could've happened."

"You dick." Josie couldn't believe he'd have
the guts to say that. Easy for him to say in New
York with his wife and his new kids and his best-
selling fucking life.

"No, listen, remember what you said that day,
about the note? Remember?"

"Yeah, I remember."

"You said, 'What do you do with this? Carry it
around all your life?' So now someone's made it
easy. No, don't say anything, just listen to me. I
know you're upset, but just stop and think.
You're very young, Josie, and at some point
you're going to need to get on with your life.
This could be a huge blessing, though I know
you can't see it right now."

She could hear he was winding it down, getting ready to hang up. Getting on with his own fucking life.

"She's still in love with you," Josie said, desperately. "She'll listen to you. Can't you call her for me?"

"Didn't you see how she kicked me out of the mourners' box that day? I'm sorry, I can't do anything with her. And not to put too fine a point on it, under the law, well . . . she is his mother." She heard the finality in his voice, like someone closing a gate in front of a store. "Now, Josie, it's very late, we're three hours ahead. Can you call me in the morning?" Impersonal as the man on a movie-theater recording. She was afraid he was going to say "Have a nice day."

"Hey, Cal? You fucking get some sleep, okay? Get some nice sleep. And fuck you very much."

She lay in bed, drunk, moving in and out of sleep. She dreamed she was walking through an enormous hall full of Chinese people at tables playing cards, throwing dice on green tabletops, money and chips, green and red, looking for the old Jewish man from the cemetery. Floppy-breasted waitresses on unicycles passed by with trays loaded with flowery drinks. Chinese people gathered around a pit, yelling, with money in their fists, like in *The Deer Hunter* when Robert De Niro and Christopher Walken played Russian roulette. But it was her at the table with Meredith, the gun between them, and Michael in a lifeguard's chair up above them. He didn't seem to realize it was her, just watching from behind his blue glasses, and the avidity of his face as he watched reminded her of the way he stared while the dog spun in the street. Meredith wore the same blue glasses. She spun the gun.

Josie glanced around, desperately, wondering how she could get out of this game, she didn't want to play, but they were surrounded, not just by Asian people but by Cal and the old men from the funeral, even Daddy Jack, and Gommer Ida, making bets, their eyes glittering greedily, but she could not tell how they were betting. She started to cry at the idea that they were betting against her. The game was fixed, she remembered. The house always won. The gun's barrel pointed at Josie. Her turn.

"Go on," Meredith said. "You wanted it."

She had no choice but to pick up the gun. She held it to her head. It was cold, and she knew there was a bullet in the chamber. The game was fixed, there was always a bullet. So what were they even betting on? She struggled to think of another way, so that she didn't have to pull the trigger — she was too young. The crowd shouted angrily for her to do it, the money in all those fists. She closed her eyes tight and squeezed.

17
Meredith's Room

The rain had stopped, but the trees still dripped all around her. No lights shone in the tall, iron-framed windows of the Dark Castle. She walked to the gate, which didn't seem so lacy and festive anymore, just heavy and cold and formidable. Now the chain was locked for real. Josie went back to her car and sat smoking, the faint verge of dawn sky glowing in the side mirror, watching the driveway with ferocious patience. They would have to unlatch that gate sometime, to let in the gardeners, the cook and the masseuse and the piano tuner. Someone would be sent to the store for salmon and Scotch. It was only a matter of time, and she had nothing but time. She could wait all day if she had to.

She hunted for a roach in the ashtray and found half a joint, a small spark of grace. She lit it and turned on the radio to the classical station. The DJ had a snooty, flat voice, he reminded her of her English teacher in seventh grade, Mr. Pella, who made them read *Twenty Thousand Leagues under the Sea* and humiliated Josie in front of the whole class when she couldn't remember any of the characters' names.

She dozed off and startled awake several times, keeping her eyes on the gate in the side mirror, fighting sleep. After a night like that, she was in no hurry to dream again. What did it mean when you died in your dream? She could guess it was not a good sign. She'd never died in a dream before, she had always awakened just in time. She could still feel the gun against her temple, the bullet drilling in, and knowing that her life was over. Game over, no reset.

She was surprised to discover how sick the feeling made her, the idea of a sudden death. Did she still want this life so badly? Was there something deep inside her, a Tyrell thing, an Okie stubbornness, that would not let her succumb? What had she done in her short time on earth

but meet Michael Faraday? It was like the
Gauloises at the liquor store. She didn't even
know what there was to ask for. She had no education, no languages. She had never so much as
been out of California. The only thing she'd ever
had going for her was a certain kind of look, the
ability to make an interesting shape in space,
and that her body remembered things.

If she died now, all that would remain would
be her image folded into some tattered sketchpads, a figure walking through a handful of student films. Her parents would remember her,
maybe. Her brothers and sisters, at least the
younger ones, Corinne and Bo. Pen would. And
Meredith Loewy. Yes, Meredith would remember
her. She would remember Josie, clearly and pre-
cisely, until the day she died.

A pickup truck moved slowly along the street
in the grayness of early dawn, men bundled in
sweatshirts throwing jacketed newspapers onto
the driveways. One threw Meredith's at the
gate, but it didn't go over, it caught in the spear
points and fell into a puddle. She was somehow
surprised Meredith even took a newspaper, that
she would be interested in such transitory
things. Josie's paper was still coming, though
she threw it out unread now, wrote *Deceased*

on the bill. There was no news in the land of the dead. No urgent meetings with heads of state. No weather, no sports.

Michael had loved his newspaper. Lying on the blue couch, he could spend half the morning reading it. Arguing with it, making clever remarks. He was obsessed with the obituaries. She'd never read them before, he couldn't believe it, to him it was like someone who'd never read the funnies. At home, they were nothing special, but in LA, you had to be someone. They were for people who'd done things — invented machines, created art, started companies, inspired people. Sometimes they were so famous, even she had heard of them. Michael always wanted to know what they died of — accidental gunshot wounds, overdose, cancer. *Was it a suicide?* That's what he really wanted to know. Tears shot to her eyes, stinging like fumes. And she hadn't thought twice about it. Just another of his funny eccentricities. Obits and classifieds. That's what he liked. There might be no news in the land of the dead, but there were classifieds. They were as much a part of it as those silvery roses. What else were you going to do with the stuff of the dead? *What would you do with his things, cart them around for the rest of your life?* Old people's dogs, the youth bed the dead child never got a chance to use. Needlepoint supplies. *Estate sale everything must go.*

A light came on in a neighboring house. A low wooden annex with square windows off a field-stone house with steep roofs, a sycamore in the lawn. Kitchen, she guessed. Someone up making breakfast. Still nothing at Meredith's. Maybe she was a day sleeper, like all musicians. Or did she sleep at all? Maybe she went down to Gardena and played cards with Morty all night. Some version of Russian roulette.

Josie sat listening to Horowitz play the songs of Schumann, sure she was still watching the gate, but when she awoke, the sun had come up as much as it was going to, somber and dull through the trees, the jays squawking. She had to go to the bathroom, she was out of cigarettes, her mouth tasted like rotting garbage. She should give up and go home. But then the maid appeared, in a brown tailored dress, unlocking the chain, picking up the newspaper from the driveway. She carefully looped the heavy links around the bars, but didn't clasp the big padlock.

After a few minutes, Josie got out of the car, walked quickly back to the gate, lifted the chain.

It groaned its iron lament, but she suspected the morning was already noisy enough that no one would notice — the traffic had already started down on Los Feliz Boulevard, and a news helicopter overhead whipped at the gray clouds. She slipped inside and rearranged the chain, quickly walked up the drive and then into the trees. She pulled down her pants and peed, watching the house, then fumbled back into her clothes.

She circled around the side of the house to the terrace, the pool. Leaves lay steeping at the bottom, like tea leaves in a massive cup. If only she could read them. If only she could have read them that first day, when she swam in all that lovely green water, Michael's eyes on her. What would she have done? Left him alone, or gone down this long dark hall again?

Edging up to the back door, she peered in through the window, the rusty screen. It was all the same as the first time, the black and white tiles, the overloaded cabinets. The maid sat reading at the small table, coffee cup in a saucer, her black hair tidy in its painful bun. Josie quietly tried the doorknob. It was unlocked, but she would never get past the maid. Michael would have gone in like he owned the place, even if it was someone else's house. Probably ask the maid to make him some breakfast. She had seen that side of him, the Little Prince.

She watched and waited. Finally, the phone rang, and the woman got up to answer it, put the receiver on the counter and left the room. Josie took her shoes off and slipped in, keeping her hand on the knob so the bolt wouldn't reengage until she had shut the door behind her. It closed with a brief click. Shoes in hand, she ran through the kitchen, ducking into the butler's pantry between that and the dining room. She could hear the maid on the phone in the hall, "The Señora is sleeping. No, the concerts have all been canceled. I don't know about that, you must call Señor Markovsky."

She waited for the maid to return to the kitchen, then crept out into the dining room, that vast lake of mahogany, the chandelier exposed now, catching every bit of light. She trotted across the terra-cotta tiles of the foyer, cold under her bare feet, climbed the stairs. She hesitated at Michael's room, the first room on the right, but something made her continue down the hall, to the last one.

Silently, she cracked the door and slipped in. The drapes on the windows kept out most of the light, thick carpet gave under her feet, and the room smelled of smoky perfume and the heaviness of drugged sleep. The dark head lay framed by the shiny satin headboard that gleamed subtly in the dark, in the very bed where she and Michael had made love that first day, those perfect hours. You couldn't tell the color in the dark but it was sky blue, as were the satin drapes that fell from a frame suspended over the bedstead where Meredith lay sleeping, hair spread on the pillow, thick and tangled as if from a bad night of dreams. She wore a satin robe over her nightgown, the covers wrestled into a heap.

Josie stood over the sleeping woman, thinking, how odd, really, that people had to do this every day. Shut down and go somewhere else, leaving their bodies behind. She wondered where Meredith went at night, was she too in the card palace in Gardena, spinning a loaded gun? Suddenly, it occurred to Josie how easy it would be to kill a person while she was sleeping, pour something into an open ear. You could slip right out of the house again, and no one would know. How helpless Meredith looked, lying there. This woman who so hated her, a woman she admired, feared, could not help wanting to know. An accomplished, remarkable person. If Meredith died right now, there would be a half-page obituary in the *Times*. Her career, her father, her famous ex-husband, the tragic death of her only son. Her skin glowed in the dark room, her eyelashes resting on her cheeks, her mouth half-open, snoring softly. She suddenly wanted Meredith to open her eyes and find her there. She gave her every chance, strolling around the room, the carpet thick and padded underfoot, taking her time, not trying to be especially quiet, looking at the perfumes in their glass tray, unstoppering a few, looking for the one that she really used. She inhaled the various fragrances until she found it. An openwork glass stopper with a silk tassel. She put some of it on her wrist. It didn't smell the same on her.

Bits of jewelry lay in a dish on the dresser, photographs massed on a bedside table. Black-and-white, in silver frames. One was of Meredith in a black dress reclining on a couch, her striking profile. Another was Cal, Meredith, and Michael as a toddler on some kind of rooftop, looking out on an Arabian kind of city, with domes and flat, cutout roofs. Cal and Meredith lay on either end of a daybed, she wore a Juliet dress and heavy eye makeup, the baby in her lap playing with her enormous earrings. Cal's hair was dark and he had muttonchop sideburns, he sported a Nehru jacket. The kind of photograph they ran in Laura's old *Vogues*. *People Are Talking About* . . . So glamorous. They'd thought they were untouchable. When they had so much to lose. And one of Michael, fairly recent, only his hair was longer. He leaned on a building, a wool scarf around his neck, thinking something funny, she could tell from the set of his mouth. Harvard. He should have stayed there. He should never have met her.

She picked up Meredith's strand of pearls and held it up to her neck. The white pearls softly gleaming on top of her hole-filled gray turtleneck in Meredith's beveled mirror. With dark hair and false eyelashes, she could be Meredith in the photograph. It wasn't so special. Just another costume. Meredith moaned on the bed. Josie quickly put the pearls back in the dish and went to the bed. She gazed down at Meredith, imagining this was what it had been like for Michael when he was little, when Meredith would sleep all morning after a concert, and he would have to be very very quiet. Hoping she would wake up but afraid she would be angry if he woke her. But she didn't wake. On an impulse, Josie left her vintage shoes by Meredith's bed, toes pointing in, just where she had been standing. She walked out, closing the door.

In Michael's room were all the things Meredith had taken from their little house. Not sorted at all, just thrown in. The paintings, the books, even the goddamn piano and the painted dresser. How had she known Josie would be gone that long? Veronica, naturally. Meredith must have paid everyone off. Josie burned to think of Meredith directing traffic on the stairs, Veronica just watching, not saying a word, counting her hundred. Shoes for the babies, gas for the car. But where were the journals? That's what she wanted. What Meredith had wanted too. Why hadn't she hidden them, why hadn't she known? She dug through the heap of his things, their things. She found the pipe-cleaner circus in a box. She looked for *The Ballad of Reading Gaol* and *The Prose of the Transsiberian,* the poems of Paul Valéry, but there was no time, her mind wasn't working, she had exhausted her burst of determination. She ended up grabbing the box with the circus, the painting of Blaise and Jeanne, and one of her in his armchair by the window, her hair a mess of gold.

The scary maid was on the phone in the foyer as she came down the stairs. "Morning," Josie said, continuing to walk without missing a beat, barefoot but regal, Elena descending, the box in one arm and the paintings under the other. "Don't worry, I'll see myself out."

18
Goodwill

There it was, the proof. The thing the mother had tried to deny. She propped the pictures on chairs, the one of herself, and the one of Blaise and little Jeanne, a sixteen-year-old poet and his innocent whore, on the road to disaster. Love pure and unbidden as wildflowers growing out of cracks in the sidewalk. *Blaise, are we very far from Montmartre?* She had the proof, and yet, what? He couldn't remember it, he couldn't remember.

She was tired, her nerves stripped like wires, the red and the white. She felt like a saint with the arrows shot through, she was bleeding to

death. Out the windows, the city stirred slug-
gishly, the day moving through blue to disappointed gray. It was already exhausted. The
prospect of going out to Northridge and posing
this body in the same tired ways, for the same
eager students, was too Cream of Wheat box to
bear. Maybe it was time to give up. Just pack it
in. Though she was dressed, her modeling bag
packed, she just ended up in Michael's chair,
next to the little circus that she had returned to
its place on the sill. The ballerina, the seal with
the ball. She never canceled sittings, prided herself on diligence, she'd always been like that,
wanting to show she was not the Tyrell everybody expected. But lately she found herself
doing all kinds of things she'd never have
dreamed, like standing over a sleeping woman
and imagining pouring something into her ear.
She called the booker at Northridge, pleaded illness, the flu or maybe cancer, it was hard to say
which. But then she found herself wishing there
were no more decisions, that it was just over,
and it scared her, so she smoked a joint and
drove downtown.

It was soothing to walk the long aisles of the
big central Goodwill, listening to the stories
whispered by the detritus of a million urban

lives. She and Michael had shared this love for hunting through old things, rescuing household appliances and dishes and outdated *Look* magazines. The happy hours they'd spent here. *Hey, Josie, look — Burroughs and Brion Gysin, it's a first edition . . .* His green sharkskin suit, her red little Jeanne fall, a purse with silk daisies blooming behind yellowing plastic. Josie pulled a dress from the Fifties from the rack, all scratchy organza skirt and spaghetti straps, held it up to herself, smoothed the skirt, put it back. A dress she once might have snapped up, but now it reminded her of a girl on a date with a boy who drove too fast, a dress that wouldn't anticipate a blind curve on Mulholland, the sheer drop to the bottom, would not imagine itself covered in blood.

A Latino family stared as they passed. The mother gave her the evil eye as she herded the children, especially the elder daughter, maybe thirteen. As if what Josie represented might be contagious, this incomprehensible white girl in torn leggings and mustard sweater that covered her ass, wild dark-rooted blond hair a punk flag. She was a girl that parents steered their children away from, always had been, though now it was something she'd chosen — *for christ's sake don't end up like that.* But the girl was still watching, looking backward, memorizing her hair, her spike-heeled boots.

Josie knew she was slipping, bagging on jobs, not to mention standing next to Meredith's bed, imagining how easy it would be to kill someone while she slept. She tried to remember how it had felt to think that, but it was like she was wearing a raincoat inside her mind, she couldn't hold it clearly.

Instead, she thought about buying something slick for the movie, to go with the ultramodern house in the hills. That made her a girl with a purpose, not someone hiding out at Goodwill because she didn't know what she might do if left on her own. *Total Sixties,* she thought. Not the fringy, fuzzy, peace-love-and-tie-dye Sixties, this was James Bond and go-go boots, *Blow-Up* and little English sports cars. The Shrimp and Edie and Warhol. Speed and vitamins for breakfast. A pink Pucci wrap dress was promising, and a color-block double-knit stewardess number, its big metal front zipper ending in a ring pull, she could sew up the rip under the arm. Her eyes shuffled through sleeves and collars of dresses so ugly even a half inch of fabric showing at the shoulder was more than enough. Then she saw the sliver of navy blue, the muted gleam of the real, like Meredith's silverware. The sleeve, unornamented, wide, and three-quarter length, was attached to a collarless jacket of nubby raw silk, accompanied by a ladylike slight-dirndl skirt. The jacket closed asymmetrically with metal fasteners like the ones on firemen's boots, high on one shoulder, then descending in a row to the left. She opened the jacket to inspect the lining. It was as beautiful inside as out, the French seams, and the label read *Made in Hong Kong for I. Magnin.* In a suit like that, you could give signals to waiters, run someone down in your Jag. You could hire a hit man or fly to Madrid first class, all for twelve dollars.

She took her clothes to the mirror. There was only one at the Goodwill, though the store was immense. They didn't make it easy to discover what you'd look like in your purchases. Naturally there was no dressing room, you had to try on the clothes right there in the open. Two large black girls ditching school tried on prom gowns — green satin, red lace, flounces in every wrong place. Josie had never worn such a dress, a dress for a girl imagining herself a princess. By the time she was that old, it was already too late for her.

Finally, the fat girls got done, leaving their dresses on the floor in a pile, contemptuous of fantasies so recently indulged — going to the prom in green satin, with impossibly long nails, acrylic, iridescent as a drum kit, their hair beaded and braided, dripping with crystals, Isaac Hayes watching from behind his shades, asking someone, *Who is that girl?* Then anger, that they never would have that, the dresses didn't fit and anyway, they had no dates, so they left the dresses behind as they themselves had been left, walking away, the way a guy who fucks a poor fat girl walks away, leaving her in a pile on the floor.

Josie rehung the dresses on their hangers, she couldn't stand seeing them there, discarded on the floor. It wasn't their fault they were ugly and not big enough. She hung the stewardess number and the suit from Hong Kong on the rim of the mirror. She felt the hot eyes of the Goodwill stock boy watching her pull off her sweater, his arms full of clothes to restock hoping for a glimpse of tit or at least a bra. She took it off the rest of the way, happy to reveal a grubby tank top and the black hair in her armpits, knowing it would turn him right off.

She purposely tried the dresses first. The

Pucci print was a perfect fit, in size 4 you could always get a good selection at a thrift store, women never stayed 4 very long, 2 and 4 were the universal recipients of used-clothing riches. The deep V of the wrap dress would need pinning, unless she wanted to go slutty in a black bra, an ugly cross. But she never chose to be ugly when she could be glamorous. There was no mystery to that, it was all right there and more than you wanted. The color-block was right on the money, sad that the mod colors taupe and blue and ivory would be lost in black-and-white, but the shape was just right, she looked like Jean Seberg, another lost cause. Finally, she took down the navy blue silk, unpinned the skirt, which didn't frighten her so much. She rolled it at the waist to the right length, she would have to take it up, it looked hilarious over the leggings. A lady skirt, like something a teacher would wear. Then she removed the jacket from the hanger, and put it on without raising her eyes, fastening the grommets, tugging it smooth. She took a deep breath and looked in the mirror.

She had never seen anything so beautiful in her life. A suit no Tyrell had ever considered. She blinked at herself and saw a possibility that had so far escaped her. Of a woman more glamorous than any rock star. Even over torn leggings in the fluorescent light of the Goodwill. She was glad no one could see her there, no one she knew, it was a transgression. Her normal clothes always had a sense of kiddie dress-up, cute vintage dresses and stretched sweaters and half-worn-out boots. But this was elegance still in its prime. There was nothing camp about it, except the fact that it was being worn by Josie Tyrell. She felt a guilty excitement, even considering *Made in Hong Kong for I. Magnin.*

She gazed at herself, her impossible hair, imagining just a short strand of pearls, worn inside the neckline, a few showing at the nape. Patent pumps, black three-quarter gloves, and big sunglasses. A slim handbag, strap over her forearm, and the gesture Jackie Kennedy once made in a photograph she'd seen, crossing her body with her arm, touching the top of her purse.

How Michael would hate her to even be thinking this. It wasn't part of the deal. Their deal was, she wasn't supposed to want what he had. They were just a couple of bohemians, that was the story. Living on air, scornful of the comfort and power money could buy. She could never say it might be nice to see what it was like, to be one of the people who counted, who could read the signs and give the signals. Michael loved her because she was so far removed, he didn't think she would even know enough to want it. One of the lies between them. Her rejection of all that was only a matter of self-preservation. Because they would never have her. And his self-deception, that she was what he really wanted. He would have gone back sooner or later. Yes, she knew this, though she pretended she didn't.

She remembered a dream she'd had a few days ago. Michael with a refined girl in the audience of a concert hall, he wore a black suit and a silver tie and looked unspeakably elegant. They were sitting in the middle of the row, and Josie stood in the aisle, trying to get his attention, but he never looked over, he spoke quietly to the girl, their dark heads together. She knew, they'd known each other at Harvard. Josie tried to reach him, stepping over people's legs as they glared at her, when the usher stopped her and made her come out, asked to see her ticket. It was for another part of the theater, he led her back there like a shoplifter being escorted from the store. They went through a door, into a back room of the concert hall, like a barroom, you couldn't even hear the music, everybody standing and talking, quarrelsome, it was smoky and loud and people were stepping on her feet. Somewhere she'd even lost her shoes.

That dark-haired girl was the one he needed, a Harvard girl who knew what he knew, had what he had, on whom it sat well, a girl who could wear a suit like this and not as a joke. She looked at herself in the mirror in the blue suit, imagining not Josie Tyrell but Elena. A girl who would not have worked three jobs to pay the bills while her lover sat before the window night after night, drinking and shredding the arms of the chair. A girl who would not have waited for him to fall to pieces on her like that. He would have stuck around for a girl like that.

Who the fuck are you supposed to be? her father said suddenly in her head. His mouth downturned, the mustache curled around it. She put her sunglasses on. It didn't matter what her father said anymore. She was a girl who didn't give a crap, that's who the fuck she was. She was someone who could have a little dignity, someone with something inside. This was what she should have been with Michael all along, something she hadn't understood, she thought he wanted her because she was so unlike Meredith, but in the end, she was just a Tyrell, grubby and stupid and vicious as a rat. There in the mirror was the girl who should have been with Michael. And her name was Elena.

19

Topanga Shoot

Birds flew across the windshield like a page of music. In the extreme range of vision, she could make out the feathery foliage of an old pepper tree, its hanging clusters of pink fruit. This was what it was like to be dead. Staring through a shattered windshield, bent into an awkward but not painful pose. The soft sound of traffic from Old Topanga Road floated through the open window. No terror, no rage, no hope, no love. Just, nothing.

She was good at being dead. She'd played it often enough. It was the only way Jeremy knew how to end a film, the Girl lying on the floor of a train station with a bullet in her heart, or slumped against the wall of a living room, or facedown on a bed, a jar of pills in her hand. And here she was again, behind the wheel of a wrecked BMW. Dead again. Acting dead wasn't hard, it was like modeling, finding an interesting arrangement of limbs and staying very still. She'd never felt like part of her body anyway. Even as a child, she could watch things happen to her and remain unmoved, like the time she cut her knee open, rolling in the spring grass, a hidden stick tearing her flesh, and she watched the blood flow, the pink of slashed muscle like a mouth. This was her secret, she wasn't what they saw, a slight girl with crazy bleached hair. She was buried inside herself like a coin in sand, a whisper in a seashell. Her neck arched at an impossible angle, but she didn't feel it. It wasn't so awful to be dead. The stillness would almost be a relief. She wouldn't want the pain, she wouldn't want to be wounded or mutilated. She could never shoot herself, or jump off a building. But being dead was not unthinkable.

She could see Sergio through the windshield, the big 16-millimeter camera on his shoulder, as one of the two camera assistants, both named Bob, pulled him along in a shopping-cart dolly. A fly landed on the fake sugar blood Laura had painted onto her face. She could feel each of its six legs. The delicate curl of its tongue. But she didn't move. What did a lifeless body care about a fly? The normally boring business of filmmaking had become a blessing. For the next ten days, there would be no time, only an empty horizon. Busy and blank, she could just think about space. Space without time. Maybe that was God. Her dead eyes registered Jeremy, the shock of blond hair bobbing in a side mirror. To think, Michael had been jealous of that. When Jeremy's one thought was who he could get to see his film, could he get it into contention at Toronto?

Through the windshield, a chunky hawk circled high in the winter sky. She watched it jump as it passed along the jagged cracks in the glass. Perhaps it thought there was really an accident, and was waiting for the crew to leave so it could feed. She imagined a sharp beak tearing her indifferent flesh. *Dilly dilly, come let us die.* The fly wandered around on her face, its tickly feet, feeding on her sweet, sweet blood.

Finally, the take was over and Bob Two opened the passenger door of the crumpled car — it was green while the real one was blue,

but it would read the same in black-and-white.
He guided her out into the weak winter sun. She
felt like she was unfurling, like a butterfly in a
science show, emerging from the cocoon all
slimy and cramped, and then unkinking, to
stretch fragile kite wings in the sun. Jeremy gave
her a hug, as if she were a doll pulled from its
box, a wonderful present. But he left his arm on
her shoulder as he called for the next setup.
"Magic hour, people. Two to go and then blacklight sombreros time."

Magic hour, when film students scrambled to
shoot as much footage as they could, while the
sun lowered and the world glowed as gold as it
could on a winter's day. She cracked her neck,
spinal segment by segment, small lateral moves
left and right. Lifted her arms up and behind,
stretching her shoulders, and in the process, dis-
lodging Jeremy's proprietary arm. *Bad faith*.

"That was brilliant, Josie. You're a superstar,"
Jeremy said, kissing her, squeezing her, handling
her. He was always handling her. How upset
Michael had been. When she tried to explain,
Michael said she was deluding herself. It was
bad faith to pretend you didn't know something
you did, bad faith to have someone kiss you and
pretend it meant nothing, bad faith to dislike

someone and stand there chitchatting. You had to be authentic. It was the only way to really know what you felt.

It was true, Jeremy took advantage. And she let him. It was his film, and she really didn't care. It was just a body, like a rented suit. Michael had tried to make her feel differently about her self, that it wasn't just for use by others, it was hers, she belonged to herself, she had to occupy herself. She had when she was with him, but now he was dead. She couldn't remember why it mattered whether she let Jeremy paw her or not. What she did or didn't do.

"We're going out after, to the Guadalajara. You're coming, aren't you?" Jeremy stroked her bare arm. "You buy me drink, sojah?" It might be bad faith to let him touch her like that, but at least it was a human connection. Inauthentic, and yet sad and real in its way.

"Maybe," Josie said, pushing back the white-blond hair that Laura had rebleached in her sink, eliminating the roots, turning her into a Hitchcock blonde with a touch of the futuristic.

Laura draped Josie's coat around her shoulders. "You look fantastic," she whispered, touching the corners of the spiky Veruschka eyelashes. "They stayed on fine." Looking over Josie's shoulder to where Sergio consulted with Jeremy, while two of Sergio's girls moved equipment for the next scene.

The actor playing Conrad sat on the side of the road, settling into his role. A strawberry blond with clear blue eyes, built like a surfer, muscled but slim, he was a real Actor. Too bad for him. Doing a student film to "keep fresh." He'd heard Jeremy was going places. It was always interesting to see who the student directors picked to play their heroes. You could make a movie just about that. It was always who they would be if they could. The actor was Jeremy without the goofiness, his self-absorption more physical, more photogenic.

While the crew set up for the shot, Josie climbed the hillside in her white patent boots and color-block dress, wading through dormant mustard and fragrant fennel higher than her head. She climbed into the low crotch of the double-trunked sycamore, its powdery white limbs glowing pink in the light of magic hour. A few hand-shaped shriveled leaves twirled on the white mottled branches. She liked it out here in Topanga, with its hippie country store and trees and stream. The film students all shot here, the closest to country you could get ten miles from

Hollywood. The sky was the pale blue of old landscape paintings. The faint breeze tousled the long-leaved boughs of eucalyptus and peppers, as if they were boiling.

She wondered what Meredith was doing right now. She could feel her, in her house in Los Feliz, standing by the window as magic hour tinged the view gold. Only Meredith would understand how Michael had stopped time with that bullet. How it pooled now, lost its course, wandered like the malarial mouth of a river, leaving the two of them stranded together in a boat, like the end of *The African Queen,* lost in the reeds, waiting for rain.

On her hands, the resinous smell of the fennel clung. She imagined how nice it would be to lie on a bed of that fragrant ferniness. She rested her cheek against the powdery white of the sycamore trunk, watching the crew swarm over the spot in the road by the crumpled car like ants over a bit of spilled jam. All that attention — the crew of eleven, plus camp followers, camera, sound, the mike like a mop hanging off a fishing pole — focused on that one human being by the side of the road. The actor was about Michael's age, full of himself, he'd had three weeks on a soap opera, big fucking deal.

Right now he was Feeling His Way into the
Scene, she could tell. Rocking himself back and
forth, working himself into a state. It was the
Method. She'd learned all about it from another
boy on an AFI shoot. You came up with memories that made you feel what the character was
supposed to be feeling. "The actor's got to be
thinking all the time," the boy said. "You can't
just 'stand here and look upset.'" And Josie had
been embarrassed, because that's exactly what
she did. God knew no film student cared
whether the Girl felt her way into the character.
They just wanted you to "stand here and look
upset." Look scared, look sexy. And for Christ's
sake remember where you put your hands. Jeremy had convinced the actor this film was
going to Toronto, a showcase, it would make his
career. She didn't tell him the truth. It was a fif-
teen-minute senior film, there'd be a screening
at USC, maybe something in a festival in San
Diego. It wasn't going to make anybody's career,
Buñuel meets Hitchcock in Antonioni's unmade
bed. All of Jeremy's heroes greased up and
writhing, an orgy of influences, where nobody
really came.

Josie never tried to feel it. She never memorized lines. She'd thrown the actor already in the

precrash scene, not giving him the right lead-ins to the lines he'd learned. She didn't ever act, she only modeled with movement. Maybe that was her problem. She didn't feel anything. She simply imitated a feeling. A lot like Jeremy, really. Because whenever she felt it, it was too much, she didn't want to feel things, and have people see it. A coughing fit seized her, and she clapped a hand over her mouth, quickly glanced down the hill to see if they'd started shooting yet, Gil the sound guy would throw a fit. He was always in a shitty mood, Sergio had the two Bobs and all his girl helpers, when Gil had jack shit. But they were only setting up.

She looked up into the great unleafed emptiness, the branches making a puzzle of the sky. Getting out of her life, coming onto the film, was just the right thing, like climbing out of the wrecked BMW. She was glad she'd told no one about Michael. If she was careful on this shoot, if she just stood where she was supposed to, ran where Jeremy pointed, if she held still and let flies crawl around on her face, the pain might be kept at a few feet's distance, just for a while, she could see it, but not let it bloom through her skin like quills.

And somewhere behind those hills, and the

ones behind them, Meredith sat in her house all alone, with all that was left of her son piled in a room she couldn't bear to go into. Holding herself just as Josie did, arms across her chest, trying not to bump into the stiletto corners of grief. The hawk flew low over the hillside and the little birds fell silent.

"Speed," Gil called, holding his mike out like a fishing pole.

"Rolling," came Sergio's bedroom voice, full of artistic ennui.

Jeremy pointed to Conrad. "And — action."

The actor lay back in the grass and forced laughter from his throat. This was his read on grief. Josie thought doing nothing would have been more realistic. When your girlfriend dies in a car accident, it takes a while to believe it. The realization comes later, when you understand you will never see her again. When you go to wash the clothes, and there are her clothes, and you don't know whether to wash them or not, and you think, *not,* because that would mean fewer particles of her existing in the world, the smell of her body which was now underground, that particular scent will never happen again.

After Conrad's scene, Josie clambered down

the hillside for the next one. She wiped off her white patent boots, and Laura brushed off the back of her dress. "Can you believe those pants?" she whispered in Josie's ear, gesturing with her chin at the blonde in violet stretch leggings. "You could get away with them, but not her. Not with that ass."

As Laura refreshed her lipstick, retouched her fake blood, Jeremy came over, glancing meaningfully at the others, and said softly, "Josie, we decided we're going to try something different."

Why was he looking at her with that sneaky smile? Jeremy's entrée to a con. "Just tell me," Josie said.

He gazed off toward the sea, flicking his hair from his eyes. "I'm seeing Elena, emerging from the wreck, walking down the road . . . a naked soul, heading into the Hereafter."

She looked from Jeremy to Sergio to Bob One, and they looked blankly back at Jeremy, and she knew the "we" was simply his collective "me" with yet another grand idea. He wanted Elena in the buff. *A naked soul, heading into the Hereafter.* In other words, he thought a naked girl in the movie would give it a sexy edge — like the people who put a topless girl holding a muffler in a car-parts ad. It had nothing to do with vision. It was just bad faith. It was one thing to model for an art class, but to let him use her that way, because he knew she could do it, that pissed her off. "Hey, fuck you, Jeremy."

"Oh, come on, Josie." He flipped his hair from his goggly blue eyes. "You're not hung up. You do it every day. Look, we're all family here."

She almost laughed. *Clink, clink.* The sound of counterfeit coins falling from his mouth like a payoff in Vegas. What in the world could Jeremy's idea of family be? Something he'd seen once on TV?

He draped his arm over her shoulder, put his face down to hers, he must have seen the gesture in a photo of some other director. "She's a pure soul, walking down the road. It would be such an awesome ending, Josie."

"My rear ending, you mean." Pulling away from him. He could get his fucking arm off her.

"I'm offended," Jeremy said. "You cut me to the core. I have a vision of Elena's soul." He framed the shot with his fingers in L's, as if he was already watching the movie. "I see her walking away from us. Nude, barefoot on a country road. She's invisible, Conrad doesn't see her, she walks right by him and down the road. She has been freed. It's over. The clothing, the trappings of her former life, all fallen away. Free of every expectation, every constraint. Please, Josie, I'm begging you, do this for me?"

She stood with her arms crossed, looking down that long road, the sun casting its shadows. Who gave a crap. It was a body. A rented suit, yes. And bodies died, they were raped, they were smashed, they were cremated, they were buried in family tombs. Though it pissed her off, Jeremy thinking he was putting something over on her. "How much to see this naked vision?"

Now he stopped playing to the bleachers. His eyes flickered back to her, he shoved his hair out of his eyes with that hurt look, like a parent whose kid got an F on his report card. "I'm already giving you top billing." The sad-eye treatment. "I thought you believed in me, in this project."

"Okay," she said, shifting her weight, digging her spike-heeled boot into the dust. "If you direct it naked. Everybody naked. We'll all be naked souls on Naked Souls' Day."

He looked at the rest of the film students, his ragged crew, the chubby Gil, the probably underendowed Bobs. The helpers were possible, and Sergio, but everyone else was finding something more interesting to look at, like the ground or the pepper tree. Jeremy came close. "Why do you hate me, Josie? Look, we're losing our light."

She said nothing, just waited, watching the light become more blue as they spoke. Waiting to see what he would do. She felt like Elena.

"Gordo? We've got a little problem here," Jeremy called out to *My Producer,* a fat boy from Denver whose uncle had coughed up most of the money for the shoot. He owned a chain of discount dental clinics in Arizona and New Mexico. Gordo came over, smoking, a blue cloud matching the black cloud of his brow. They conferred, heads together. Finally, Gordo opened his wallet and counted his money, nodded once.

"A hundred," Jeremy said very quietly, right over her ear. "An extra hundred." She was already getting fifty a day, twenty-five more than everyone else who was getting paid.

She wanted to ask for something else. She really wanted everyone to know what it felt like to shed their clothes in front of strangers, be just a body for a few minutes, get real, not just her. She wanted Jeremy to know, but what was the point of wanting Jeremy to know anything? He was as self-involved as a toddler in a sandbox. She'd just have to take the hundred.

"You want me to clear the set?" Jeremy asked, ever the professional.

Josie looked around. She wanted to laugh. Who was there to clear? The ragtag bunch of film students, Sergio's followers, Gordo? She unzipped the color-block dress, handed it to Laura, added her stockings, her boots, her underwear. Laura was pale with sympathy, thinking her brave, she could tell, but in truth, she always felt more like herself without clothes. She walked down the road to her mark. Everyone was looking at her. Let them. She was a dead girl. Everybody looks at a dead girl's body, her bush, her naked breasts, poke at them until they harden up. The cops, the mortuary. Some of them might even fuck her corpse, knowing she couldn't reject them now. But Elena was beyond feeling it. She was free in the way only the dead are free. That was fucking true. She stepped to her mark.

"Okay, Josie, ready?" Jeremy called. Sound came to speed, camera rolled. He pointed to her. "And — action."

Josie began to walk down the dirt road, past Conrad sitting with his head in his hands, shedding actual tears. The silky cold dirt and sharp pebbles of the road alternately soothed and jabbed the soles of her feet. January, the sun going down, a good day to be dead, she could just forget the living now. Whatever she had wanted from this boy crying in the grass, she didn't even remember. This was what it was like, you were cold, you didn't have clothes, you remembered nothing, you just walked on down the road. She imagined Jeremy was disappointed now to have wasted a hundred dollars this way, when he saw how thin she was, how unsexy her body would look on the screen, that her glamour was an illusion now revealed to be thin as a dress. She walked farther and farther from the square-shaded lens of the camera, wondering if for that extra hundred he would make her walk all the way to town. She kept walking until she heard Jeremy yell, "Cut."

He met her halfway on the road and wrapped her in a blanket, it was sandy and smelled of mold and sea. He put his arm around her as they walked back to the set, kissed her cheek. "Fantastic, Josie. You'll see. It's going to make the movie. I'm eternally grateful. People are going to remember you."

At least they would remember her ass.

A noisy bar on Sunset near Virgil, the Guadalajara featured Day-Glo sombreros suspended from the ceiling, all bathed in black light. The crew's teeth and shirts glowed. She didn't know why she had come, what she was doing with these strangers, only that she didn't want to go home. She was the Girl in the Movie, a girl whose boyfriend had just killed himself, going out for drinks with the film crew, drinking tequila shooters and not telling anyone about the source of her desperate gaiety. The Girl was glamorous, and the boys crowded around her, trying to amuse her. The Girl in the Movie flirted with the director and played bar games with the camera assistant and the pink-haired wardrobe girl, spinning quarters and drinking a whole beer without taking a breath. The Girl whose boyfriend had just killed himself pretended to listen to the handsome young actor talking about a TV pilot he was going to be in, as she downed tequila until she was really too drunk to know what he was saying and didn't give a crap anyway. At least he was young and sweet and they danced to "La Bamba" on the jukebox. She could sense the director was unhappy with this turn of events. He was the director, the Girl in the Movie should be his. But the actor was sexier, handsomer, and she wouldn't see him again after the shoot was over.

He followed her home. They stumbled down the stairs to her house behind a house, so empty, cold as the produce section at a grocery store. The walls with their bare hooks. The artist was gone. She was glad the actor was there, and she screwed him in Montmartre, in the white bed, the very bed where another girl and another boy had made love like gods. Until they didn't. Was it supposed to be a shrine? Should she be Meredith, put a rope across the doorway, light candles, burn offerings? The actor screwed her and screwed her, he was too drunk to come, and suddenly she came out of the drunk and the role of the Girl and it was just her, being fucked by some stranger when Michael was dead, in their own sacred space, but by then it was too late.

"That was great," the actor said when he finally came.

What movie was he in, she wondered, wiping herself on the sheet.

20
Sweden

Her headache wound around her forehead, a crown of tequila thorns. Light inflamed the uncurtained windows she had not had the foresight to cover. The clock said 3:00, but it always said that now. She guessed it was more like seven. The light slashed across her eyes like a belt with a metal buckle. Sombreros, a drinking contest. And there next to her, on Michael's pillow, lay a glowing reddish blond head. *Oh God.* It had not been a dream. She was fucking strangers in his very own bed.

She staggered into the bathroom, crouched over the rust-stained toilet in which someone had pissed and not flushed, and vomited into the stench. The bitter twice-tasted tequila flooded out in a yellow gush. She waited to vomit again. And then again. She wished she could vomit herself to the bottom, until everything that made her Josie Tyrell came up and there was nothing left but a dried skin, a bug crackle blown by a breath of wind.

She lay on the cold bathroom floor, dragged the bath mat over herself. She could have gotten up, but knew she'd have to vomit again, so she lay on the tiles, shivering, imagining Michael watching her, with that man, that actor, in his bed. *This is how much you cared. This?* She might as well have taken Nick Nitro up on his offer at Lola Lola's. At least they would have gone back to his place, not done it here. Fucked in an alley standing up in garbage and been done with it.

She crawled to her knees, pulled down the kimono hanging from the back of the door. It wasn't warm either, but she didn't want to be naked anymore. There was only so much nakedness a person could stand, and she had had it. She pulled herself up on the doorknob and tied the robe, the ties so long, she was growing thinner, like a refugee. She ran some water and brushed her teeth. The new tube of toothpaste tasted too strong, she had grown used to Michael's old-fashioned tooth powder, now buried somewhere in his dark childhood room.

She leaned in the bedroom doorway, wanting to go back to bed, but she could not lie down next to the actor. She felt dizzy and sick, hot and cold all over.

"Get up," she said hoarsely.

The head didn't move.

"Get up," she said. "Wakey wakey." She went to the bed and shook him.

He groaned. "God, what time is it?" Groping on the bedside table for his watch, knocking over the vase of peacock feathers, that fell heavily on the floor and rolled under the bed. He squinted at the watch. "It's early." He sank back down to the pillow.

"No, it's late," Josie said. "You have to go now."

He focused, his arm shielding his eyes from the light. A weak smile came over his face. "Hi, you."

"Get up."

He opened the covers to show his muscular body, the ripped abs, the morning hard-on. It was a bit of a wonder, considering. "Come on in, it's early." Stroking himself, cradling his balls. His pubic hair was red. She hadn't remembered that.

She picked up his clothes and tossed them onto the bed. He really thought she was going to fuck him again? She struggled not to cry. Wasn't she being clear enough? "Stop jerking off and get up. I need some time before work." She didn't have to be out at Cal Arts until one, the shoot wasn't until dark, but she found it unbearable for him to still be here, where the ballerina and the artist could see him. She would set that bed on fire before she let him lie there on Michael's pillow one more minute.

"Fuck and throw the guy out, huh?" He pouted.

What was his name, Conrad? No, Conrad was the character. "Yeah, every guy's dream, huh?" she said.

"You don't know me," he said. "I'll stick around. I'll make you pancakes."

After how many tequilas, he was thinking of food? Even the thought made her belch.

"But first I'll make you," he said, turning onto his side, head propped on his hand, a sexy pose, making the most of his distended cock. Christ. Such an obvious move, but it must work or he wouldn't do it. You do the shtick that gets you approval. She knew that better than anyone. Michael never posed, never. His body completely natural, awkward or at ease.

"Wade," she said. That was his name, Wade. She hated to play games when all she wanted to do was get rid of him, the better to beat herself up in private, but she was willing to do whatever it took. "Listen, honey, I like you a lot, but I really need to be by myself now. It's part of my process." She remembered one girl talking about her process. It seemed like a good way of making demands without admitting it was just a whim, all those rituals and routines. "I have to have time alone. To meditate," she added for good measure.

Thank God Wade knew nothing about her. She wasn't even a real actress. She'd never meditated a day in her life. This was the wonderful thing about strangers. They were big blank pieces of paper, you could draw whatever you liked on their impressionable surfaces. Was that what Michael had seen in her too? Yes, of course it was. Yes. She waited until she saw him rise, then retreated to the kitchen.

Out the window over the sink, the panes on the houses across the glen flashed with eastern light, traffic on the 2 and the 5 creeping into downtown. How could people bear it? Waking up every day, living their lives. While God the Chinese grandmother picked them off one by one. *Even my looking at things turns them ugly.*

Painting his face in the mirror. Long and mis-shapen, his eyes too large and set too high in his head. He hadn't said more than four words to her all that day. Wouldn't touch her. She sat on the rim of the tub, painting her toenails blue, trying to get him to relent, it had been such a terrible summer. She couldn't figure out what she'd done to deserve this, how mean he'd become. She wore her blue slip from St. Vincent de Paul, hoping to seduce him, he was still a man, his body could be reached if he'd let her. "Why do you have to make yourself so ugly?" she asked.

"I am ugly," he said, face inches from the mirror, his voice so matter-of-fact. "Fifty-something kilos of gristle and hair. Not even enough for a lampshade. Look at that." He gestured to the glass. He was wearing shorts but no shirt, his beautiful arms, his chest with the sunken place in the middle, the square but lean shoulders. But he hadn't been sleeping well, his skin was more sallow than usual, circles around his eyes. He frightened her when he was like this, staring in the mirror as if it was a freak show.

"Let's go down to the park, you can paint the lotus. Or the bridge." Down in Echo Park, they could take a paddleboat under the red Chinese bridge, they could float in the shade of the Canary Island palms, drift through dark pools of shadow. He'd play her little blue guitar and sing her funny songs from the Twenties, imitate Louis Armstrong doing "Big Butter and Egg Man," or Bing's version of "Just a Gigolo." "It'd be cooler there. Can't we get out a little?"

"It's cool enough here." The tiled bathroom, he'd been in here for days. "Anyway, I wouldn't dare paint anything else. Even my looking at things turns them ugly. I'm a Gorgon, Josie. You shouldn't be here, you should hold up your shield."

Trying to get rid of her.

Now, staring out at the traffic, she finally knew just how he felt.

Her eyes blurred with tears. Fuck it. Maybe Cal was right. Everything had a memory of him, maybe it was better for Meredith to have it all, keep it in his old room like death's junk shop. All the paintings, for better or worse, the beautiful ones and the hideous, his painting of the faucet in the bathtub with its rust stains on the worn enamel that looked like blood, the mad monk with his black cloak and furious eyes. She would never have been able to get rid of them, they would only remind her of how useless she'd been, she hadn't been able to think of a thing to say when he said he made the world ugly just by looking at it.

The actor finally staggered into the bathroom, she could hear him pissing, like a horse. "Don't forget to flush," she called out.

"Come and help me," he called back.

She went down to the garden, the cracked stones they had placed in sand like a puzzle they'd worked until all the pieces fit. In the days when things came together. She picked a handful of mint. It was quiet down here, even the dog at the bottom of the hill hadn't begun to bark. Green and fragrant, the morning glories glowing at their margins. Not like last summer, when it had been just filthy hot, the view out the bathroom window shimmering like a dirty mirage, the colors all bleeding to white.

The actor was showering when she came back up. She let the mint steep in the little pan, poured a mug and took it into the living room, where she could watch the traffic crawl, sitting by the window, the pipe-cleaner circus. She picked up the horse and girl rider, straightened the feather on the horse's head. Why hadn't she done something? Gotten him some help. The darkness a side of him she hadn't seen until that summer. His cruelty, his obsessiveness. Though she'd tried. Hadn't she? "Maybe you might want to see someone —"

"I am seeing someone. You." He gestured at her in the mirror, over the painting, and she shuddered as she remembered the way he had looked at her, like he didn't even know her, as if some stranger was glaring out of his eyes. He couldn't see her anymore, not Josie, not little Jeanne, his lover, not her.

"I mean, like a shrink or something."

He leaned in close to the canvas, working green into the skin. "There's no cure for the human condition, Josie. For the condition in which we find ourselves. For instance, did you know there's a dish they make in Spain, called *cipriones en su tinta.* Ever hear of it?"

Christ, what did this have to do with seeing a goddamn shrink? He was getting so convoluted, it made her head ache. "No, Michael, I haven't. Do I flunk your little class?"

"It's squid," he said. "Cooked in its own ink."

She waited to see if he would make the connection for her, or just leave her scratching her
head, a sentence without a period. "Yeah, and?"

"It's you, Josie. Don't you see? Cooked in your
own ink."

She wished she could touch him, shake him,
remind him somehow that she was the girl he
loved. The one who gave him permission, they
had been to Siberia together, all the way to
Japan. They had opened all the doors. She
wanted to touch him, but she was frightened of
what his pale eyes accused. What had she done
but love him? "You want to tell me what you're
talking about? I'm sorry I'm so fucking ignorant,
but I just don't get it."

"Your calling attention to my needing to see
someone. When in fact, I am seeing someone
very clearly. You, and your boyfriend Jeremy."

She sighed, put the bottle of blue nail polish
on the back of the toilet. "You know, you're right
about one thing. You make everything ugly just
by looking at it." And yet, there was also the thin
shudder of fear.

He never considered it might not be Jeremy.
Jeremy was someone he despised but secretly
envied, someone who could create without
worrying whether it wasn't the finest thing that

had ever been done. But Nick Nitro was simply beneath Michael's field of vision — a screamer, a punk rocker, a broke speed guitarist who rode a junk Japanese bike and looked like the guy who worked on your car.

At the time, she hadn't considered fucking Nick the same as having an affair. It wasn't as if she had started something new. She didn't tremble when she took Nick on his dirty sheets. Having sex with him was more like picking up a jacket or a record album she'd left behind in the hall, or eating cold pizza when she was stoned. Who would know or care what transpired between them? At the time, she thought it was Michael's fault. If he would only touch her, smile at her. Make love to her the way he could if he wanted to. But that summer all he wanted was to be left alone to make ugly paintings in the mirror and listen to Schoenberg on Deutsche Grammophon, that fragmented, half-mad music.

So she started going around to the Franklin Fuckhouse. Not often, just three or four times, to put off going home. Just somewhere to go to avoid the gathering gloom.

Liar.

It was way, way more than that. She was angry and hurt and it was payback for being treated like

garbage. When she would do anything for him.
She paid the rent, bought food and did the laundry, paid for his canvas and fucking paints now
that he'd quit Señor Reynaldo, up and quit, for no
good reason, suddenly he didn't like the way Reynaldo hovered over him, said he was sick of
clumsy infants and playing the same music over
and over so many times he was hearing it in his
sleep. That's what he said. Poor Reynaldo probably had no better idea than she did why Señor
Music had suddenly grown so sulky and difficult.
He hated everyone that summer. Leaving her to
bust her butt while he was painting his ugly pictures, guide to his own private Bosch, and then
not even kissing her, flinching when she touched
him as if it burned. So she would go to the Fuckhouse and get laid hard and good with no questions asked. Honestly, she'd liked Nick better
then than in all the time they'd been actually together. He was the ultimate anti-Michael. He had
no ideas, he didn't think their sex meant something. He didn't wonder if they were getting back
together or even ask if she had changed her mind
about him being an asshole. The very thing that
had been so annoying about him was now his
strong point. Didn't Michael always say your
virtue was your vice and vice versa?

Peter, Peter, Pumpkin Eater. She had Michael but she couldn't have him.

Though he could come to life for his mother, oh yes.

When she'd started calling him from Leningrad and Denmark and Sweden. They'd gotten all chummy again. The woman couldn't leave him alone. And she knew just how to reel him in, calling from her tour, lonely, *missing you.* At the beginning he was short with her, but after a while their conversations lengthened, and the worse he was feeling, the happier those calls made him. He still wouldn't let her give them any money, oh, he was too proud for that, Josie could work three jobs a day and that was okay. But his mother knew just what to say to him, what he would respond to. By the end of summer, they were thick as thieves. *You know how they were.* Oh yes, she knew.

And when Her Highness called, she wouldn't even acknowledge Josie with a hello. Treating her like the goddamn answering service, Stepin Fetchit to the Crown Prince.

"Hello, can I speak to Michael, please?" The crackle of the long-distance line.

It was the wrong day to pull that shit. "The name's Josie," she hissed into the receiver. "You can fucking say my name, Meredith, or kiss my fucking ass." It felt fantastic to hang up on her, brilliant.

Michael appeared in the doorway, hands covered with paint, squinting like a mole after the dark cave of the bathroom. "Who was that?"

She turned to him, leaning on the wooden counter. "Who do you think? She calls and doesn't even say hello. Like I'm the maid or something. *No habla inglés.*"

"What did she want?" He pushed the beads out of the way, there was still paint on his hands.

"I don't know, I hung up on her." She held out a glass of iced tea for him.

He didn't take it. He just stared. "You hung up on her."

"Yeah," Josie said. "I hung up on her." Her heart beat fast, he was seeing her now. She'd finally gotten his attention. What would he do, hit her? She hoped he would. It was life at least, a reaction.

"She's in Sweden," Michael said.

Josie put the jar with his tea down on the counter, backed away. "Well break out the brass band."

"She's my mother," he said, coming toward her. "You don't just hang up on her."

"Why the hell not?" She pressed up against the counter, her free hand braced in an attitude that was pointedly casual, afraid and excited by the outrage on his face, finally some emotion there besides his stupid funk. She took a drink of tea, eyed him, waiting to see what he would do now. Would he strike her? Realize how pompous he sounded, like somebody's father? She wanted to push him hard, see what would happen, though it frightened her too, she wasn't sure if she was really ready to know. "Your mother's a snotty bitch and I'm not putting up with it anymore."

The phone rang again. Michael brushed out through the beads, answered the phone himself, glory be. "Hello? Meredith?" He rubbed his forehead without thinking of the paint on his hands, leaving a green streak. "I know she did. It's hot here, it's making us both kind of edgy."

"Tell her we've been together a year, when's she fucking going to get used to it?" Josie called from the kitchen, but he didn't appear to be listening.

"Everything's fine here," Michael said.

At least he had the decency to lie.

He sat on the blue couch in front of the fan, picking his toenails, settling in to a nice long chat, the gloominess of his face lifting like tule fog when the sun starts to burn it off. Talking to the great love of his life. It was so painfully clear. Josie felt like crying out of sheer jealousy. How a woman calling from five thousand miles away could get that reaction, when she couldn't with all her clothes off six inches away. Meredith hadn't spoken to him for months after she'd cut him off. Now she was calling all the time, talking about her tour, the conductors, her exciting life. Michael said she did it when she was all jazzed from a performance, or bored or lonely in her hotel, it wasn't just him, she'd call everyone she knew and talk forever. Her phone bill was the equivalent of a small country's gross national product.

"Where are you staying? Sure, I remember Mr. Eriksson. He's got to be ninety, he's still there? No, in Sweden it's the midnight sun. The white nights are Leningrad." It was more conversation than Josie had had from him in weeks. "How's Sofía?"

Meredith took the maid with her on tour, to do all the packing, make the travel arrangements, get the cabs and make phone calls and pick up the mail at American Express, do the shopping and cooking. Meredith stayed in suites with kitchens, so she could be sure of eating well on the road. When Michael was a kid, Sofía and the tutor flew coach while Meredith and he went first class. That said just about everything.

"No, I can't," he was saying. "Yeah, it sounds great, but we're pretty busy here." He glanced quickly at Josie, then away.

She knew what Meredith was up to. She was inviting Michael to join her in Sweden. To seduce him back into his old life, maids and hotels and white nights. *Why are you sitting in that hot squalid little shack when you could be here in Stockholm? I'd love to see you, why don't you ditch Mimì and come out? I'll send you a ticket.* And it filled her with such love for him, that despite everything, his crazy accusations, the nights he spent in the chair by the window avoiding her bed, the way he would shudder if she touched him, he would not leave her to run off to the midnight sun with his mother. He knit his forehead streaked in green, making those planes he liked to turn into tumors in the paintings. "Yeah, well I never fit in either, so I guess that's two of us."

They were still the two of them. She knew what the mother was saying. *She wouldn't fit in. She's not like us. I don't know why you're with her, I really don't.* But still he chose her. He still loved her, he did. He would not leave her for his mother's siren song. She vowed she would never fuck around on him again, that they would deal with their problems, she would wait for him. They'd get through this together. In her own way, she saw, she'd given in to despair as much as he had.

She dropped the shoulder strap of her slip, so her breast would peek out, the nipple like a bouquet, so he would remember what she could do for him that his mother could not. He rolled his eyes at her, *oh please,* picked up a drawing pad from the orange footlocker, and tucked the phone against his ear, so he could listen and draw at the same time. "I had that piece in the show at Barnsdall, did you get the clipping? A gallery's even interested in representing me."

Barnsdall Park's municipal gallery was a big deal, lots of famous artists had had their first show there. And out of all that art, the reviewer from the *Weekly* had mentioned his specifically. Though it shocked Josie that he was talking about it with Meredith. At the time, he'd dismissed it — the show, the review, everything. "They let everybody in, Josie," he'd said with a sneer. "It's not the Whitney Biennial. Me and four hundred of my closest friends." He hadn't even wanted to attend the opening, but she'd made him go. People loved his painting, Josie nude on the couch in black stockings and her red little Jeanne wig. The reviewer called it Schiele-esque, which Michael hated for some reason, all but called her an idiot. Now he was bragging.

This was the part of Michael she found so impossible — the way he could take a position and then later completely reverse his point of view. He hated it when other people did that, *re-visionists* he'd call them, but he couldn't see how he did just the same thing. What was worse was that he believed the new version as much as he had the old one. And she was afraid that someday he'd do the same thing with her, the story of his love.

"Yeah, well, the photo wasn't that great." He frowned, turning away from Josie, not wanting her to watch him reel out his revised version of reality for his mother's inspection. She was clearly finding something to criticize. That bitch. She never wanted him to be a painter. He was supposed to become a famous art critic, a *curator,* so he could travel with Mummy and yet still have something she could point to and say, *Oh, my son's not just hanging out, he's here for the*

Schiele auction. Fuck her. She probably knew Schiele and didn't think it was Schiele-esque enough. Josie could tell Michael wanted her to leave, to let him talk to his mother in private, but there was nowhere else to go — was she supposed to sit in their hot, stuffy bedroom? And anyway, this was her place, really, she was paying for it, she'd goddamn sit anywhere she wanted. She conspicuously plunked herself in the chair by the window, where the smoggy haze stalled over the giant ryegrass and nothing moved but the fan, waving its blue and green ribbons. A toy car on the toy hillside drove past little houses like the models in a race-car set. And beyond, the painted backdrop of a city through smog. What if it was all just an illusion, a diorama at the Museum of Natural History, and they were in it, she and Michael, locked in a two-dimensional world. But not Meredith. She was out there in three dimensions, with her concert halls and Stockholm and breezes off the fjords.

And Michael chatting away as if everything was fine, great, neato. She couldn't help wishing she could rate that kind of heroic deception, instead of him saving her for the grinding reality, his terrible gnawing doubts about his life and everything around him. The true world so far away, it hadn't been seen for so long, only this opaque day-to-day shit they were living. She had to admit, it was a relief to hear him happy, to know he was still capable of it. She had to give that much to Meredith. When he got that stranger's face, and started in on one of his rages, Jeremy or some other crime she'd ostensibly committed, there wasn't much that could snap him back out again.

She should have made him see someone. She should have not let him distract her. Even if he broke up with her. But she hadn't been willing to take that chance.

Now, she could hear the actor in the bathroom, showering, singing "Number One," going up into falsetto. God. She hadn't thought there was that much hot water. She drank her tea. To think that she'd let him fuck her in Michael's own bed. Christ. Well, at least she hadn't enjoyed it.

She remembered joining Michael that day, on the blue couch in front of the fan, how she'd spread her legs and let the air go up her naked crotch, hoping to remind him just what they had seen in each other, how good it could be, but he put the phone on his lap and turned away, concentrating on Meredith in Sweden, which she could only picture as a loose collage of blond stewardesses in blue uniforms, bad disco bands like Abba, or else men and women in horn-rimmed glasses walking on rocky coasts in Bergman films. No wonder Meredith wanted Michael to come out.

He wouldn't look at her. His mother said something funny, he laughed, and though it was good to hear him laugh, it pissed her off, too. Why could he pull himself together for Meredith, but not for her? It was exhausting to listen to them, they made the air hotter, more oppressive, how could they find so much to talk about?

She put her foot on the fly of his shorts, to see if she could rouse him while he was distracted. He frowned, trying to concentrate. She pressed gently, working the toes and the ball of her foot, feeling him harden despite his frown. She walked her toes up his cock as he kept talking to his mother. She could jerk him off like that, if he'd let her. Keep talking, she thought. It's Meredith, your mommy.

He didn't look at her, but slid his hips forward on the couch as he listened. She took a chance and slid her hand into the fly of his shorts. He covered the receiver and mouthed *cut it out.*

But the look of his mouth and the way that he swallowed, she could tell it was turning him on.

"Pretend I'm not here," she whispered. Like he'd been doing for weeks. She wanted him to want it, she knew there was a spark to be lit, it was still there. This holding her off was a punishment, but for whom, and why, she never could tell. When you loved someone the way she loved Michael, you couldn't help being punished no matter who it was he was trying to hurt. All that love, all that joy, she knew it was in there, in that body, under that skin, in those green eyes, she'd lived with it, knew it, where could it all have gone?

She could feel the velvety skin of his cock, at least that still knew her. It always remembered her, and she touched him there, light and gentle, not rhythmic, yet it moved under her fingers, on its own, as if he were not attached to it. There was the Michael in her hand and the Michael who was talking to his mother in Sweden, and finally he sighed and shut his eyes, pretending she was not there, his unfaithful mistress, pretending it was the breeze, or the stirring of a thought, a womanless hard-on that grew and sought, without a head or eyes or ears, without knowledge or wonder, but a wanting that came before all of those things. Maybe he was imagining it was Meredith. Was that it? Was that what would get him off? His legs sagged apart, although his face was still turned, and she bent her head and took him in her mouth. At the contact, he gasped involuntarily and put his hand over the receiver, but as Meredith talked he let Josie run her tongue around the head of his cock, he thrust himself in her mouth, "Uh-huh," he choked into the receiver, then covered it again, and arched and the sinews in his legs were hard as roots, covering the receiver as he bucked and groaned and then his hands in her hair as Meredith told him stories from over the sea.

"Okay, you," Wade said, coming into the living room, all dressed, showered, and combed — cowboy boots and black jeans and leather jacket. "See you in a couple."

"Yeah," she said, not turning, so he couldn't see the tears streaming down her face. "See you."

She still wanted him. Fiercely, as she had on that day, as much as she had the first day at Meredith's, the way she'd always wanted him. He just wasn't like anybody else. She'd fucked a lot of boys but never wanted any of them, that was the truth. That was the goddamn truth. She'd never felt a fucking thing. And now she'd lost him, those hands on her body, those bony hips, his lips on her breasts, his tongue in her, his cock, *never and never.*

She lay on the couch for the rest of the morning, like some crazy girl in a locked ward crying and masturbating all the day long.

21
Sunset Plaza

Orange crime lights illuminated new blacktop along Sunset Plaza as she climbed, her headlights washing the fronts of low modern houses crouching windowless to the street. The concrete walls and ivy and crushed white rock glowed in the artificial light. She parked a dozen houses up from the location, dry swallowed a cross top, and walked down, carrying Elena's clothes in a bag. She'd just driven in from a four-hour sitting in Palos Verdes, it was going to be a long night. Greek statuettes flanked the flat black double doors she walked through without knocking, hoping she had the address right. The slate entry, walled in frosted glass, gave way to an expanse of immaculate white shag and a sheer wall of windows. *Total Sixties, it'll blow your mind.* Beyond the white leather and glass of the sunken living room, past manicured lawn and bright swimming pool, lay the vast jeweled vista of night-crawler LA, spread out like a careless club queen passed out on a bed, skirts hiked above her waist, for anybody to fuck any way they wanted.

The crew had already trashed the carpet, black grimy cable smears and cigarette ash, wires snaking through the shag to feed light stands propped with sandbags. Jeremy and *My Producer* Gordo conspired, heads together, on a couch of ivory leather. "Whose house is this?" she asked. "Are they crazy, letting you use it?"

Jeremy pushed his lank hair back from his face, goggle eyes alight with a guilty excitement. "Actually, they're in Aspen," he said. "Actually."

These people hadn't dreamed how dangerous it might be to befriend a student filmmaker, and then say when they'd be out of town. How little he cared about them, compared to his need to use their perfect Sixties house for his movie. She felt like a burglar. Then she thought better of it. She wasn't going to feel too sorry for people like this. They thought they could seal themselves away behind glass and white leather, but they were mistaken. Perfection was no protection. Disaster had a way of dropping by just when you least expected it.

Film students swarmed the set, drinking coffee, dropping cigarette ash, dragging lights, and setting up reflectors. The blonde in zebra pants knelt, taping cords. Her ass looked like a traffic island. Josie wished she had gotten some sleep. Her eyes kept catching on patterns, edges and corners, unpredictably threatening. She picked her way down the hall, found the master suite, blessedly all white. In the center, a white-leather-edged waterbed sat, plump as a fat bride. She lay down on its fur spread, let the water roll out from under her, slapping the far edge to recoil beneath her again. Suddenly, she remembered a boy from school who'd had a waterbed, what was his name? Steve something. They'd met at the Circle K, he took her home on his bike, a piece-of-crap Honda. She could picture his room, the AC/DC poster, the cheap tapestry of a bighorn sheep, but she couldn't recall his face. Just the feel of the waterbed and his monotonous thrusts, and that stately ram.

She got up and changed into the Pucci dress,

pinning the front closed — Elena was not the type for walking around with her black bra showing. Elena had never been to a Circle K, never lain down under a bighorn sheep rug. Josie examined her face in the mirror. After four hours in Palos Verdes and an hour-and-a-half drive into town, she needed to wash and start over. In the sparkly Formica bathroom, she taped the picture of Veruschka to the mirror under the space-satellite fixture, trying to remember how the face was created. Too bad Laura had quit the night of the sombreros, when Sergio had gone home with the blonde. Jeremy told her all about it. He had no personal life but he relished the dramas of others.

Josie opened her makeup kit, her bag of tricks, and began the slow transformation into Elena. Base, like gesso on a canvas, erasing the traces of her own personality, her dark eyes staring through the mask of her face. Then layer upon layer, building up another face, brown in the hollows, dark under the jaw, white on every bone. The two sets of eyelashes, giving Elena that Sixties look of pampered ennui. White shadow, black in the crease. Two broad bands of liquid liner, the spiky mascara. Pink lipstick, and a pale one over it. She brushed out her new-dyed hair, ratted it up, then swept the top layer over it, twisting it into a tiny chignon, no bigger than a silver dollar. She pinned and sprayed, then threaded plastic disc earrings through her earlobes.

And there was Elena.

She stared at her, this girl she had created. *Who are you? What do you know that I don't?* Elena gazed back, that sweep of remarkable eyelash, a Jeanne Moreau smile on her downturned lips, and said nothing. She was a magician ready for the show, every ace in place. She didn't let herself hang out, raw and ragged as a torn hem. Michael should have been with a girl like that. Someone smart, sophisticated, who would have loved him less but understood him better, anticipated his needs, handled him with dexterity. He thought he wanted Josie Tyrell, her scruffy innocence, to impregnate with his dreams. But he was mistaken.

The lights blazed in the living room now, generator outside humming like a fifty-foot hornet, a sound she knew would give Gil hemorrhoids. Jeremy hovered over the camera with Sergio and the Bobs, gesturing scene movement. Then he saw her. He straightened, and came to her on his storky long legs. "Josie!" He peered into her face. "My God, how did you do that?"

A small man with a strawberry birthmark on his cheek sat nervously on the white couch, his tiny feet in polished loafers that barely touched the floor.

"Who's that?" Josie asked.

"My bank teller," he confided, in his version of *sotto voce* which could be heard across the room, he had only two levels of volume, loud and louder. "Don't you just love him?" Jeremy couldn't resist the deformity. "So Mr. Cairo."

"What are you going to do with him?"

Jeremy shrugged. "I'll think of something."

Poor Tellerman. He had no idea Jeremy was using him because he looked like Peter Lorre and had that thing on his face, and a toupee. He wasn't in the script, but Jeremy would find a use for him. The potential for cruelty here was too painful to contemplate, so she walked outside, past the generator and the pool. It was damp and cold. She wrapped herself in her skinny arms, her thin poly dress no protection from the night. Down below, car lights snaked along the Strip with its hookers and dazed tourists and excited kids, too young for the clubs, but not too young to want to come down and be part of the scene, maybe catch sight of Debbie Harry or Joey Ramone. Josie had never hung out in front of the Whiskey, watching for the band. She might have been a hick from Bakersfield, but she always knew how to get past the box office.

One broad band below Sunset ran the double slashes of Santa Monica Boulevard, with its handsome, hungry boys watching the river of cars, hopeful thumbs ready, their cocks and asses. You could have anything for twenty-five bucks. So many lost boys and girls, even more lost than she. She'd given them rides, knew their stories, even pressed a few bucks into grubby hands. And above them all, the giant Marlboro man squinted down from his billboard with testosterone scorn, like God sneering down on Creation.

And where was the true world? Hiding its face behind this one like stars behind clouds. If it had ever existed. She didn't know anymore. *You'll have to remember for both of us* . . . But she couldn't hang on. She pulled the half-pint of Smirny from her modeling bag, felt the hot burn of it in her throat, in her nose. She hadn't slept in who knew how long, she felt like a puppet with somebody else's face. From the lawn she could look down on God, be even more indifferent than He.

"Hi, you."

Wade, standing beside her, his arms crossed, wearing his character's costume, his suave Movie Director dark turtleneck and leather sport coat. "Saw you out here."

Josie put the voddy away, didn't offer him any. Serious actors didn't get loaded while Working. *Tant pis,* as Michael would say.

"That was great," he said, taking in the view. "The other night."

Josie tasted vodka on her lips, rummaged in her bag for a ciggie, wondering what this would look like on film. She could almost see the script he was reading from, *It was great, the other night . . .*

"I know that we're working together," he said, coming closer. She could smell his aftershave, Jovan Musk for Men. "I usually believe in waiting until things wrap. But you know, we've got a lot of chemistry, you and me."

"There is no chemistry, Wade," she said. She found the box, put a Gauloise in her mouth, and lit it with her father's Ronson. Maybe she could light her breath on fire. That would make him think twice. "I drank half my body weight in tequila, that's all."

"We should try sometime without that." He grinned. "Nobody's ever complained." She was afraid he was going to adjust himself in his pants. Thank God all he did was brush his hair back with his hand.

Nobody ever complained? Girls were kind. No one ever told him, *I could barely stay awake. If only you'd come faster, I could have ignored it altogether.* Girls were born knowing how destructive the truth could be. They learned to hold it in, tamp it down, like gunpowder in an old-fashioned gun. Then it exploded in your face, on a November day in the rain.

Conrad, the Famous Movie Director, comes home to perfect Sixties house and his girlfriend, Elena. He's upset about problems on the film he's working on, and she listens, saying nothing, mysterious and haunted. It was even in the script. *Mysterious and haunted.* "Think *Belle de Jour,* Josie," was how Jeremy described it. "Like *Blow-Up* meets *Belle de Jour.*" She saw it perfectly. Antonioni buttfucking Buñuel in Hitchcock's basement apartment.

They blocked the scene, and then shot it. She

liked being Elena, it was interesting, she could play with it — she'd never bothered much about one of her characters before. She'd just been the Girl. But Elena had little rooms you could walk into, the coldness behind the mask of her beauty, the edginess behind that. *Blah blah blah,* the Conrad character ranted, about his adversaries at the studio and how they were trying to take his film away from him, as Elena watched, pretending to listen. Josie could feel her, watching, not like a lover, but like a leopard contemplating its next meal. She could feel Elena's remove. Elena was the star of a very private movie, herself as director, actor, and sole audience. All Elena's admiration was for herself. She knew that's how Elena got off in bed — she would watch herself getting laid in the mirrors of a man's eyes.

Suddenly Wade was on her, his smell of leather and musk, his fat tongue in her mouth. She gagged, struggled, pushed him away. The feel of his tongue, the foreign taste. She wanted to spit.

"Cut!" Jeremy yelled. "What? What was that?"

Her face was red, she could feel it hot and prickly under her makeup. She'd fucked up the whole scene. But her mouth still knew Michael's kiss. The way he would run his tongue along the inside of her downturned upper lip, or just brush her mouth with his. This was like eating garbage. *Since when did you mind eating garbage?* But she did. Surprisingly, something or someone in her did not want to anymore. She thought furiously. "Listen, she's not really in love with this guy. It's the other guy, what's his name, Franco, that she wants. She can fake it until he kisses her."

"Oh, Gawd . . . now you're having ideas?" Jeremy looked at his watch. "Listen, Josie, I appreciate the insight, it's terribly important to me and all, but we've got a long night. Can you just do it?"

Of course she could do it. It was only a movie, just a goddamn movie, what difference did it make if fucking Wade stuck his tongue down her throat or up her ass, she'd already slept with him. What did she think she was betraying that hadn't already been betrayed? It was just a body. *It was just a body.* She had always had such a sense of that. But not now. It wasn't just a body anymore. It had once been loved. Her body. Hers.

"She's forgotten about Franco. This scene is about her being totally into Conrad," Wade said.

The actor was pouting, like any man whose kisses hadn't been received with ardor and gratitude.

Jeremy looked from Josie to Wade, she could tell he was weighing who it would be easier to blow off, her or the actor. Jeremy sighed and turned to Wade. "Look, maybe a little more *romanza,* yeah? That'll set Conrad off from Franco. Not so much full-frontal attack. I think that's legitimate, don't you?"

Wade struggled to contain his masculine ego, to pretend it was only artistic differences, not a girl who obviously wanted to vomit because he'd kissed her. "I was only doing it the way it's written."

"Okay, let's be a little flexible, people. Take two."

She still had to eat garbage, but at least it wasn't being forced down her throat. She thought it wasn't so bad being Elena, people listening to her for a change, being in possession — of her body, of a certain power. She didn't know what else Elena had that she didn't have, she was looking forward to finding out.

They broke around two for dinner. Just the look of the pizzas made her ill, their red splatter and stringy white cheese, grease pooling at the top. Gil and the Bobs scarfed down their slices like grinning hyenas. The little tellerman, Mr. Cairo, had brought a carton of yogurt from home. He ate meticulously, scraping his underlip with the spoon, like a mother feeding a good baby, glowing with excitement about being on a real movie set. Wade lectured her about the difference between Conrad and the dangerous Franco, whom he also played, while Jeremy went over a blocking with Sergio, dripping grease on the pages. Sergio glanced across the table, ignoring the blonde in the zebra pants and the willowy brunette, both bristling with the stress of romantic contention, sending Josie sexual messages with his bedroom-soulful eyes. She wanted to go over there and kick the crap out of him. Sergio was a man in a candy store who was never hungry. She wanted to tell him that love was something people lived for, even died for. It wasn't a chocolate cherry you ate half of and put the rest back in the box.

Wade wouldn't shut up, and her head hurt. She went out into the living room, got her bag, and swallowed three aspirin with a swig from her can of Seven Up. Outside, she glimpsed a coyote trotting across the grass from the wild part of the slope onto the brightly lit dichondra. She held the cold soda can to the knots in her forehead. The gray long-legged beast stopped and gazed right at her. A small head, pointed muzzle. Its gold eyes were crazy and fearless. Hunting up its midnight meal of Chihuahuas and overfed cats. It frightened her, how boldly it stared. What was wrong with it that it wasn't afraid?

She waited, and so did the coyote. What did it want? Why was it staring at her like that? She felt a chill. Was she supposed to lope off with it, off on four legs, into the wild, like in one of Shirley K.'s Castaneda books? Maybe it was a witch. Maybe it was Fate. Like Elena's destiny, meeting her out on Old Topanga Road. Maybe it was the message she'd been waiting for. All this time, some sign he was near. "Michael?" she whispered. "Michael?"

She cracked the door, slowly, afraid it would come right into the house. The glass slid easily on its tracks. "Michael?"

She stepped out onto the grass, just a few yards from the doglike creature. It wanted to tell her something. She could feel it. "What is it?" For the longest time, they stood in the misty cold, staring at each other, like a whisper of the true world.

Then Jeremy came crashing into the living room behind her, his booming voice. "You're going to love this, Josie, it's totally brill."

The coyote broke its gaze, started, and trotted away.

"No," she called out, but it was leaving, out past the irradiated blue of the pool and down into the brush on the far side. "Come back." Its tail disappearing into the night.

"Josie, come hear this," Jeremy yelled.

The last of him. She'd finally had a sign, and then fucking Jeremy had to fuck it up. She turned back mechanically into the room. She wanted to die.

"Rick?"

"Yes, I'm here." The neat little man with his small hands and feet, the gold chain around his wrist.

Jeremy held up a sheet of paper, scrawled over with notes and spotted with grease, a dream sequence he'd concocted, she couldn't follow a word he said.

"He's Death, come to settle her account. Get it?" He made quotation marks with his fingers in case she didn't. "'Settle her account'? God, I'm such a genius. No no, hold the applause." He shoved the shaggy blond hair from his eyes. It fell right back in.

They used the same setup as for the Conrad shot, the same blocking. He pushed the little tellerman into position. "Stand right here." He tapped the spot with his foot, Conrad's mark, noted with duct tape. "Give Elena the envelope. All you have to say is, 'I'm from the head office.' Got it?"

"'I'm from the head office, I'm from the head office.' Oh, I know I'm going to mess this up, I just know it." Mr. Cairo's birthmark flamed even redder. Poor little tellerman. Rick the bank teller had no idea why this was all happening, as Bob One measured the distance from the lens to his birthmark. He was shaking his hands in panic.

"It'll be fine, you'll see," Josie finally said, the way Michael used to say it when she started feeling sad. When she was afraid, he could always calm her when he wanted to. How good that had felt. When he still wanted to. She gazed at this poor little man, the bank teller, visiting this cold woman in the cold glass house. "Her account's overdrawn. She thought she had plenty of money, but she'd spent it all and more. You're cutting her off."

Mr. Cairo nodded gravely. He knew about that, all right. "Shouldn't he have a briefcase?" he asked. "He would have a briefcase if he went to see her in person, wouldn't he?"

Of course he would have a briefcase. Of course he would. What was scary was how this movie was starting to make sense. She'd gone beyond tired, she was in the Zone, where everything made sense, in a surrealistic way. Coyotes, and the Bank Teller of Death and his Briefcase of Destiny. "Gordo has a briefcase. Gordo, can Tellerman use the Samsonite?"

Gordo looked up from the couch where he sat on the phone, scribbling some figures, the ashtray overflowing with butts. "Just don't mess with it, okay?"

Once the prop was in his hand, Mr. Cairo seemed to find himself. The Great Teller, coming to Settle Her Account. *Get it?* Like goddamn Fellini. The zebra-pants blonde put a piece of paper in a big envelope for him to hand her, and once the Bobs cut some of the lights and Sergio changed the filter on the lens to blue, Jeremy walked them through the scene once more. "And if there's something you're not sure about," Jeremy stooped over the teller, his arm around the small man's shoulder, "just stay in character.

Don't stop. And for God's sake don't look into the camera."

Rick nodded, holding his envelope, putting it into the briefcase and taking it out, balancing the open hardsider on his knee, practicing saying his line and then handing her the deadly notice.

They took their places, Josie on the couch, the little man by the front door, ready to enter her dreams. Jeremy called, "Action," and the teller moved to his mark, clinging to Gordo's battered briefcase. He stared at Josie with his bulgy brown eyes, sweating in great rolling drops, counted to five as Jeremy told him to do. Then he whispered his line. "I'm from the head office."

Serious, and so nervous, this little Death in his tasseled loafers. She could feel Elena, watching him through her eyes. He looked like a bug to her. So far beneath her she couldn't be bothered to crush him. "I'm sorry, you must be mistaken," she said, in a tone so much like Meredith's. Melodious, icy. Yet at the same time, she knew, under the curtain of her certainty, there was no mistake. She became even haughtier when she knew she was wrong.

He handed her the envelope.

She opened it. Inside was just a piece of scratch paper Gordo'd used to work out some figures, but she imagined it was another piece of paper, another overdrawn account. An overdraft of the worst sort. *I hope you find someone who can meet your needs better than I could.* She'd overdrawn her account, all right, down to the last penny and beyond. The tellerman knew. The head office had it all on file. Death's little bureaucrat in a crisp white shirt was here to tell her it was over. Account closed.

She folded herself onto the leather couch like an accordion receding between its two plates. She pressed her hand to her forehead, fighting panic. "Maybe it's a mistake."

He dropped his eyes to the gold chain circling his chubby wrist, rotated it with the hand that held the briefcase. "You can talk to management," he ad-libbed.

"You're from the head office. You can do something." She was cornered, she needed a friend. She felt Elena's fear, suddenly exposed, and immediately covered it up — everything was fine, under control. Smiling, showing off her mouth, her legs, the silky hose whispering against itself. "I know you can help me." She stood, slowly, coming close to where Death's tellerman stood on his mark, fearing to fall out of frame. She fingered his lapel. "You can do it for me."

He stiffened. "I'd lose my job," he said starchily. *Faggot.* He wasn't interested in her legs, the flirt of her eyelashes.

The way he said it infuriated her. Death didn't care about sex, about love, human weakness. It had what it wanted, a toupee and a gold chain bracelet, tasseled loafers and a part in the movie. She never thought Death would be so petty. It had Michael, this vain little creature, and for what. "You love this, don't you. Playing with us all. You get your little scrap of power, that's what you care about. You — bureaucrat."

She could see the sting of humiliation on his prissy face, and knew she was right "You don't have to get personal, miss."

"You think this isn't personal?" She held out the paper. *I hope you find someone . . .* Her voice rising. "There's nothing more personal." Tears, her eyelashes unpeeling, the liner running. She reached out and slapped him, hard, in the face.

The Teller of Death's eyes opened wide, he turned on his heel and left, Gordo's briefcase in his hand.

"Cut!" Jeremy yelled. "Oh Josie, you angel."

Josie walked past Jeremy and the stricken Mr. Cairo in the foyer rubbing his cheek, out of the flat front doors into the surrealistic night. She climbed up the dark street to her car and let herself in, and sat, listening. There was nothing but silence, the distant noise from the Strip. She howled, stretching her face up to the sky, but the only response was from dogs across the street, breaking into furious salvos. She fished in the ashtray for a roach, but found nothing. Her fingertips were black and she wiped them across her forehead, like the Catholic kids on Ash Wednesday. *Forgive us . . .*

Of course Jeremy would have to use it in the movie. Nothing escaped the movie. The movie was the black hole in the universe where everything went in but nothing came out.

The Mysterious Phone Call. Elena sat in the white leather reading chair with an art magazine. Her legs in their slick white boots crossed on the footstool, the shot was all about her legs. The set phone rang, like the clamor of a bad conscience. She lowered her legs, the whisper of nylon, the slight animal smell of the raw silk of her suit, the glide of the pearls she'd found at a yard sale, as she walked elegantly to the couch. Picking up the sculptured Sixties handset from the coffee table, she answered, "Yes?" But there was no one. "Who's there, please?" No one.

She returned to the reading chair, crossed her legs Elena's showy way, the top parallel to the lower, at a perfect diagonal. She was a girl who played to the back of the house in an empty room. As she flipped through the magazine, she paused at a painting of a boy standing in a rubber pool, masturbating. The light like the light from the pool outside, lurid and underlit. *None of us is quite himself these days,* she thought, her own audience.

The phone rang again. She crossed impatiently. "Hello? Who *is* this?" Again, no one. She hung up slowly, then suddenly reached for it again, sensing it was about to ring, though it didn't. She drew her hand back and waited, calm but nervous under the calm. Like a painting they'd seen once in Venice Beach. It was a big abstract oil that was just green stripes. She never understood art like this, but Michael explained, "It's not a green painting, see? It's a red painting under a green one." He pointed to the edges, where the green didn't quite cover the red.

That was Elena. Red under green. Her rawness just visible around the edges.

She sat still as a cat, her whole body listening, motionless but for the tip of its tail, never taking her eye off the phone. Her number was unlisted. No one knew she was here, she had no friends, only the Movie Director, whom she was fattening for the kill. Yet someone knew she was here. Maybe they were watching right now through those plate windows. She looked up and saw herself, her reflection on their print-free surface, the corona of blond hair, the couch, the navy suit *Made in Hong Kong.* Perfectly poised. Red under green.

Someone was trying to get through. *Remember me?*

She didn't want to remember. Elena had it good. A cushy house, an important boyfriend. She opened the box on the table, full of cigarettes, Kents. Even the ciggies were period. She put one in her mouth, and flicked the free-form lighter, knowing with certainty that people who would fill a vintage box with vintage cigarettes would keep the lighter filled. It sparked and lit. She inhaled and stood, graceful and controlled as a leopard on a leash, and walked to the windows.

Left foot, right foot, with the slight crossover of a runway model. Elena didn't miss a trick.

Her reflection in the plate glass. A woman who had overdrawn her personal account in the worst way. She'd been skating along the surface, imagining nothing would touch her. But the end was coming. She was pounding away on a piano, when children were sealed in the walls.

He loved you. And you killed him. How could you have forgotten so soon?

And there was her face, smooth and untroubled, a face that could shoot a man in the heart and leave him bleeding on a sidewalk in November. She wanted to hurt her, make it real. *You bitch.* She banged her face into the glass. She didn't know she was going to do it, but then she did it again. *You evil cunt.* Now she wanted to cut that face, with glass edged with green. It felt crazy good. She knew she shouldn't, the glass could break, but she couldn't stop. She thought someone would stop her, but nobody did. Bang. Bang. Finally, it didn't break, and it hurt, and she'd exhausted her fury. She pressed her arms against the glass, cradling her head, smoothing back her hair, and she smoked the rest of the cigarette.

"Cut!"

And everybody clapped. As if it was a goddamn performance. She could have put her
head through and nobody would have lifted a
finger. She was in trouble here. On the high wire
wearing nothing but a tutu, holding a parasol,
over the eightieth floor.

Jeremy threw his arms around her, picked her
up, twirled her around. "My God, Josie! Ab-so-
fucking amazing! Now that's acting!"

She wriggled and kicked until he put her
down. Acting? Was that what it was?

Talking, everybody talking at once. She knew
she shouldn't cry, her eyes would take a half
hour to repair. She concentrated on getting the
end of the cigarette to her trembling lips. Jeremy was framing the reflection in the glass
with his fingers formed into double L's, imagining the reverse shot. Wade, his hair dark for
Franco, the alter ego, came up and whispered,
"Fantastic, Josie."

She smiled and backed away. He shouldn't
even stand near her. Her life had become a stage
tilting toward the edge, she didn't know what
she would do next. She shouldn't be allowed to
walk around. She might hurt someone.

She went back to the bedroom and closed the

door, sat at the dressing table. In the mirror was a face Michael would have recognized, spectral, all in pieces. The eyes too big, the forehead too high. She was seeing it as he had, everything was broken. The brunette came in with some ice in a bag. "I was holding my breath the whole time," she said.

Josie pressed the ice to her forehead with her left hand, touched the lashes with the pinkie of her right. She was going to have a whacking big bruise, but it wouldn't show until later. Like everything. She pulled out the voddy and had a shot, eyeing Elena's face, that mask. And her own face underneath, also a mask. And under that? What was under that, Jeanne of Montmartre? Daisy Mae? Something hideous, that Michael would paint in the mirror? Maybe you just kept peeling and never got down to the real face, maybe it just got smaller and smaller until there was nothing at all.

22
Nick

It was noon by the time she arrived home, her nerves jangling like a great set of keys. One more scene, always just one more. She wished she hadn't done those white crosses, even though it was how she always got through those long shoots. Wired was the last thing she wanted to be. She pulled the noose on the gate and walked down to the house. As she neared the bottom, she slowed, stopping before the door. Something in her didn't want to go inside, as if there were something terrible waiting for her. Ridiculous. She forced herself to open the door. An empty living room with four empty

walls, nothing to be afraid of. *Get it together,
Josie,* she could hear Pen's voice in her head.
*Don't go fucking psycho on me, okay? We'll go
to the Rose Bowl, we'll buy some new fucking
stuff. It ain't pretty but you'll live.*

She was exhausted, she'd been up some
twenty-eight hours now, she needed some
sleep. She sat on the blue couch and smoked a
ciggie, staring out the windows at the flat light,
overcast, a weird greenish tinge to the sky, like
an old bruise. She thought she heard something
coming down the stairs outside. Damn it. She
felt so exposed in there, suddenly. She half rose,
listening, but then she didn't hear it. She got up
and opened the door, but everything was the
way it usually was, the splintered stairs, the peeling pipe-railing, the giant birds-of-paradise, purple and vaguely mocking. She closed the door
and locked it. Though the door itself would give
way to one well-placed kick.

The windows suddenly looked so raw without curtains. As if they had never moved in. They
used to love it like that, but now all those houses
on the opposite hill stared, without compassion.
"What are you fucking staring at?" She got her
purse and went into the kitchen that was less
exposed, sat in the breakfast nook with the

cutout hearts, and drank the last of the vodka, wishing she'd put away something before the shoot. She should have known she'd be like this, a night shoot. What she wouldn't give for one of those Percocets now. Almost worth going in for some emergency dental work. She thought of the Diazepam bakery, but it was too early, the stone-faced Salvadoran didn't come in until five.

She missed the painting of her cooking that always hung there, above the nook. Everywhere, the ghosts of the vanished objects glared — missing paintings, absent china, furniture, along with the boy who made them, bought them, loved them. *What isn't there.* She didn't want to look at any of it anymore, she hated this place, she should move, if only she had somewhere else to go, but she didn't want to see anyone, explain anything. She retreated to the bedroom, where Montmartre still covered the walls. *La Bohème.* Lucky that Meredith hadn't figured out how to steal the walls. When she did, no doubt she'd be back, and the walls too would disappear, the whole house, folded up and carried away.

She drew the felt curtains and lay in the fusty bed, willing sleep, the bed where he'd lain with his headaches, his mind grinding like a mill, just like this, grinding him away. She wanted the grinding to stop, the clocks. The Duke of the Dark Castle with his frozen hands. She had to sleep. She needed a pill, Christ, something that would knock her out cold, hide her in sweet oblivion. Compared with her, Michael was brave. He always moved toward the thing he was afraid of. Sitting in that chair, night after night, looking right into its face. Painting it in the mirror. When she couldn't stand much at all. If only she could make it just stop.

She went out and phoned the house on Carondelet, but nobody was home. She called Tilly's Cafe but Pen wasn't there either. Genghiz answered at the salon on Melrose, Shirley was there but she had her hands in color, could she call Josie back? She tried the pay phone at the Teriyaki Oki Dog, a boy answered it, Matt somebody, but she didn't know anyone who was eating there. She finally got hold of Paul at Cashbox, he didn't have anything better than Sudafed. She washed dishes, she folded and restacked her clothes, mopped the kitchen floor, made the bed. Shirley never called back. At three in the afternoon, she put her dress back on and drove over to the Fuckhouse.

It was a broad-porched, two-story Prairie-style

house on Franklin Avenue, built in the 'teens for a big, prosperous family, but the block had declined considerably since those old dirt-road, pepper-tree Hollywood days. Making what seemed to her to be a thunderous amount of noise, she clattered up the wooden steps, past the broken furniture on the porch and through the unlocked front door. In the living room, a boy she didn't know with spiky red hair sat on the couch watching a nature show on TV with the sound off, listening to Dead Kennedys. On-screen, an alligator was eating a heron. The house smelled of garbage and cigarettes. The ashtray had overflowed onto the coffee table, but she didn't live here anymore, she didn't give a damn. "Where's Nick?"

"He's not up," the boy said, then finally turned his head, saw her in her newly bleached hair and the Pucci dress. "But I'm here."

Josie checked in the kitchen to see if anybody was in there, Hector or Robbie slurping down a first mug of resinous coffee, but only the cockroaches were up, busy in the sink, feasting off the dirty dishes in their bath of filthy water. Back copies of the *Weekly,* old *Creem* and *Crawdaddy, Puke,* buried the wobbly table. Bags full of beer cans and bottles rested by the back door, waiting for someone to turn them in for cash when money was tight. She'd once lived like this. Had even thought it glamorous, the bands, manic boys and outrageous girls, and she had been the homecoming queen, a sort of Chelsea Girl in the movie of her mind.

She heard the water come on upstairs, someone in the bathroom taking a shower, and she climbed the bare wooden steps, white boots clattering on each step. She wondered how late they had all gotten home. The walls were covered with spray paint, drooling down the dirty white surface, *NO GOD. WHO CARES? NO ONE HEARS YOUR CRIES*. She touched her own name in the stairway graffiti, *JoC,* and in the *C* a knifed heart. It seemed like another life. She walked down to the door at the end of the hall, plastered with stickers for bands and motorcycles, Nick's two chief loves, and opened it without knocking.

The sun tried to penetrate the red pull-down blinds that bathed the room in a spooky daytime glow. It smelled like seven days of sex and three of speed, and Nick was fucking some skanky brunette doggie-style in his rumpled bed, the mattress half-exposed where her grip on the sheets had pulled them away. His poor face looked harsh and thin and hagged out, but his body was tight as a wire, a body somebody should cast in hot metal.

She knew she should just close the door and let him finish, but she was feeling difficult, a prima donna, and yes she had to admit it irked her to see her ex fucking such a cow, reminded her that for Nick it didn't matter what pussy he got, it was all about as personal as a public toilet. So she threw a load of clothes onto the floor and sat on the butterfly chair with the tiger-stripe cover she had made for him when they'd been together, crossed her legs like Elena, and watched him do it, as if she were at the symphony. She lit a cigarette, threw the match on the floor.

"Watch me make her scream," he said. He changed his rhythm from slow to little fast jerks, then plowed all the way into her, holding a fistful of her dirty hair like a rider holding a horse's mane, and even now she knew what that would feel like, though she pretended she didn't, just an indifferent spectator. Sure enough, the brunette went from her deep-in-the-throat moans to a real earsplitting howl as she came.

Nick arched back and froze, gripping the

girl's ass so hard she'd probably have bruises, and then collapsed on top of her like a toad on a rock, then rolled over, his cock still hard in the red window light.

"Like her?" Nick asked, slapping her big ass. "There's enough for everybody."

The girl turned over. She recognized her, somebody's girlfriend, Tammy, Terri, she waited tables at Canter's Delicatessen. "Hi, Josie," she said, pulling the covers up over her big beach-ball tits, looking uneasy, as if she wasn't sure if Nick and Josie might have gotten back together again. *Trini.*

"Hey, Trini," Josie said. "Nick, I want to talk to you for a second."

Trini yawned, stretched, and snuggled down in the dirty covers for a postcoital snooze.

"So talk."

"Alone."

"You sat there and watched me fuck her, suddenly we've got secrets?" Nick said. "Gimme a ciggie."

Josie threw him one of her Gauloises. He pawed through the debris on the bedside table — it looked as if he hadn't cleaned since she left — found a cheap Bic lighter and shook it, struck the flint, took a drag, frowned. "Shit, what are these things?" He pulled a shred of tobacco off his tongue.

"Dried moose turds," Josie said.

"Yeah, I guess. So, what are you doing here, I thought you'd be all in mourning. *She walks the hills in a long black veil* and whatnot." Nick squinted against the harsh smoke, pushed his long stringy hair out of his hypothyroid blue eyes. "You couldn't even talk to me that night at Lola's, you think I was too stoned to remember? You were really a bitch."

"Sorry."

"You should be," he said. "You can't take that shit out on me, I didn't even know the guy."

"He was beautiful," Josie said. "I was in love with him."

"Well, what am I, last night's cumstain?"

She said nothing. Next door, she could hear Robbie's hacking cough. "Hey, I didn't say it."

She read the hurt in Nick's jaded blue eyes. "So what do you want from me?"

"Who said I wanted something?" Josie rounded the cherry of her cigarette on the bottom of her boot.

"You're here, you must want something. You don't come over just to hang out." He flicked his ashes in the direction of the bedside table, the sheet up around his waist, his other hand reached out and appreciatively jiggled Trini's round haunch through the dirty sheet. "So what is it? No, let me guess." He looked her lazily up and down. "By the way, I love that outfit." She watched him stroke his skinny, tight-muscled chest, the small hard nipples. "You don't want to get laid, I guess, so it must be dope. Am I right, Bob? A little something to settle your nerves."

Needing something was such a drag. She wished she could tell him how bad it had been, the sleeplessness, the sense of something evil about to happen. Living with Michael's death all day and all night, replaying the fights they'd had, the sight of him at the morgue. How it must have been for him, pretending things were fine while he was weighing his life in his hands. She should have known, it was right in front of her, all around. She didn't know what was real anymore. She had stood over a sleeping woman and thought how easy it would be to kill her. She had almost put her head through a window. Coyotes were coming out of the hills for her. A little something to settle her nerves? "Something like that."

Nick blew red smoke up into the red room. "So what are you going to do for me, Josie T.?"

Asshole. She couldn't believe he thought he loved her. He loved Mickey's Big Mouths, and d'Andrea guitar picks. He had no idea what it meant to love someone. Just like her, before she'd met Michael. To think she had fucked him when Michael was in the house on Lemoyne, struggling with his darkness. Who was the skank of all skanks? Not Trini, that was for sure. "What, you want me to suck you off in front of all your friends, is that what you had in mind? Why would you even ask me a question like that?"

He dropped the butt in a beer can, by the hiss you could tell it wasn't quite empty. "Okay, dope it is. But you better not pull that shit anymore, like I'm some shit on your shoes." He threw the covers back, his small electrified body with the oversized cock, and moved his skinny, sinewy legs to the side of the bed, took his jeans off the floor and put them on. She never knew a boy in rock and roll who wore underwear. "I may not have gone to Harvard, but I didn't off myself. I didn't lay that on you. I do give a shit, ya know." He stood up, hitched himself inside his pants. "Although if you wanted to suck me off in front of all my friends, I wouldn't say no."

She drove him in her car over to his friend Red's on Fountain Ave, where he lived above the old market, the oldest building anywhere in Hollywood, two storied, wooden with a peaked roof, it looked like a feed store. She stayed in the car — Red didn't like Josie, from the time he was living with them at the Fuckhouse, freebasing off the electric coils on the kitchen stove. Well, what did he expect, he was a creep magnet, she couldn't live in a house with that kind of dealing going on, it was just too much, she'd made Nick kick him out. "Get me some barbs, as many as he's got, and some pot." She gave Nick fifty bucks.

"What do you want with the downs?" he asked. "Not that it's any of my business, but you're not thinking of pulling a Marilyn, are you?"

She hadn't been. Or not this minute anyway. "Well, it's not any of your business. But no, I just need something to sleep. I'm so wired I can hardly blink."

He gave her an extrahard look, but went in with the cash. In a few minutes he came back with an envelope of reds and Nembies and the weed. They sat in the car and she rolled up a doob, lit it, and punched in the tape. Nick startled when he heard the opening notes. "What the fuck's that?"

"Rimsky-Korsakov," she said. "Elegy for Tchaikovsky."

He laughed, quickly, like he always did, his young face already lined. She could see how he would look at forty. "Roll over, Little Richard."

She felt the tension slide off with the first wave of the high, like sandbags she could let slide to the ground. She reached over and turned up the volume.

Nick adjusted the outside mirror toward him, examined his eyes, his stringy sandy brown hair. He fluffed the strands, gazed at the hairline. "You think I'm gonna go bald?" He angled the mirror a different way, craned his neck. "Hey, see that gray Olds? Just about five cars back? I swear I saw it when we left the Fuckhouse."

Nick's paranoia. He was famous for it, especially when stoned. He'd been busted twice, and now he was always seeing cops. She glanced in her own rearview mirror until she saw the car that bothered him, the gray American car. Though she was pretty sure it was just Nick, she tucked the dope under the seat anyway.

"Let's drive off, see what happens," Nick said.

She pulled away slowly from the curb, drove to the stop sign, no car following them. "Pot's just not your drug."

"Wrongo, baby doll," Nick said. "Here he comes."

The gray car crept along about half a block back. She drove down De Longpre, took a right on Las Palmas, left on Santa Monica, left on Cahuenga, and the Olds stuck like chewing gum. It was very quiet midweek in the winter, a bum asleep in the sun, two men in tight white jeans going into the Spotlight.

"One guy in the car," Nick said, still watching out the side mirror. "Flattop, he looks like fucking Joe Friday. You can lose him in the alley."

She turned left up the side street and up the alley past the Masque, dodging potholes, stacked wooden pallets, and a homeless guy with three mismatched dogs pissing on the wall, it was way too narrow for a whacking huge Olds to get through. She threaded her way to Vine via alleys, then made a series of fast turns, Selma to Argyle to Yucca to Gower, making sure he was gone before ascending the hill to Franklin. She stopped at the curb in front of the Fuckhouse, let Nick out. He leaned back in the door, his hair hanging around his gaunt face. "I'm serious if you wanted to stay here. And this ain't some kind of bullshit seduction."

"Thanks, Nick," she said.

He reached out and stroked her cheek with a rough guitar-calloused thumb. "Bye, Josie. You take care of yourself."

She drove back to Echo Park, shivering in her white vinyl boots and poly dress. That was exactly what you'd expect, a bust, to completely fulfill the Tyrell curse. First you lost Michael Faraday, then you went up to Tehachapi on a drug rap. Her daddy was right, you could never get a break in this world.

As she approached the house on Lemoyne, clinging by its toenails to the side of the hill, she had a sudden instinct to circle the block, the way she used to when she lived at the Fuckhouse, just to see who was out on the street before she parked and made her way back to the place. There it was, the gray Olds, down on Scott Road, parked in front of the elementary school. And Joe Friday nowhere to be seen.

He was no cop. She understood that now. If it had been about Red and the dope, how would he have known where she lived? *Five grand and you'd just disappear.* She swallowed, still feeling those hands around her neck, the rage in those fingers. She thought of her shoes by Meredith's bed. When your only son killed himself, that was enough to drive anybody over the edge. Hadn't it done that to her? Hadn't she stood right over Meredith's bed, thinking, *I could kill her right now.* What had she thought she was doing, going into the house in Los Feliz like that? How had she expected Meredith to react?

She hadn't thought about that at all, just wanted to hurt her the way she had hurt Josie, remind her that no one was safe. After all, the woman had come in and taken everything Michael had ever touched. But Josie hadn't thought through, hadn't considered how far Meredith would go. She'd thought a rich, glamorous woman like Meredith Loewy would be too civilized, would back off. Evidently she had been mistaken. Maybe she should have poured something in that sleeping ear while she could. Elena would have.

23
Stalked

Josie stood in the dim back hall of the Lotus Room, her drink on the tray underneath the phone. Phone numbers and erotic graffiti and flyers for bands covered the Pepto-Bismol pink wall. The idea that Meredith could hate her this much, that she wanted her dead, like Michael, a body in the morgue. No, it was crazy, her imagination was going wild, she hadn't slept in so long. And yet, the memory of Meredith on the phone, whispering *five grand and you just disappear.* Those enormous hands closing around her throat, the fury in them, her body remembered — the glands in her neck, the tendons, even now. Her own bizarre thoughts. She focused her Veruschka eyes and stared at the phone dial, tried to think what to do next.

Every time someone came out of the bathroom, the disinfectant smell billowed, gagging her, but at least the bar was filling up, the afterwork crowd stopping in from downtown for a weak drink and a botulistic plate of Chinese short ribs. They wouldn't try to get her in here, not with all the City Hall types around, people with connections. She took the change out of her purse with a freaky thin, Blue Period hand, set the coins up on the shelf in piles, dropping several onto the floor in the process. Her hands were so cold, they wouldn't bend right. Her mind was as stiff as her fingers, trying to close around the idea that someone was out there with a job to do, and the job was to end the life of Josie Tyrell.

Would he shoot her, or just grab her on the way to her house and strangle her with a wire, the way they did in the movies? She was shaking uncontrollably, she needed to get the goddamn money into the phone. She took a swallow of vodka, and put the coins into the slot, hearing them drop inside. She dialed Pen, but there was still no one home, the ring ring ring like the universe's answer to any cry for help. There was never anyone home. Only the neat gentleman with death in his eyes. She let it ring, hoping against hope that Pen was at the door with her key, she might run in any minute. But she didn't. Josie hung up and the money came chiming back into the coin return. She struggled not to cry, not to break down, she had to do something, she couldn't freak now. A man went into the bathroom, giving her a long look.

She turned away from the stink of the men's room, called information, and got the phone number for Tilly's. She tried to memorize it long enough to dial the numbers, repeated it over to herself, what she thought she heard. She was infinitely grateful to hear Tilly's growly smoker's voice on the line. She asked for Pen, hearing Dave the cook yell something in the background, the crash and bang of dishes, and Pen came on.

"Pen, I think Michael's mother's taken out a hit on me. I'm at Sammy's and I don't know what to do. She threatened to do it and I was out with Nick and we saw this guy, and now he's here at my place."

Pen sighed wearily, as if she had been talking about invaders from Neptune. "Oh, fuck, Josie, don't get psycho. Be reasonable. You know she's not going to take out a hit on you, you know that, don't you? Have you slept at all?"

"No, but it's for real, I swear."

"Go take a pill, sleep it off. You shouldn't have taken on this movie, I told you not to. You need to just fucking kick back. It's too fucking much. Give yourself a goddamn break why don't you?"

Josie knew what it sounded like — like Nick having a paranoid fit. Not even Pen believed her, it sounded crazy even to herself. "Fine. But if I show up dead, tell the cops it was Meredith Loewy, okay?"

She could hear the cook shout, *Number three, hey, stop jerking off over there.* "Okay, I will. Now you swear you'll go to sleep, okay? I'll call you when I get off. You're going to be okay, Josie," Pen said. "It's a bad day, that's all."

Josie hung up the phone, lit a cigarette, leaned against the pink sticky wall across from the phone trying to gather her thoughts. Down the hall, the Buddha altar by the kitchen glowed in the light of the flickering candles in their red votive cups, the potbellied deity surrounded by tangerines and incense, things printed in gold on red paper. She didn't know how to pray, especially to some collection of dime-store knickknacks, but she tried to. *Please, let someone fucking care about this.* She wouldn't call Nick, she didn't want to go back there anymore. It would be too fucking easy to start all over again. She called Phil Baby at Otis and also at home, she called Henry. She called Shirley at Genghiz's. Paul and Ben's apartment phone had been disconnected. Well, the universe had spoken. There was no one left to turn to.

On the wall by the phone, under Cassiopeia's phone number, someone had written, *Man cannot stand very much reality.* How true that was. She tilted her head back against the wall, trying to keep the tears inside. What she wanted more than anything was to take a few of those reds in her purse and check out. Just for a little while. But she didn't want to nod out at Sammy's, slide down to the sticky floor, her legs spread like an obscene doll's, she had to keep on top of this, she had to live out this moment as she had lived out every other goddamn thing since Michael's death, second by excruciating second, it seemed an impossible mass to climb over, a pathless mountain range.

Why did Meredith have to hate her so much? They had both lost Michael, it should have drawn them together, not set them tearing at one another like the dogs her brother Tommy and his friends used to set on each other in the tow yard after dark. Snarling and ripping at each other, you couldn't help but hear them. She wanted to be with Meredith the way they'd been that night in Los Feliz, talking about the good things about him, when she'd gotten to see the human side of her. She'd only wanted that woman to like her. But Meredith had decided from the very first instant exactly who and what Josie Tyrell was, what she wanted from her son. And Michael had made sure of that, waving her in his mother's face like a cape before a bull.

She drank her watered vodka, staring at the phone, the constellation of messages and numbers and scrawled genitals. The Loewys and the Faradays. People like that. The whole world was theirs, why did they have to fuck with people like her? Couldn't they just be satisfied with ruling the planet? No. Look at Michael, he had everything, but it had combined inside him like a lab experiment gone wrong. It festered, it grew, it took away everything good and left him with a yawning emptiness she could never have filled. Look at Meredith. Aside from her music, what was she anyway? Just a frightened, middle-aged woman with money in the bank, money that couldn't keep her safe, money that couldn't keep her son alive, that couldn't do anything but call out more death.

She kept watching the door into the hall, for a man in a flattop. A girl came down the hall, a short, wide dyke with pins in her nose and her ear, a chain between them, her hair in a short shaved Mohawk. Josie recognized her, she was a drummer in a dyke band that played sometimes at the Hong Kong Café. She stopped at the phone, saw the drink and the coins and the purse. Josie quickly pushed off the wall, got her hand on the receiver first, wondering if the girl would punch her. "Sorry, I've got just one more call."

The girl heaved a sigh, but made a gentlemanly gesture of "you first," though she made no move to go, propping herself up on the facing wall, her big drummer's arms akimbo. Under her gaze, Josie turned away and put coins in the slot, concentrating not to drop any, and dialed.

"Loewy residence," the Spanish maid answered.

"Yes, Meredith Loewy please. Tell her it's Josie Tyrell." She stood taller, under the Mohawk girl's scrutiny. Straight girls weren't necessarily losers.

She heard the maid's steps walking away, listened hard for how the conversation would play. *It's that girl on the phone.* Her boss would know which one. She tried to imagine Meredith's reaction to the fact that she was still alive, irritation well concealed, red under green. Would she even talk to her, or would the maid lie, say Meredith wasn't home? Some music was playing in the background, strings, something sweet and whipped creamy, Mozart maybe, or the other guy, Haydn. Steps again, the rattle as the phone was retrieved.

"Josie?" Meredith said. She sounded surprised to be hearing from her.

Josie took a sip of vodka, the ice trembling against the side of the glass.

"Josie?" Meredith said impatiently. "Is that you?"

"Thought I'd be dead by now?" She looked over at the drummer, who stuck out her lower lip in a gesture of *that's a new one.* Now Josie was glad she was there, in case there was trouble, she looked like someone who could handle herself in a fight.

A long pause then, she could hear Meredith clearing her throat. "Why, were you planning it?"

Josie tugged at the metal-encased phone cord,

imagining how it would feel wrapped around her neck. "Gray Olds? Guy with a flattop?"

"What *are* you talking about?"

All her fear turned to anger, with just that snotty emphasis, the better-than-everybody cadence. "Five grand, remember? Couldn't you think of something better to do with that money, like clean out your pool? Killing me won't bring him back, Meredith."

There was a silence on the line. "You really think I'm capable of that?" She could hear Meredith's careful breathing. "I was just talking. My God, you really think I could — Really, Josie, your imagination is getting the better of you."

Josie frowned, looking up at a white-shirted City Hall type coming out of the men's room, zipping up his fly. The heavy drummer girl crossed her arms, as if to protect Josie from his interference, or maybe just protecting her place in line. He scuttled back down the hall.

"So who's this joker who's following me around, Santa Claus?" She could hear the Chinese cook in the kitchen yelling at someone, rapid fire. The Buddha grinned mockingly. "I want you to know I told people. If anything happens to me, they'll know it's you."

"Oh, Josie, you didn't." It came quick, defensive. Like it was civilized to hire a hit man, but barbaric to let people know she'd done it.

"You didn't think I'd let you get away with it."

She heard Meredith heave a shuddering sigh that had levels to it, like a house running down-hill. "You think I hired someone to kill you. You're insane."

"Maybe," Josie said. "But listen, anything hap-pens to me, they go straight to the cops. I fall down the stairs, eat a bad sandwich, you're on the hook." Her punk audience nodded approvingly.

"All right," Meredith said. "All right. I did hire someone. But not to kill you, please, try to be-lieve me."

She just wasn't sure. At the end of the day, she did not want to think that this woman hated her enough to want her dead. It was one thing to suspect someone you knew wanted to murder you, but another thing to have it be real. A very, very big difference. But she had been Elena. She knew it was possible to be that cold.

"Josie, try to understand. You broke into my house. You came into my room while I was sleeping. You . . . let's say you seemed some-what unstable. I hired an investigator to follow you. I just wanted to know where you were, that's all."

It sounded reasonable. Meredith Loewy wouldn't jeopardize everything she had to do something to Josie. Would she? But Meredith hadn't thought twice of robbing the shit out of her. On the other hand, would Meredith have any idea how to set it up, whom to call? She didn't exactly hang out in the right crowd. Josie would probably have more success in that area.

Still, reasonable didn't mean true. Just because murder for hire seemed overly dramatic didn't mean Meredith hadn't done it. Michael had blown his brains out. Anything could happen. Reason was seductive, it gave the appearance of truth, but they were smart, Meredith and her family. They knew just how to bend the truth to suit themselves. Josie felt herself back off from belief like a dog that smelled poison in a chunk of meat. "Just because I didn't go to college doesn't mean I'm an idiot," Josie said. "If you were really afraid of me, you'd hire a bodyguard, not a private eye."

A Chinese woman in her fifties squeezed by. The punk girl had given up on the idea she would ever get to use the phone. Now she was just enjoying the drama. Meredith cleared her throat but said nothing. Mozart burbled in Los

Feliz, while out in the bar, the jukebox was playing Elvis, "All Shook Up."

"I can prove it," Meredith said. "Let me meet you somewhere."

"Why? So Flattop can come and finish the job?" Though she knew chances were slim he'd come blazing away at the Lotus Room. No, she wouldn't show and then he'd wait for her on the way to the car.

"You told all your friends, remember? I'm not planning on spending my golden years in prison. Orange isn't my color. Come on, Josie. Anywhere you say."

24
Lotus Room

Josie, on her second vodka, sat in the corner banquette where she and Michael had liked to sit, in the beginning. Their heads pressed together, making up stories about everyone. From here she could watch the door. She itched to take one of the reds, but this was no time for a blackout. She shook her hands, blew, and rubbed them together, trying to get some feeling back. All around her people were talking, laughing, their jackets hung on the back of their chairs. Nobody else seemed to be cold. She flexed her fingers, trying to get some of the stiffness out of them, they were so clumsy, she was spilling her drink. But as long as she stayed in the bath of colored lights from the Lotus Room's Chinese lanterns, nothing could hurt her. She could always get someone to walk her to her car. Like that big bus-driverish man with the salt-and-pepper hair, or the dyke drummer, watching her from the bar. How fast would a bullet be, she wondered. Would she even hear it?

She kept thinking about that night, when they sat around in the big living room, talking about Michael. It should have brought them closer. But Meredith was as unpredictable as her son, one minute they were friends and the next, she was ripping off her stuff, trying to get her killed. If Michael was here, what would he say about his mother now? *Please,* she prayed to the vacant universe, *don't let this be happening.* All she'd ever wanted was to be accepted by people she respected, and look where that had gotten her.

The Lotus Room door opened and closed, she watched each new figure, waiting for Flattop, or perhaps someone she hadn't even seen yet, but the black portal only admitted more civil servants in high-water pants and office workers dressed for success. When Meredith finally arrived, however, there was no missing her. Tall, wearing a sable brown coat and matching narrow pants, a turtleneck. She had forgotten how beautiful the woman was, even at her age. Her luminous eyes caught what light there was, and her skin glowed unnaturally, like she was some kind of phosphorescent fish. Even the drunks at the bar looked up from their Old Grand-Dads, astonished. She came into the room a few feet, blinking, trying to adjust to the light, peering through the gloom, ignoring the gazes of the men around her — no, more than ignoring them. Not even seeing them, as if they were just so many trees or bushes.

Josie didn't wave or help her, just watched Meredith hunting for her in the crowd. For some reason she found it intensely satisfying. When in the world had a Loewy ever looked for a Tyrell? She waited until the older woman found her. "Josie." Meredith slid into the banquette, her purse firmly wedged on her lap. She gazed around her, her clear eyes taking in the tables of civil servants in cheap loud jackets, the pulsing disco lights on the jukebox, the tables of early rockers, Willie Woo scolding someone at the bar, the TV turned to the news with the sound off, smiling Ronald Reagan, stern ayatollahs, something about the hostages. Jerry Dunphy's white hair like the crest of a wave.

"You know, I've been by here a thousand times, but I've never been inside. You look different," Meredith said. "Your hair."

Josie felt a flush of pleasure, automatic, it pissed her off. She dropped her eyes so Meredith wouldn't see it. Christ. "I'm on a movie."

"The dress is good too," Meredith said. "I used to have one just like it. Must be a collector's item by now."

Meredith had had a Pucci dress like this? She didn't want the woman to flatter her, and yet, she was flattered. Even now, she was glad Meredith could see she could be chic, put together, she had her own kind of glamour. Then furious at herself for caring what this woman thought, this woman who'd emptied her apartment, who'd walked in as if she owned the place, as if Josie was just a slight obstacle, a minor nuisance, a squatter in her own home. This woman who wanted her dead approved of her dress.

"Want it?" Josie asked. "You've got everything else that belongs to me."

The old waitress, Helen Chow, tiny and vivacious in an embroidered sweater, her black-dyed hair arranged on her head like something you'd see in a cake-decorating class, threw a napkin in front of Meredith and switched out the ashtray. "What can I get you gals?"

"I'll have a J and B on the rocks," Meredith said in her breathy, elegant voice.

"Another voddy." Josie drained her glass and put it on Helen's tray.

Meredith fingered the stained appetizer-and-drinks menu. "How's the food?"

"Diabolical," Josie said.

They watched Helen walk away on her tottery high heels. Meredith crossed her arms on the tabletop and gazed up at the lantern above and the table across, men in short sleeves and ugly wide ties, they looked like engineers from Water and Power. They'd been stealing glances at her, but quickly looked away as her gaze drifted over them, terrified of what might happen if she caught them staring. Like the Gorgon, who turned people to stone. "Did Michael ever come here?" Meredith asked.

"Lots of times." Charmed by its cheapness and its jukebox full of kitschy old music, and Willie Woo and Helen Chow. The rockers irritated him, though, Ben Sinister and David Doll. He thought they were ignorant, crass. The truth was, he was always uncomfortable with people his own age. He felt they judged him and so he rejected them first, and the fact that Josie knew them made him feel more of an outsider. So he came less and less, did his drinking at home in the chair by the window.

Helen brought their cocktails. Meredith took a sip of hers and made a face. "I don't think this is J and B."

Helen shrugged, unapologetic. "You want something else?"

"I never said this was a good place," Josie said, sipping her own drink.

"I suppose this will do," Meredith said.

They sat quietly and drank their weak drinks in the dark booth, Meredith's face stark in the light from the lantern over the table, like an old movie star shot in black-and-white, very high key, the sculpture of her brow and cheek thrown into relief. She traced a circle around the mouth of her glass, around and around, but it didn't make a sound. "Really, I'm surprised you didn't see the man before. You're not very observant." She put a manila envelope on the table, slid it to Josie.

Josie opened the brass claw, saw the thick packet of photographs and typewritten pages, and swallowed, feeling the tightness in her throat. How far someone would go. She had always underestimated that. She was still so naive, right off the turnip truck, Daisy Mae from Dogpatch. She spread the photos out on the table, not bothering to wipe off the wet and sticky surface, hoping it would ruin some of the expensive surveillance. She was amazed at how many there were. Her, coming out of her apartment, wearing the yellow coat, though it was gray in the photograph. Morning light, her breath in a cloud. Her on the movie that day in Topanga behind the wheel of the crushed BMW. Walking naked on the road. They were grainy, shot from a long way off, he must have been up on the hillside. Like a sniper with his gun. Here she was walking around the lake in Echo Park, wearing a hooded sweatshirt, looking like a monk. Her and Pen having coffee at that Scientology-run hamburger place on Fountain. Now what was that supposed to reveal? That she drank it black? That she was a lousy tipper? She felt flayed, gutted like a fish caught and cleaned right on the dock before it was dead. It felt just like when she got back and found her place stripped. Meredith thought she could get away with murder.

Here was Jeremy, coaching her, arm around her shoulder. Jeremy kissing her. Josie fought the urge to explain, to defend herself. If Meredith wanted to invade her life, she could bloody well guess what it all meant. *Your boyfriend Jeremy, the fake Englishman.* Her trying on clothes at Goodwill. It was like God, watching you. She wondered why people found this idea comforting, someone always watching, when it really made the world a giant prison camp, with God and his angels the warden and guards.

"And where's the one of you, stealing my fucking stuff? Look at this shit." She pushed the pile over to Meredith. "What's it prove except you're one controlling bitch. Did you find anything? I mean, what were you looking for?"

"You're the last piece of him left," Meredith said simply. "I needed to know you."

She flipped through the reports: *Subject meets white male, early twenties, Canter's Delicatessen. Subject attends concert with Hispanic female, Penelope Valadez, Palladium, Hollywood. Subject modeling, California State University, Long Beach; instructor Gloria Reyes.* Dates, times. It was a movie without sound, the movie of her own life, and only she knew the story. To Meredith she was a mystery to be solved, and no amount of detective work would solve it all. *You're not very observant.* But Meredith could look at these pictures all day and have no idea what she was seeing. How oddly fascinating, really, to be of such interest to another human being, her life such a riddle, and still, Meredith would never know the answer. But in the end, all people were like this, standing outside a telephone booth, trying to understand some stranger's conversation.

Stupid not to have known she'd been followed, and for such a long time. Like being raped while you were asleep. Her in Life Drawing at Otis, how had he gotten those? No one ever came in, only the models and students. In the photo, she looked painfully tired and thin. The strain was showing. Talking to Phil Baby after class, their heads close together, Christ, anytime someone touched her, the little man with the camera was there. No wonder Michael had been so eager to move to Echo Park, away from his mother's prying. Pictures of her and Pen sweating at the Elks Club, Pen laughing at something, Josie looking the other way, a glass halfway to her mouth.

"You're very photogenic," Meredith said, angling her neck to see the picture better, her thick dark hair falling forward. "I had no idea."

Josie couldn't help liking the compliment and

it made her angrier still. "Add that to the list of the things you know nothing about."

Meredith plucked a photograph from the mass and set it on top. "Like this?"

She should have known it was coming, but had not. The actor, Wade, coming out of the gate of her house. She had almost succeeded in forgetting about that. But here it was. She stared down into her hands, feeling like she would burst into flame. Michael had been dead for five weeks, and there she was already, fucking some actor. Josie leaned back against the banquette and closed her eyes. *It was a mistake, I was drunk, it's not what you think.* But what excuse could there be? Her throat hurt. She waited for Meredith to say something. *You slut, you unfaithful slag.* There it was, proof, what she had obviously been looking for, proof that Josie never really cared about him, that her love was a fiction, that she couldn't stay true to him, dead or alive. But when she opened her eyes, the older woman was just gazing down at the picture, sorrowfully. Wade in the sharp morning light. The sun on his strawberry hair, he looked so smug in his leather jacket.

Meredith's hand went to her own throat.

"This was the best you could find?" she whispered. Her voice hoarse as if it had been grated.

Did Meredith think she was the only one, that she had a lock on the mourning department? Did she think the only way to mourn was to stay home and play Brahms and walk in a rose garden? "He's dead no matter what we do," Josie said.

Meredith sagged back onto the banquette, stared up into the light. Her skin looked bruised. Her gaze dropped to the table, cluttered with images of Josie's days and nights, her friends and colleagues, Josie full face and in profile, Josie dressed and naked, Josie with this man and that one. "What was it I thought I'd find out?" Meredith said, picking up the shot of her at the Elks Club. "What did I think you were hiding?"

She felt sad to see the woman like this, so suddenly helpless and lost looking. It scared her worse than seeing her powerful and in control. If Meredith was lost, what did that make Josie? "You could have just called."

"You never pick up."

She thought of phones ringing, a city of phones ringing and no one picking up. A universe of people in need, and nobody answering.

"I think about dying," Meredith said, looking

into her drink. "I think about it all the time. I don't know what I have to live for now."

"I know the feeling."

The table of Water and Power engineers across the way burst into laughter, one had a bray like a donkey, high-pitched and silly. How strange, Josie thought, that people could still laugh like that. She felt like a Martian, all these people living their regular lives, having a laugh with their coworkers, stopping in for a little camaraderie before they went home to families or empty apartments, their cat and TV. Whereas this was her only comrade, the only person who understood just how empty a house could be.

"You have your music, that's not nothing."

Meredith sighed. "You know, I was about your age when my father killed himself. I don't know if Michael told you."

"He told me some," Josie said.

Meredith arranged her coat around her shoulders, the cold that only the two of them seemed to feel. "I'd been working with Rudolf Serkin at Curtis, just before he died." She leaned forward, elbows on the table covered with photos. "A very great pianist, one of the three greatest of his time. It was terribly important. Anyway, he was going to play with the Philadelphia Orchestra in

New York, Carnegie Hall. The Brahms Second. And he got sick, I don't remember with what, but he recommended me to Ormandy to replace him. I was all of twenty-one. One day's notice, the Brahms Second. It's a monster concerto. A huge responsibility."

All these names, floating like buoys in a sea of the things Josie didn't know. *Serkin* and *Ormandy* and *Curtis,* but she could understand that Meredith was her age and suddenly she was supposed to play at Carnegie Hall. It had to have been a super big deal.

"It was like something right out of an old movie, where the star twists her ankle and the girl gets her big chance. I was so nervous I threw up just before the concert, then went out and something took over. It was like being lifted up on wings. Harold Schoenberg called me a goddess. Hurok signed me the next day, and within a week, he'd organized a tour. It was like being in the nose cone of a rocket, the momentum, how fast it all came. Everything I'd worked for since I was four years old. Like breaking free of earthly gravity."

Josie imagined the glory of that moment, Meredith walking onstage, very straight and graceful with her dark hair and her pale skin, in

a green dress maybe, and sitting down to play at
the great black piano. Like a girl lion tamer. How
thrilling it must have been, to be suddenly so
successful, in front of everyone. Showing what
you had inside of you to the amazement of the
world. How daring Meredith had been, to go on
with one day's notice. Josie would never have
been able to do something like that, never. The
dizzying achievement.

Suddenly the light went out in Meredith's
face. She reached for her glass, drained it, shook
the ice, looking sadly down into its emptiness.
"My father shot himself a month later."

She could feel the woman's pain, even now,
after all this time. Could feel it across the wet
photos, the dark table. "Didn't he know?"

Meredith laughed bitterly, twirling the ice
with her long, smooth finger. "Sure he knew.
Couldn't even wait until I got home." The same
sardonic curve of lip that Michael had in his dangerous moods. "He always had to be the star. He
wanted to make sure I wouldn't enjoy it, that it
would always be about him." A tear ran down
Meredith's cheek, just one, sliding unstopped in
the bluish light.

Josie wanted to say something, but how did
you comfort someone whose father would do

something like that? Sometimes things that happened were just too solid to move, like some huge bookcase or black breakfront that had dug its legs into the floor over the years.

Meredith leaned her forehead on her hand, looking up at Josie, making no effort to hide her face. The water glistened on her eyelashes, her nose was red. She took the bar napkin and wiped her nose, spoke in her peculiar soft husky voice. "I couldn't even come back to LA, I just couldn't stand it. I didn't go to the funeral. I let his friends bury him, those old men. I had them close up the house for me. And I toured, just living in hotels or in people's homes like the Man Who Came to Dinner. I was playing with Von Karajan, with Solti, all the great orchestras, and I couldn't stand to be by myself in a room."

She hadn't even gone to her father's funeral.

"There were men, of course," Meredith said, signaling to Helen Chow, not a big wave like anybody else, just raising one finger, and then pointing to her empty glass. And Helen nodded. The code even worked here, at a dump like the Lotus Room. "Men are easy. I suppose I shouldn't begrudge you that. I know what it's like to be alone and to take someone just because you can." She turned the picture of Wade facedown, so all that showed was the stamp on the back, Fred Bauman Investigations, an address in Culver City. "Just because there's nothing inside."

Josie didn't want to think about Meredith sleeping with strangers, her aging body naked and vulnerable in a faceless man's embrace.

Helen came with another drink for Meredith. The older woman drank deeply, wiped her mouth on the back of her hand. "It was only when I fell in love with Cal that I suspected it was possible to live without this pain. I felt maybe I'd paid enough."

"Paid for what?" Josie asked. "You didn't kill him."

"Of course I did. In the Oedipal sense. I outshone him. So I had to be punished. Then Cal came along and I felt, maybe it was over. Maybe I'd paid enough. Maybe there was a chance at happiness." She drew in the wet on the table, five lines, the vertical bars, a musical staff. "We came back to LA. I reopened the house. We had Michael. For a little while, it looked like the curse had lifted." She began to place notes on the staff. "Then Cal left me, and I knew it would just be one disaster after the next until the day I died."

Michael had told her it was Meredith who left

Cal. She didn't know whom to believe, how you would know the truth. She tended to believe Michael, but Meredith had been there. Anyway, this was her story, and it was true for Meredith, part of the map of her own inner landscape. In a way, it didn't matter — who could tell where a rift between two lovers began? "But I always had Michael. Until you came along." She wiped out the staff and the music with a quick sweep of her hand.

As if the fact of her coming along would change anything. Meredith was like a cancer in-side Michael, one that had spread to every organ of his body. There was no chemo for that, no ra-diation treatment.

Josie thought of Meredith's life, the combina-tion of great wealth and talent, with a black thread of tragedy running through. Was it worth having the one if you had to suffer the other? And yet, she reminded herself, poor people had tragedy too, and they didn't get to play Carnegie Hall, travel the world with their picturesque agony, they didn't have a beautiful gift. They acted out their tragedies in trailers and dingbat apartments, shacks and slums, every day. Why were the tragedies of little people less profound than those of Meredith and Michael? What was it about having enormous advantage that made tragedy seem so much more tragic?

"I'm thinking of selling the house," Meredith said. "Getting the hell out of here, I could buy an apartment in New York. Or go back to Paris."

She would sell the house? Josie felt panic leaping up. The house was part of Michael. Her swim in the pool, the satin bedroom where they made love the first time. The famous people who had come through, Stravinsky and Hedy Lamarr. The way it smelled, the quality of the light. The beauty, the history. She couldn't sell it. Josie loved the house, everything about it, even its tragic moldiness. If Meredith sold the house, there would be no more Los Feliz, there would only be Echo Park and Launderland and Sammy's Lotus Room. "It won't help," Josie said. "What happened, happened. But the house —"

"It's a curse. Think how painful it is for me. I grew up there, you don't know what it was like, how wonderful it was, he knew the most creative, dazzling people. The way we lived . . . But he died there. Those memories, now."

"But how could you sell it?"

"I haven't been able to, have I?" She glanced over at Willie Woo, yelling at one of the drunks at the bar, upbraiding him in his abrupt, barking

Chinese. "Some nights I think the only way out is to just burn it down. Preferably with myself in it. At least then it would all be over. But I'm too much of a coward. If I was braver, I would have done it a long time ago."

The Lotus Room began to empty, cocktail hour over, the downtowners heading home, only the regulars staying on to nurse their dollar well drinks through the evening soaps.

Suddenly, Meredith choked and closed her eyes, eyelashes lying on her cheeks the way Michael's did. "We're just cursed. Every last goddamn one of us."

Josie put her arm around Meredith's shoulders, trying to reassure her, her head against the woman's dark curls. The smell of her incense-like perfume combined with the smell of the house, the Michael smell of mothballs and cedar. She knew it was fucked up, what she was doing, it was wrong, she should be running out of there, but she couldn't get enough of that smell, and the breathy murmur of that elegant voice, of being allowed this close. "My family's like that too," she admitted. She didn't know who was the more cursed, the little people or the big-deal ones. Having your composer father kill himself just after your Carnegie Hall debut, your famous novelist husband leaving you, your brilliant son killing himself, or being raised with nothing, having nothing, being nothing, and then losing the one fucking decent thing you ever had.

She felt Meredith's hand slip into hers, cold as her own, and wet from the drink, big and yet delicate, just like his. It was a shock, like holding Michael's hand all over again. "Josie, would you consider coming and staying with me for a while? It's so lonely up there, I feel like I'm going mad."

Josie pressed her head against Meredith's skull, two hard heads, like two rocks. She knew there was some reason she should not agree, but she couldn't remember what it was.

25

Los Feliz

Through the live oaks and rusted screens of Michael's old room, the full moon appeared, painting shadows onto the silent walls. This room, where she had pictured him, painting. Moonlight washed the old piano and gilded the Madonna, outlined the heap of records and paintings, the books that held only a fraction of what he'd once known. In dying, the worlds he'd taken with him. More than she would know in her next seven lifetimes. *Each man kills the thing he loves,* and Michael had killed what lay coiled in his head.

She turned over in the narrow bed, the pillow

smelling of him, a scent that would never again exist in the life of the world. That smell cut her and filled her and cut her again. She let tears slip down her nose into the goose down. How many times she would catch the scent of him still, in her hair, on her body, while pulling a dress over her head, and have to just stop, halted by the strange power of it. These sheets hadn't been changed in all the time Michael had been away, coarse and gritty and slightly damp, but permeated with him.

Under the boiled-wool blankets, despite sweatpants and a turtleneck and a white sweater she'd found in the bureau, the kind people wore for tennis — *I am not sportif* — she shivered spasmodically. You'd think people as rich as the Loewys would have heat, but the drafty room was stone cold. They must not have thought they needed heat upstairs, when all they were doing was sleeping. After all, California wasn't Vienna.

Although she was giddy with exhaustion, sleep was a lover who refused to be touched, who wanted to stay up all night painting ugly pictures and staring at Bosch. Who held himself at arm's length, shrinking back as she approached. She'd done one of Red's downers before bed, but still hadn't felt the warm fuzziness, that deep puffy nothing. Instead, she lay with her cold clanging heart like an empty drum, sticky with tar and half-eaten with rust.

Opposite the bed, she could see the heaps and piles of paintings and drawings leaning against one another like a playing-card house. The Chinese bridge with its palm grove, and the blind Merediths climbing the white stairs. Little Jeanne in black stockings, the piece he'd submitted for the Barnsdall exhibit. That expression of pure quiet trust. So vulnerable, not a trace of Elena or fox-faced Tyrell. She couldn't even remember what that had felt like. Like Michael, not remembering. *We loved each other once. . . . Didn't we?* The love in the picture had gone missing, like an arm she'd lost in a war, leaving only the sensation of absence. Her face, so full of belief that it would all just go on and on.

She lay under the weight of old blankets, their funky, musty smell, shivering, trying to recall the feeling of being in love, when it was light and kisses and music, when they could pass through space and time riding a line of poetry, the night he put on Louis Armstrong and taught her to Charleston. How well he had danced, easy and natural, unaffected. He'd said all he learned in

Cotillion was how to talk to dull girls, but that was only another story, a picture he'd painted of himself for her collection.

And how they had sprawled on the blue couch, their compartment on the Transsiberian, passing the domes of Moscow *smooth as almonds*. The rush of words creating a world they could ride inside. Blaise and Jeanne slid the door open, put their one suitcase up on the rack, they were seven days from home and *the Kremlin was like an immense Tartar cake iced with gold* . . . And now it was just a watery shadow, a world lying at the bottom of the sea.

But it had been real. *We loved each other once* . . . It was up to her to remember, and the look on little Jeanne's face, yes, there was the proof. Propped against the old piano, resting on the dresser. The poet's lady, adored for the turn of her mouth and the twist of her spine. Reading in the breakfast nook, wearing the sun like a shawl. One moment out of time, locked onto a piece of stretched cloth that would never change, though the artist was dead and his model shipwrecked. She struggled in the sheets that wound clammily around her like a web in a nightmare. She remembered having been in that sun-filled kitchen, but not how it felt.

That kind of tenderness couldn't be permitted to last. Nothing that beautiful could live long. It wasn't allowed. You only got a taste, enough to know what perfection meant, and then you paid for it the rest of your life. Like the guy chained to a rock, who stole fire. The gods made an eagle eat his liver for all eternity. You paid for every second of beauty you managed to steal.

She turned over and over in the hot gritty sheets, trying to find a place where her heart didn't twist and wring itself like wet socks. Lucky for her, Meredith hadn't made any effort to arrange her plunder from the shack on Lemoyne. The crippled boy's room wasn't so much a shrine as a U-Store-It where the woman had gathered the broken pieces of her son, piled them up, and closed the door. Heartbreaking to see this hurried deposit, and yet just as well. The progression of the paintings would have told his mother far more than Josie would have wanted anyone to know about what had happened between them, the progression from little Jeanne, the poet's lady, to the bruised girl, with her cubist pelvis and red sliced cunt.

She turned over, her limbs tender and burning. She hadn't had a decent night's sleep since that day at the morgue. Her body felt like it had been beaten with a hose. This must be what it felt like to get old. It wasn't that your body fell apart from living so long. It was that you had to take so many stompings from life that you'd be happy when the time came to close your eyes and never open them ever again.

She shivered, despairing of ever feeling the bathwater-warm Seconal creep through her veins. She wondered if Red knew they were for her, and had given her some ancient crap left over from Valley of the Dolls. She closed her eyes, trying to seduce sleep in the fragrant darkness the way she used to try to coax Michael away from black moods. It hadn't worked then and it didn't now. Her lids kept opening like a window blind with a sprung catch. Opening onto the horrible self-portrait he'd painted this fall. The dark monk, or saint, clad in his rusty black robe, with crazy overlarge pale eyes in a dark face that followed you around the room, accusing you. It hated her, blaming her for everything. She thought saints were forgiving, you could turn to them in the night, but Michael had couched his fury there, in his murderous holy man.

How much his art had changed since she'd

known him. Better? Yes, probably, she could see the impact of the work increasing from the Jeannes and Blaises to the Merediths and the horrible monks, but all the love had gone out of them, replaced by layers of disgust and rage and self-hatred. Now there would be no more, no redemption, just this pile of canvases in a room his own mother couldn't bear to enter. Meredith had tried to give her the guest room, but Josie wanted to be with Michael, his things, smelling him, feeling him, though it was death all around.

I should just burn the whole place down. Maybe right now, right at this moment, Meredith moved about the house, wadding up newspaper. Now that Josie had come, there were no loose ends, they could have the cremation Michael had wanted. She eyed the oak door with its inset panels, and imagined it locked from the outside. Meredith splashing gasoline, saying a last twisted prayer. Well, why not? If Michael could be dead, what difference did Josie make? She wouldn't have to go through all that working and cleaning and shopping and paying the bills. Who said she had to go on? Why need a library card, a gas bill, a book of appointments?

Her eyes followed the moonlight shadow of an oak branch stretched along the wall, wide around as the trunk of a tree and almost horizontal. A limb that begged for a noose. She wondered why Michael never thought of it, why he had to go all the way to Twentynine Palms when he could have hung himself here? Or cut his throat with the straight razor that he'd always used. Maybe that's what he'd thought about every morning, as he gently shaved his neck. Already handling it, the idea of it. But in the end, nothing less than blowing his brains out onto a wall had satisfied him.

Oh, she knew about rage, knew plenty, but she hadn't known how it could go inside as well as out, could smash things you couldn't even see, you carried the pieces around forever, and then they worked their way out through your skin years later, like her father's friend Denny, who'd been caught by a mine in Vietnam. The pieces of shrapnel still working their way out of his flesh all those years later. When he'd been drinking, he'd show you where one was coming out, a dark patch under the hairless, scar-shiny skin. Was that how Michael felt all the time? And how she would feel the rest of her life, pieces of this disaster coming to the surface, cutting through her from the inside out.

She hurt. She hurt like she'd been in a car

wreck. Her armpits, her throat, the small of her back, every joint, burrowed into the covers, shaking, but grateful for the quiet. No sounds at all, not the rustle of a leaf or the gurgle of a pipe, no passing cars. Just the cocoon of the night. In Echo Park, the noise never stopped, helicopters and the demented barking of neglected dogs, time-delay soccer games from Ecuador and Brazil, and the pop pop pop of boys settling scores. The time the fucking helicopter cops caught her in the searchlight, outside in her underwear, they hovered overhead, thought it was pretty damn funny. Here the darkness wrapped itself around the house like black mink, a rich woman at a funeral, all decorum and softness and mourning.

He should have taken her with him. He should have killed her first, he should never have left her behind. She had wanted nothing more than to be with him, to belong to him always. If she had found her way here, to the place that made him, he shouldn't be surprised. She wanted her clothes in the closet next to his, the way they had always been. Her clothes were lonely for him. She liked the narrowness of the bed, like the bunk on the train, rocking on the rails. *Blaise, are we very far from Montmartre?* His arm around her, his mouth to her ear. *A long way, Jeanne. Everything gone except cinders . . .*

Now she felt the drug coming on, its creeping warmth. Sleep, a butterfly, uncanny blue, fluttering in the moon-filled room, loosening the grip of the world on her exhausted body, letting her drift. As good as being buried, the earth close around you, heavy and soft, lovely with silence. She wrapped the house around herself, the depth of the walls, massive as a fort, spongy like the insides of a giant cork tree. Wasn't this what she wanted? Yes, this was why she had come.

She dreamed of a beautiful train with flowered curtains on the windows, little brass lanterns swaying. They were on their trip, the Transsiberian, she couldn't believe they had made it. And here was Michael, sitting in the seat next to her. Alive. He kept talking to people, just when she wanted in the worst way to get rid of them and have him all to herself.

They pulled into a station, and he wanted to buy them wine and something to eat while he could, it was going to be a very long trip. She didn't want him to go. She wanted to make love, but he wouldn't listen. He kissed her and got off the train. Out the window people crowded around the train, pleading to get on, fights broke

out, there were soldiers and Michael wasn't
back yet. People trying to climb on the train,
holding out their hands in the window. Soldiers
hit them back with the butts of their guns. Why
had he gotten off here, of all places, there was a
war going on, a revolution, she opened the window to look for him down the platform and a
starving man tried to crawl in, his hands, his
skin, his mad eyes, and she banged the window
closed on his arms and neck to make him let
go, chopping at them, and then the train started
up, slowly pulling forward. It was leaving. She
opened the window and screamed for him, but
the train picked up speed, leaving the town and
Michael behind.

Someone shook her. "My God, what are you
screaming about?" Meredith, the moon on her
wild dark hair, glazing her quilted, aqua blue
robe. The flood of light as she turned on the
lamp. Her fingers on Josie's face like a blind
woman, reading. "You have a fever." Piling the
blankets back onto her when it was already so
hot. "I knew you shouldn't be in here. Why is the
heat off? Sofía!"

The mad monk stared evilly at her. *How could
you leave him at the station?*

But she hadn't wanted him to go, hadn't

wanted him to get off in the first place, not with the war on, hadn't she told him not to go? "I told him not to. I told him." But she had let him get off, she should have known better.

"Told him what, Josie?"

The dying people reaching through the window, wanting her to save them, but she couldn't, and the way she banged the window on them, and Michael . . . "We were on a train, I told him not to get off."

Meredith's night hair frizzed around her diamond-shaped face, a night face pale and unreal as a woman climbing white stairs. "I know you did," she said. Her hands, smelling of her smoky, Japanese-incense perfume, were cool on her face. "I'm sure you did, Josie. We're going to put you in the guest room. This is no good."

"No. I want to stay here." Josie clutched at Meredith's hands. "Please." She turned her head to the side, in the pillow that smelled of him, the one thing she knew, sleeping here was like curling up inside his mind, she could hear the hum of his brain, the thump of his heart, if only she could have kept him on the train.

"Josie, you're going to listen to me."

"No." Her throat was so raw. "I'm sorry I

screamed. It was a bad dream. I won't be any trouble, I promise."

Meredith's cool hand against her cheek. "Just lie still."

"Please." She threw off the covers, tried to prop herself up, but she felt so heavy, weak as water. Meredith did something with the blankets, turning the edge of the sheet, making a smooth edge over the blanket stitching. Such a kind gesture. Something a mother would do. "Please?"

The maid appeared out of nowhere like a ghost, wearing a plaid bathrobe, her hair down around her face, cascading down her shoulders, far longer than Josie would have thought. "We need some aspirin," Meredith said to the woman. "A thermometer. Something for her to drink, too, some water, no, tea. And a washcloth. Her lips are all chapped." Meredith, shining in the satin robe, pulled a chair up to the bed. The tight line of the Spaniard's mouth, the arch of her nostrils. The disdain, having to wait on a girl like her.

Meredith settled into the chair and pressed her cool hand to Josie's forehead, that scent of incense and cedar. "When I was a very little girl, and I was sick, my mother used to put her hand across my forehead, like this, and sing me a song." Her huge hand, and she sang. "*Oh, what a beautiful morning.*" She had a terrible voice. How sad, a woman with such music in her soul could not sing. Everyone in Josie's family could do more than justice to a tune. "*There's a bright golden haze on the meadow . . .*"

Josie wondered if Meredith Loewy had ever seen a haze like that. When the almond trees were blooming, and the new leaves came out on the grapevines that were trained like so many Christs strung up by their wrists. Meredith's bare night face, the deep eyelids shining in lamplight, her voice cracking like a junior-high boy's. Josie wanted to tell her, it was a hard song, you had to have a good range and the ability to hold a note without wavering, and Meredith had neither.

The tea came. A washcloth. Aspirin, scratchy and bitter. They propped her on the pillows, tipped tea to her lips, too hot, she spilled some on the sheet. Meredith filled a spoonful, and blew on it, her lips pursed, his lips, blowing. Her mouth opened as she spooned it into Josie's, her hand underneath to catch drips. Her breath smelled of Scotch and chamomile. Taking care of her. Michael said Meredith never took care of him when he got sick. Said she was terrified of illness. Too many people depended on her, she couldn't afford to catch anything. Yet here she was, blowing on tea, spooning it into Josie's mouth. How astonished he would be. Jealous. Yes. He would be jealous that his mother would take care of Josie like this when she wouldn't do it for him. It should have been Michael. But Michael was dead. Michael didn't need anyone to spoon tea for him now. She could be Michael, just for a little while. The mad monk glared at her over Meredith's shoulder. *Impostor.* But she ignored him. She needed someone, and Michael didn't anymore, it wasn't her fault, anyway she was too sick to resist.

She let them change her, Meredith and the maid, like a child, stripping away the sweat-sodden clothes, the tennis sweater, the leggings, toweling her off. They threaded a nightgown over her head, over her arms, the soft cloth that smelled of mothballs. She understood she was shedding her skin, she was being given a new one. They changed the sheets, folded her into them like a letter. She felt better in the high-necked flannel gown, a blue and green plaid, the white embroidery on the yoke, and drifted back to sleep, and dreamed of a boat, a canoe made of stone, on a dark river, and three dark fuzzy-haired people paddling her away from the shore. The snaky roots of trees growing out of the water. *Is he here? Is he near here?* she kept asking, but nobody would tell her. She was afraid of the dark and the fuzzy-haired people and where they were going.

In the morning, music rose through the floor, filling the bright room, drenching it in light like a sponge cake in bourbon. Lords and ladies drifted down wallpaper, ladies on swings, ladies with parasols, ladies with crooks and lambs. Where was she? What room was this? But the music told her. A guest room, they must have moved her in the night. And she was secretly glad of it. That room bred nightmares, the pile of their sad things, the mad monk, all the hundreds of books that hadn't helped him live. They should be locked up and the key buried. How much better to be in this bright place, a good place, like light in a fog.

She had forgotten the fog. A game they played, from a book, *The Pillow Book of Sei Shonagon.* These wonderful questions. *What was the best kind of fog in June? What scenes improved from being painted?* The book had opinions, the way Michael did. She never would have thought about it, how should June be, what was the best kind of fog? She'd always had to take life just as it was. She would have been afraid to consider an ideal, knowing how unlikely she was to ever achieve it.

She edged her head closer to his on the pillow, so she could look up into the green-lined paperback he held over their heads. "What's the best kind of fog?" he'd asked.

She tried to think about kinds of fog. "When it's sunny and foggy at the same time," she said. "Like being inside a paper lantern. And it's your birthday, and you wear a party dress, and you're inside. And everything's bright, nothing but brightness. And you disappear into the fog." If death could be like that. Just disappearing into the soft and white.

Sweat dripped down her back, slid into the crack in her ass. She liked the light but it hurt her head. She turned, and kicked off the covers, looking for a cool place on the sheet, and faded back into sleep, dreamed she lay in bed with her mother, watching *Giant* on TV, the part where Elizabeth Taylor meets James Dean. The boss's wife and the oil rigger, but they were somehow her mother and father, and you could read their tragedy a long way off. "He died just after they finished it," her mother said in the dream. "Why are you all in such a hurry? All you young people."

Later, the Spanish maid came and Meredith, they wiped her face with cold cloths, fed her a boiled egg like a sun in a spoon, walked her haltingly to the bathroom, her legs wouldn't stay up. Cold marble underfoot, the white rug. Music. A flower in a vase on the tray. A January rose, it wouldn't last long, all big and full-blown like that. He loved things like this, fragile, that wouldn't last. She touched its silver-mauve petals, a hundred layers like an old-fashioned petticoat. *The Japanese would say that's their elegance, the brevity of their beauty.*

But Josie wanted things you could lock away, she wanted time to stand still. The rose would bloom and drop its petals, the rose would break her heart. If only she had known Michael would be like that. Slipping through her fingers like mercury from a broken thermometer. *What's the best kind of fog? What should the weather be in November?* His birthday, that he shared with Spiro Agnew and Hedy Lamarr, *Kristallnacht* and Dylan Thomas's death.

"What is the best kind of November?" she

asked, looping her leg over him. He was good at this. Like the book, he knew how things should be.

"In November in LA, it should be murky and warm." He took a drag of his cigarette. "The haze takes on a blue tint toward evening, and there's a hint of smoke in the air. The sun sets bloodred, and there's a sprinkling of lights in the hills. It makes you think of Istanbul, or Cairo. It makes you want to be somewhere else." And she could see it, the reflection of the bloody sky in his eyes.

"I've never been anywhere," she said, watching smoke ripples arabesque overhead, into the painted lanterns.

"What about Paris?" He rested his head against hers. Temple to temple, the love flowing back and forth, better than sex, better than anything. *I remember, Michael . . .*

But truth shuffled in, that bitter old woman, opening her toothless old mouth. *There never was Paris. You just dreamed it, on a salvaged mattress, in a room with a floor that sagged toward the windows. No Paris, no Japan or butterflies from Brazil, it was all just a hash pipe you smoked.*

She turned and watched the ladies pour

down the walls, ladies and their pudgy courtiers. Such fragile moments, but they'd been real, they had been, and she would do anything to have them again. The touch of his chest on her cheek, his smell. The way he described his roommate at Harvard, Odious Thomas, who left his coffee cups around the room, growing mold. He'd been a scientist, and believed only in reason. Michael imitated a ritzy East Coast accent, with its own funny drawl. "'There's your God, old son,'" holding an imaginary, moldy cup up to her nose. "'There's your Platonic Ideal.'"

She dreamed she'd gone back to her parents' house. And the coyote came for her, its crazy gold eyes. It trotted away through the cars in the impound and she followed it, in her nightgown, barefoot, her gown kept catching in the cactus, except there was no cactus in Bakersfield, even in the dream she knew that. They were on the desert, in the starlight, and suddenly there were helicopters, sweeping the ground with their beams. She hid behind rocks, but they found the coyote. Its eyes glowed for a second, like a small devil caught in God's headlights. And then they shot it. Leaving her alone in the middle of nowhere.

"Josie." Meredith shook her. "This is Dr. Edelman.

He's come to take a look at you." An old man with very blue eyes. He leaned over her, his hands gnarled as roots, his face full of canyons. She knew him. He'd been at the funeral, he'd carried Michael's coffin. His old fingers probed her neck, he looked at her throat with a Popsicle stick, scraped it. Meredith sat her forward and the old man listened to her back with a cold stethoscope, thumped her. What was a pallbearer doing here? Shouldn't he be a bank teller? Rick, from the head office?

He gave her a shot. Her body seemed far away. She was mesmerized by the crevices in his old man's face and the clarity of his eyes, as if his old face was a mask and his real face peered through. He and Meredith stepped away to talk in the doorway, she knew they were talking about her. What were they saying? She felt a spark of fear. What if the doctor wasn't really a doctor, and even if he was, doctors could kill you in ways that wouldn't even show up. Who knew what might be in that shot? She waited to see if she felt any worse, if she would suddenly stop breathing.

The doctor left, and Meredith, wearing a soft blue sweater like clouds in the morning, settled in the chair next to the bed, a wing chair upholstered in white silk. "You're a very sick girl," she said.

A very sick girl, somehow it seemed like a title in an old silent movie. *Josie Tyrell* as *A Very Sick Girl.* Even a bit of prestige. Was that it, her role here? Meredith held Seven Up to Josie's parched lips, the bent straw. A girl who needed taking care of. Those long leopard eyes. Wiping Josie's face and neck with a cold cloth, always a fresh one, they never smelled like mold, like when her mother would wash their faces in the bathtub, she and Corinne and Bo, all in the dirty water together.

"Feeling better?" she asked.

"A little," Josie said, though she didn't know if it was true or not. She did feel better with Meredith there, taking care of her, paying attention to her.

"Let me brush your hair." She had a soft burnished-silver brush in her hands, its bristles yellow with age. "Would you like that?"

Her sweaty, repulsively dirty hair? She didn't think the old brush would get through the bleached strands — when they tangled, they matted like felt. But Meredith had already started, working the sweat-dampened tangles, brushing it back from her forehead, and talking to her the way you talk to a dog when you're grooming it, no point to the talking but filling silence with sound. Her deep voice hypnotic and musical.

"That nightgown, you know where that came from? There was once a store called Lanz, down on Wilshire near Fairfax. My father got all my clothes there, they imported them from Europe. I had to be *comme il faut.*" She stopped to tease out a snarl with her bare fingers, and then took to brushing again. "It means 'just so.' That's what he was like. Just so. Completely old-world. I don't think he ever got used to being in California. These were his brushes. They had the same hair, my father and Michael. Only my father's turned silver. He was quite vain of it, most of his friends went bald." Brushing, the rhythm, her hair all smooth now, the rhythmic stroking, the slight scratching of scalp, like being pushed on a swing, it soothed her, made her sleepy. "Women adored him of course. We had wonderful parties here, all the émigrés, the writers and directors, the actors. Vicki Baum and Galka Scheyer. Rita Hayworth danced the tango with Rudolph Schindler, the architect. Do you know who Hedy Lamarr was?"

"The movie star." She'd been photographed

nude in a movie in the Thirties, Josie went with Michael to see it once at the New Beverly. Hedy backstroking in a pond, like a white mermaid in the water. The dark water. *Ecstasy.* Meredith's father had scored her studio movies in the Forties.

"They were good friends," Meredith said. "Sometimes she stayed over. She'd sleep in this very bed."

Hedy and Michael and Dylan Thomas, all linked in some mysterious abacus. Dylan Thomas died in a bar in New York after drinking eighteen whiskeys in a row. He was a man who wanted to die but didn't want to know it. A fat man with bulby eyes, she'd seen a picture of him on the cover of his poetry book. Dylan Thomas wasn't beautiful like Hedy Lamarr but his words soared like music. *A stranger has come to share my room in the house not right in the head, a girl mad as birds . . .* Michael loved that poem. And she was that plumy girl.

How sleepy she felt, warm and clean, her thoughts untangled along with her hair, under Meredith's hands, her perfume, the sound of her voice, instead of out in the dark with the dead coyote.

"I've missed having someone to take care of," Meredith said. The brush, caressing, comforting.

Michael used to draw self-portraits with night-mares hidden in his curls. "I'm taking good care of you. You're all I have now."

You're all I have. Yes, that was right, they needed each other. Who else was left? Although somewhere under what the doctor had given her, a small cowlick of mind rebelled, twanging alarm. *Don't buy it, kid. You were the one stand-ing there, thinking how easy it would be to kill her in her sleep.* But the sound of Meredith's voice was so soothing, the brush in her hair. And she was tired of being afraid of her, circling her beauty and grace like some abused dog. The rhythm of the brush, Meredith's father's brush from Europe, *comme il faut,* and her deep voice, inviting Josie in. It felt inevitable, this was why she had come, and she would let herself fall into the bright fog. The small voice went inside a trunk and sank to the bottom of the sea.

26
Pen

In the cold green brightness of the living room, Josie lay under a woven throw, drinking smoky Chinese tea and listening to Meredith play Debussy on the black Steinway. After her illness, she felt empty and purified, light and bleached as driftwood left on a beach, like the abandoned clothes of the people who rose for the Rapture. Her aunt Cora used to tell her all about it. People going to Heaven without having to die, leaving behind their clothes and their cars and their shopping carts, the ice cream melting in the parking lot. She never thought about going to heaven herself, it was all those shopping carts that caught her attention. That's what it felt like to be up here in Meredith's living room. There was no *after,* no *next.* Everything that was going to happen already had. What tremendous safety, that it was all just over.

Through the tall windows, camellia bushes twenty feet high strained noon's passage with their winter green. They were so old they had grown into trees, bearing white flowers, a few of which floated in a crystal bowl on the table. This was all she wanted, to be allowed to lie still and drift and listen to Debussy, hidden away from the clear light of day that stood you against a wall and frisked you like a cop. A little softness was all she asked for. A stopped clock.

She could see her feet sticking out from under the blanket. How absurdly small they looked in flannel quilted slippers that matched the green and blue plaid of the gown. She touched her hair, washed and neatly combed, tied with a ribbon. She had sat at the mirror while Meredith parted her hair, combed it smooth. Josie didn't tell her she didn't wear her hair parted on the right. She knew without a doubt that this was how Meredith had parted Michael's hair, combing it just so. *Comme il faut.*

On her lap lay Michael's Dylan Thomas, she'd found it in the pile on his piano. The fat man with the bulby eyes, who wanted to die but didn't know it. Scores of little paper slips marked the yellowing pages, Michael's precise vertical handwriting with its *g*'s like *8*'s and *e*'s like *3*'s filling the margins. She turned to the poems he had marked, letting their strange phrases jump out at her like faces in a crowd. *Altarwise by owl-light in the half-way house, the gentleman lay graveward with his furies* . . . In the margins, he'd written things like: *Death in the tomb of the Christ. Hangnail=nail=Christ to Cross. Remainder of creation's expermt.* Such a fury in him to climb inside the world and look out through its eyes. He was ravenous for that, had to conquer it like a mountain. . . . *And, from his fork, a dog among the fairies* . . . Michael lay graveward with his furies, leaving her, she supposed, the dog, dancing with its mouth open.

"Michael loved this piece," Meredith said, starting something new, quiet, intentionally hesitant, odd stops and starts, a little oriental sounding. "It's called 'Jimbo's Lullaby.' Debussy wrote it for his daughter, Claude-Emma. Jimbo was her toy elephant."

Josie could see the stuffed animal lumbering

through a dream jungle, running, coming out into a clearing in the moonlight. She liked Meredith telling her things. It was like Michael, the pleasure of him showing her something. He gave her so much, when she gave him nothing, though it was all she had.

I am the long world's gentleman, he said, and share my bed with Capricorn and Cancer.

"If you're feeling better by the twenty-eighth," Meredith said, "Pierre Boulez is going to be in town, an all-Debussy evening. They're sending me tickets."

She would wear her blue silk Elena suit. She would know enough not to clap between movements.

The maid came in, her starched apron and starched face. She checked the small fire, put another log on, then leaned across the low coffee table, filling Josie's teacup from the porcelain pot without once looking at her. "Thanks," Josie said, hoping to win a smile, but it was like talking to a chair. The woman despised her, treating her like a bit of dogshit Meredith had picked up on her shoe, that she had to keep cleaning up as the boss tracked it around the house.

Josie sipped the smoky tea, Lapsang souchong, propped on the plump pillows, wearing her gown and robe and slipper set from Lanz, the flannel that smelled of mothballs and time. Meredith's own childhood. Full length, the gown was too long for Josie, making her feel more childlike than ever, like a pampered invalid in a movie set in the Victorian era, fussed over and propped before sunny windows in a wicker wheelchair.

How beautiful Meredith looked as she played, the fine head bowing over the keyboard, dark hair held off her face with a barrette and curling around her shoulders as she played the falling-water music that soothed Josie like fingers across her brow. Not doubting, questioning, like Brahms, Debussy was forgetfulness, dreams, life malleable as green water. Meredith knew Josie liked it, she was showing it off like a dragonfly showing a new set of wings. And it occurred to Josie how tortured Michael must have been by the way his mother's gift just flowed out of her, so clear and certain and unobstructed, like a spring. How painful it must have been for him to watch this. Michael had that genius, maybe even more than Meredith, but he couldn't let it out like that. Just pour it out. And no matter how good he was, even if he was the one picked out of a whole show, he could never feel it. He could do everything except find a way to satisfaction.

The doorbell rang its old-fashioned carillon, eight notes that repeated, but Meredith did not even lift her head. Josie was gripped with admiration for the woman's cell-level certainty that someone else would answer it. It was so much like Michael. Whether it was aristocratic egotism or the sense that what they were doing was more important than what was coming to them from the outside, it didn't even matter. Josie arrayed the blanket over her knees, lay back in the cushions. Sofía would get it. The chimes rang again.

Finally, the maid bustled across the red-tile entryway, and they could hear a male voice, and then a higher one, female, she almost recognized it, but could not place it until the visitors were admitted, and she saw them at the top of the steps.

A cop, and Pen.

Over the top of the book, the shock on Pen's face mirrored her own. Pen's mouth an O edged in dark lipstick. Her face and the studs on her jacket gleamed in the dark foyer. Pen took the whole thing in at a glance, the robe and the tea and the good-girl part in her hair. Josie could hear the judgment as loud as if Pen had screamed it. *What the fuck do you think you're doing, Josie Tyrell?* The maid showed them into the living room, pressing a finger to her lips to instruct them not to speak while the Señora was playing. As if it were church.

The cop took a seat on the couch opposite Josie, she was lying on the near one, taking up the whole expanse. Pen irritably folded down next to him, her face as white as Josie knew her own to be, eyes and nostrils flaring messages of outrage. Josie concentrated on the black words on the white page, avoiding Pen's glare. She'd really screwed up. Had completely forgotten Pen and her instructions to call the cops and everything else. She wished she could disappear. She looked at Meredith but the woman kept playing as if she were absolutely alone. She realized that she'd wanted to be forgotten, had wanted to step into brightness, and disappear. But when had Pen forgotten anything?

She could feel the heat of Pen's outrage, but she kept her eyes on the page, and groped for a likely story in the swirl of thoughts, the way a woman gropes in her purse for her sunglasses. It was an honest mistake, it wasn't her fault. She was *a very sick girl,* she'd had a fever, it wasn't her fault she'd forgotten about the world *down there*. She had arrived in the place where the clocks had all stopped. But Pen was a clock that kept ticking, she would open the drapes, drag her out into the cruel noon light.

Maybe this was just a hallucination left over from the fever, Pen sitting in Meredith's living room next to a cop. Look how absurd it was, the cop's hat held respectfully over his crotch, goggling around as if he had never been in a room before. This was exactly what her father used to tell her about people like the Loewys, how they could get the Man to take his hat off and make him wait while they finished their Debussy. Leaving him gawking around the room like a hick. She was embarrassed for him, disgusted with how impressed he was, eyes leaping around like a badly trained dog, jumping from the gilded mirror to the silver candelabra to the Chinese horses big as deer, the oil painting of Meredith as a girl posing at the keyboard, blue ribbon in her long dark hair. Across the leather-topped coffee table, Josie still couldn't look at Pen in her studded miniskirt, eyes narrowed to furious slits. Pen knew exactly what she was doing there, what she was betraying. The little world they had created of the torn scraps and broken pieces of *down there.* Like abandoned children holding hands and singing bravely in the dark woods. There was no solace there, no beauty, only make-believe. Though she knew Pen saw it the other way around, that *down there* was the real world, and this was the elaborate charade.

Josie played with the fringe at the edge of the blanket, hearing the final spill of notes, which bled in the air for a long time before fading away. Only when Meredith's fingers left the keys did she look up and notice that she had guests. She blinked as if she had just arrived off the plane from Paraguay. "Can I help you?"

The cop rose and introduced himself as Officer Ricketts, a stocky young white man with razor burn and a few bruised-looking pimples on his jaw. "We had a missing-person report, ma'am. One Josephine Tyrell."

Josie pulled the blanket up higher, waiting for them to disappear as you would wait for the sun to set, as you waited out an acid trip that wasn't going too well. They couldn't stay here forever, it would be over eventually. They would go and the peace and the music would return.

"It's been five days, *Josephine,*" Pen said. "Nobody's seen you, heard from you, *Josephine.*

What was I supposed to think? You said she took out a hit, for Christ's sake."

Josie glanced over shamefaced at Meredith, who had risen gracefully from the piano, giving no sign of having heard a thing, and Josie was reminded just how good she was, exactly Elena, the control that could come and go at will. Worlds away from Pen with her purple-streaked hair, the broad studded bands on her wrists, seething like a jealous lover. *How dare you lie there, how dare you seek refuge in the enemy's lair?* This was how, Pen. This was how you shed your skin, how you walked out on a country road and left yourself behind.

Meredith came around the white couches in her fluid hip-walk, like a stalking cat, and stood behind Josie. "There's been a misunderstanding," she said, her hands covering the balls of Josie's small shoulders. "The girl had the flu, she was delirious. I've been taking care of her."

Pen knit her black eyebrows, her mouth fell open with disbelief. She turned to the cop. "She said this bitch had hired someone to take her out. Tried to kill her at the funeral, you should've seen the bruises. Josie was terrified of her. Tell him, Josie."

Josie blanched. She wished Pen would just stop talking, would see how it was and drop it. She didn't have to keep this up, pin her to the wall, force her to lie. "I — I was upset, I wasn't thinking clearly."

"What funeral?" the cop interrupted. "Wait a second." He pulled out a little notebook and set it on his knee, the pen hovering.

"My son." Meredith's voice came from behind her. "Passed away. December fifteenth. This girl was his . . . dear friend."

The warm weight of Meredith's hands on her shoulders. She felt them both looking at the cop in exactly the same face.

"Sorry for your loss, ma'am." The cop wrote in his notebook. "Cause of death?"

No one said anything. Josie met Pen's eyes for the first time. *Don't say it. Just don't.* Pen stared back at her, *You are so fucking full of it,* but she said nothing out loud. Meredith's fingers tightened. The cop glanced under his pale eyebrows from Josie to Meredith.

"My son was depressed," Meredith said quietly, over the choke in her voice. "He had — mental-health issues."

"I see." The cop folded the notebook and put

it away. "Sorry to have troubled you, Mrs. Loewy. My condolences." He looked down at Pen accusingly, his signal to vamoose and make it snappy. Pen stood. There was a hole in the knee of her tights, a red streak on the toe of her motorcycle boot.

"I'd like to talk to my friend for a minute. In private," Pen said.

The cop looked to Meredith to say yea or nay, as if she was the parent. "Of course," Meredith said in her deep, cultured voice. "Josie, why don't you use the study. But, please, don't tire her, she's just starting to feel better."

"Oh, I won't *tire* her," Pen said.

Josie didn't want to, she wanted to stay there, *a Very Sick Girl*, where Meredith and the cop would keep Pen from ragging on her, but Meredith nodded her on, like a reluctant toddler, so Josie removed the blanket and sat up. Her head reeled for a moment, then stilled. She stood slowly, steadying herself on the back of the couch, took her cup and saucer and, lifting the hem of her gown, shuffled across the wood in her too large slippers, across the worn carpets which she had come to learn were extremely valuable, eighteenth century, through the tiled foyer and into the study where Mauritz Loewy had shot himself in the head. She sat down on the tufted leather couch, set her tea on the table, and crossed her arms, sulky, like a child caught in a petty crime.

Pen closed the padded leather door behind her. "What the fuck do you think you're pulling, *Josephine?* Fuck, man. I was worried about you." Standing over her, on the rug into which Meredith's father's blood had seeped. She imagined she could still see a slight discoloration in the light portions of the pattern. But Pen wasn't looking, not at that. She was not looking at the gold spines on the books or the tassels on the velvet curtains or the crystal decanters in the bar or the painting of the weird, long-bodied thoroughbred over the fireplace. Pen was glaring at her, sparks flying from her eyes. "What kind of shit is this? I'm all worried about you, and then I find you here like this, some fucking little princess? What the fuck was going on out there?"

Josie shrugged. "I got sick. She decided she wanted to take care of me." She looked down at the overlong robe, the slippers, knowing she looked like a first-class idiot, but she had never had a pair of slippers that matched the robe that matched the nightgown. Neither had Pen, of course, and Josie knew just how you had to hate things you could never have. But it was such a little thing. She had lost Michael, couldn't she have the slippers, and the tea, to pretend for a little while what it might be like to be him? "I know it's a little strange. But she's lonesome. I give her something to do, I'm sort of a project, I guess. We're all we have left."

Pen threw herself into the studded wing chair, put her feet up on the table, her Doc Martens with their thick soles. "That's so bullshit, Josie. This stinks to high heaven. You saw her that night and suddenly you're sick, she's got you up here like some goddamn invalid, don't you think that's a little suspicious? What if she's, like, poisoning you or something?" She eyed Josie, who was lifting her cup of tea to her lips.

Josie looked into the cup. Yes, she could be, it was possible. The doctor and his needle. *A Very Sick Girl.* But she drank it anyway, gazed into the cup, the little shreds of Lapsang souchong clinging to the eggshell porcelain, the little flowers painted at the bottom, flowers that would never grow old and die. "Pen, the truth is I don't really care. I'm tired of my fucking life."

"Don't say that! You're depressed, okay, you're depressed. But this fucking house, shit, Josie . . ."

Pen put her hands into her pockets and shivered, though it was warm in the room. "It's a fucking creep factory, and she's got you brainwashed, I mean, look at this place — they ought to rent it out for slasher flicks. And you're in some kind of trance. You gotta snap out of it. Get your stuff and let's get out of here."

Josie lowered her eyes and shook her head softly. "I'm not leaving. There's nothing down there for me, Pen."

"Are you goddamn nuts?" She slid her boots off the table, leaned forward, her black eyes flashing like pinwheels. "Don't even say it. Fuck, Josie! You got friends! You got modeling, and what about that fucking movie guy, he's been looking for you. You're disgustingly gorgeous. Jesus, if I was you I'd be rolling in clover."

Rolling in clover. Pen sitting there, blinking at her, having no idea what it meant to have your heart ripped out by its ragged roots and then be expected to walk around like that, with a big black hole in your chest. "Guess what, I'm not rolling in clover. Guess what, I really loved the guy. Guess what, I like being in his house, it makes me feel closer to him. It smells like him. He's everywhere here."

"He's fucking dead, *Josephine*," Pen said. She

was digging with her thumbnail into the leather arm of the chair. Outlining the letter *P.* Christ, she was going to gouge her name into Mauritz's leather armchair.

"Pen, don't do that."

She looked up, amazed. Josie had never told her what to do before. "Do what?"

"Fuck up that chair."

"Fuck the fucking chair, Josie." She stood and kicked the chair over with a heavy boot. She knocked the table with its magazines to the floor, the teacup and saucer. The teacup cracked into three pieces. "Fuck this house, fuck all this shit. What's wrong with you? You don't need this shit. These are not your people." She grabbed Josie by her arm. "She is not your fucking friend, Josie. We are. Me and Shirley and Paul and Nick and that guy Jeremy, Phil Baby, we're your life, Josie. Not this. Now get your shit and let's go." She yanked on her, trying to pull her off the couch. "Get the fuck up!" Josie struggled but Pen was stronger, she had a grip like handcuffs. It was just like at home. Nobody reasoned with you, they just dragged you where they wanted you to go.

Suddenly, the door opened and Meredith and the cop stood in the doorway, staring, Pen with

Josie's arm in her leather-studded grasp, the overturned chair, the mess on the floor.

"That's quite enough," Meredith said.

"Josie," Pen pleaded, but she let her grasp loosen. "Listen to me."

"She doesn't have to listen to you, not one more minute." Meredith strode past Pen, put her arm around Josie. "I think it's time you go. Are you all right, Josie?" The extralong nightgown and robe pooling around her. The toppled table, the broken teacup.

"I'm all right." She leaned on Meredith, her head spinning, *a Very Sick Girl*. Meredith helped her toward the door, leaving everything where it was, the chair and the cup and the ashtray and the magazines.

"I'm awfully sorry, ma'am. We'll be leaving now," the cop said. "You. Let's go." He went to take Pen's arm but Pen pulled away.

"And you can kiss my ass, Josephine. Listen, when you need a friend again, don't think of me."

Josie gave Pen one last look as the cop led her to the door. "I'm sorry." Knowing she was choosing against her all over again, Michael over Pen, Meredith over Pen, Loewy over Tyrell. Traitor.

"Fuck you, Josie. Just fuck you up the ass."

Then the cop and Pen were gone. Josie and Meredith settled back into the living room, Meredith at her piano, playing Debussy as if nothing had ever happened. Josie picked up her Dylan Thomas, pretended to read it, though her hands were still shaking. Pen was gone. Her last link to *down there*. And she was here, in Meredith's house, she was staying.

27
Phone

Josie sprawled on the couch in Mauritz's study, smoking, wearing her own clothes now, since Sofia had brought them up from the house on Lemoyne. She enjoyed the red-paneled room, it was nice and gloomy in there, smelling of leather and cedar, the oaks barely admitting the afternoon sun. On her knees, big as an atlas, lay the musical score she'd pulled from Mauritz's bookshelf: *Schubert Symphonie Nr. 8 h-Moll D 759, "Unvollendete."* The long page of lines covered with music, like wash hanging in the sun. Each line was assigned a different instrument, *Ob., Fl., Timp.* Oboe. Flute. Timpani. Even the drum had music. She liked the look of the sweep of notes, their shapes on the pages, trying to imagine how it would sound all together.

At every moment, each instrument knew what to play. Its little bit. But none could see the whole thing like this, all at once, only its own part. Just like life. Each person was like one line of music, but nobody knew what the symphony sounded like. Only the conductor had the whole score.

The doorbell rang, and she could hear the click of the maid's shoes on the red tiles, polite sounds of greeting. Through the open door of the study, she could see old men coming into the hall, their black instrument cases bumping together, and Meredith sweeping down the stairs above them, a flash of sea green sweater, a skirt with high heels. She spoke to them in German. It was always strange to hear someone you knew speaking another language, they were somehow different than they were in English. In German, Meredith was more girlish, her voice higher pitched. A girl who'd once spoken German with her father.

Meredith came through the study door, still looking back at the old men over her shoulder, then glanced over to where Josie was reading on the couch. "Josie, do you have a moment? There are some dear friends I want you to meet."

Did she look like she had a moment? Oh, she was much too busy. She put the Schubert down and followed Meredith into the living room. The old men were opening their instrument cases, hanging their jackets on the backs of four straight-backed chairs. She recognized them from the funeral, Death's string quartet. "*Herren,* I'd like to introduce Josie Tyrell." Meredith put her hand on Josie's shoulder. "Michael's fiancée. Josie will be staying with us for a while."

Josie watched their faces, to see how they would react to this latest version of reality, when they had all seen Meredith wrap her hands around Josie's neck at the funeral. Not one of them expressed any trace of skepticism at Meredith's new daughter-in-law.

"Mr. Weinstein." Meredith indicated a frail old man with a delicate face, who shook her hand with a dry small one. "Mr. Cousineau." Short and chubby, smiling under a cloud of white hair. His plump hand pumped hers enthusiastically. She noticed with a shock the blue numbers peeking out from under his shirt sleeve. She knew what that meant. Such a happy, chubby man.

"A great pleasure," he said, flirting.

"Mr. Palevsky." A tall, mournful man with bushy eyebrows, dark eyes sunken above enormous bags, extended a giant hand speckled with age spots. "How do you do." Another accent, different, but how, Josie couldn't say.

"And you know Dr. Edelman."

"Good to see you, Doctor," Josie said, easily as Elena would. All these foreign hands. Those blue numbers. History close as a handshake. That's what she felt in this house, intensely. It was why Meredith and Michael were here in the first place. Right on that man's arm.

"Yes, dear, how are you feeling?" Dr. Edelman said. His accent not as strong as Cousineau's.

"Much better, thank you," she said. And none of them seemed to wonder what she was doing there. No amusement or surprise on those ancient faces. She'd gone from pariah to family member with the wave of Meredith's hand.

"Such a loss," Weinstein said.

"Yes, thank you," Josie said, glancing at Meredith, who smiled back. Her new mother-in-law.

"Feel free to join us, Josie," Meredith said, moving behind the great piano. "We've got Brahms today, the piano quintet."

"Oh, let her go, we'll bore the poor creature to tears. We have to argue over everything," Cousineau explained. "Everyone must show off. A quartet is a very dangerous thing."

"Unstable," said Palevsky.

"And add a pianist, you know what they're like. Unbearable egotists," said Weinstein.

Had they done this when Michael was alive, had he heard these same jokes? Maybe the routine dated from the days of Mauritz, whom she felt everywhere in the house. Describing music as if it was some dangerous mission.

"As the amateur, I feel fortunate simply to keep up." Dr. Edelman eased himself into the second chair, pulling up one pant leg and then the other, showing his socks. He took his violin out of the case and tucked it under his chin.

The others began to tune their instruments. Weinstein on the other violin, Cousineau on cello, and Palevsky next to him, his must be viola. Meredith rolled her eyes as if telegraphing to Josie that this was not exactly of her own choosing. And Josie understood this wasn't an everyday get-together. It was a musical shivah. The old men had taken it upon themselves to keep Meredith company, the best way they knew. *Those old men, they know what to do.* It was their version of dragging you out to the Hong Kong Café.

"What's *Unvollente* mean?" she asked Meredith. "The Schubert."

"*Unvollendete,*" Meredith said. "Unfinished."

So much music. She settled back down on the red-leather couch, ran her fingertips along the page of the grandfather's book, *Symphonie Nr. 8 "Unvollendete."* The shapes of the notes, strung along the staff like birds on wires. Michael could read a score like this and hear it in his head. Meredith too. All these people. She looked at the page, imagining what the notes would sound like. Clusters, sections where sets of notes repeated, you could see where it was frenzied, notes jammed in together under double and triple bars like people under an awning, and where it was quiet. She felt like a deaf-mute watching a pianist. *They always sit on the left, so they can see the pianist's hands.* Even without knowing the notes, you could see there was form here, meaning.

But still, she could never hear it. Just as she could act like Elena, but never be her. She was always just staring at shapes on a page.

As the Brahms played, she flipped back to the first page. *Franz Schubert. Symphonie Nr. 8 h-Moll D 759, "Unvollendete."* Unfinished. She wondered why. Had Schubert died? Or didn't he like it? Maybe inspiration simply abandoned him. The way she'd left Jeremy with his movie. Poor Jeremy. She'd never left someone in the lurch like that before. The project souring in his hands. All the money Gordo had sunk into it. No, she shouldn't think of it. It wasn't her problem. She was no actress. She was just killing time.

Out in the living room, she could hear their voices, arguing about some fine point of music. One of the violins played, and then the cello played alone, slower. More arguing. On Mauritz's big desk, where Cal had found the suicide notes, stood an old-fashioned cradle phone, sitting on a crocheted doily, like something Gommer Ida would make. She was surprised to even think of the film, or anything else happening *down there*. But something had happened that night on Sunset Plaza, something she had never felt before. She wasn't a creative person like Michael or Meredith, like the art students or these old men or even Jeremy. She was just a girl who went along, who could remember where she put her body, could *stand there, look upset.* She wore clothes well, put on her makeup with flair. But things coming out of her, visible to the world? It was in a strange way another loss. You gave things away you couldn't afford to lose. Private things. You showed yourself and you couldn't take it back. Yet, she couldn't stop thinking about it, how exciting it had felt to have all that come out of her. Creating something that hadn't been there before. Like painting a canvas. Like the music coming out of Meredith and her old men.

She picked up the phone. The receiver was heavy in her hand, back from the days they made phones from Bakelite instead of plastic. She wasn't going back down or anything, she just wanted to apologize. Suggest someone else who might be able to do it. Two different girls, Jeremy would think of a way.

She counted the rings, hoping Jeremy wouldn't have gone out so early. Unlikely. Film students, like musicians, were vampires. They didn't come out till the sun went down. *Ten, eleven* . . .

" 'Lo?" Jeremy's voice sounded tentative, like someone searching for his glasses, though he didn't wear glasses.

"It's me," Josie said.

"Josie?" Now he was awake. "Where have you been? Your friend Pen said you're being held hostage in some voodoo mansion. Are you okay? How does it look up there?"

She had to smile. Already thinking about a turn in the script that needed a voodoo mansion. She faced the wall, kept her voice low. Somehow she knew it wouldn't be kosher to be discovered using the phone. Reaching outside the circle of grief to the living world. But the piano heaved a great waterfall of sound, the strings commenting and scolding. Then the music stopped and the arguing began again. "I'm staying with someone. Sorry I didn't call."

She could hear him choosing his words. She knew he wanted to chew her out, but something was keeping him from doing it. "Josie, I heard about your boyfriend." He said it in such a human tone, unlike him. "You should have told me."

She slid her hand down the old-fashioned cord. It didn't coil. She wondered when they started to make them the curly way. "I guess I thought if people didn't know, I could just get on with it. I couldn't take it if everybody knew. They either feel sorry for you or think it's your fault."

There was a rustle on the other end. "What are you talking about? Nobody would think that. That's delusional."

"But if I told you, you might have used someone else." Something he would find easier to understand. *God, you look like crap. Take some vitamin C, eat a steak.*

She could hear the sound of his breathing. He couldn't deny that. He might've felt sorry for her, but success was a train that only made scheduled stops. "Well, that's moot. I've been desperate to find you. I edited the footage. You've just got to see it, Josie. I kept thinking, 'Who is that?' " He laughed, short, apologetic. "Not that you weren't *always* good, but *entre nous,* you never worked up much of a sweat. Now you're mesmerizing. We don't know what you're going to do next. Are you coming back soon? Please say you will, I beg of you."

"I don't know," Josie said. "Jeremy, I —"

Suddenly there was Meredith, in the doorway, her face flushed from the effort of the Brahms.

"Look, I've got to go." She hung up without even a goodbye.

Meredith brushed her hair from her face and held it back tight to her scalp. "Who was that?"

"Nobody," Josie said. "A wrong number."

She reached for her cigarettes, remembered she'd smoked the last one. She crushed the box and threw it at the wastebasket, but it only clipped the side and ricocheted onto the polished floor.

Meredith's sweater was exactly the same color as her eyes. His eyes. It disturbed her that the longer she knew Meredith, the harder it was for her to remember Michael, his face was so much like his mother's. The same lanky grace, the same eyebrows, the wide mouth, smiling, though her eyes didn't smile.

"Are you done playing?"

"Mr. Weinstein had to use the facilities. I didn't hear the phone ring."

Josie turned away, toward the window dappled with the tiny triangles of blue February sky. She opened the window, leaning out, breathing the fresh air. "It was just some business I had to take care of. Don't worry, it was a local call."

"Josie," Meredith said, crossing her arms, lounging against the doorjamb. "I don't want you to take this the wrong way. But I'd prefer you not tell your friends where you are. Not if that girl was any indication."

Josie stood looking out at the hills, the green domes of the observatory. Somewhere up there, in the clumps of oak and eucalyptus, they'd made love on the picnic table at Dante's View. Could she have seen them from here? "Don't worry, no one's coming."

"Not the man in the photograph, was it?"

Josie smiled to herself. Meredith wanted to know more. The identity of the man she'd called. *You're all I have.* And the woman wanted her too, every bit of her. Now Josie was starting to understand how Michael felt if she ever asked him where he'd gone, what he'd been doing. He hated to be questioned, and here was the reason, the source of all his locked doors, his secrets. This woman in the green sweater, still stunning at forty-whatever. "No, it wasn't. Someone else," she replied. Did Meredith think she was lying? It made her smile to think so. Like the photos her private detective had taken. She would never really know. The blown roses clung to the bushes outside.

Meredith turned to listen to a voice from the living room. "If you need anything, don't hesitate to ask Sofía. This is going to take a while."

Josie stretched, her hands linked overhead, then twisted from side to side. "I could use some cigarettes."

"It's a foul habit," Meredith said automatically. "And anyway, you just got over being sick."

"I'm an addict," Josie said.

Meredith gazed at the window, touching the soft sleeves of her sweater. The shadows played across her face. "Well, perhaps this isn't the time for further renunciations. Just tell Sofía."

Josie leaned over, picked up the crumpled packet from the floor. "They're Gauloises. She can't get them at the market."

"I know what they are, Josie," Meredith said.

"Michael used to say the smell of Paris was Gauloises and dogshit in the rain."

Meredith was looking at the volume of Schubert she'd left on the couch. "What are you doing with this?"

"Reading it," Josie said.

Meredith lifted her thick, shapely eyebrows. "It's a beautiful piece. Would you like to hear it sometime? I've got some of the most wonderful recordings. Furtwängler, with the Vienna. And Bruno Walter did a marvelous one with the Chicago, few people know about it." She picked up the book and paged through it. "You're looking very pale, Josie. You should sit in the sun. I don't want anyone accusing me of *poisoning* you." She slid the symphony back onto the bookshelf where it came from. "Let Sofía know when you'd like lunch."

"Sofía doesn't like me much, if you can't tell," Josie said.

Meredith laughed, musical. "Josie, who cares if Sofía likes you? If anybody likes you."

Josie tried to imagine a person who wouldn't care if people liked them. What about Meredith? The way she spooned tea for her, the hand on her shoulder. Didn't Meredith like her? "Don't most people? Want people to like them?"

Meredith perched on the arm of the leather couch, her heavy hair falling over one shoulder. "At one time, there were a handful of people I cared about, but their numbers seem to be diminishing." She sighed, tried to smile, it twisted her face into an awkward grimace. "In any case, don't worry about Sofía. She's a servant, she'll do what she's told."

Michael told her Sofía had been a young widow in Seville when Meredith hired her, during her first European tour, back in the Fifties. Josie didn't like her any more than Sofía liked Josie, but she'd never heard anyone described so callously. *She's a servant, she'll do what she's told.* She could imagine Elena saying it, though.

As if a servant was somehow different from a real person. She wondered what Meredith would think if Josie told her that she'd scrubbed toilets in the Sunnyvale Motel, scraped down the grill at Rollerama.

"Now I've offended you." Meredith stood, brushed down her skirt, her dark hair rich around her pale face. "I didn't mean to sound so Marie Antoinette. It's just the way we live. Is it so hard to get used to, getting what you want, when you want it? Having someone taking care of your needs?"

Her needs. Christ.

Josie wondered, who was that *we* in *the way we live?* Did it mean her and Meredith? Meredith and Michael? Mauritz and Meredith? Or just people like the Loewys. Was she included in that *we?* It was true, it wasn't hard to get used to. Josie suddenly felt as strange to herself as a fledgling must feel when it sheds its baby down and feels the sharp feathers piercing its skin from the inside out.

As commanded, Josie lay by the pool in a patch of weak winter sunlight, wearing her yellow coat and sunglasses, a scarf tied Grace Kelly–style around her head and throat. She listened to the instruments, each with its own voice, meeting, arguing, separating, coming back together again. She felt grand, pampered, at ease. It was warm in the sun but an underlayer of cold revealed itself whenever a cloud came by. Watching the surface of the dark water, the ripples when a leaf fell in, she felt herself sink into a sweet lethargy. She had the sense that the phone call to Jeremy might be her last volitional act. From now on, she would float like a leaf on Meredith's pool, like a phrase of Debussy.

At some point, she heard clicking heels on the concrete. Sofia approached and stopped at her side, stiffly asked if she needed anything. Where before she might have asked *if it was okay, would she mind,* now she just said, "Yes, I am a little hungry," the way Michael would. Not saying what he wanted, but just that he had a need, and it was the rest of the world's job to fill it.

"You want I make you lunch?" The woman didn't look her in the eye, but gazed somewhere over her head. With her thin face and sharp, high-bridged nose, she spoke to Josie the way you'd talk to someone taking a crap, at an angle, as if they weren't really there.

"Breakfast, I think," Josie said. She could feel herself wanting to add *if that's okay,* but forced herself to leave it off. Every attempt to show herself a good person in Sofía's eyes had failed anyway. Maybe she preferred the Loewy imperial style. Or maybe it just didn't make any difference. But it maddened her. "Sofía, you don't like me, do you?"

The woman's full mouth drew into a sudden line.

"What did I ever do to you?" *Who cares if Sofía likes you? If anybody likes you.* "Look, I'm here now. I'm not going anywhere, so you might as well get used to it."

"I make you breakfast." Her low-heeled pumps clicking away as she marched back to the house.

"And if you go out," Josie called after her, "I could use some cigarettes. Gauloises, in the blue box."

Sofía ran her hand over her slicked-back hair, touched the chignon, and kept walking.

Well, where had wanting to be liked ever gotten her? People liked people who didn't care. She lay in the sun behind her dark glasses, listening to a jay argue with a squirrel, and the Brahms. How cold it was, even in the sun. Michael was always cold. Maybe that's why he headed for the desert. Maybe he hadn't gone there to kill himself, maybe he'd just hoped it was warm. The desert was a mystery to her, why people went out there, where there was nothing but a bunch of rocks. It wasn't even beautiful, like Sequoia, or the beach. Why would he go there? Why didn't he just do it at their house? Maybe a gesture of caring, that he hadn't blown his brains all over their bedroom, where they'd made love and spawned their dreams. A last act of consideration. That or a final fuck you.

After a while, Sofía returned with her breakfast, set up on a linen mat — a boiled egg in a cup, toast, honeydew, and the thin dry Spanish ham that Michael liked. She set it on a small table by the chaise, and never once looked at Josie. Sofía might have to wipe her Tyrell ass, but she'd still manage to regard her as untouchable.

"You know, Sofía, I'm really not so bad," Josie said.

For the first time, the other woman met her eyes. And the expression in them was a surprise — not loathing but stranger, almost pity. Josie felt a surge of confusion, anger, humiliation. Pity? How dare Sofía pity her? But then it was gone. Sofía straightened and went back to the house, her apron's crossed straps and bow starched as a napkin.

28
Photo

While Meredith was occupied downstairs with the string quartet, Josie ripped through the pile of raided items in Michael's old room. His things. Their things. All jumbled together. The dresser and toys and pictures, records and books. *They had to be here somewhere, they had to be here.* Those black sketchbooks, in which he had told the truth, all the things she did not know about him. She wanted them. The thought of them invaded her nights. But Meredith had clearly stashed them elsewhere.

Defeated, she sat on the crippled boy's bed, contemplating the massive heap of objects. If she were an artist she would draw this, the angles of paintings and falling books, the points and bundles of soft clothing. A cubist rendition of a stillborn life. But she wasn't an artist, she couldn't depict the abandonment of things the way Michael could. He could make a simple object mean something, touch you.

His fiancée. What she wouldn't have given. Though she never mentioned it to him. It would have ruined their fantasy, that it was just the two of them in their private true world, forever and always. She loved that dream, tried to live up to that. Their love as a dragonfly, skimming over Echo Park, stopping to visit the lotus. They weren't going to be like everyone else, they were Blaise and Jeanne, eating dreams and drinking blue sky.

Out in the brighter studio, the winter light fingered its way through the leaves of the live oak. The last time they had been here was when they packed him up for the move to Lemoyne Street. They'd had the house to themselves. He made her dinner and served it to her in the vast dining room. And she'd imagined someday she would return here, yes, and it would really be their home, why not?

And now she was here, without Michael. The irony. She could dismantle this jumble, clean it up, put the things that upset her in the back of the closet — the mad monk, the Merediths — hang some of the other pictures. But she doubted Michael would have wanted it. He would have wanted the mess to be out, for them to have to look at it. *See what you did to me?* The mad monk glared. *All you bitches.* She had to admit, she preferred the luxury of the guest room, the blue and white wallpaper, the gilded white wood, to the monastery library. She could hear Pen yelling, *You're just like everyone else.* Maybe she was. But Michael hadn't thought so. She had to hang on to that.

But maybe he was just seeing himself in her mirror. Michael had purposely made this room severe, to distance himself from his mother's indulgence. He wanted something harder, purer. He wanted to feel real to himself. She lay head to foot on his hard narrow bed and looked up at his Mexican Virgin. Who had not protected him. Who had not spread her wings around him and hidden him from the light. Her feminine uselessness with her big brown eyes. One more woman who had failed him. Across the room, the blind

Merediths still climbed the white stairs. Josie in her black stockings, her own idiotic tenderness.

She wished Sofía had brought her cigarettes. It was the only thing she still needed the world for.

She picked up an armload of clothes, opened the closet and turned on the light, began hanging things up, shirts, pants, but the smell of the closet overwhelmed her, the scent of pine and moss, that cedar. And here was the green silk tie he'd bought for three dollars at the Salvation Army, the one he wore to the symphony. She slung it around her neck, remembering how it made his eyes so green she could hardly bear it. She pressed the silk to her lips as if she could kiss him through the fabric. Looking in the mirror at the back of the closet, she tried to tie it, the way he had shown her, around and around and through. It was lumpy and lopsided, hanging over the raveling knit of her sweater. She could still see his fingers making the knot, neat and precise. A three-dollar tie, but those fingers knew what to do with it.

She looked in the mirror, the very mirror that had seen him as a child, as a fuzzy-lipped teen. It had drunk his image ten thousand times. She leaned against the mirror, her face against the cool glass. *Michael, why'd you have to do it? Why did you leave me here all alone?* Smearing her wet cheek on the glass. Then she saw the knob. A doorknob of faceted glass, like all the other knobs in the house. The mirror was hung on a door. A door inside a closet. She took the knob and turned.

It opened into another closet, but this one was all white — white painted wood, white carpeting. Light streamed in from the next room, while Brahms came up through the floor, accentuating the silence. The smell of cedar and smoky perfume.

Connecting closets. His and hers.

The thought gave her a headache. She was tired of learning new things about him, each revelation further watering down the memory of the boy she'd known. She wanted to hold on to the way she remembered him, to what she'd thought was true. She was losing him and then losing him some more. She was tired of the truth.

And yet she couldn't help but walk through.

The white closet in fact was even larger than his, a complete dressing room with a window and a white tufted hassock. The walls of neatly hanging clothes, garment bags and racks of shoes and shelves of purses. In a series of quilted bags hung long gowns, sea green and dark green, black and burgundy, white and flowered. She couldn't help running her hands over the silks. A rough nail caught on a sea green chiffon. Crap. She shouldn't be touching these things. She zipped the bag hurriedly. Meredith wouldn't know, it would be a while until she wore these dresses again.

Here were not one but a half dozen fur coats, a dark brown plush, a full-length black mink, a long-haired spotted chubby — lynx, she imagined. Her shoes were like a display in a museum, there must have been a hundred pairs but only one of tennis shoes, Keds, three eyelets, perfectly white. Even the flats were leather. Josie couldn't resist trying on a pair of black satin strappy sandals woven into an intricate Chinese knot, and held up her jeans legs in the three-way mirror to see what they looked like. They were way too big, but they made her legs look like a movie star's.

Wool suits and silk suits, each type arranged by color, from white to buff, sea green, French blue, navy, black. Coats, trenches and overcoats, leather jackets, even a long black-velvet cape with a red satin lining. What kind of woman could wear a full-length velvet cape and get away with it? Who could walk into a room and own it like that, used to people standing up when she walked in? Signing autographs without even blinking.

And just on the other side of the door, her son. Nipping in and out the back way. Getting him to zip her up. Maybe he spied on her this way, too, watching her dress. Of course he would have. He could not help watching, he could be caught through his eyes like a fish on a hook. It was something she hadn't needed to know about him, that he could come into his mother's room this way, and she into his. *You know what they were like.* This door had always been there. Their secret passage. He hadn't known Josie then, but she still felt as if he'd been unfaithful, not to have locked it years ago.

She wondered if the journals were here. She looked in cupboards above the closet. Hats and suitcases, boxes of letters, but no journals. No, Meredith would have them under lock and key by now. Down in her father's study? Maybe not even there. After all, Cal had breached security. No, they were in a safe-deposit box in some bank downtown. Fuck. She should know better than to underestimate Meredith. She had it all thought out.

In the bedroom, light filtered through the trees and the raised blinds, the blackout drapes tied back, everything fresh and white and blue — the pleated and tufted blue satin of the headboard, the gleaming silk of the spread, where she and Michael had made love that very first time, a year and a half ago. His closed eyes flickering. Where he whispered, *Show me, show me what you want.* And she'd thought he was a virgin. Christ, what a fool. Could a virgin have made love to her like that? Did she really think she could have taught him so quickly?

And where his mother had lain in her drugged sleep, Josie standing by the bed, thinking how easy it would be to kill her.

She glanced around the room. She could hear the Brahms from downstairs, the complicated patterns of music. She knew she should not be here, what if that sneaky maid caught her? And yet, she was family, now. *His fiancée.* And family made itself at home, didn't it? Michael wouldn't have hesitated. She imagined belonging to a room like this, the dresser gleaming in the early afternoon light, its inlay of flowers in a basket set like a marvelous puzzle into the cinnamon-colored burl. All that work, so Meredith would have a place to put her underwear. She ran her hand across the top, with its perfume tray. She could see herself in the fancy beveled mirror over the dresser, wearing Michael's tie, her scroungy punk hair with the roots already starting to come in. She was going to have to decide soon, if she wanted to be a woman who deserved to have a room like this, or to stay the ragged innocent Michael had loved.

In the top drawer, Meredith's stockings lay in neat rolls tucked between dividers in a long satin case like bees in their comb, scented with sachets of sandalwood and winey roses. Slips, all embroidered, exquisite, lay in a perfect stack. She touched the smooth needlework on a white satin half-slip — appliquéd flowers, their petals drifting toward the scalloped hem — taking care that her rough fingers didn't snag the silk. She flushed to think of the bra she had bought from the Goodwill, that she had tried to impress Michael with. How pathetic she must have looked, the scratchy turquoise lace and her torn underwear. In the next drawer, sweaters, cashmere, lamb's wool, thin, soft as clouds. Below that, bigger sweaters, shawls.

Who was Meredith Loewy? The woman down there commanding the Steinway, leading the strings, she had performed this Brahms piece in great concert halls. The woman who had raised Michael, the woman who could say one moment, *She's a servant, she'll do what she's told,* and the next could beg, *Don't leave me. You're all I have now.* Into whose hands was she giving herself? She didn't understand Meredith any more than she had understood Michael. They both had such secrets. She didn't know if she'd even recognize them if she found them. It might be like sitting in Mauritz Loewy's study reading the Unfinished Symphony. Clues could be staring her in the face right now, and she would have no idea.

The Brahms turned tender through the floorboards, the yearning of the violins, one higher, one lower, the brightness of the piano, the sadness in the cello. The sadness everywhere. She sat in Meredith's satin-striped lounge chair, listening. The photographs in silver frames rested on the bedside table by her elbow. Michael gazing out at the camera over the tops of his Ben Franklins at Harvard. Where he went to try to best his father. His green eyes teasing, she could tell he was about to say something witty. She touched his face, the cheekbones, the planes, the wide mouth, the way it curled in the corners. *What didn't you lie to me about, Michael?* She wanted this photo, she had no photographs of him. It would be so easy to turn it to the back, open the hooks, slide it out from the frame. But she let it stay.

She wondered who had taken the picture. Whoever it was, she was already jealous, that Michael would have looked at her that way; she knew that look, it was intimate, his guard down. She had already seen *People Are Talking About* the Loewy Faradays, in their groovy Sixties getups, on the Arabic rooftop, tiles and domes. The picture that caught her attention now was Meredith in her pearls, propped on a couch, one arm thrown back behind her head. Michael once had Josie pose exactly in that position, on the furry blue couch. So here was the original. Meredith, regretful and yet seductive, polished and sophisticated in a linen sheath dress, the bare underarm, eyes rimmed in dark eyeliner. She was a woman for whom a man would buy a diamond ring or a new car, just to cheer her up. She tried to gauge Meredith's age, but it was hard to tell with her. She hadn't gained any weight from then to now, and the simple clothes could have been from any era. She wore her hair loose, to her shoulders, it could have been yesterday or twenty years ago. The light flooded out any possibility of wrinkles on the black-and-white film.

Who was the photographer, admiring her like that, bathing her in such tenderness, such sympathy? Cal. Suddenly she understood it was a way of having him without copping to the fact she was still carrying a torch for him. *It's what's not there that's most important.* A photograph she chose to look at every day of her life. Though she surely must have liked the way she looked, the sexy seriousness of her face, the large breasts evident but not overexposed, it was a way of keeping Cal without admitting she still cared.

The music stopped. Josie listened, holding her breath to hear better, but they were just discussing something about the piece. She waited until they started again, the same section they had just played. She felt a bit the way she used to feel in Bakersfield when she would touch herself in the bedroom she shared with her sisters, listening in case anyone was coming.

She saw that the round table holding the photographs was actually a small bookcase that revolved on a pedestal of white wood and brass, rising from three clawed feet like a drum on stork's legs. She rotated it, allowing the titles to flow past, *Immortal Beloved,* Anna Mahler, Arrau. Books about Horowitz, Rubenstein. *Life and Liszt.* A group of unmatched leather-bound books caught her eye, all different colors, black, red, brown, green, blue. She pulled one out, bound in black pebbly leather, full of old photographs, mounted on thick black paper with black photo corners, each one carefully titled in white ink in a spiky handwriting. Pitched roofs, houses, people. Cafés, funny old-fashioned cars. It had to be Europe. She had always thought she would go to Europe with Michael, sit at café tables like these.

Café Central, Wien. A lively group of people, the women in pulled-down flapper hats and T-strap shoes and sweaters with fur collars, men in coats and vests and ties had pushed several small tables together and grinned for the camera over coffee and cigarettes, their names all listed below their images, *Schatze, Siggy, Jan, Hector, Kaspar, Mauritz, Lisbeth.* Mauritz. There he was — young. Dark and animated, with wavy black hair and a sexy smile, his arm around a dark-haired woman, Lisbeth. She could see why women had wanted him. Laughing against a stone wall, his arm thrown around another man. How affectionate he was, she wouldn't have guessed. How free. *Herrengasse, August 1928.* At a table with a group of people on a sidewalk, holding his glass up for a toast. In a darkish room, writing in a music book at a piano, wearing a tie but no coat. *Klaviersonate cis-Moll, 1929.*

The woman, Lisbeth, was more serious than Mauritz, more direct in her gaze, and they were almost always together. Walking on the river. Waltzing, Mauritz in a tailcoat, Lisbeth in a long gown with a handkerchief hem. *Musikverein Ball, 1932.* Obviously a hot love affair. The woman looked a little like Meredith, but it couldn't be her mother, Meredith had been born in the U.S., her mother's name was Pauline. Such handsome people talking, laughing, playing instruments, skiing in old-fashioned black sunglasses, waiters on ice skates. She envied their progress through life, carefully annotated in the white writing, their names, the places, the dates. The liveliness of their faces. Those times were so much more real, those people more alive than people today. The living had a deadness now, where the dead had been so alive. She envied them, each and every one. Mauritz and Lisbeth,

Schatze and Kaspar and Jan. She could imagine herself and Michael among them, laughing. That's where they should have been. If only there had been a way. He would have found himself there. It would have been the right place for him, with Schatze and Kaspar.

The next album, a light brown cowhide stamped in gold diagonal lines, opened in Los Angeles, a jump cut without the help of a train or boat shot, no waving goodbye, no Statue of Liberty, no "Welcome to California." It made you wonder what you'd missed. Only the dates showed it was the next album, it had to be. The paper of this album was a soft cream, the annotations in black, a round, more childish hand. In California, Mauritz was tanned, he smiled, there were new friends. Dinners with white tablecloths, here in this house. A woman in shorts laughing under a eucalyptus. *Galka Scheyer, 1933.* Mauritz at the beach, the men wearing bathing suits with tops, *Salka and Eisenstein.* But Mauritz had changed. He reminded Josie of today out by the pool — warm in the sun, but just underneath it, cold like an undertow.

A blond woman with pale eyes made her appearance, wide shoulders in a halter dress before a microphone, her hair in a marcel wave.

Lounging at a pool, her long fleshy legs. *Ambassador Hotel, 1933.* Wearing a corsage and a lace mantilla, Mauritz's arm around her neck — you could tell she was taller than he was. Their wedding picture. *April 1934.* Even at their wedding dinner, they were an odd pairing — together, but not in the same way as Mauritz and Lisbeth had been in Vienna. The blonde seemed out of her depth, even at her own wedding, as if she had just been brought along — sitting uneasily with the men smoking cigars around a table full of drinks — she was not intrinsic to the party, not part of it as Lisbeth had been in the black album. She was just with Mauritz.

Suddenly, in a bed jacket, a dark-haired baby on her lap.

Josie bent down to look closer at Meredith and her mother. The eyes were the same. But it was strange, Meredith more closely resembled Lisbeth than her own mother. Many shots followed of Mauritz at parties, *Salka Viertel, Garbo, Huxley 1937.* Mauritz with Meredith, her Shirley Temple short dresses from Lanz with smocking across the front, *comme il faut.* But there was only one shot of the three of them together, at the table in the garden, she recognized it — it was in this very house, at the same table where Michael had sat when he drew her that day in the pool. Mauritz had Meredith on his lap and Pauline smoked sulkily. She recognized that sulk, oh yes. Pauline at a party with Mauritz, who turned away from her to talk to the dark-haired woman on his right. *Hedy Lamarr, Billy Wilder's 1939.* Pauline had a nugget-sized diamond on her finger and an expression like the woman in *Citizen Kane* in the vast empty house, working the jigsaw puzzle.

Suddenly, no more Pauline. She wondered what had happened to her. Michael only said his mother's mother was a singer who left when Meredith was a little girl. But now, Josie realized there was more to the story, though whether Michael knew it and didn't say or really had accepted Meredith's version was unclear. Because really, what woman ever left a small child behind with its father? Seeing that look on the woman's face in the garden, that mix of boredom and disgust and hopelessness, she imagined a different scenario. An affair, with a musician maybe, a horn player with the band at the Ambassador, someone who didn't look down on her because she was big and blond and uneducated, just a big American dummy compared to Lisbeth. But she wouldn't have run off and left her child with Mauritz. No, he must have discovered her affair, and offered to pay her to get lost, if she just left the girl with him. And Pauline took him up on the deal. He never loved her. She had only brought Lisbeth back to him. He didn't need her anymore.

As Josie looked through the ensuing years, the procession of people, Meredith becoming the kind of girl that people who have children hope for — curly dark hair and the translucent eyes, she couldn't see their color in the black-and-white photographs, but she knew they were green green green — she couldn't help but think of Pauline. How she took the money, in an envelope maybe, or one big check, and her furs and the ring, took it all and opened a bar somewhere, a little cocktail lounge in the desert maybe. She was probably out there even now, some blowsy granny who could still belt it out when she'd had enough to drink. Probably counted herself lucky to have gotten out of here with her sanity. She might have married the horn player, who would be the bartender, and had a couple more kids, and they would all have green eyes. But none with the hypnotic quality of her first daughter's. Just ordinary people, ordinary kids.

Josie went to the window, looked out. Was this the secret to Meredith — that she had replaced her mother in her father's affection? Just as Michael had replaced Cal. *Screws up the whole Oedipal chain of command.*

Oak leaves whirled in small eddies over the bricks. Everything so empty. She flipped listlessly through the red album, the green one. Baby Meredith shakes hands with people, baby curtsies, baby sits at a monstrous keyboard next to proud papa. *First recital, June 1942. Wilshire Ebell.* Meredith at the keyboard, various ages, an extraordinarily beautiful child in dark dresses with white cutwork collars and cuffs. Piano teachers. Meredith with her father, now silver haired, holding up a cup or a certificate. Parties, *Arnold Schoenberg,* an old man with big ears, bald with a drawn face, white handkerchief in his pocket. *Cyd Charisse, Igor and Vera Stravinsky.*

The teachers disappear, leaving just the young woman, triumphant, alone. Tall now, dramatic, skin very pale against the black dress, her dark hair lost in the blackness of the hall. Her luminous face attracting all the light. *Royce Hall, 1948.* Back East pictures, brick buildings, trees without leaves. Meredith in a dark coat with a tormented-looking older man. *Serkin, Curtis, winter 1954.* Serkin, her teacher, it had been a big deal.

A picture of a sign, *Carnegie Hall. Philadelphia Orchestra, Ormandy, Serkin, Oct. 27.* Carnegie Hall. It didn't look as fancy as she thought it would. Then the grand piano, the hall, a girl in a sleeveless dress, her long white arms, an orchestra behind her, her face almost ugly with the effort of what she was performing. Then flushed and triumphant, holding a bouquet of roses, a fat old man beaming at her.

Then another unnerving jump, this time to travel shots, cities, landmarks. *Berlin. Covent Garden. Concertgebouw.* Men in tailcoats, with rumpled hair and foreign-sounding names. *Von Karajan, Boulez, Juin 1956.* Boulez. They were going to see Boulez on the twenty-eighth. This very same man. This world was still going on. Would she too be in pictures like this, *Josie and Boulez, 1981?* She ran her hands over the postcards from opera houses, postcards from hotels: George V, Hôtel de l'Europe. Meredith in conversation with famous people, you could tell they were famous, there was an aura about them, even the fat old men in heavy eyeglasses. Now the stars are there to see Meredith — *David Niven, Simone Signoret, Maria Callas,* a handsome woman with striking features next to whom Meredith seemed very young and otherworldly.

But not a trace of Mauritz, who killed himself a month after her Carnegie Hall debut.

No little pamphlet from the funeral which Meredith had not attended, no photograph of the grave, no obituary, no pressed flower. *Let's not say any more about it. Let's just go from here.* No indication that anything had gone awry, only his absence, everywhere. First Lisbeth, then Pauline, then Mauritz. Death, disappearance, what you didn't talk about, like a sewer running under a street, the shit was down there, out of sight, but you could smell it, it didn't go away, it didn't vanish. It was the absence behind everything. The album ended with the picture of Meredith that was on the table. Lying on the couch, her long arm behind her. And now she saw it, the sadness, the absences in her eyes. Just under the sun-warmed surface of her new life.

People showed you everything in what they left out. No father, but suddenly, here was Cal in the green album, *Cap d'Antibes, Juin 1957*. How beautiful the letters looked, a place, a season. She tried to say them under her breath, *Cap d'Antibes. Juin.* "Zhwain. Antibe." The handwriting less childish now, less round. Cal and Meredith, both very tan, on a terrace of a restaurant in the evening. Both so handsome. Cal's hair was dark like hers, and longer than was the style. The remains of a meal, dishes and bottles and wineglasses crowded the white-clad table. Sitting very close together for the picture — Cal must have asked the waiter to take it. She noticed that Cal's hand was under the table, she wondered what it was doing as they smiled for the picture. Meredith's face so poised, so assured, but was that hand between Meredith's thighs? Pushing aside her handmade lace panties while the waiter told them to get closer, closer?

Cal and Meredith in white, riding a motor scooter up some steep road paved in cobblestones. *Grande Corniche, Juillet 1957.* "Corniche," she whispered. Meredith sidesaddle, in a dress and sandals and big sunglasses, clinging to his back. Josie's heart pounded. Never was she with Michael the way Meredith and Cal had been. Such life in them. Rich and famous and young, beautiful like a matched set of horses.

She turned the page, startled to find a shot of Meredith topless, lying on a striped lounge under an umbrella, her long body tanned against the paler stripes, propped up on her elbows, her breasts large, her nipples dark and erect. Just a photograph like all the others, affixed to the page with the little black stick-on corners. She stared at the shot, trying to understand how Meredith, who was so proper, who labeled in a clear hand all the pictures in a family album as if it would go into a history book, who couldn't get over that her son had fallen in love with an art model, would include a picture of herself lying on a beach in public with her tits out. Hypocrite. And there was Cal, wearing a tiny racing bikini, his cock's outlines visible for anybody to see. She flipped ahead to see if there were any shots of them actually getting it on. *Oh Christ, Josie, don't be such a hick. It's Saint-Tropez. Don't be such an Okie. You shouldn't even notice that Meredith has no top on, that you can see that Cal is uncircumcised.*

More dinner shots, Meredith with Cal, Josie recognized Leonard Bernstein, she'd seen his face and thick hair on album covers. She looked more closely at this one. Meredith wore a strapless dress and white gloves over the elbow, and she listened to Bernstein on her left who was talking to her. Cal had his arm stretched across the back of her chair. Territorial. He was listening too, but not as entranced as Meredith was. It looked like they were already married now.

Other men vying for his wife's attention. Already problems, she could feel the strain between them.

And then Michael made his appearance, the small blue-edged birth announcement, date, weight, length. Jesus, how many pictures could they take of one little baby? Cute, with those eyelashes, he looked like a baby in a Disney cartoon.

She envied him. Even dead, she couldn't help it. How many pictures did her parents have of her in the family album? The family album, such as it was. A shredded white cloth-covered volume with its discolored plastic overlay that never quite stuck down, later photos just thrown in there loose. There were three. One of her with Corinne and Bo in the bathtub. The one of her and Jimmy in the tow truck with their father, and one of her at sixteen on roller skates serving Cokes at the Rollerama roller disco. And that was it. The unfairness of it grabbed at her as she looked at the photo of the three Faradays in a hammock under a live oak. These people living important lives, assuming that posterity would need to know what they were doing in June 1960. Documenting. The photos in her parents' family album were purely accidental. Someone had a camera, thought something was cute or funny — Uncle Dave passed out on the couch at a party, someone put a bra over his head and ears like earmuffs.

But there was no posterity for the Faraday album. They were a dead end. All that documenting for nothing. Meredith and Michael, sharing a secret on the couch, their foreheads together, his little hand on her breast. God, if she could have had his child. That sweetness, she practically couldn't look at it. Cal at a book signing. Cal, smoking a cigarette at his typewriter, at the desk in Mauritz's study, handsome in that craggy way, every shot looked like a book-jacket photo. Meredith on the glider in the yard, reading with Michael, him in diapers. Meredith with Michael on her lap at the keyboard of the big concert grand in the living room, his small hands striking the keys, her big hands on either side of his. *You know what they were like.* Michael on a plane in a shorts suit, solemnly talking to the captain. Michael at four or five, naked in a hammock, reading a book, not a kid's book, something hardbound, and absently fondling his baby dick. The book was heavy, he propped it on its side. If it had been anyone else's kid, and he wasn't masturbating, you'd think it was a staged photograph. The cloud of dark ringlets and the long eyelashes, he looked like a child in a fairy tale, a child who lived in a blackberry bush.

Michael with his six-year-old fingers in Meredith's long hair, sucking his thumb. Meredith listening to a short black man in a jacket and tie, both holding drinks. Then no more Cal. Another sailor overboard. Exit one husband.

His vanishing fuels a second expeditionary period. *British Museum, January '64. Bodleian Library.* Michael and a young man studying at a table by a tall window, the shapes of tree branches falling across them. *Bloomsbury.* Michael meeting a hairy, grinning Indian guy, making that bow with his hands pressed to his forehead, *Maharishi Mahesh Yogi.* Parties with brightly dressed groovy people in shades and floppy hats. Meredith in her black concert dress, shaking the hand of a young woman who looked like a horse. *Command performance, Windsor, April '64.* Meredith sitting on the steps of what clearly was Greece, *Parthenon.* Her dark hair long, she wore an oatmeal-colored shift and sandals that wove up her legs. You could see up her skirt to a pair of white panties.

The two of them, then, Meredith and Michael, very tanned, on horseback, on camels, in a tiny plane. Broken columns rising out of the desert like the backbone of an immense dinosaur. *Palmyra.* Latticed windows above worn three-story houses on crooked streets, *Constantinople.* Birds in cages, a tiled dome. *Isfahan.* Smoking piles on steps leading down to a river. *Benares.* The pyres on the Ganges. A dead body burning, right out in the open, black as a barbecue. Not at all as she had imagined, not at all. You could actually see the corpse through the flames.

Michael dancing with a miniskirted blonde, ballroom-style, looking away over the girl's shoulder as she stared up into his face attentively. *Cotillion, '70.* Michael playing tennis, the shot that his father carried around in his wallet. *I am not sportif.* Skiing. She could feel the slow drip of anger running down her forehead. Why would he want to present himself as the crippled boy to her, when he could ride a horse, play tennis, swim, drive? What did he get out of it — was it just a put-on, was he laughing at her the whole time? Could she have been in love with someone who didn't even exist, some puppet he had invented, a life-sized puppet whose strings he pulled?

Michael carrying a bouquet of red flowers. *Siena, '71.* Michael lying on the couch reading. *Köln, '72.* Meredith at a café, looking out at the traffic, her bare shoulder. *Café de Flore.* And another shot, the same café, of the two of them, the waiter must have taken it, Michael was older now, fifteen maybe, their heads together, the same eyes, the same expression.

Meredith and Michael on a striped chaise lounge under a beach umbrella, white boats in the background. *Saint-Tropez, Juillet '73,* she even recognized it by now. Meredith, with her teenaged son, wearing nothing but a string-bikini bottom. She leaned forward, her tits out, not as high, but still attractive, and Michael knelt on the lounge behind her, rubbing suntan oil on her back. She had her head turned, talking to him. Their two dark heads, their faces were so close together, they could have kissed.

Josie's lungs grew stiff, pressing on her heart. She squinted at Meredith's serene face. They looked like lovers. Christ, they looked like lovers. She turned back to the café shot, it was there too, sharing a secret. Their heads together. This was not a boy with his mother. A boy with his mother was goofy, sulky, solicitous, tender at best. She returned to *Saint-Tropez,* looked at that picture until she thought the image would begin to dissolve off the page. His face, the eyelashes lying on his cheeks like that, like a sleepwalker. She knew that look. The dreamy look of his sexual face.

Oh, don't be ridiculous. Someone took that picture, some friend or other. They weren't alone. But her brain kept balking, smashing into that picture like waves crashing into rocks. Cold, salty, choking. These weren't people like the people she knew. Maybe they were like prizewinning dogs, or racehorses, so finely bred they could only fuck each other. They thought Okies were like that, marrying their cousins and so on, when it was them all along.

She turned the page, but it was just life as usual in the Loewy/Faraday household. As if nothing had happened. Michael at a school with horses, leaning against a fence. Michael sulking dramatically in a chair. Meredith with people in evening clothes . . . but now she knew what to look for. The story wasn't in the pictures, it was in the jump cuts. *What isn't there.* Suddenly they weren't traveling together anymore, suddenly Michael was in school at Ojai, suddenly there were no more intimate conversations over café tables and back rubbings in chaise lounges in France. She gazed at the photo in the silver frame, Michael glancing over the tops of his Ben Franklins against the ivy wall of Harvard. That expression, all his irony, sad and humorous and Bosch, was this what it held, *Saint-Tropez, Juillet '73?*

She touched his face, his lips, the wide mouth curling. Had he ever really been hers? Or was the only person he ever loved behind the camera? Meredith's shadow over everything.

She put the album back in its slot. Now she wished Meredith had burned down the house as she said she would. Before, when there had still been something left of their love, troubled but possible. Now there was nothing but the disgraceful, unavoidable truth that she was nothing to him. An aberration, a failure in judgment, maybe a desperate attempt to hold back the night.

Well, she had known it all along. Hadn't she asked herself a million times, what was he doing with a girl like her? It wasn't her at all. How absurd. How ridiculous. She was just a decoy, something you threw out of the car to slow the cops while you made your getaway.

She went back through the closets, then out into the hall, the maid was coming up with a stack of towels. She looked up just as Josie came through Michael's door.

Josie spoke first. "It was more than just

mother and son, wasn't it? Between them. In France. You were there. You knew."

Sofía said nothing, just held out two packs of cigarettes, Gauloises Bleues. "You should never come here. This is no your home." She reached behind Josie and closed the door to Michael's room. "Leave us."

"Maybe I will. Maybe I fucking will."

Josie went into her own room, the room she had come to see as her room, the guest room, unwrapped the cigarettes and lit one. Just like Cal had said, it was Michael and Meredith, from the start. She could tell herself all the pretty stories she wanted, but she was no better than her mother, living in her movie-matinee fantasies of Elizabeth Taylor and James Dean and Natalie Wood in the middle of a tow yard. She'd walked off a cliff into thin air, not realizing she'd been walking on nothing at all.

29
Paris

Josie lay on the chaise in the last patch of sun. Inside, the quintet had stopped, they didn't seem to be starting up again. She held the photo in her hand. Her suitcase was packed, just with the things Sofía had brought from her house, she was taking nothing Meredith had given her. The sun moved toward the observatory. Soon it would be dark. *The brevity of beauty.* She rested her head against the back of the lounge, feeling the last warmth on her face. How elegant, finally, she had become. It was the coldness, she hadn't understood that before. Coins of light played across the top of the pool, tiny dapples of gold above the dark.

Finally, Meredith emerged from the French doors onto the brick terrace above the pool, like an actress making an appearance onstage. Stretching, first lifting her arms straight over her head, turning her linked hands palms up, then, elbows cocked, bending from side to side, she let her arms drop with a contented sigh. "Ah, that was wonderful. It's been too long, I've been gathering moss. So what have you been doing with yourself all this time?"

Then, Meredith noticed her suitcase.

Josie waited. That's the way you handled a scene, you controlled the silences. She crossed her legs Elena-style, on the chaise, and lit a cigarette. She felt the cold rage coiling inside her, watching how Meredith moved, her body so like his, that flowing-sea quality, the long legs, long forearms, the looseness of hip and shoulder and wrist. The utter selfishness. There was her rival, right there. All along. She tapped the photo in her hands, drawing Meredith's attention to it, though the older woman was pretending she saw nothing. Instead, she picked off some dead leaves from a straggly fern growing out of a stone urn, one of the set that flanked the steps down to the pool.

"She's being mysterious," Meredith said to the plant. "Nothing like a good mystery at the end of the day."

Sofía emerged from the kitchen door in her neat day dress and heels, her starched apron, bearing a tray, two tumblers, a Scotch on the rocks for Meredith, the other glass containing something clear. She served Meredith on the terrace, at the table just where her mother had sat that day with Mauritz and herself as a baby, then brought the second drink down to Josie, at the other end of the pool. Sofía managing to offer the tray in a way that she wouldn't have to actually hand the glass to her. The woman's narrow face worked with the effort of withheld information. Josie could see that Sofía had not told Meredith about catching her coming out of Michael's room. *Leave us,* the woman's eyes said, reflecting her tiny image in their obsidian mirrors — the yellow fake fur, a white dot of bleached hair, the Jackie O sunglasses.

Meredith sat at the table, drinking her drink, and Josie imagined a leopard, spread out on one of these heavy branches overhead, waiting for something sizable to fall down on. Impersonal as God. Though not to the deer, who would feel the fatal drop, the deer who would take it all very personally.

She took a deep draft of her own drink, Stoli on the rocks, the clean burn of it in her nose and throat. It was just what she wanted, that heat, she felt suddenly warmer. It was what you wanted to drink if you were going to Siberia, to see the dead piled by the train. If you were going into the tiger cage.

The woman was up again, prowling around the upper terrace, looking up into the trees, across the valley to the observatory's domes. Then she swung down the steps, on a diagonal, her stride like a big cat's slink, weighty and silent. Josie drank again, watching her, you couldn't take your eyes off someone like that, she could see how she would take possession of a concert hall, no one would be able to look anywhere else. Meredith prowled down the outside of the pool, drink in one hand. Behind her, the gold of the setting sun bathed the heavy-branched live oaks and outlined Meredith's sable hair. She stopped to tear some browned flowers off a pink camellia and threw them into the bushes. She leaned over and broke the leaf off a plant, tore it, sniffing.

"I love these scented geraniums. We've got lemon, there's peppermint and even chocolate. Have you smelled this?" She came around the foot of the pool, extending her hand, close enough that Josie could see the wet hair around her face from the exertion of the Brahms quintet.

"Tell me about Saint-Tropez."

Meredith halted in midstep, it was just an instant, but Josie could see her every gesture, as if magnified, the way her eyes paled, pupils contracting. Then she smiled, relaxed, lifting the shredded geranium leaf to her nose. "Just a resort town. A little tacky. People go to Ibiza now. Why do you ask?" And Josie knew that Meredith could see the photograph now. Playing innocent, as her silent leopard's body came nearer.

She took another big slug of the Stoli, felt the flush in her head. She wasn't cold anymore. Heat filled her as she stared at Michael's mother, the source of all disaster. "Was it tacky in 'seventy-three? When you went with Michael?" Clicking her nail on the edge of the photo.

"Maybe," Meredith said. "But we had our traditions. That was Michael, he loved traditions. I think it gave him structure. We're a nomadic people."

"Something different happened that summer." She could feel the Stoli singing in her ears. She had been so lethargic lately, sedated. It was good to feel the rush of energy, her heart full of blood and outrage.

"Maybe." Meredith passed behind Josie's chaise. She could hear the ice rattling in Meredith's Scotch.

She didn't want to strain to follow her, she just tilted her head, as the voice moved from her left to her right. She didn't like Meredith being behind her. Anything could happen when you couldn't see them. You had to watch them every second.

"What happened in Saint-Tropez, that you didn't go back?" The damp sheets, the smell of the sea, nobody but the two of them. Who would know? They could pretend it hadn't happened. They both loved pretending things that weren't true.

"I have no idea what you're talking about." Now she could see her, she'd moved to the edge of the pool, squatted down, tested the water with her fingers. Then she glanced up at Josie, pinning her with those green eyes.

"I always wondered what your hold on him was. I couldn't figure it out. Like you were some heroin he couldn't put down."

Meredith stopped then, her bullshit testing of the water, it was damn freezing, you didn't need a college degree to figure that out. She straightened, very fast, it startled her. Was Meredith going to hit her? But the woman only shook the water off her hand. "Where did this all come from? Really, Josie, four hours ago you were happy as a lark. Maybe you shouldn't mix your meds." She came and sat down on the chaise just next to Josie's.

Josie blew a smoke ring, another inside of it. Inside and inside. That's the way it played up here, one ring inside another. Just when you thought you knew what was up. "Let me tell you something about your son. You know what he liked?" She took the last drink of Stoli, exhaled the heavy fume. "He liked doing things when he was pretending to be doing something else." She put the glass down on the table between them, just a tiny table. She leaned over so her face was only inches from Meredith's and lowered her voice to a whisper. "For instance, he liked me to fuck him while he was talking on the phone with you."

Now Meredith seemed to get it. Josie wasn't going to be intimidated by her high-class bullshit anymore. This wasn't going to go down that way. She could smell her smoky perfume, the sharp sweat from the session with the old men.

The older woman blinked, set her Scotch down on the table, leveled her green gaze at Josie. "Why are you trying to hurt me? When I took you in. Treated you like my own child."

"What happened in Saint-Tropez?"

She flicked the corner of the photograph. Meredith and her leopard son, him rubbing her, her purring. Still the woman made no move to see it, just kept staring at Josie, as if she might sprout another head.

"Michael never got past it."

"Is that what he said?" Meredith said sharply, then backed off, taking a drink of her melting-ice Scotch that smelled like a forest fire. She smiled. "Oh, Josie, you know what he was like. How self-dramatizing he could be." Red under green. So it was true.

"You fucked him. In Saint-Tropez." Josie dropped the photograph onto the table. One Card Pickup.

Meredith leaned over and looked at it, but didn't pick it up. Didn't touch it. She took a long breath, not a gasp but a sensuous inhalation, a long, luxurious outbreath. "Where did you get this? Have you been going through my things?"

"Are you insisting on privacy all of a sudden? You, of all people?" Josie stabbed at the photo with her forefinger. "Explain that, if you can."

The smile widened and a laugh broke over her like a wave, a full-throated laugh, giving her a view of her fabulous square white teeth, even as pavement, and her long column of neck. "Josie Tyrell. What a prude you are. Who would have guessed? You take off your clothes every day, but Lord, see a mother sunbathing with her son, suddenly you're the morality squad." She wiped the corners of her eyes, wet with laughter. "God, you're so American. Terrified of the body, terrified of sex, while being completely obsessed with it. What is it that bothers you the most? That you weren't there, or is it just someone my age still comfortable in her own skin?"

She could kill her. *Saint-Tropez, Juillet '73.* "That's too fucking comfortable," Josie said, pointing at the picture. She wanted to bash Meredith's face into it. "Way too fucking comfortable, Meredith. That's your goddamn son."

Meredith gazed down at the photo, her and Michael, and sadness replaced the smile that had just swept her face. "Our last good summer," she said, pushing back her dark hair. "Maybe one day you'll have a son. Then you'll know. It's a special relationship."

Josie grabbed the photo off the table and thrust it in front of Meredith's face so she could get a good look, a good close look. "You didn't want him to have a girlfriend. You fucked up everything you could and now I know why." *Civilization and Its Discontents.* She held out the photo the way a cop holds a badge. *Argue with this, motherfucker.*

Meredith didn't look. She was looking at Josie, her cool gaze unwavering. "Try to understand. I've lost so many people. We were close, yes. Have I ever denied it? And yes, I disapproved of you, I thought he could do better. Maybe I was wrong about that and a million other things, and I've told you so. But what you're picturing goes beyond anything I would do. Ever. You've got to believe me."

Josie kept holding out the photograph, but she felt less sure than she'd been. She reached for her glass but it was empty.

Meredith put her cool hand on Josie's wrist and gently pressed her arm down. The sight of her wrist under that enormous hand shocked her, it looked like a twig under a tiger's paw. She was suddenly tired.

"In Europe, women sunbathe with their families, and nobody thinks, God, they're having sex. I swear to you." She gently pulled the photo out of Josie's hand, then stood up, facing into the setting sun. The last sunlight licked the domes of the observatory and the oaks and the pool, it was a poster for California from the orange-grove days. "I don't even care that you went through my things. Go through everything, it doesn't matter anymore, wear my clothes. Just stop thinking of me as a monster every time you see something you don't understand."

She had felt it so clearly before. But now she wasn't sure. Maybe they hadn't actually fucked. Maybe it just was what it was, something with a line so fine, it didn't exist. One more sad thing. She would never know. After all, she hadn't been there, in that room. She couldn't be sure. *And what if it had?* There was nothing anybody was going to do about it now. The shape of her back, so much like his. The squared shoulders, the slender hidden strength. She missed him so much. She was so tired, she felt like crying.

Meredith looked at the photo, then slipped it

into her pocket. "As a matter of fact, there's something I wanted to talk to you about." She came back over and sat on Josie's lounge chair, down by her feet. "I've decided to close up the house. I'm going back out on tour."

Closing up the house? Just a moment ago, Josie could have killed her. Now she felt abandoned. Leaving? Just like Cal. Picking up and going back on the road, Buenos Aires, Bombay. Leaving her stuck here, discarded, forgotten. Just as Michael had left her. These people, they picked you up and played with you and left you lying in the rain. Meredith back on tour. Applause and fans and five-star suites, while Josie — yeah, what? Went back to the shack on Lemoyne. Insomnia and the hulls of dead dreams blowing across the floor of the empty rooms like dry leaves. "So when did you decide this?"

"I just decided."

Punishment was swift. Christ. "Because of me. Because of this."

"No. No, Josie." She reached out and took Josie's small hands in her huge ones. "I'm a musician, that's all. It's what I know." Gently, she pulled Josie's sunglasses off, and looked right into her with that gaze that was like touch. "Look, this isn't going to get any better. Believe me, I've been here before. They say time heals all wounds but they're lying." She folded the sunglasses and put them on the table with their watery tumblers. "I know it sounds heartless to go back on the road, but it isn't what you think."

Josie hated people assuming what she thought. "How could you know what I'm thinking?"

"It sounds terribly glamorous. Room service and white-tie dinners, limousines. When it's really a string of practice rooms and rehearsals, and more taxis and train stations than you can imagine."

That was what she'd thought, but what difference did it make now? Meredith was closing up shop. Taking her ball and going home. Sofía would cover the chandeliers and the furniture and double bolt the door, they would head out for Tunisia or Timbuktu. Just like fucking Cal. Moving on. These fucking people. Leaving her with Michael's death in her lap. She strained at the air, groped in her schoolbag for her cigarettes.

Meredith reached over and Josie jerked her head back instinctively, but Meredith just tilted Josie's chin up to look her in the eye. "I want you to come with me."

She heard it, but so faintly through the roaring in her head she wasn't sure, maybe she'd just imagined it.

"It's meant so much to me to have you here. Even if you are a pain in the ass, who else do I have now?"

The world, which had just shriveled to the size of a pea, suddenly opened again. Going on tour with Meredith? *Wien, Hamburg, Edinburgh, Concertgebouw?* Her? Was she serious? Her heart thumped in her chest so loud she could hear it like a kick drum. She tried to remember, this was the woman who had eaten him away, who had destroyed him. But she was more afraid of being left behind. She knew she was being asked to forget what she knew, in exchange for something she'd never had. But who would blame her? *Everybody.* But whose business was it? There was nothing stopping her. A jay swooped across the silent pool, retreating to squawk among the camellias.

"But what would I do, when you're off doing all that?"

Meredith laughed softly, stroked her face with the back of her forefinger. "Well, what do you do here?"

She tried to think, what did she mean, but it was just the giant blank screen, she didn't even know what to ask.

Meredith embraced her. Took her in her arms, fake fur and all. She could feel the woman's strength, inhaled the smell of her, the Scotch she'd been drinking. "Josie, you're my son's fiancée. My daughter-in-law. You're all the family I've got left. We'll make sure you have a good time. I promise."

She heard a small voice, her father's jealousy. *You got a family. You know where all hers ends up.* But where did Josie's own family end up? Bakersfield. CYA. Revival meeting. Some shit job if she was lucky. "How long would we be gone?"

Meredith left an arm around her shoulders, still holding her tight. "I don't think I'm coming back, Josie. I've had it with this place. I hope this whole godforsaken city falls into the sea."

She could really go away like that? *Never,* the sound of it, so big, so final. And yet, it was everywhere, wasn't it? That was how things went. Things *were* big, they were final. *Never and never.* The person you loved better than anyone in the world died and then you left and never came back.

"Well? You want to come?"

Josie drew in a deep breath, nodded. A very small nod, but it was enough. Signs and signals.

"Good. I'll call Markovsky. We'll be off in no time." She squeezed her shoulder once again and stood. "We'll start with Paris, I know you'll love that. I have a flat in the sixteenth, just off the Avenue Foch." She brushed the wrinkles from her skirt. "Actually, I'm surprised Michael never took you."

A flat in the sixteenth. Off the Avenue Foch. She felt like lightning had hit her and cut her in two top to bottom. All those evenings, dreaming of Paris in their shack on Lemoyne, when they could have just fucking gotten on a plane and gone? While Josie was working like a donkey, trying to put together the money for rent and food and art supplies? A flat in the sixteenth? *Was it very far from Montmartre, you fucking asshole? Was it so very far?* They could have gone anytime. But he didn't want to. He didn't want her to come in from the cold. He wanted to keep her in the dark like some goddamn potato. As their lives closed around them.

She was glad for the gathering night, she could feel her face burning with anger, her eyes stinging with sudden tears. *Who the fuck were you, Michael?* A figment of somebody's imagination, but whose? Hers? His? Or some mutually agreed upon fantasy?

Meredith just chattered on, walking around, picking dead flower heads off the bushes. "We'll have a little stopover in Paris to get our bearings, and then pick up the tour in Frankfurt. It's six weeks in Germany, three in Switzerland, and then on to Vienna. We'll stay at the Imperial, you'll adore that. I've got the Brahms Second, God knows why I did that, threw myself to the lions, but it seemed like a good idea at the time."

Café Central, Wien. "I don't have a passport."

"Well, I wouldn't think you would." Meredith laughed, and came over and picked up the two glasses from the table. "Never mind, Markovsky knows how to speed things up. It won't take long."

Even the federal government bent to Meredith's will. Josie should be outraged, but now she was on the other side of the have-not divide. Not idling beside some Dust Bowl highway, stuck at the California border checkpoint with a mattress and the kitchen stove tied to the roof of the truck. This was a flat in the sixteenth, off the Avenue Foch. She couldn't have Michael, but she could take his place on the train, his seat in first class. Unlock all the doors. She picked up her suitcase. It seemed ridiculous now, a child running away from home with her teddy bear and a peanut-butter sandwich. She was going all the way now.

30
Drown

Time was moving again. All speeded up. All wrong. She had never felt wronger in her life. The house was supposed to be the place where the clocks had all stopped, but they'd all started again. *Tickety-tock.* Her passport had arrived by special messenger. She'd been a good girl and had her roots erased by a Beverly Hills salon, the picture was a girl she didn't recognize. They were leaving Tuesday morning, first class, Air France. *Première classe.* Meredith up in her room, on the phone. Talking the night away. *Yackety-yack.* Ever since she'd decided to leave, Meredith was like a woman on crank. Contacting her buddies from Brussels to Berlin. She gained energy by the day, like a radioactive mutant in a horror film. Up at nine, practicing until three, running through her repertoire, Bach and Schubert and Beethoven. Mendelssohn and Schumann, Dvořák and Bartók, and the big Second, over and over and over again. The music chased itself in Josie's head until she had to sit outside and play something on the blue guitar just to get a different tune in her ear. *Saint Louis woman, wears her diamond rings* . . .

She was getting it, humming under her breath. She took a hit of the cigarette she'd wedged between the strings, up by the pegs, the way her daddy played, and tried not to think about Europe, coming at her like a truck that had lost its brakes on the Grapevine. The clothes Meredith bought her, at Saks and Magnin's and Bullock's Wilshire, hanging in the closet upstairs. Heavy clothes for the European winter, Christ, she'd never even seen snow, except that once when she and Michael had driven up the 2 into the Angeles Crest. It was hard and crusty and they made feeble snowballs and threw them at each other. "Not warm enough," Meredith kept saying. "You're a skinny little kid, you're going to freeze." She got lined wool pants and long skirts and high leather boots, a down cocoon and a cape and a brown and white pony-skin coat that cost five hundred dollars. Dresses for receptions and dinners, velvets and chiffons and even an evening gown.

Boulez was in town, they went to see him rehearse at the Music Center. He'd been all over the orchestra, pointing out everything people did wrong, it was excruciating. He called out the third horn player or the second bassoon, made them do bar 49 over about three times in front of everyone until he thought it was all right.

"Are they always this mean?" she'd asked Meredith, sitting next to her in the red-velvet seats of the empty auditorium.

Meredith smiled. Leaned close to Josie, explained in a low voice, "He has a vision of how the music should sound. This is how he shapes the performance. You should see some of them. Especially the ones who hate women. They love to see if they can make you cry."

Josie imagined some old guy trying to make Meredith cry. Good fucking luck.

Up close, Boulez wasn't as scary as he'd seemed, a nice old guy, with deep indentations in his cheeks and bright brown eyes. Again,

Meredith introduced her as her son's fiancée. "I'm very sorry, my dear," he said, holding her hands in his.

She had to admit, it had been interesting to go to the concert after watching them pick the Berg apart bar by bar. Now she knew what to listen for, and afterward, they went to dinner with Boulez and some other people, an unbelievably expensive restaurant with frosted-glass panels like perfume bottles. She sat between Boulez and some guy from the Music Center, at first she'd been flattered that he would sit next to her, ask about her so-called career, the acting and modeling, and tell her a bit about Berg, but then the critic chimed in, and soon they were all talking about some other conductor's treatment of Berg, which bled into some juicy gossip about the conductor, then a play they'd all seen, a song cycle presented at a Schubert festival, names and places, *Salzburg* and *Aspen* and *Bayreuth*, somebody's recordings of Poulenc, she might as well have been a nicely turned-out store mannequin someone had propped in a chair as a gag. She could see, it didn't matter how pretty you were in Meredith's world, or smart, or original either. If you weren't Somebody, you just didn't have a thing to say. She didn't know how drunk she'd gotten until it was time to go home.

And now they were leaving. Or someone was leaving. Somebody whose passport said *Josephine Tyrell.* Leaving Michael behind in his grave on the hill. Leaving it all behind.

Out by the pool tonight, the dappled clouds spread against the sky like tufts of wool on an old stuffed animal. The moon, bright behind them, held the dark cloud forms against the lighter backdrop of the night. She gazed down into the pool at the sky. She was finally, perfectly high, the exactly correct balance between pills and booze. Weightless, suspended between two brightnesses. In the daytime, the pool was the dark thing, but at night, it was the bright thing in the dark. She concentrated on the simple chord changes, *Saint Louis woman, wears her diamond rings . . .*

She leaned over the edge of the pool, ran her fingers into the cold water, rippling the sky. "So what do you think, Michael?" she asked the dark water. "I'm a-goin to Paree. I be sleepin in your bed, whaddya think of that?" The jittery image of herself peered back across the dark mirror, the white of her face, the silver of her hair. "It should have been us." They could have gone anytime. But no, he wanted to keep her down in Echo Park, scratching like some Okie chicken, like she'd done all her life. She could feel the tears coming. She was really getting to be a sloppy drunk. She wiped her tears, her nose.

Down in the water, her face like a full moon over the tufted yellow fake fur coat. That same fucking face, that face. "What are you looking at, piece of shit? You just shut the fuck up." Sliding right into his chair. Still warm from his body. Right at home with the leopard people.

In Paris right now it was daytime. That's what she had to remember. People on bicycles, taking the Métro, drinking Pernod in sidewalk cafés. Splashing water into clear liquid and watching it turn white, the way they used to in Echo Park. Now she'd see the real thing. But not with him. Not even on her own. If she had one stitch of honor that's what she'd do, just scrape some bucks together and get on a plane. Meredith didn't have a patent on air travel. But no, that wasn't what she wanted. She wanted the whole nine yards. His world. His life.

"You shouldn't have said you loved me if you didn't," she whispered to him, in the trees, in the night. "If you really wanted her." She leaned over and picked up her tumbler of Stoli from the lip of the pool. Felt herself coming out of the chair, she righted herself just in time. Didn't even spill her drink. "You know you fucking played tennis. You played everything. Why couldn't you tell me?" He could tell her about Meadowlands, but not about Meredith. Not about *Saint-Tropez, '73.* And now she was going to try to wear his shoes. Move into his room. Yeah, making herself right at home. Leaving him behind in his dark bed, all alone.

Well, wasn't this what you wanted all along? something whispered.

It wasn't true, where the fuck did that come from? Christ, she'd loved him more than she had imagined it possible to love.

But she was remembering it less and less. *You'll have to remember for both of us.* She wanted to. But how could she, all on her own? It was hard, she needed to forget as well as remember. A fine line. And Meredith being around complicated it even more. She was so goddamn much like Michael, Josie was forgetting what he looked like. She couldn't remember what his voice sounded like. She didn't even know whom she was grieving for anymore, at times it felt like she'd just made him up.

You didn't love him. You just wanted to be him.

No! That was a lie. But . . . what if it wasn't? That underneath it all, what if this was what she loved? Not who he was but what he was. If what she really wanted was to sit in his seat, eat with his spoon. Her reflection beamed back, down there in the dark, like an unknown moon.

She hadn't wanted him to die, what was she thinking? She loved him! She'd always loved him, even when it got bad, like last summer when he pulled away from her, as if her touch was diseased. When he tormented her with his doubts, until she wanted to scream. She'd tried so hard to reassure him that she'd loved him since that first day, when she'd swum here, bathing in the greenness of his gaze. *You envied him, his years in Europe, his family and passports and maids from Seville. You tried to destroy him.*

Fuck. She put the guitar down. These were not her thoughts, they frightened her, the way they came out of nowhere. But truthfully? Honestly, she didn't know what the truth was anymore. She took another swallow of Meredith's good Stoli, lit a cigarette, let the smoke tumble out of her nose. The reds weren't working as well as they should have, that piece of shit Red must have sold Nick a bunch of outdated pharmies. She took another slug of Transsiberian firewater. *Moscow, city of a thousand and three bell towers* . . .

And now she was on her way to Europe. Josie Tyrell, Bakersfield High Class of Nothing Rien Nada Niente Null. "Well I'm going," she said up to the black stars. "Hear that? And if you don't like it you can go screw." Except that he couldn't. "No screwing for you," she said. "Nevermore, croaked the raven." That beautiful body she could screw all day long when he'd let her. Just to touch him. But he didn't want to.

And then the fucking dog came along. Every dog had his day and that dog fucking had to have his.

She leaned forward to see her face in the bright water. So treacherous, her and her moon face, her big innocent eyes . . . She spit at herself but her face reassembled, it wouldn't go away.

In November it should be murky and warm but it wasn't, it had been cold and pissing down rain. Michael curled in the passenger seat, mute and sulky, he'd been like that all day. They'd gone to the museum, she thought it might help for him to get out of the house, but he hadn't liked anything, from the show on down to the cup of coffee he bought — took one sip and threw it in the trash. Staring out at the rain through the heartbeat of windshield wipers. And the dog ran out into the street. It would have made it to the other side, but a car came over the crest of the hill, a patched little Toyota in primer gray, and honked, and the fucking thing lost its nerve and turned back, flew to the curb. The car never stopped.

She should have kept going, she should have just run the fucking thing over, kept going and never looked back, that was the thing to do. But she stopped. Everybody's fucking Good Samaritan. Ran back to where it was rolling around by the curb, swimming with broken back legs. "Hey, boy, hey." Holding out her hand the way you were supposed to, but it growled, snapped at her while it kept swimming, she would never forget the way it swam in circles in the dirty water. It was mangled and hideous, still alive, they had to do something, she never knew the right thing, it was what she hated about herself most, being so stupid and useless, and she called out for Michael.

Why hadn't he just stayed in the car? If only

he had just turned up the radio. But he came out into the rain and stood next to her, staring at the dog, the way it was swimming, with its dead hind legs. "What do we do? Michael?"

But he just stood there, staring, like it was some picture in a gallery, like a Lucien Freud or a Francis Bacon, staring the way he stared at himself in the mirror, paralyzed and utterly fixated. She shook her hands as if there was something on them. "Do something. For once, for Christ's sake!" But he couldn't. He was just like her, useless, but it was worse because he was a man. And she needed him to do something when she didn't know, but he couldn't, and after so many nights of him staring out the window like this, his sulks and depression and his fucking mother, while she was working her ass off like a donkey to pay for it all, and he never fucked her, at least he could do something about a goddamn hurt dog instead of going into the Zone, leaving it all up to her, Christ, her little brother Bo had been more of a man.

And so she started screaming. "What good are you? Do something for once, can't you?" She just wanted him to scream back, to fight, to wake up, but all he did was stare at the dog dragging itself in circles, its brown coat matted with mud, whining and growling, making her more and more furious, she wanted him to do something, anything, just make a move. And it all came pouring out, the things she had not said in those awful months. "You useless son of a bitch. What good are you? You don't fuck, you don't work, you're taking up air somebody else could be breathing. You mama's boy, you faggot!" She walked away from him, screaming up at the houses on the hill, their windows closed against the rain. "Isn't there a man here somewhere? Does it always have to be me?" She stormed back to the car, and threw open the trunk, to see if there was anything there she could use to put the fucking dog out of its agony. It was howling, she couldn't stand it one more moment.

This was what she had been trying so hard to forget, and now the memory was all coming out like a clown's handkerchief, one moment tied to the next and the next, how she had stormed back to the car, her piece-of-shit Falcon that kept breaking down though he could have bought her a new one, but no, it was all up to her, all the time. There must be something, a jack, a wrench, she didn't know what, and there was the brick. She stripped off her leather jacket and wrapped it around her arm and the brick, and the rain was coming down, so cold, and she shoved Michael aside and brought the brick down on the animal's skull, hard and round as a kneecap, as the dog bit at her leather-wrapped hand, and she pounded and pounded it, gritting her teeth as she hit it again and again, venting her fury at Michael and every boy who hadn't come through and the world that didn't care about a damn dog and left it all up to people like her who didn't know what to do, there was blood on the brick, and on her jacket and her hands, hit it and hit it until the dog was done.

Panting and weeping, she stood in the water by the curb covered with dog blood and the dead dog at her feet, and Michael's hand came on her shoulder, touching her with more tenderness than he had showed her for months. And she bared her teeth at him, just like the dog, she would have sunk her teeth into his arm if she could have. "Don't you touch me," her face contorting with rage and disgust. "I'm sick of being the man. I'm going to go out and find someone with a big cock and I'm going to fuck his brains out, and forget all about you. You go back to your mother and let her clean up after you, I sure as hell ain't gonna do it no more. I didn't sign on for this shit. I thought you were a man. Guess I made a mistake."

She wanted him to make her stop but he didn't, he could never give her what she needed and she knew she should stop, but now it was coming out, hot and bitter and it felt hellishly good.

"Don't, Josie. Please." He straightened so she couldn't see behind his Ben Franklins, but his mouth was trembling.

"Don't fucking what? You don't want a woman, you want a goddamn nurse. Why didn't you just say you were in love with your mother? Maybe you ought to fuck her. Maybe you did, some lonely night in Sweden or somewhere."

It made her dizzy, she laid her head on her knees. Of all things. She started to cry. She had not even known. But if she had, she would have said it anyway. She was going for broke then, she was giving it every evil thing that she had, she had reached her own heart of darkness. "You were right, you know? I am sleeping with some-one. But it's not Jeremy, it's Nick, what do you think of that? He fucks me standing up out with the garbage, which is just what I like. I'm so sick of you I could puke."

He was shaking like eucalyptus in the wind, staring at her, the way he stared at the dog. "Josie, don't." He was begging her, not to kill their love, not to do it, they had problems but she didn't need to pummel it into the ground with a brick like the dead dog. But she was every rat-faced Tyrell woman who'd ever screamed at a man, holding her face up to be punched, waiting for the blow, but defiant, because she was getting hers in for once. But Michael wouldn't hit back, he just kept retreating, she needed someone to stop her but nobody would. "Yeah, sometimes I need a good screw, I can't live on poems and silver lilies and shit. Sometimes I just need a good fuck, Michael. And where have you been for me? Nowhere." She felt like a blacksmith hammering a horseshoe on an anvil, hammering that thing for all it was worth. "You don't want a woman. You want someone creeping around going, 'What's Michael gonna think? What's Michael gonna do? Is Michael going off the deep end today?' Well you know what, Michael. I don't give a shit."

It was in her blood after all, how to wound and belittle, she'd grown up with it and now here it was, streaming out of her like gasoline, scalding the person she loved most in the world, and yet unable to stop herself. "Guess I'm just not some silver lily, huh? I'm just po' white trash like your mama told you. Why don't you just go on back to her, then, and if you happen to grow a set of balls, you let me know."

She'd done it right then and there, killed the thing she loved.

She was only trying to get him to wake up, wanting him to see what he had driven her to. She got in the car and drove home, letting him hoof it, fuck him.

And now, in the dark above the pool, her moon face on her knees, weeping, rocking back and forth, she remembered it all. He should have hit her. He should have stopped her. That's all she wanted, for him to stop her, to say she was wrong, to put his arms around her like a man and say that he loved her. When she got home the silence in the apartment reproached her, his art on the walls, the girl at the piano, Blaise and Jeanne together on the blue train seat, staring at her . . . *don't you remember?*

She wept into her hands, slow racking sobs made slower by the booze, but no less painful. Why hadn't she stopped that day, why couldn't she have just driven home, they could have had tea, she could have tried to cheer him, ask him something, God, he loved to teach her things . . . She just hadn't realized how angry she was, hadn't known she could do something so horrible to the boy she loved. *Registered as Oscar Wilde.* Wilde knew what he was talking about, all right.

And when he'd finally gotten home, dripping wet from the rain, she got down on her knees and begged him to forgive her, but it was too late. He couldn't hear her anymore. He slept out on the couch, cold and rigid, staring up at the ceiling. "Don't even try," he said. She tried to make him understand, she was crazy mad, she would have said anything, what could she do to make it up to him? She knelt by the couch and begged him. "I was just mad, I didn't mean any of it."

"You meant every word," Michael said.

"I wanted you to stop me. I wanted you to tell me you loved me."

And he laughed then, a tear-filled laugh. "When I grow some balls, I'll think about it."

It was a mistake you could never recover from. Though he pretended he had, he never did.

And now she was going to Europe with his mother. It was like murdering someone and then moving into his house, taking his job, his lover, eating his food, sleeping in his bed.

She reached down for her voddy and then it was like a series of photos, a film in slow motion. The chair tipping, her falling, she could see it, like stop-action, the dark water coming closer, her own bright reflection. Her head hit first, shockingly cold, her shoulders, her chest, *this is it,* she found herself thinking. She assumed she would float but no, her coat filled with water, pulling her down, surprisingly heavy, and the water closed over her, like a book.

Swim, the thought came, but from very far away. She could see the moon through the water, shimmering high overhead, she knew she should swim, but she was too heavy, the moon was too far. She was so tired, it was simpler just to sink. It made sense. At last, she could stop fighting, it could just end.

31
Sofía

Get off me, she said, or thought she said. She took a deep breath and vomited. Lying in the wet and the cold, she started to cry. She didn't know why, only that it was deep and sad, it felt like it was coming up from the bottom of the sea. Shivering on the bricks. Cold and wet.

"Why you no go? You say you were leave and then you stay." Someone had her by the hair. "Why you stay?"

She curled on the bricks. Fucking Sofía. She should have left her down there. She was ready to die. "Where's my fucking coat?"

Sofía hissed an exasperated sigh, standing,

wringing out her long hair, water raining down on the bricks. Josie looked up at her. How tall she looked from down here. Furious. So fucking what. Fuck her. Suddenly, the woman was jerking her. Pulling her up. Her legs buckled, but the woman held her up, keeping her from falling. The bright pool was dappled with clouds. Darkness under the bright. Waiting for her. Peaceful. She had no problems there. Where was her guitar? Her little guitar. There. She bent down to get it, lurching forward, and Sofía grabbed her, wrenching her arm as she started to lose her balance again. God, she was fucked up.

She clung to the little guitar tight, tight, as Sofía hauled her toward the house. Yanking, shoving. Why was everybody pushing her around? Nobody would just leave her the fuck alone. If she wanted to curl up and sleep at the bottom of the pool, what the fuck did this bitch care? Sofía just didn't want her croaking on the property. It'd look bad for the boss. Josie felt her putrid life inside her, heavy, like a bad meal. She wanted to vomit it up. Her evil, foulmouthed, ignorant life. What had Michael ever done to anybody, compared with her?

The Spaniard pushed her into a chair on the checkerboard kitchen floor, went out, the door swinging back and forth, back and forth. Her eyes skittered over the checkerboard pattern, the tiles. Maybe it was a message. Checkers, chess. *Marcel Duchamp played* . . . But what was she? What kind of chess piece, and what was the game? She shivered spasmodically, though she felt nothing. She needed a cigarette. She pressed the tuning pegs to her cheek. She was crying again. *Oh God, oh God.* Though there was no God. No rest, no beauty, no truth.

After a minute, Sofía came back with clothes in her arms. She pulled Josie into a room she'd never seen before, small and yellow, with high windows, giving the impression of being taller than wide. A single bedstead in silvery nickel sat demure in one corner. A crucifix. And on the dresser, Michael gazed out from the bricks of Harvard. She'd surrounded him with candles in tall glass holders, a single pink rose.

It was a shrine. Josie hadn't thought to do that. She had no shrine, no candles. She didn't know how to do these things. She only knew how to kill the thing she loved. The expression on his face — as if he'd already known what she was going to do, how it would all end up. *Ming.* "Why'd you save me?" she said. "You should have left me there." Sofía shook her head, yanking off Josie's wet clothes, rubbing her hard with the towels. "Hey," she said. "Ow." The woman worked fast, shoving a sweater over Josie's lolling head, jerking on a pair of underwear, jeans, her old leather jacket. No pony-skin coat from Saks.

Sofía sat her on the bed, where she lay down and watched Sofía turn her back and take off her own clothes, towel herself dry. She wore a crucifix around her neck. Her body was thin and her tits sagged and her butt was flat as a frying pan. She dried herself in the same rough way and hurriedly dressed in an ugly white bra and panties. A dress of black wool. Slid her feet into a pair of flesh-tone knee-high stockings and then into pumps. She propped Josie up again and hung her schoolbag purse from its strap around Josie's neck. Like a fucking Saint Bernard dog's cask of brandy. Josie was impressed by the efficiency with which Sofía pulled off Josie's remaining wet boot, then shoved her feet into her Docs.

She got Josie under the armpit, hustled her out like a cop. Josie wanted to go back to the yellow room, where the shrine was. But she was moving despite herself. Stumbling out of the house, into the dark, the garage, the musty oily pine smell, strong and dark. Wet wood. Sofía leaned her against the fender of a station wagon. There was an old Chrysler, and a little sports car, and the Jag. The station wagon's door came open and the woman pushed her inside. Josie lay on the bench seat, the cloth was warm, it smelled like the couch at home, a comfortable smell, she felt she might even be able to sleep. Sofía got in behind the steering wheel and backed out, through the courtyard, the bump of the bricks, back through the opened gate, out into the night.

"Hey," Josie said, and it took a long time to say it. She didn't want to leave the house. Where was this woman taking her? She didn't want to go back down there. Josie sat up, tried to open the car door.

Sofía reached across and slammed the door closed. Josie tried to open it again. The Spaniard leaned over and grabbed the handle, and they struggled. The older woman slapped her face. "Sit still, bad girl!"

Josie let go of the door handle. She could feel it but only just.

We'll go and never come back.

Josie leaned against the window and gazed muddily at the glow of the lights as they wove down the empty streets of Los Feliz, past all the pretty mansions lit up like dollhouses, Sofía's long hair curling and wet on her plain black dress. Her Spanish eyes glittering with determination as if she was fleeing a fire.

"Why do you hate me so much?" Josie asked.

"You fool. You are confuse," Sofía said. "Who hate you."

The big houses, going away, the bright windows, the unnaturally green lawns under the streetlamps. The woman's mouth was set in a line of pure contempt.

"She's taking me with her. To Paris."

Sofía hissed like a teakettle. Josie watched the houses. A big Great Gatsby one, with a rubber tree in the sloping front lawn, striped awnings over the windows and all the lights on.

The night sky was thickening, the tufts of clouds coming together in a sad blanket across the moon, forgetting how beautiful it had just been, smearing itself all together. The old ficus trees planted in the parkway glowed yellow in the light from the short, old-fashioned streetlights, and the monstrous entwining roots rose two feet out of the ground.

They came off the hill, down to wide Los Feliz Boulevard, lined with its immense deodars. Sofía flicked on her turn signal, watched the traffic for a break. It was painful for Josie, even fucked up as she was, to watch the Spaniard drive. Sofía was one of those drivers who put the seat all the way forward, and hunched over the wheel, clutching it hard.

"Did she fuck him, Sofía?" Josie asked. She pointed at the Spaniard's sharp nose, the only thing in focus. "You know."

A big space opened in traffic, but Sofía didn't take it. She just kept sitting there watching the oncoming lights, the corners of her lips severe. She shook her head. "Poor Miguel. He hate he love her that way."

The blinker ticked. *Tick, tick,* as they sat looking through the windshield at the empty street, the big houses, once decorated with thousands of lights, now dark and silent. Had he loved Josie at all, had he ever loved her? "I loved him, Sofía. So much."

"*Sí,* I know." She sighed. "Miguel, he have too much *alma.* You know what is *alma?*"

Alma. Just a name. "No."

"It mean soul. You take care your own soul, Djossie." It was the first time she'd ever heard the woman say her name. "Have more respect yourself." Sofía made her careful left turn.

"You think I have a soul?" Sagging down in her seat, finally resigned to being driven away. "Maybe I just borrowed one."

"Poor fool."

They drove down Los Feliz and turned at the big fountain on Riverside Drive, sitting inside its giant ring. The fountain, rainbow colors inside its crown of shooting water, was built in honor of William Mulholland. The one from *Chinatown,* who got killed in the runoff. *Drowned.* He didn't really drown though. Not in real life. The dam burst and he died from the guilt. *Fuck,* she could understand that. Fuck yeah.

So many memorials. The whole city filled with them. Bridges and statues and buildings. Michael was the only one who ever gave a crap. He was the one who remembered. *You'll have to remember for both of us . . .* But how could she, she didn't know anything, how was she supposed to do it, all on her own? When she had killed the thing she loved.

The long silent blocks, the last bit of Griffith Park. The World War I bridge, the lightless stretch by the 5 where the homeless lived. Their old vans and trucks, a tent city in the bushes, the hillside melted all down into the street, creeping in on Riverside Drive. Sofía's headlights caught a ghostly, fuzzy-haired homeless man crossing the street in too-short pants, his dog tied to his waist by a rope. Sofía had to swerve to avoid them. Josie watched them through the back window. Was that Death? Somewhere along the line he had lost his toupee and his birthmark, his tasseled loafers and his job at the bank.

The turn on Allesandro. She wasn't going to help Sofía find it, fuck her. If she didn't know the way, they would have to go back. But the woman turned right at the school, the pictures of children along the vast cement wall, the silent tractors under the overpass. She knew the way exactly.

"Were you there? When she ripped me off? Why'd you let her do that?" Her eyes kept closing.

Sofía gave that teakettle sound and just kept driving. *You fool.* The houses seemed worse than ever, tumbledown things clinging to the steep hillsides, the rank vegetation.

She felt drearier than ever, drowned and then dredged up again. She couldn't even do that right. Sofía should have just left her in the water. Her and what was left of her *alma.* What good was it to have a soul when you did the things that she had done? "Why do you even bother with me?"

"You are like a . . . one who walk in sleep. After you say you leave and then not, I think, something happen to that girl. So I watch for you."

A good-sized skunk shambled along the side of the road, in the sick light cast by the orange sodium crime lights. Garbage and abandoned cars. Back home again.

"Does she have *alma?* Meredith?"

Sofía made that hissing sound again. "She have music. *Es todo.*"

Josie pictured a scene from a horror movie, the vampire that looks in the mirror and sees no reflection. "So why work for her, if she's got no soul?"

Sofía shrugged again. She was a handsome woman. Her hair down, curling as it dried, the sharp nose with its high bridge, narrow tip, the fine dark eyes. "I work to her a long time. I know very well. She suffer many thing. Her life very sad. Sometime she does bad thing, I know. But I know to her. No good for you."

They pulled up in front of the house. It looked small and overgrown and run-down, the fence leaning from the weight of the plants. Sofía parked behind César's white Riv, pulled Josie from the wagon. She half walked her, half carried her through the gate and down the long flight of stairs, the air smelled of water. The door wasn't locked. They staggered through the living room like a four-legged beast, edging their way to the bedroom. The woman dropped her down on the bed, tried to pull her guitar away, but Josie fought her for it. She gave up and took off the Docs and pants, pulled the covers over her. "You sleep. And hold on your *alma*. She is what you have now." She closed the felt curtains, turned out the lights, shut the door.

32
Soul

She dreamed she was an inmate on a prison island. It was completely surrounded by a malarial
swamp, everything shades of gray and murky
green. Nothing for miles but dead water, a
labyrinth of roots. It was hopeless, no possible
way out. But among the prisoners, it was said
there was a place you could swim out, a hole
down at the very bottom of the swamp, that let
you swim through and come out somewhere
else, somewhere clean and beautiful, with transparent water and brilliant sky. Although it was
just a prison rumor, she came across the spot she
was almost sure was the place. She dove into the

murk. Down, down, into the ooze, away from the sun, away from the light, and there it was, she saw it, the mouth of a cave. But just as she was getting there, she found she didn't have enough breath, she couldn't make it all the way. She turned back and tried to swim to the surface, but she couldn't reach that either, she'd miscalculated the whole thing, she was drowning.

She fought her way into wakefulness, still smelling the swamp, the dead water clinging to her. Where was she? Her lungs ached, she needed aspirin, but didn't want to move. She rolled over, sank into the pillow as it all came back to her. The black pool, the darkness and forgetting. That moment of surrender.

You stupid motherfucker. Falling into a pool on pills and booze like every dumb-ass rock-and-roll accidental suicide. If it wasn't for that flat-ass Spaniard, you'd be dead now. Lying on the bottom of Meredith Loewy's pool, like Marianne Faithfull in that Shakespeare movie, a crazy girl who'd drowned in a stream because some prince wouldn't fuck her. Fuck. She was lying here breathing only by accident. She could still remember what she thought when she went in. *Yes,* that was what she was thinking. *Good. Here it is.*

She lay in the stale bed, in the musty room, staring through the darkness to the wall where the dresser had been, their green dresser with its silver paisleys, now at Meredith's, along with everything else. A slit of light barely illuminated the empty room. *There aren't any accidents,* Shirley K. always said. If you left your jacket or ran into a post, you must have wanted it. Josie lay in the bed like a shipwreck on a beach, her lungs still hurting. Tears slowly slid down the sides of her face. Was that what she really wanted, just to die? Follow Michael down to the bottom? Like Dylan fucking Thomas, drinking himself to death that night in New York, wanting it without wanting to know it. By any rights, she should already be gone, a bloated potato girl in a fake fur coat. That was what she really wanted. To forget so thoroughly she'd never have another memory again, the bitter so bitter you gave up the sweet.

She shivered with the cold and the dank and the swamp. *You take care your own soul.* Her soul. She tried to picture a soul. A white feathered thing, like your lungs, those wings. But hers was more like a rotten old bathing suit that had molded on the hook, it would tear clean apart if she tried to put it on. A moldy old scrap only fit for throwing away, not even the devil would take it on consignment.

What was she doing here, alive, when Michael with his beautiful *alma* was gone? He was the one who cared about things like that, the true world, God, having a soul. Yet what had kept that fucking bitch Sofía awake that night, had not let her drown? Was that God? Was that destiny? Or just sheer fucking dumb luck. She thought of a kid on a skateboard by the sea, the wheels going around and around, praying without knowing it for a girl who didn't know how to pray for herself.

Her nose was running, she needed water, she had to take a leak. She rolled to the edge of the bed, gingerly pressed herself to a sitting position, waiting for her head to settle back onto her shoulders. It was the worst kind of barbiturate headache, she felt her skull was going to crack in two, like an egg. *Duck eggs.* Not so elegant today, Michael. Not very elegant at all.

Holding her head, she stood up, groped her way to the toilet, bare feet on cold tile, eased herself down, tried to connect to make herself go. The empty bathtub gaped, an enormous sarcophagus, an empty boat. The hours they'd spent in that tub. Letting out water when it got cold, putting more hot in. Goofing with armies of plastic toys, flotillas of little boats. He once reenacted the whole Battle of Trafalgar for her. The bigger boats were Spain and the little ones were England, they were faster, and the general, Lord Nelson, was seasick the whole time. He died and said, "Kiss me, Hardy."

She would lie against Michael, away from the faucet, and dream of their room in Montmartre. In the shadow of the Sacré-Coeur. The kitchen behind a curtain, the brass double bed, pancake saggy, the view of all Paris. She felt a rush of nausea. So many things he'd failed to mention, like an apartment off the Avenue Foch.

Her head throbbed like a smashed finger. She flushed and went to the medicine cabinet that was hung so high she could barely see herself, Michael had had to install another over the toilet so she could do her makeup. But she could see well enough to take in her matted hair, her face gray and gaunt, all shattered apart, she was getting a cold sore on her upper lip. She took out the aspirin, shook four into her palm and took them two by two, with swallows of water from the spigot. Who was she? Who was he? Nothing was familiar now, she could take nothing for granted.

She went back into the bedroom, opened the windows, though it was cold, she had to get rid of the swamp smell that still clung to the bed. She buried herself in the covers, as Montmartre came back all around her. She remembered how he used to make coffee in the morning and bring it to her in bed on a tray. He'd come in under the covers and tell her stories about their life on the Butte. The café on the corner, where they drank their café au lait from big bowls standing up at the bar. The dwarf owner, Madame Sorel, who had a platform built up the length of the bar, so she could look the customers in the eye.

"But what are we doing up so early?" She pinched his nipple, he liked that more than you'd think. "We were at Cocteau's party until dawn, remember? You were Pierrot, and I was Columbine." The moon-drunk clown and his silver lady.

He dangled a stem of grapes above her lips, so she could reach up and bite them off one by one. "We have to shop," he said. "Before it's picked over. Monsieur Clemenceau *le boucher* always tries to sell us the worst meat. We know if he wants us to buy the veal, it must be old. *Non, monsieur, les côtelettes d'agneau, s'il vous plaît.*"

"You go shop. I'm staying in." Drinking the coffee, which he had ground in the brass tube he'd bought in the market in Istanbul.

"Ah, but sometimes I forget. . . . Last time the daffodils were so pretty, I spent all our money on them, remember? A whole armload, and dropped them onto you one by one while you slept."

The idea of him, embracing an armload of flowers, dropping them on the bed in Montmartre to wake her up. All that yellow, lighting their room. They could have had that. They should have just gone. Tears flowed down her temples into her hair. She couldn't understand. All these things had been within reach. But he was so damn perverse, he preferred to dream it than to make it come true.

Of course, it wouldn't be *La Bohème* in Meredith's flat in the sixteenth. She knew what it would look like. Plaster leaves on the ceiling, striped-silk drapes and chairs with pale wood legs. Not their artist's room in Montmartre. But couldn't they have had just as good a time in the luxury of Meredith's apartment off the Avenue Foch, antiques and wallpaper, clean sheets and a maid?

Maybe. It would have been fine for her. But

she knew it wasn't what he wanted. He wanted Montmartre, where he was the young artist, fighting his way to himself. The Montmartre of their dreams, the two of them, living on their wits and what they could scrape together from odd jobs. Him playing piano in cafés, her modeling and singing in bars — really, just what they were doing in Echo Park. But in the flat in the sixteenth, he would be the son again. Like a prince, both important and irrelevant. His value only by association. And Michael had been trying so hard to matter to himself. That's what he was doing here in his own just-starting life. The real Paris, that you could get to on a plane, wasn't their Paris. There was no Cocteau anymore, he'd been dead for years, no Duchamp or Apollinaire, no Blaise or Jeanne, they were gone even when the poem was written. For all she knew, the Sacré-Coeur might be a disco by now.

She lay in the stale bed, gazing up at the ceiling, its tongue-and-groove surface bare of the pagoda paper lanterns and painted birdcages, the spiral of tassels they'd found in a box on Alvarado and tacked up there. This had been their Montmartre. Right here. This haven they'd made. The afternoons they lay in this bed, making love so slowly and thoroughly it wasn't even sex anymore, it was a world of its own. And he read her his books, filled her with light, he changed her, he dreamed her up and there she was. He hadn't told her about the flat in the sixteenth because she wouldn't have understood, that *this* was their Paris.

She hadn't understood him even that well. It was right there in front of her. Her idiocy made her lungs ache.

So why had it stopped being a refuge, and become something else — a dogtrack, a bullring, where there was nowhere to hide from his dark drama? July, or August. Things had been fine up to then. They'd gone to TJ and Ensenada — and he'd had that show, the review in the *Weekly.* He'd painted the Meredith picture, an exorcism. Was it her working on that film with Jeremy? Was it Reynaldo, the strain of supporting himself? First he quit, and then he was painting those mad monks, and then he stopped painting altogether. His mood moving from twilight to midnight. She remembered walking on Cerro Gordo by the water tank, and pointing out leaf patterns impressed in the sidewalk, that unexpected beauty, and he said, "Some leaves blew into the wet cement, Josie, it's not the miracle of the loaves and the fishes." The world that was the emanation of the divine had been reduced to a handful of dust.

He was the one who had taught her to watch for signs of the true world and suddenly it was as if all that had never happened. She was left alone, and he began to stiffen when she touched him, when once he would have pulled her into an embrace. "What did I do?"

"I just don't want to be pawed," he said.

She never knew what she'd done to deserve that. She'd thought it was his painting not going so well. Then the accusations, the jealousy, before he had any reason. Accusing her of lying to him, when it was him all the time. From the beginning. Pretending to be a virgin. Saying he didn't play sports. Letting her believe there'd been no other girls, that he never talked to his father. He'd lied to her from the very first day. Shaping a picture of himself that had certain things in common with the real Michael, but left so much out. He wanted to appear much more helpless than he was. He certainly didn't trust her enough to tell her about Saint-Tropez.

He hate he love her that way. There it was. Josie may have pulled out the rug from under him, but it was Meredith who put it there. Unthinkable. And yet, why not. All kinds of things happened in this world, a brother, a sister, a mother, a son. She could picture it. It wasn't such a stretch.

A hotel room with shutters, like that painting by Matisse. She'd come in, just to say good night, talk over the day. Adjoining rooms, of course, you wouldn't have to go through the hall. The line that was so thin, it was not even there. She could see it. His mother walking in on him reading a book. Stroking himself as he read, he liked that, doing things while he did something else, to know and not know in that way. Meredith in a light robe, maybe her hair up in a towel. "Busy?" Probably half-crocked, she was disciplined in some ways but not in all. Lonely. No man in Saint-Tropez to flatter her, only the handsome son. Seeing him pull his hand out from under the sheet, pretending not to, yes, they both were like that. Talking to him as if nothing had been seen. Lounging around, having a good little chat. Her robe falling open.

He always said he loved Josie's delicacy, her lightness, her small neat form. *For she is my love, and other women are but big bodies of flame . . .* But maybe he'd just been looking for someone who didn't remind him of Meredith, and that night in Saint-Tropez, the woman who came in through the closets of a dream. *Was that all, Michael? Was I nothing to you but the anti-Meredith?*

It started with those goddamn phone calls. Stockholm, Reykjavik, Hamburg. *July, August.* Though maybe he'd been making collect calls to Meredith the whole time, what did she know? She was as blind as the blind Merediths times ten. Restless, not sleeping, the painting had taken a bad turn. Had he longed for her, the room in Saint-Tropez, her warm full body exposed in the light robe? His eye drawn to the dark patch at the V of her legs, Meredith saying, "If you didn't know me, would you find me attractive?"

Michael wouldn't have stopped it. He always moved toward the thing that frightened him. *The two of them, you know what they were like.* The crippled boy, the deaf-mutes. He once told her Meredith liked to pretend she was his mistress in public, it was a game they played, in cafés and in galleries, the handsome boy and the elegant woman, a game and not a game. The boundaries already so blurred. He'd been taught since he was a baby how different he was from everyone else, how different they all were, the Loewys, rules didn't apply. *Did you touch her,*

Michael? Did the smell of her make you dizzy, so familiar, the smoke of perfume, the dark musky smell of her body? It was a night which had been brewing for years. He just wouldn't have known how it would feel, to carry it around, his judgment of himself.

His erection visible under the sheet, hard and flat against his belly. Maybe she laid her head on the pillow, her breast falling from the robe. "What if we were strangers." He so loved to pretend. Her hand caressing his face, how it might have happened. Maybe kissing him a bit open-mouthed, letting herself forget for a moment it was her son, just a handsome young man, the feel of him jumping under the sheet, her hair a mess on the pillow, how warm she was, how familiar, her breast in his hand, *it's only a dream, Michael, it's not real,* something he must have dreamed about, dreamed and feared. Afterward, listening to the sound of the surf . . . *Shhh, don't think about it, don't say anything . . .* her hand to his mouth . . .

He hate he love her that way but he was helpless to stop it. There was your fucking sad destiny. There was some fucking *ming.*

And the next day Meredith would have tried the adjoining door, for the first time found it locked. She would have knocked, called out, but he wouldn't answer, never again. And when he came down to breakfast, he wouldn't have met her eye, would have answered her superficial remarks in monosyllables. That day he didn't go down to the beach, he stayed in the hotel, called his father collect, said he wanted to come home, wanted to go somewhere to school, could Cal arrange it? Be like the other boys, though it was already too late. His father got him into Ojai, it must have been Cal. And she let him go, knowing she had gone too far, knowing she had lost him. He didn't want to be her little husband anymore, now it was way too real. He ran. Threw himself into school and played handball, *fast and mean,* yes. And all the rest, everything that had come after.

And Josie understood why he couldn't tell her. Because, unlike Tommy, he had loved that dark damaged woman. He couldn't betray her, who had betrayed him in the worst way. He started calling his father, just to shoot the shit. But he could never admit how twisted things had gotten with his mother. His loyalty to Meredith was absolute, to the end. Yes.

So who was Josie Tyrell in the story, really? Someone who would stir no memories, who

might help break the bond? *And was that all?*
We loved each other once . . . Didn't we? Until
now she would have said, *Yes, of course we did,*
what do you mean? But now she didn't know.
Maybe that summer, when Meredith called him
from Hamburg and Denmark, he started to see
Josie as she was, not as a project, but the bare
fact of her, unsophisticated, half-literate, without
much to recommend her at all. And maybe he realized the world he had chosen was really very
small. Perhaps it had all started closing in.
Maybe he had grown tired of playing artists in
garrets, just as Meredith had predicted, and
didn't know how to stop. The pressure building.
He'd made a mistake. Had wanted to give Josie
up but couldn't bring himself to. Couldn't betray his dream of a man's life for himself.

She reached for her purse, hanging from the
doorknob of the bedroom, but her damn cigarettes were in Meredith's pool. She could go
down to Gala's, but she didn't want to go out into
all that light, it was too much to bear. She felt
helpless, exposed, like Dave in *2001,* the com-
puter closing the spaceship doors behind her.
Cut off in deep space. *Open the bay doors, Hal.*

She hauled herself out of bed, went out into
the living room, it smelled like swamp and dead

plants. It was so bright, it cut her in two. She
found a few long butts in an ashtray, opened
them, rolled the tobacco into a bum's cigarette
that tasted like trash and burned leather. She
knew she should go into the kitchen, get rid of
whatever it was that was stinking so badly, but
she'd used the last of her energy. She sat heavily
at the peeling dining table, smoking the acrid
cigarette, opened the drawer, hoping to find
some decent smokes, but there were only scis-
sors and pins and her old tarot cards, folded in a
Moroccan pinch-dyed scarf.

He was going to design a whole pack for her,
but he'd only done the one painting and a series
of sketches. She spread them on the table, not
reading them, just looking at their pictures, like
old friends, the Empress, the Chariot, the Fool.
The Fool, the Zero card, dressed in motley, daz-
zled face to the sky, foot about to come off the
cliff. Pierrot. It wasn't Michael at all. It was her.
You fool. She brushed at tears with the back of
her hand.

And which one was he? The Magician? She'd
thought he was. She'd thought he had it all
lined up. The world spinning on his little finger.
Or else the Hermit with his lantern, looking for
the true world. But no, here he was. The

twelfth card. The Hanged Man. Lashed upside down to his crosstree. Unable to go backward or forward.

The phone rang on the orange footlocker. Michael once told her about Zeno's paradox, that showed there were an infinite number of small movements to doing anything, and you could divide them smaller and smaller, so that you never really arrived at the final point. You swam toward the surface but you never could reach it. Josie saw herself going through the infinite number of small gestures that arrived at picking up the receiver. "*Oui, c'est moi.*"

"Josie? Thank God you're all right." Meredith. Chipper as hell. "I went into your room, I knew you couldn't possibly still be sleeping. And you were gone. Sofía said you went home. What, did you forget something?"

And who was Meredith? The Empress? The High Priestess? Or only the Queen of Swords, ruining everything she touched, the Typhoid Mary of *ming.*

"I had some things to think over."

You're not nervous, are you? Trust me, Josie, it's going to be fine. The presenters take care of everything, and I'll be right there showing you the ropes."

The ropes. Which ropes, the ones that bound the Hanged Man to his fatal cross?

"Josie? Are you there?"

She found the Queen of Swords, saber in one hand, the other outstretched, beckoning. "Just thinking." She looked through the deck, found the World. Put it between the Queen and the Fool. She could have the world. But at what price? The Hanged Man gazed up at her from his gallows.

"Josie, listen to me. There's nothing to think about. It's not an organ donation. Four days we'll be there, and I'll treat you to the best dinner you ever had."

But what of her own shredded bathing suit of a soul? Wouldn't there always be a dark swimming pool, a murky swamp, waiting in Zurich, Vienna, even an apartment in the sixteenth? How far could you run to escape a boy in his grave?

"Josie? Josie, you know, it's all right to give yourself something good. After all you've been through." Her voice was low and confiding, persuasive, a beautiful voice, so understanding. "You deserve it. As you yourself said, he's dead everywhere." But Josie couldn't get away from the sickening feeling of the cliff crumbling underfoot. Like that night at dinner with Boulez. Everything that Michael had loved about her gone. *Smart, original.* She'd been unrecognizable.

"Think of it, you'll have a whole new life, a fresh start."

Josie walked her fingers up the curly cord of the phone. The picture of little Jeanne and Blaise in the blue train compartment, their heads together, watching her. *Remember.* "I'm not sure I can."

Meredith's voice came like a whisper, like a voice in her own head. "Think how you'll feel if you're not on that plane. Someday, you'll be washing dishes in a trailer in Lancaster. You'll have four screaming brats hanging on to you and you'll look out the window at the laundry hanging in your yard and think, 'I could have had a different life. I could have had something better.'"

Like Pauline? she wanted to ask. Her mother had met all those famous people. Tagged along, tried to fit in. She'd started as someone and became nothing at all. Finally, she had a chance to redeem something of herself and she hocked that ring and headed for parts unknown. Left a child behind, that was how bad she needed to go. Josie ran her fingernail through the fake fur of the couch, parting it like hair, like a furrow for seed. She wanted to ask, but she had done enough damage. "I just need to do some thinking."

"I just don't understand you!" Meredith snapped. "You've got a seat on the plane, I've got your passport. I'm offering you everything. What in the world is bothering you?"

Meredith thought none of this would ever catch up with her. Michael, her father, her mother, Lisbeth and Wien, 1934. Saint-Tropez. Everything. She thought all she had to do was stay in the spotlight, keep moving. But it was like the swimming pool. She could go to Paris or Bayreuth or East Fuckwalla, it would still be there waiting for her. She was the most frightened woman Josie had ever seen. "Look, Meredith, I'll either be there Tuesday or I won't. I have to go now."

She could hear Meredith breathing, her lips close to her ear. When her voice came back it was flat, businesslike. "Ten o'clock Tuesday, Air France. It's up to you now."

You take care your own soul. She is what you have now. Josie gathered up her cards and put them back in the deck.

33
Drive

The clogged arteries of the 210 snaked east through Pasadena, Arcadia, Monrovia, suburbs that splashed up against the dark bulk of the San Gabriels like water thrown on a dirty floor. It wasn't such a hard drive, more like taking your place in line at the DMV. Thousands of people, all caught in profile, locked into their mobile fish tanks. Each face, each car, transporting grief, boredom, rage. Someone in one of these cars was contemplating murder. Someone, right now, in the privacy of his aquarium, threaded the beads of his suicide through his fingers, praying along the chain like a rosary. Someone begged

615

for help from a God he didn't quite believe in, yet had no one else to appeal to. The rest thought only about dinner, tonight's episode of *Dallas*, the day's argument with the boss.

In an alternate universe, she would be going home from a day at the bank, the Auto Club, the State Farm office, thinking about her own kids and what she would make for dinner in her suburban kitchen in El Monte. Tuna casserole with potato chips crumbled on top. Her young husband picking them up at day care. What was so wrong about that? Something simple and basic, attainable. She wanted too much, that was her fault, not just Michael's love, but everything everything everything. Genius and wealth and culture, art and achievement, that whole Loewy trip. If she had just stopped. Had taken off the blindfold of her magical thinking.

On the tape, Patsy Cline sang *I fall to pieces, each time I see you again* . . . She'd bought it at a gas station in Glendale, it was the closest thing they'd had to the blues. How Pen would have laughed if she could see her now, singing along, she knew every word, every cowgirl hiccup, like her own heartbeat, she could hit every high note, and capture the quaver and the chin-up bravery. Patsy was Piaf in fringe and white

boots. But Meredith had the Piaf, she had Louis and Django and Bing, right along with Brahms and Bartók, she'd even swept Josie's old Merle Haggard into her net. Sitting now in a heap in Michael's old room. *I don't think I'm coming back, Josie.* She would lock up the house and never return. Fifty years from now, that stuff would probably still be sitting there, the pile of their things covered in a layer of dust thick as felt. They'd all be dead, but their things would still be waiting, the records still playable. Who would it go to when Meredith was gone? Knowing that woman, it would just go on and on. Some bank paying the taxes, the whole house silently crumbling into the ground.

She should think about her own soul, what she was going to do with this funky tattered pond-dank item. Dark and stained, a ruined thing. She could not do what Meredith was planning, just lock the house and leave town without a forwarding address. Although she was a girl who killed the thing she loved, she could do one thing that that frightened woman could not — go to the end with him. She could take it all the way.

Traffic inched down the valley, past Azusa and Glendora. In the orange-grove days these had

been real towns, each with its railroad siding and general store, but now it was one big snail track of suburb, one great sleepwalking sprawl. Yet, still, what she wouldn't give for a piece of that ordinary life, to share with the boy she loved, like a loaf of plain, warm bread.

Out in Pomona, ghostly white balloons hung in the night sky over the car dealers lining the freeway. Weird white surreal clusters against the black, tugging at their tethers. She could feel them in her throat, in her chest. The dark batons of palm trees shot up darker than the sky. The moon rose above a bank of clouds, the great grinning Oz of a moon. Was that God, she wondered, just the man behind the curtain, working his cranks and levers? Covering His own inadequacies? Just a cheesy music video made in someone's garage, with lots of Mole fog and up-lighting?

Michael had driven this same road, past these very same car lots, these exact palms. Did he know just where he was going? Or did he rent a car from the National counter at the Ambassador Hotel and just spin the keys? East was the desert, a dead sea, salt flats, the great missile testing range. Did he know it would be Twentynine Palms, or had he just passed each exit in turn,

waiting to be moved by a fatal instinct? Why not one of the eight exits of Pomona? She watched them go by. *Fairgrounds, Garvey, Towne, Indian Hill. Etiwanda,* why not Etiwanda? Or Montclair, or Ontario. How far did he think he had to go to meet what could have been met right there in the house on Lemoyne?

Finally, the suburbs loosened their grip on the land, the commuter traffic thinning toward Colton. She could tell, no one lived in Colton and worked somewhere else. People didn't even commute to Pomona from here. The billboards changed from gentlemen's clubs and car lots and overnight communities to fantasies centering on the vacation traveler, women in feathers, or else floating in pools, men in white pants playing golf. Spas and the hotels of Palm Springs and Las Vegas. *Feeling lucky tonight?* She couldn't remember the last time she felt lucky. She thought of that old man, Morty, and his wife, driving out here on their way to Las Vegas, their big Caddy on cruise control, listening to Sinatra on four-speaker sound. She liked knowing he was awake down at the Four Queens in Gardena, that he'd be awake all night. She wondered if he thought of her when he visited his wife. Did he ever look over at Michael's stone

and wonder what happened to that girl in the
yellow coat, who had never known anyone
who'd died? Now it seemed unbelievable, the innocence of a girl in a fairy tale.

The train yards in Fontana sat forlorn under
orange crime lights, empty cars waiting on sid-
ings, full ones moving slow as a dream, going
somewhere with their load of steel and oranges,
trains without beginning or end. But not their
train, Blaise and Jeanne's, the one that started in
Paris and went through a war in Siberia to end at
the sea in Harbin, China. *The Kremlin was like
an immense Tartar cake* . . . Easy enough to die
in Fontana, you could lie down on the tracks and
be divided neatly, top and bottom. Or you could
just pick a fight in a beer bar, expending the
smallest insult, and let someone else do the job,
bashing your skull against the concrete curb of
the parking lot.

This very second, she could jerk the wheel of
the car to the left just ever so slightly, and the
sixteen wheeler with the slick, shiny cab could
crush her like a candy wrapper. Her hands
sweated. She tried to think of something else,
but she could not stop thinking how it would
feel, how long would it take. Just an accident.
You didn't really have to know what you were

doing. You could deny it all. *I just fell asleep for a second.* Swilling barbs and voddy and falling into a pool. The brave thing was to admit it. To say, *I have fucking had enough.* To take the fucking gun and put it in your mouth and pull the trigger. *I'm doing this, assholes, and it ain't no accident. Look, here's how.* If you were going to do it, you should know that's what you were doing. Your eyes wide open.

She wove through the serpentine knot of freeway exchanges, the split between the 10 and 15, one heading to Beaumont, Banning, and Indio, the other moving north to Las Vegas. She felt panic, imagining Mort and Dotty turning off here, leaving her alone to continue east, she had almost believed they were with her. She drove on.

Redlands 10. She thought of Pen, growing up out here, scrappy mad and dreaming of LA so hard she could taste it. She missed her like an arm — Pen, with her great love of life, her sense of fun and her rough practicality, that gap-toothed smile. Pen had never considered taking an extra pill or five, crashing into oncoming traffic. How furious it made her to see Josie succumbing to the Loewy spell. She could never explain to Pen why she was going to Twenty-nine Palms, why she had to know, once and for all. Why she had to take it all the way. She didn't fully understand it herself, but she felt if she was ever going to save that last shred of soul, she had to go into it, right up into the asshole of death.

In Redlands, a little carnival churned and blinked, a Ferris wheel, a miniature roller coaster, her favorite kind of ride. But she would not stop to investigate. He hadn't been looking for a carnival. *Carne* for meat. *Carnevale.* The feast before Lent, getting ready for Easter, the death of Christ and His miraculous recovery.

He'd taken her to Easter Mass last spring, in a pink brick church on Vermont. It surprised her, but she liked when he got an idea in his head, to do something weird like this. She put on a nice dress and heels. "What if it happened?" he said on the way over. "What if they rolled the boulder back and found the tomb empty?" They came in late and sat in the back. The church was packed, every kind of person, hair color, fashion choice. Big flowers in front filled the sanctuary with their scent, and honey candles, full-voiced choir. The larger-than-life Christ sagged on his cross. How thin he looked, such a terrible fragility. Broken. Forsaken. The priest spoke, the congregation responded. Suddenly, everyone turned around and shook each other's hands, saying, "peace be with you," "and with you." How seriously Michael had done it, said, *and peace be with you.* She wondered what they would have thought if they knew he was half-Jewish. A priest walked down the aisle with an altar boy carrying a bowl of water, and shook a bell-like contraption on a wooden stick, watering them with a sharp hard rap. The surprise at the cold water, amazing it didn't raise blisters, considering who they were. Michael's eyes shining. What was he thinking he was doing here, she'd wondered, a Jewish boy whose grandfather had to flee Nazis with the clothes on his back? But now she understood. He wanted faith, that the boulder would some-day roll away, and the Son would walk free. That he would be released from the tomb he was sealing himself into.

She felt such searing pity, she had to pull over. The cars crashed by as she sat trying to breathe, her chest tight as a fist. Why had she not seen it? She'd just watched, without a thought in her head except when would they go and have lunch. Afterward, they'd stopped at a side altar, he lit a candle, knelt and prayed before a beauti-ful Virgin with flowers around her neck. Josie paid the dollar and lit a candle, but it was just a game. She thought of the Virgin over his bed in

Los Feliz. Why a Virgin, instead of a Jewish candelabra or star? She had always thought it was just a piece of kitschy decor. But it wasn't. This was the Mother he wanted to watch over him in his anxious sleep, someone who could love him without condition, take his pain away. Not one whose genius taunted him at every turn, a mother who raised him up with one hand just to cut him down with the other, who blurred all the lines, who tunneled with secret doors into his soul. He wanted to be loved purely, simply. No expectations. And she herself wasn't free from that guilt. She had wanted things from him too, needed as much if not more.

And so, she and Meredith, the women who'd failed him, were left with their sins, and the boulder never did roll away. She sat and smoked a cigarette, the tears drooling down.

After Redlands, the road climbed into some sort of pass. In the dark it seemed lush and wooded. But on the other side, she was met by wind that shoved the car halfway into the next lane. A Buick blatted its horn. At first she thought something was wrong with her tires. It would settle for a minute, five, she thought it was gone, and then suddenly the car skidded sideways again. She fought her way through battered

Calimesa, a town from the Forties, pickup trucks and small-town feel, its Bob's Big Boy the center of visible nightlife. And all around in the flat western landscape, scattered lights winked way off in the distance. She understood people who'd choose to live like that, isolated in a dry, hard terrain, so far from comfort. People who didn't want to love their neighbors as themselves, or rather, loved their neighbors about as much. Hard people, whose own company was even more than they could stomach.

She fought the wind for an hour, her arms weary and aching, her nerves peeled to a thread by the time she pulled into the Denny's in Beaumont. She was glad just to be somewhere. Raw cold cut her as she left the car, all she had between her skin and the wind were a pair of dirty jeans and a sweater, a dog-torn leather jacket. Well all right. She didn't need a five-hundred-dollar pony-skin coat, a new full-length down cocoon. You couldn't swathe yourself in goose down when you were taking it all the way. It was cold and hard and it was her choice.

The hostess took one look at her punked-out hair and jacket and seated her away from the families, at a window where she could watch the lights on the highway, and her old Falcon with the marks of a hundred small-time bands. She ordered a burger from the bow-tied waiter, a middle-aged Latino. "You're not from around here," he said. "Have a hard drive?"

She smiled, declining conversation. Maybe she was wrong about the people out here. Maybe it was herself she was thinking of. The windows bowed as the wind hit them. She imagined them popping, the customers all sliced by glass, blood flowing, pooling on the patterned salmon and teal indoor-outdoor carpeting, the brightness of heart blood. Did Michael sit here in the Beaumont Denny's with a cup of weak coffee, listening to the wind and the trains going by? It was a Dust Bowl sound, it stirred something in her own blood. She had never felt so lonely in her life as she did at that moment, listening to the train whistle cry.

A man with a gray crew cut and gray eyes and gray skin sat in a booth facing her, his hands cradling his coffee. His body was there but his eyes were a thousand miles away. She wondered what he was seeing, where those eyes had gotten stuck. She ate half her burger, but wasn't hungry after all. The meat made her ill, the pickle. She ate a few of the fries and let the waiter bring her more coffee, she lit a cigarette and watched the gray man, a dead man in a coffee shop under fluorescent lights. The papery crinkles of his skin, the gray eyes staring at nothing. She understood just how that could happen. She understood very well. She finished smoking, her Gauloise as odd in a Beaumont Denny's as a fur at a Fourth of July jamboree.

After Banning, there were no more towns. No roadside lighting, just the glow of rock off hardpan earth and the dark wall of mountains against sky. The blasts of wind threw bursts of sand against the thin skin of the Falcon. In the moonlight, she could see the mountain's ghostly topography, its crushed-velour flanks. It wasn't that the mountain seemed particularly threatening, but like the gray man, it was just eerily silent, utterly sad, untouchably distant. It was the valley of the dead, the mythic underworld, shadowy yet defined, gray on gray. Some sort of big-trunked shaggy trees sucked a living from the desert floor.

The wind batted from the left, always the left, like a one-armed boxer. Tumbleweeds flew and rolled across her headlights. And yet cars still passed at 90, 110, a Beemer, a Porsche, a Rolls, two Mercedes, a Cadillac, all heading for the oases of Palm Springs and Palm Desert, Rancho

Mirage. Rich people who knew where to go, traveling in their fast, safe cars to solid destinations . . . but she knew better now. They thought they could hide in the right clothes, the right resort towns, but they were the ones who disappeared from Meredith's photo album, one by one. They thought they'd found the safe place, the good place, that knowing how to dress and what to order would save them, but they were still out here in the night, swatted by the same giant hand, going somewhere incomprehensible. Palm Springs would not save them.

The fancy traffic turned south, but she kept hard east through the terrible landscape, dark and open as the moon. It was like something from Castaneda, wind and forms so dark they were almost invisible, but not quite. And there, in the road, a silver coyote. She swerved to miss it, fuck! The car fishtailed wildly, she suddenly saw herself flipping, ending up upside down off the side of the road. *Go with it ride it out ride it out.* Her father's voice, it must have been. She steered with the skid, staying off the brakes, until the car straightened out. Her heart thumped like the bass in a gutbucket band. She would stop but there was nowhere to pull over.

The fucking coyote had vanished. Maybe she should have hit it. Got rid of it once and for all.

A U of lights opened before her, a wide valley, *Desert Hot Springs,* she saw what she had been looking for since Pasadena — *Hwy 62, Joshua Tree, 29 Palms.* She exited the highway and bumped onto a two-lane road that went past a little hamlet and then up into the night.

The rough, narrow road was protected to some degree from the wind, but the Falcon slowed ominously, chugging up the grade. She watched her temperature gauge rising. No lights at all, no car behind or in front. The road reminded her of the tarot card The Moon, the road winding into the dark mountains, and you couldn't see the end. The Moon hung her tragic head. No light, no vista, the hills closed in, and she could see faces in the eroded sandstone. The claws of telephone poles menaced like the forelegs of insects. She could smell the metal of her own fear. She might blow a tire, break an axle, the car could overheat, a belt could pop — but Michael had driven this. He had felt this very thing. This was what he chose. Like a sick dog, trying to find the farthest, most remote place to do his dying. Though if she had ever seen a good place to die, this was it.

Motorcycles droned behind her, their lights glaring in her rearview mirror. Four bikers coming on fast, then they were all around her. Longhairs on chopped Harleys, wearing the leathers of their local club. The nameless anxieties of the lonely drive were quickly replaced by the focused danger of the human element, now surrounding the car. There was nothing between her and gang rape but the forward motion of the unpredictable Falcon. She had known what to do in a situation like this since she was ten years old, the acting that was more than natural, it was necessary. She forced a tired, bored look onto her face, as if she did this every night, coming home from her job cleaning rooms in Desert Hot Springs. *I know you,* her body language was saying. *I shop with your wife at Stater Brothers. I dated your brother Spider.* One of them, riding abreast of her, grinned and blew her a kiss. She raised two fingers from the steering wheel in a neighborly salute. And then they took off, leaving her the vacant road.

Sweaty and shivering, she reached the summit, blessedly untenanted, and began to descend to a little town amid chaparral and tumbleweed. *Welcome to Morongo Valley.* Rough and sparse and without cachet. She felt a sudden fondness for its clutch of residents, dug in just under the summit. It was a place to hide out, a sanctuary for people with records, people on the lam. Bigamists and repeat offenders, women with violent husbands. A place for girls who have killed the thing they loved. But she didn't stop at the Blue Jay Inn, though its painted wood sign said *vacancy.* Michael hadn't holed up, hunkering down until the storm blew over. He had another destination in mind. He had not stopped short, and neither could she.

She fought the wind, her arms aching, but now it seemed right, it seemed almost like company. She was tired of listening to Patsy, she turned on the radio, but all she could get was TJ, and a hellfire preacher from Hemet. She fumbled for a tape from the pile on the passenger seat, Germs, X, Joan Jett . . . She wanted something bluesy but not desperate. Not *Pierrot Lunaire,* Christ . . . finally she came up with an old Lou Reed, it was the best she was going to do. *Holly came from Miami FLA . . . thought she was James Dean for a day* . . . She fought the wind, listening to Uncle Lou, his New Yorky sneer covering what junkie transsexual heartbreak, she only now was starting to imagine. Tumbleweeds paced the car out on the coyote-

side, the dark thorny arms of Joshua trees im-
plored the sterile moon.

She stopped in Yucca Valley for gas — it
wasn't a place that would have called to
Michael, four lanes through a suburbanish town,
not the haphazard clump of Morongo Valley —
Allstate office, car lots, a Safeway store, A and W
Root Beer. It was 11:00 p.m., everything was
closed but the gas stations. She noticed the tow
truck parked next to the garage, *24 hour
service,* an old-fashioned lift. Couple of junked
cars and one in the bay. The man wheeled himself out from under the car, came over, wiping
his hands. He had *Dale* written on his me-
chanic's uniform. He reminded her of her uncle
Dave. A small man, wiry, with a hard face, about
thirty-six, but thirty-six the Bakersfield way, that
made them men at twenty and old at forty. Not
like the photographers and art teachers and
casting agents of LA, who could be any age at all.

She popped the hood and got out, leaning
against the car. She lit a cigarette despite the
sign that said *No Smoking.* She could hear
Dale's radio playing in the service bay, faint
against the wind. Johnny Cash, "Folsom Prison
Blues." "Is it going to keep up like this all night?"
she asked.

"Could," Dale said. "This ain't even bad yet. How far you going?"

"Twentynine Palms," she said.

"That's not far," he said. "Stay to the center of the road, you'll be okay. Want me to check your tires? It ain't a night for a blowout."

She agreed it wasn't, and he checked the tires. They were low. He filled them, but they were pretty bald. They'd probably get her where she wanted to go, as long as she didn't try to go very fast. "I could make you a deal on a new set, you're gonna be around awhile."

She smiled and shook her head. "Is there a liquor store open this late?"

Dale grinned. "Only thing that is. Not much else to do 'round here. I don't drink no more so I work nights."

"Is that a fact," she said, just the way her uncle Dave would have said it.

She paid him and he took her money into the little station to make change.

Up here, the wind sounded like bombs, booming in the wide, high valley. A truck pulling a four-horse trailer slammed past on the high-way, empty, wagging in the wind. She'd looked up Twentynine Palms on the map before she started. To the east was a vast nothing. The road just kept going, out to the state line and the shallow trickle of the Colorado River, no town until then, only the giant marine base to the north — nothing but mountains and valleys you've never heard of — Ward Valley, Sheep Hole Mountains, even a clutch of mines, the Virginia Dale, Lone Mine, the Gold Standard, the Rose of Peru. She could imagine lost prospectors wandering around out there with donkeys and beards like someone had forgotten to tell them the Gold Rush was over.

She hoped she could find the motel. *The Paradise Inn.* She should have made sure, found an address. But how big a town could Twentynine Palms be, anyway? She'd know it when she saw it. And if she didn't, it wouldn't be hard to find out. People in bars would still be talking about the suicide, some kid from LA who checked into the Paradise and blew his head off. If she didn't find it tonight, she'd look in the morning.

She drove around the corner to Jerry's Liquors. Dale was right, it was the only thing open. Jerry was a fat man watching pro wrestling on TV. The place was too hot. He looked up at her when she came in, then turned back to the TV. "I'd like a half-pint of Smirnoff, please," she said. "And some Camels."

He ignored her.

"Hey," she said. "You open or what?"

"Read the sign, Blondie." He pointed to one of the myriad signs behind him, counterfeit twenties, big-breasted beer models. An American flag. A Marine Corps flag. Oh yeah. The sign said *We Reserve the Right to Refuse Service to Anyone, and that means YOU*. And again in Spanish, in case you didn't get it the first time. How could she have gotten all nostalgic for the Folsom Prison blues? Patsy Cline and all that crap.

"You keep the swastika in another room?" she asked.

He was looking at her now. "You want me to come over there and pierce your ears in a few more places? Get your freako self out of my shop. This is a decent place. We're Americans here."

Yeah, it was America, all right. "Hey, motherfucker. Sit on this." She gave him the finger and left his shop quick as he stood and started around the counter.

She walked out into the wind, got back to the car. Her filled tires felt strange on the road, like there was something wrong with them. She pulled out on the highway, taking Dale's advice to hug the yellow line. No voddy tonight. Well. Just as well. You were either in or out. You wanted to know or you didn't. No more of these blurred lines. No more taking the edge off. She needed the edge. The edge was all there was. She ought to thank old Jerry for being such a Nazi prick.

Just as the little man had told her, twenty minutes and she came over a rise to see the twinkling lights of spread-out Twentynine Palms in the distance. And there, close on the right, a one-story L-shaped motel at the ass end of the world. *Paradise Inn.* She pulled into the parking area before its sign. *Vacancy.*

34
Paradise

In the elbow of the L-shaped motel, she found the door with the hand-lettered card saying *Manager.* Light shone through dingy curtains behind yellow panes that were marked off in diamonds in a mistaken attempt at down-home charm. She rang the bell. The screen door rattled in its frame in the bitter wind, and the oleanders, growing in the gravel yard, shivered like dogs. A Joshua tree vibrated, stiff and stoic by the empty pool. The chain link sang. If Michael had come out here hoping for warmth, how desperate he must have felt right about now, in a cold that was bleaker than anything in LA. She banged on the door. "Hey!"

A silhouette appeared through the curtain, the fabric inched to the side. A girl in a knit cap, startled and suspicious, peered out as if she had no idea why someone would be banging on the door of a motel with a vacancy sign at eleven-thirty at night. The face disappeared and the lock scrabbled open. It took her a while to re-lease the screen-door latch, she wasn't looking at what she was doing, she was watching be-hind her. Finally, the girl managed to get the screen open and let Josie in.

She was about Josie's age, nineteen or so, pale, with ashy brown hair and frightened eyes under bushy eyebrows. She moved behind the pine counter with its hooks for keys and kitschy calendar of Montezuma and his feather-clad court. Beyond a doorway, in what was clearly the rest of the apartment, a man and a woman reclined on matching plaid couches. The man, about fifty, also wore a knit cap, turquoise, on his bald head. The woman, hatless and just slightly older than the girl, glanced at Josie, said some-thing to the man, who laughed.

"I'm looking for a room," Josie said to the girl.

"How many night?" she asked.

"I don't know yet. Listen, you had a boy here, about eight weeks ago. He registered as Oscar Wilde."

The girl flashed her a white-eyed look of fear before she dropped her gaze to the registration card she'd pulled out.

"He was here, wasn't he? Tell me."

The girl wouldn't look at her. The man said something to the girl in a language that wasn't English — French maybe. And the girl said something back. Angry sounding.

The man hauled himself off the couch, came out to the little office. He was hammered. "A room for this young lady," he said, replacing the girl behind the desk. Not quite French. His eyes were astoundingly blue. There was something wrong about these people. Over his shoulder, Josie could see the girl going through a card file, glancing up at her suspiciously. Wasn't this a public business? And why was the girl wearing fingerless gloves inside? The man smiled, leaning on the counter, as if he was enjoying a joke at her expense. She'd thought he was drunk, but he didn't smell of booze. High on something, that was for sure. "Maybe we have a room."

The keys hung off the hooks behind him, it didn't look like many were missing.

She'd normally have left by now, they were weird and she didn't like being jerked around. She wondered if the Frenchman had given Michael this same shit. She imagined not. Michael spoke French. He spoke everything, he could go into a Thai restaurant and chat up the waitress. Michael would've known enough to wipe that smile off the man's face. Very, very far from Montmartre.

"How many nights do you stay?"

Just one, she imagined. "You had a boy here," she said. "He killed himself."

She thought that would have wiped the smirk off his face, but it didn't. Only a slight narrowing of blue eyes, and the girl playing with the card file trying not to look at her. "Not here," the man said. "People are happy here. It's Paradise." He opened his palms as if to let a bird go free.

The woman giggled from the next room. The girl with the fingerless gloves shot her a fathomless glance. She knew. If Josie could only get her alone.

"How many nights did he stay?" Josie asked.

"Who?" the man said.

"The boy. The boy who didn't stay here."

The bald man turned to the rack of keys, ran his fingers along them, as if they were chimes.

He pulled a key off the hook, the red plastic tag said *Room 4.* "How many nights?"

"Don't know yet," she said, taking the key.

"Got a credit card?"

She stared at him impatiently. She wasn't exactly a girl credit-card companies opened their arms to. *Art model. Actress, freelance.* But then again, this wasn't the Hotel Diplomat, Stockholm.

"Thirty-five for tonight," he said.

She pulled out a crumpled twenty, ten, and five ones. He recounted them briskly, snapping the bills, creasing them longways like a gambler. Someone used to dealing with cash. "You have a suitcase?'

"In the car." She had all the essentials — a toothbrush, a change of underwear, nine assorted barbiturates, and a blue guitar. She took the key off the counter as the girl watched her, then quickly looked away.

Outside in the darkness, Orion hung, wind-scoured and sulking in the face of the accusing moon, like a man being scolded by a woman, as an unblinking planet looked on — Venus, or Mars? She remembered looking through the big telescope on the rooftop of the observatory, on a night just like this. All four planets, Mercury,

Venus, Mars, and Jupiter, lined up in a row like mismatched chorus girls. Michael stood behind her on the ladder, his breath on her neck. How huge their garden was then.

So this was where he came, this shitbox motel, crouching low in the wind, yellow bug lights over the doors. She gazed up at the planet that stared without blinking, wondering what it thought of her at the Paradise. She preferred to think it was Venus, the only one likely to understand her being there. Jet trails scraped the sky with their long fingernails, lacing marks through the dark silhouette of the poolside Joshua tree.

She got her things from the car and headed down the flank of the motel to her room, bracing against the wind. Suddenly, a dog appeared, slim and smooth coated. It stopped right between her and the room. She wondered if it would attack her, its wide head up and alert. "Good dog," she said, hoping it was true. The wind cut her, but she was afraid to move, all she needed now was a dog bite. Trying to find the closest hospital this time of night. "Go home," she said. "Beat it." Finally, it shambled away, behind the pool and off into the desert.

Crunching gravel under her boots, she saw room 3 but not 4. The next door had no number, it had to be right. Just as well, 4 was unlucky. Four was difficult and misunderstood, a genius before its time, it belonged to the planet of unexpected disaster. On the other hand, what did it matter if it was 3 or 4? She was past all that now, pennies in fountains, wishes and ladders and good and bad numbers. Once the worst had happened to you, all the rest was just stuff and absence.

Standing under the yellow porch light, she inserted the key into the cheap metal door and opened it. The smell of something sweetly chemical met her before she'd even turned on the light. Not disinfectant, but some kind of dry rot or ant powder. She turned on the switch. A bare lightbulb gazed down on a sad room with blue-shag carpeting, fake knotty pine paneling, a plastic chair, pressboard furniture. It looked like a set from a porno flick. That dreadful anonymity. She hadn't expected better and yet, she must have hoped. That he had had that, on his last day on earth.

She closed the door and discovered there was no dead bolt or chain, just an insignificant door-knob lock which Bo could have opened in kindergarten. Did he give her this room on purpose, so he could pay her a visit in the middle of the night? Was that the joke the Frenchman made to himself?

She sat down on the defeated expanse of the bed, breathing in the poisoned air. This dirty quilt, navy and rust in a vaguely western design. This bedside light. These rust-colored ripcord curtains that didn't close all the way, and the stink of ant powder. Not a single picture. Nothing to distract him or give him one shred of comfort. This is what he'd driven three hours to find, the boy who hated to drive, hated to be part of a machine. For something this ugly. A home for his death. Yes, you'd sit here and think, *There's nothing worth living for.* Here you could convince yourself.

In the next room, somebody was watching TV. The buzzing sound of a newscast. A man with sprayed hair pointing to a map, charting winter storms in the Inland Empire. Maybe this was the last sound Michael heard, a bland recital of the weather tomorrow. Weather he wouldn't be there to see. The storm inside never made the news, its fronts and eddies, unstable layers, sandstorms, Santa Anas.

The wind slammed into the window in a sudden punch, making her jump. The slit in the dusty curtains leered. She got up and tried to close it but the fabric had been cut badly, the two halves naturally fell away from each other. She could imagine the Frenchman or some other perv standing outside her window, jerking off. She found a roach clip in her purse and clipped the bottom of the curtains together. But that feeling, that someone was watching, continued to tug at her. She took the blue chair and edged it under the doorknob, tried the door. It slid out. She wedged it more firmly until it held.

In the bathroom, she pulled the chain that turned on the light. Broken bubbly blue tiles surrounded the mirror. The toilet seat had been repainted but the paint was peeling, rough against her thighs. No ants though. Washing her hands, she gazed at herself in the mirror. Hollow eyed, with a cold sore making her look like a kid's Halloween corpse. She got her toothbrush and brushed her teeth in alkaline desert water, washed her face, and dried it on the small rough towel.

Sitting quietly on the bed, listening to the wind and an occasional truck banging past, she peeled back the weeks and hours to the day Michael had arrived here. Pulled up in his rented Chevy, took the room, found a gun. But how? How did you decide to take your own life?

How did you get to the Paradise? How did you get this far?

In stages, that's how. First you let go of the things you loved. Blaise and Auntie Ono's guava cake and Louis Armstrong. You gave up Oscar Wilde and the shadow theater of M. Rivière, the domes of Moscow. Brahms and Schiele. The smell of laundry and moonlight on Echo Park lake. Tangerine sunsets from Dante's View. Making love as breezes trailed through open windows. He had so loved the world, its ten thousand things, but he'd peeled them off, one by one, dropping them to the floor like a woman stripping. That was how you did it. You let go, you left all that behind, you refused to remember. You let the dark in. You let your head become a ruined flower bed, overrun by rank growth, coarse and ugly as castor beans on a neglected hillside, monstrous and throbbing with cancerous life, the red and green poisonous leaves, the spiny testicles of its seedpods. Your black thoughts colonized you like a disease, the absence of faith most of all.

Finding your way here was only one of a series of choices. By the time you got to Twenty-nine Palms, your world was already vanishing.

Then came the smaller choices, one by one,

until the last one. How she wished Zeno's paradox really worked, stretching out forever the small divisions between zero and one.

But wasn't it possible he had simply wanted to get away from her, from Meredith, their feminine agendas, their judgment, their unfillable need, their awful possessiveness? From them and from Cal, the father he could not equal, who had replaced him with other children, again and again. Haunted by his nightmare of failure, thoughts of it hounding him, running him to ground — failure everywhere he looked, failure to find the true world, to be one with the people, to achieve greatness by age twenty-two.

He came here. Not to Palm Springs or Rancho Mirage, white golf shoes and hyperfertilized grass, but to this elemental place, wind and rock and sand. He turned off the main highway onto the two-lane, looking for a harsh solitude, like a prophet in the Bible. Seeking some final truth.

She imagined him sitting there, at the rickety table, writing his notes on motel stationery. His dark cropped curls, his feverish face with its week of stubble, sleepless glitter in his eyes. She went to the low dresser beneath the TV. In it was only a Gideon Bible, and a slender phone book. No stationery. She picked up the Bible and opened it at random, the way Michael would have, pointed to a line. It said, *Therefore shall the land mourn, and every one that dwelleth therein* . . . She closed the book and put it back.

He'd asked for it at the desk. He'd wanted that stationery. *Paradise Inn.* It was so like him, like checking in as Oscar Wilde. She'd thought a sense of humor proved you hadn't gone to the bottom, but that wasn't true. He could sense the ridiculousness of life even as it tore the guts out of him. She saw that now. And death lay coiled in the dark between the perception and the pain.

And so he'd poured himself a drink. Sat down to write. Tequila, maybe mescal. He loved knowing the right thing, so Sei Shonagon. *In Twenty-nine Palms when you are preparing to kill yourself, you should drink mescal while you're writing your suicide notes.* She wondered what he'd written to Meredith and Cal.

He'd been so angry. Always, even at the beginning, but it was outside the circle of their love. She didn't know how it would prowl there in the dark, like tigers outside a campfire's glow. Rage at Meredith, rage at Cal, rage at his own weakness. And she'd known it, a fury no less than any Tyrell's. It was the dark streak in all that brightness. So he came here, to punish them all for an infinite range of failures and sins. He was his own hostage. He pushed you away and thought that's what you were doing to him. Like her father yelling *Don't you raise your voice to me* before he belted you. Michael had wanted to hurt them back the same way.

Just like her and the dog. She said she had just wanted to shake him up, but that was both true and a terrible lie. She wanted to wake him up, but also to hurt him. For treating her like garbage, for flinching at her touch. For saying his life was shit, which meant her. She wanted to make him see what he was doing to them, but if she couldn't, she'd show him what it felt like to hurt. That was the truth, and there was no hiding from it.

In the next room, a man and a woman exchanged listless but antagonistic dialogue over the background noise of the TV. Lives separated by walls as thin as want ads in local newspapers. Life was just like that. Like people in a motel. You checked in for a few nights, and for a short time, you lived side by side, you heard their voices over a TV broadcast, they heard you weep in your dreams. But you never really knew what went on in the next room. You listened, you made your best guess. But when you saw them outside, you stared at each other blankly, pretending they'd never heard you weep, you'd never heard them cry out. Parallel lines met only at the vanishing point, that's what they taught the baby artists.

What a shithole this place was. Ten times worse than the Sunnyvale, where she'd worked in Bakersfield, full of thrifty travelers on old Highway 99, retirees and families, salesmen who sold things like gaskets and pneumatic wrenches. No salesman would stay at the Paradise, unless he was setting up a drug deal, enough weight that it was worth thirty-five dollars to buy some anonymity. Good enough for hookers, or if your car finally died and you were waiting for parts, or for truckers to catch a few hours' sleep. A place to plan a crime, or have an affair. She imagined a housewife from Yucca Valley coming here, waiting for her lover — the front of the L would conceal her car from the road. But the affair would be over soon. Love could never bloom in a concrete-block room that smelled of ant powder, no matter how great the need.

But it was the perfect place to gather your courage to put the barrel of a gun in your mouth. This oxidized paneling, the western bedspread. No one would disturb you here while you wrote your letters, while you sat on the bed with the gun in your lap and readied yourself for the dark. No beauty to distract you from your intention to depart.

That gun. Tomorrow she would go into town and find the motherfucker who'd sold him that gun. Who looked into his face and told himself the kid wanted a gun for target practice, home protection. She would find that son of a bitch and break his motherfucking face. *What were you thinking, you piece of unholy crap?* But she knew. She could see the whole thing. A concrete-block building on the edge of town, the firing range in the desert behind. He'd paused for a moment before going in, working out his story. *Just window-shopping. A gift for a friend.* How fascinated and equally repelled he must have been in the supermarket of death.

The owner would spot him as soon as he came in. A hard man with a hard face like her uncle Whitey, who was like her father but without Glenn's charm and with a double helping of *fuck you.* Watching Michael eyeing racks of hunting rifles, knowing he'd never shot anything more alive than an arcade duck. The city-boy skin, circles under his eyes, that tweed jacket, he'd have thought, *College boy. He'll be good for it.* Wondering coldly what he was after, suicide or murder. Clearly no case of home-owner anxiety. This was a gun about to be used, and no doubt the hard man approved. Probably it pained him more to think of a poor gun in a shoebox in somebody's closet, uncleaned, un-fired, forgotten.

He'd show him handguns on a pad on the counter, felted, like a pool table. Snub-nosed re-volvers and sleek automatics. Long-barreled Colt .45's. Michael would ask intelligent questions and the man would be surprised, he'd show him some of his treasures — assault rifles, dueling guns, Chinese souvenirs from Vietnam. Then fi-nally, after circling the matter for a half hour, they'd get down to the thing itself, tailored to his needs. It nauseated her to think how he lifted the various candidates, weighed them in his hands, sighted down their barrels. Then finally decided, like a man choosing a whore. *This one.* Paying — with what? Where had he gotten the money? Cal. Of course, Cal. Christ. Poor Cal. She thought of his red eyes at the Lotus Room bar, the weight sitting on those broad shoulders. Of course it was Cal. He could never ask Mere-dith.

The man would invite him to shoot a few

rounds, out behind the building. To get the feel of it.

She pictured him in earmuffs, squeezing off shots into a paper target on a bale of hay. She wondered if he was a good shot. Probably. Probably left the guy's jaw hanging in the dust. Hadn't he lied about everything else? He was probably a sharpshooter with certificates up the wazoo. She imagined he stood behind the gun shop that day, killing them all. In the end it was easier to kill them inside his own head.

It was late. What she really wanted was some vodka and a red, but that was all over, she was going to the end now, one way or another, to the place where the bodies were piled along the train tracks. Why did she never pay attention to the end of the poem? She just wanted to think of the golden domes of Moscow, the thousand and three bell towers and seven train stations. But now she would take it all the way. Give up the picture he had painted of himself and know who he was, what he'd suffered. Be there for him as she hadn't been when he was alive. He deserved that. She wasn't going to be Meredith, skipping over the gaps, running off to Frankfurt and Hamburg, Salzburg and Vienna, as if what had happened couldn't catch her if she ran far enough. There was no end to that. Josie had once loved him enough to let him have his secrets. Now she had to love him enough to know it all.

She was tired, but the room was icy cold, she couldn't even take her jacket off. She went to the wall heater, tall and narrow, its ancient metal vents clogged with dust. She ran her hand along the cobwebby grate, felt the hot air coming out, but it still hadn't heated the room. She pushed the thermostat to eighty degrees in hopes it would do something, but then thought of the manager's girl in fingerless gloves.

She doubled the quilt, lay under it in all her clothes, shivering spasmodically, it wasn't getting one bit warmer. Finally, she pulled the mattress pad out from under the sheet and made a bedroll of the pad and the spread and the thin blanket and sheet and got in again, turned off the light. It was a little better. She wasn't planning on sleeping but she dozed off, listening to the wind.

She dreamed she was in Red Square. It was wintertime, and the colored domes of a great church rose over her head. She knew she was little Jeanne, bright and hopeful in a rat-fur coat and a hat with a brave feather, picking her way through the snow, slippery, so easy to fall. She was supposed to meet someone inside the church, someone had something for her, but it was intimidating. She pushed open the enormous carved-wood door.

Inside was much darker than in the brightness of snow, the colors of the fantastic domes replaced by gloom. Light flickered only from small smoky lamps, and the gold of the icons glowed faintly in the dark. The strong smell of smoke and incense, pine and mothball. It was no warmer inside than out, her breath made clouds in the air. The icons glared in mute outrage, knowing she, a whore and a stranger and an unbeliever, was violating the church with her presence.

A monk stepped out from behind the screen of gold icons. His matted hair hung long and dirty around a face distorted behind a long beard, his skin darkened with grime and soot. He wore a coarse black robe that smelled moldy, and his pale glaring eyes stood out in his dark face. His teeth were all rotten. It was Michael. She was shocked, how had he let his teeth get so bad? "Michael, it's me," she said, trying to show her sweetness, hoping he would see her face and remember that he loved her, that she was kind, and harmless, on the side of good.

But instead of allowing her to embrace him, he grabbed her, knocking her hat off, yanking her toward a basin of holy water, it was filthy, rank with algae. She thought he might just put some on her forehead, but then he was pushing her face into the basin. She flailed but he was too strong, she could grab at nothing. He was determined to baptize her in the murky tub, whether or not it drowned her.

35
Room 12

Josie jerked herself awake, out of the font. Dark, and cold. The cold, the bedroll. She sat up, still feeling his hands on her head, the smell of dank water, the feeling of being drowned like a cat in a pond. He knew she was a whore, that she'd violated his sanctuary by entering there, with her ridiculous hat and rat-fur coat. But who had left such a magnificent church in those grubby, long-nailed hands? He'd lived in its darkness too long, brooding behind that golden screen of saints. Jeanne wasn't the only guilty one.

She turned on the light. The raw, ugly space

swarmed with bad dreams. The TV still murmured next door, the people had crashed and just left it on. Now what? She rubbed her face, cold as a rubber ice bag, lit a ciggie and sat in the heatless glare of the bare bulb. The emptiness of the room was so profound, it was as if the world had turned itself inside out, like a pocket. Michael was gone, and there was only the mad monk. This was the end of the road. What did she think she would find here anyway, some answer, like a comet blazing with light? There was nothing to understand. It was chaos, it was madness, and now he was gone.

She reached for the envelope of barbs in her purse, counted them. Nine. She could take one and sleep the rest of the night. Or she could take them all, and just sleep. *Pull a Marilyn,* why the fuck not? Even Marilyn had more to live for. How much longer could a person go on, living from one breath to the next?

You take care your own soul. Have more respect yourself.

She was trying to, but it was getting hard to even imagine.

A sound stirred outside. Crunch of footsteps on gravel. Someone walking around, the Frenchman? That weird fucking asshole, thinking he

was going to have a little fun with his new
guest? Well, he'd better fucking get ready. She
wasn't a girl like the ones he was used to. She
swept the reds back into their envelope, turned
off the light. Unclipping the curtains and parting them ever so slightly, she peered out. There,
in the yellow bug light, bouncing on the balls of
her feet, arms tight around herself, stood the
manager's girl. It had to be four in the morning.
She reclipped the curtain, yanked the chair out
from under the knob, opened the door. She tried
to smile, but her face wasn't cooperating, not
after this kind of night. "Hey."

The girl glanced back toward the office, then
at Josie, her clear blue eyes wet and frightened.
She opened her mouth and then closed it again.

"Come on in," Josie said.

The girl slipped inside. Josie locked the flimsy
door, turned the lights back on. The girl's gaze
rattled around the room, panicked as a squirrel
that comes in through the dog door. It came to
rest on the linens still folded in their bedroll.
Sense of duty seemed to focus her. "Oh, you are
cold?"

Josie opened the roll and flicked the bed-
clothes into place over the stained mattress.
Fuck the cold. She didn't want the girl to feel

accused of anything. "No big deal. Hey, have a seat."

The odd mousy girl sat on the edge of the bed with her hands folded in her lap over a bulky, fuzzy hippie purse that looked like it was made out of a rug. "I see . . . your light on."

Josie sat in the plastic chair, making no sudden moves, not wanting to spook her further. The girl clutched her purse, hands like little traps.

"I don't sleep too well these days anyway. Not since Michael . . ."

Those prominent blue eyes searched Josie's face, the ravaged, broken-apart face, as if asking something, but what? Then they skidded away, dropped to her hands. "To me he is Oscar," she said quietly.

So she had met him. Josie had guessed right. This weird little girl. But to her he was Oscar Wilde. "Oscar Wilde's a poet," Josie said. "His name was Michael. But he liked poetry."

Picking at the wool of her hippie purse, the girl nodded.

Josie didn't want to ask the hundreds of questions that seethed in her tired mind, afraid the frightened bird would bolt. Instead she stood, very slowly, and walked around the bed to the nightstand, lit a ciggie. The packet of reds lay by the lamp. Now she was ashamed that she'd even thought of it. Wasn't there enough suffering in the world? She picked them up and pocketed them. "Yeah, he liked poetry, and old records. Garage sales. He played the piano." Quietly, she returned to the plastic chair, opposite the manager's girl in her dirty blue parka. "We loved each other. But he didn't remember."

The girl's cheeks grew even paler. Finally, she burst out, "But why? Why he do this?"

The thing they all wanted to know. "Did you guys talk?"

She nodded again, wiping her eyes on the back of her fingerless glove. How pale she was, paler even than Josie. Where did they keep her, locked in the basement?

"He speak German." She smiled, a wavery, watery smile. "Like a Viennese."

German, that's what it was. Not French. And not just any German, *Viennese*. How like him. *Café Central, Wien*. Michael had never even met his grandfather, but he'd made a shrine to him, out of his own flesh and bones.

"His mother, his father, he miss them. Climbers." And now she could hear it, yes, *muzzer, fazzer*. Not French at all. The girl pronounced the *b* in *climb.* "They send him to America for study. All over the world they are climbing."

Like Godzilla and King Kong. Making it theirs, making sure he had nowhere to go that could be his own. So he could end up in this godforsaken corner of the universe, lying to this wretched girl. Creating himself on the canvas of her mind, the picture of himself he wished were true. *It doesn't help, Michael. It just hurts more.* Darkness coiled between what he wanted them to believe and the self he despised. It only made him more alone. How could you save someone when he didn't let you know him? Not really, not all the way.

But Josie knew about that. The glamorous model, the silver lily. She'd been the same kind of liar.

"How long was he here?"

"Almost a week. I did not know he will do this." Her begging eyes. Her forehead pleated like a lampshade. "You must believe."

A week. Josie leaned back in the molded chair, staring at the lightbulb, the chunky white ceiling, trying not to cry. A week meant he'd never gone to Meredith's at all. It meant he knew what he was going to do the day he kissed her goodbye. That day, she'd kissed a dead man. Jesus Christ.

"Here he is happy," the girl said, leaning forward, trying to convince her, trying to convince somebody. "Very much he is liking it. He hike. Always he draw. Look." The girl wiped her nose on the back of her fingerless glove, and fumbled from her fuzzy hippie purse a picture drawn on thick unlined paper. Where it had been torn from a notebook, the edge was ragged. Josie held it up, let the light come through. Pen and ink, of the girl posed in the L of the motel. It perfectly captured her kicked-dog expression. Composed into a corner, you could see how boxed in she was. *Or who was?* It was good, probably took him all of five minutes. What waste. The beauty he murdered in this place. He could never see what he had, only what he failed to achieve.

And she thought of the barbs in her pocket. So what was it she had that she was forgetting?

Take care your own soul.

And he'd chatted away with this poor little girl, his plan stinking under the floorboards like a murder victim. Telling her only a piece, the piece he thought she wanted to hear.

Josie handed the drawing back to the girl,

who looked deeply at it, as if it was water and she was dying of thirst. "So *schön.* In New York, don't go over the fifth floor. The tall ladders nobody climb."

Josie knew the poem. The skyscrapers on fire, and the ladders nobody would climb. Elevators that went right to the floor of the fire, their doors automatically opening. *These are the warnings that you must forget, if you're climbing out of yourself, if you're going to smash into the sky.* His Sexton, all the beloved suicides. Plath, Rothko, Van Gogh. He was telling the girl without telling her, knowing she wouldn't understand. Leaving him safe with his secrets, like a man sitting on a grenade.

"I — he . . . he make you feel . . . *Wert.*"

Worth. He made you feel worthwhile. That was his gift. If this girl hadn't been so pathetic, Josie would have been jealous of her, that he'd shared that with her, after kissing Josie goodbye. "Did he say anything about . . . having a girlfriend?" Who was the pathetic one? *Did he talk about me?*

The girl dropped her eyes to her hands. They were surprisingly beautiful, with healthy, clean nails in narrow pink beds. "I ask if he have a girlfriends . . ." She shrugged, flushed red in the cheeks and the ears. She was in love with him too. Well, why wouldn't she be? When would a girl like that ever meet someone like him, talking to her, bathing her in his attention? She knew what that felt like. Like heaven. In that she and Josie were exactly the same.

The girl shrugged again, brought her hand to her red face, spoke from behind her glove. "He say she die. In Siberia. A train . . . smash. In his arm her last . . . breathe." She dropped the hand, let Josie see the quivering mouth, the liquid eyes. "Please, I did not know. How I know? I believe him. Everything . . ."

Gazing up at the ceiling, Josie traced lumps of stucco like gobs of dirty snow. So that was how their story ended. Jeanne dying in a train wreck, in Blaise's arms. *What was it that died, Michael?* His love, his faith? Little Jeanne had been his hope for love, for the true world. Once she was gone, all that was left was war, cholera, a new .38.

The girl fidgeted unhappily with her ugly purse. She wiped her nose again on her glove. Josie wanted to offer her a tissue but the place was so cheap, there didn't even seem to be a tissue box in the room. The girl's skin was creased with worry, fine lines already etched into her forehead. Josie got up and, hesitating, hoping it wouldn't frighten her, sat next to her on the bed. "None of us knew. He was keeping a secret."

The girl's mouth twitched and then she broke into heavy sobs. Josie put an arm around her, awkwardly patting her knit cap, her frizzy ash brown braids. "Shhh. It's hard. I know."

She stopped hiccupping and looked Josie in the eye. "It is me. I find."

It took a moment for her understanding to unfold, like a paper flower you drop in a glass of water. This girl had been the one to find Michael. She had found him like that.

Wiping her eyes with the glove that must have been sodden, she continued. "I go in to change the room. He is in the bed. The wall, the . . ." She pressed her hands over her eyes — it was too late. There was no shutting out that sight. "*Mein Gott. Mein Gott.*"

They held one another tight tight tight, Josie's cheek against the girl's knit cap that smelled of old cats. This was what she had been spared. It could have been her, in her house in Lemoyne, but he'd come out here to keep her from that. The girl went on, "The blood, everywhere, so much blood. How he can do this . . . I just see . . . we just talk . . . nothing he say, nothing . . ."

"I know." Yes, that was how it was. You were just talking. About an art project, about baked beans. And then suddenly you were on your knees cleaning up bits of brains and freshly spilled blood. You were at a funeral. You were living in an empty house, like a dog waiting by the door.

"And then I must clean. After the police go."

That fucking Frenchman German whatever he was had made this girl clean the motel room where Michael had shot himself. That bastard. She'd kill him. She'd go in there and beat his head in with a brick. She could imagine the blood on the wall, quarts of it, the smell of it, butcher thick, and this girl on hands and knees with a bucket, weeping. There was no justice. To think that this girl could have had the strength. The girl sobbed like she was going to vomit. Josie kept holding her until she was just sniffling.

Finally, she sat up, wiped her eyes. "I want to tell you, but *he* don't let me." She knit her bushy eyebrows. "So I wait until they sleep. Look." Out of her fuzzy hippie bag, she pulled a black notebook. "I don't give to police." It was one of Michael's journals. *What the fuck was this girl doing with his journal?* She'd stolen it, or maybe he'd given it to her. In any case she'd been protecting it. From everybody, Meredith, the cops. She'd probably never done anything so brave in her life, but she'd wanted it that much. The girl hugged it to her parka'd breast as if it was Michael himself, her eyes red, nose red, but her chin raised in defiance, as if daring Josie to rip it from her arms. Then she thrust it out. "Here. You take. Is better."

She felt the heat of the girl's body still on the black cover, as the girl stood. From her pocket the German girl took something else, that jingled. A key, with a red tag. She gave Josie a quick hard hug. "Bring back before *he* wake up," she said. She smiled weakly, and slipped out into the night.

Josie sat on the bed, looking at the key and the book in her hands. She gazed at the tag on the key. *Room 12.* Twelve, the number of the Hanged Man.

Outside, it was even colder than it had been, bleaker, more forsaken. The stray dog lay curled under the block wall of the patio, as if it was warmer there, outside a room where a human being breathed. She walked quickly down the long side of the motel. Half the doors had no numbers, but the last one was marked 12. Of course, it would be the last room. *Something quiet, please.* The young gentleman wouldn't want to be disturbed. She glanced over her shoulder toward the closed door of the manager's office, fumbled the key into the lock. She let herself in, closed the door, turned on the light.

It was the same as number 4, though the bed sat against the other wall. Table, blue chair, bare bulb. And then she saw the paneling. No longer the dark knotty pine, some lighter wood. The headboard was new. She swayed, sat down on the blue chair. *You wanted to see it. There it is.*

She could taste his blood in the air. She was breathing his death, under the ant powder. If only she had known how desperate a person could be. There, with a gun in his mouth. She could taste it, the metal, smell the gunpowder, the bite of it. Why couldn't he have just told them all to fuck off? He could have disappeared into a new life. He didn't have to do this. He could have remembered pedaling a boat on Echo Park lake and playing the blue guitar and singing "Just a Gigolo."

And that girl had cleaned up the mess, bucket running bloody.

Here it was. Everything she hadn't wanted to know. He sat in *this* room, and wrote his notes, and put the gun in his mouth. Alone, in this dismal cell, inscribing smaller and smaller circles around himself until there was nowhere for him to go but out. He was the one in the corner, not the girl. Now she was here. She could not keep it from happening, but she could keep him from being alone.

The journal was number *XX*. She'd never opened his journals before. Even now, it seemed like the last violation. *Forgive me, Michael.*

The pages were dense with drawings, ink and charcoal, sticky with the hair spray he used instead of fixative. She was surprised, she thought there would be more writing, but these were just pages and pages of drawings, mostly self-portraits. Himself with three eyes. With one eye. Eyes on the same side of his head like a halibut. A truncated body with a second set of legs where the arms should be, limping past a shell and a human skull. Heads with faces tangled in the hair. Snatches of writing, chains of words in blotchy pen, running downhill, the backward-leaning *d*'s, the *e*'s like *3*'s, *Can't get back into the parade. Even tried to make a virtue of it.*

WHERE IS THE ROSE GARDEN GODDAMN IT WHERE IS IT? A hand with six fingers, severed from a wrist, the blood running down onto a piano keyboard. A series — severed hands, severed heads, arms without hands, a man carrying his own head in his arms.

And there was her name, *JosieJOSIEJosieJOSIE.* Written in chains, in suns of *Josies.* Her face, over and over again, he could do it from memory. *Don't leave me, please God don't leave me.*

I'm such a piece of shit. I disgust myself. How can she still be in love with me. She should leave. I would if I were her. Everything I touch turns to shit. Her love just makes it worse.

She shivered, she couldn't stop, it was so cold in here. *Her love made it worse.* How could that be? She couldn't understand, why was she so stupid, she read it over and over again but she still couldn't take it in. She hit her forehead with her fists, trying to wake her brain up, trying to force this into her head, how such a thing could be.

I don't know how. I don't know the first fucking thing about life. I wish she wouldn't look at me like that, for Christ's sake. Like I had crushed her last dream. What does she think I

*am, Jesus? I'M NOTHING. I HAVE NOTHING.
STOP LOOKING AT ME LIKE THAT. STOP LOV-
ING ME LIKE THIS I CANT BEAR IT.*

*Josiejosiejosie, you're all I've ever had. Every
scrap of joy. Don't leave me, please God, please
God.*

She read that part over and over. He had loved
her.

But it hadn't helped.

He had loved her, but he hated himself more.

Such suffering, so much pain. And he thought
it made him hateful, as if suffering were shame-
ful, disgusting. As if pain were a crime. Why
didn't he tell her? She could have helped him if
only he'd let her. She could have done something. But it wasn't what he wanted. How hard
he'd pushed her away. And then said, *Don't
leave me, please God. You're all I have.* He'd
loved her, he had. And he knew she loved him,
he knew it! But it wasn't enough. She couldn't
have imagined such a thing was possible. Love
wasn't enough.

Her mouth bent itself square in mute anguish,
but she kept turning the pages, trying to see
through the blur of tears, the marks they left
spattering the pages.

Clocks. Pages of them. Grandfather clocks in

black cases, dense charcoal marks. Wristwatch with a broken face. A clock nestled in the crotch of Michelangelo's *David. What's the good of all my so-called gifts? I would be a pair of ragged claws . . . HURRY UP PLEASE ITS TIME.*

After clocks, the mazes. Naked men up against the blind ends of passages. A labyrinth that bled into the distance, as if it covered the world. A labyrinth in a graveyard, the space between tombstones. A self-portrait, a labyrinth superimposed over his features.

And carefully, lovingly rendered, a dead man, lying across the lap of a huge mother, in the pose of Michelangelo's statue of Jesus and Mary, only the dead man had a bull's head. *Minotaur.* She remembered the story. A queen who fell in love with a bull. They had a child, half bull, half human. And the queen was ashamed of it and kept it in a maze under the palace. It turned murderous, the king fed it youths from Greece. *Feed me,* he'd written. *I strip your living flesh from your bones.*

And here was Josie, trailing a ball of string. The black mouth of a cave in the background, the entry to the labyrinth. The string was the way out, it was how the hero killed the Minotaur and escaped. But Michael wouldn't take the string, would he? He wasn't the hero in the story he was telling himself. He was the monster. And the maze wasn't just a prison, it was also a palace, his dark home.

She needed a cigarette, needed to breathe air that didn't stink with death. She opened the door, leaned in the doorway, sucking in the night air. She gazed up at the stars, which had retreated still higher. *We don't know, we don't have problems like yours.* He'd loved her, and she'd loved him, and it wasn't enough. She struggled to understand how that could be possible. Love, it seemed, wasn't as big as she'd thought. There were bigger things. She felt her heart being crushed, it was going to pop like a grape. But she closed the door and sat back down at the table. The black book had not finished unfolding its black tale.

Across two pages, he'd drawn a picture of a man on a bed, feet closest to the viewer, wearing black pants and a white shirt. It was an iron bed like Michael's at his mother's, the bars of its headboard and footboard like a jail. He'd splattered black ink on the wall behind the bed — just shaken the pen. Underneath, he'd written, *Mayakovsky criticized Esenin. Who can judge another man's suffering?*

She gazed at the blobs of India black, brushing her tears with the back of her hand. She had to look at that. She had to look and let it come in. It was one thing to say, *Why couldn't you hang on, why couldn't you have gone somewhere, started again?* But she could never know what he suffered, there, under the palace. Even if he had told her everything, could she have known, understood, the depths of his despair? And what if she had? In the end, she couldn't go there with him. She couldn't follow him the rest of the way. She'd tried to remind him about life and a way out, handed him the end of the string, but he'd only backed deeper into the labyrinth.

Who can judge another man's suffering? Was this before or after the dog? There were no dates anywhere, it wasn't Meredith's chronicle of her historical life. What went on inside had no time. Did it matter whether it was before or after the dog? It wasn't about what she did or said or hadn't done or hadn't said. She'd been cruel, but he knew why, that she loved him, that she wanted him. The dog day had been one more cruel thing, but not the darkness itself.

Large, Gothic German lettering: *Mauritz Friedrich Loewy, 1898–1956.*

Ming.

But she didn't believe in destiny. She refused to believe. Even if the game was rigged and the house always won, you could still go on playing, even as you lost.

Who can judge?

She turned the page and there it was. The mad monk. Wrapped in his black cloak, gaunt, hungry, smoldering with fury. Underneath, Michael had written, *I accept you, demon.*

She stared into the seething eyes of the wretched monk. How she hated that thing. She could taste the murky water of the baptismal font all over again. *His* demon? *His?* She'd always thought the monk was accusing *her,* punishing *her.* Her body felt pierced, like the chests of Indians who flew on windmills, hanging from hooks through their flesh. He was depicting his own madness, the thing that tormented *him,* accused *him. But of what, Michael? You didn't do anything wrong.* It wasn't the dog, it wasn't even Saint-Tropez. But what? She stared at the large crazy eyes of the monk, his bony body in its crow black robes like the wings of a dirty bird. *What did you accuse him of?*

WHERE'S THE GODDAMN ROSE GARDEN? WHERE IS IT?????

It was a poem too. *Down the passage which we did not take towards the door we never opened into the rose-garden.* That was all he wanted. Simple happiness. But the mad monk tortured him because he wanted it. The monk despised it, mocked it. He couldn't let him believe it was possible. That was the thing stopping him. That mocking, evil thing that had his own face.

She covered her eyes with the heels of her hands. The anguish of missing him, all these days since the cops called, since seeing him in the morgue like a giant, wooden mannequin. With his poor battered face. That fucking crowbodied thing had won. How gleeful it was now. All because he'd wanted to live, forget genius and destiny, and simply be happy. And it wouldn't let him.

It had all come to this, like poisoned bread squashed to the size of a pill. Death like a lover, caressing him, promising him peace, running its fingers through his hair, its tongue in his ear.

They have ladders that will reach further but no one will climb them.

I would have, Michael.

But maybe she wouldn't have. Maybe she would have had to stop somewhere, unless she'd wanted to follow him into the night. She didn't know what she believed. In any case, he didn't want her to save him. He had retreated into his labyrinth, out of reach.

The ant powder was making her dizzy, the stink of fear and his despair under the sweet poison. She lay down on the bed, on his side. But as soon as she did, she knew he would have taken the other side, her side, a last shred of comfort, like the dog curled up by the patio wall. She moved onto the right side. She sat in the bed, arranged the pillows behind her. He'd poured himself a last shot of mescal. *I'm sorry. I just want to stop now.* And put the gun in his mouth, sour, cold, smoky. She put her own two fingers in her mouth. *I'm so sorry.* And pulled the trigger.

36
Rock

Dawn tinted the darkness like watered ink. She sat outside number 4, wrapped in the spread she'd pulled off the bed, her chair tipped back against the rough stucco, smoking. The smell of the tobacco didn't begin to offset the smell of Michael's death. The landscape stared back at her, obstinate in its silence, spiny and hostile as the Joshua tree stretching its twisted limbs to the slate-colored sky. Dry and empty, where everything not mineral armored itself with leather and spines. The dog had gone.

She thought of Michael on the porch on Lemoyne, holding a cantaloupe like a skull on his fingertips. Mock-heroic, tilting his profile like Laurence Olivier. "*To be or not to be . . .*" She hadn't even known that speech was about suicide. "It's the only question, really," he'd said. "Zero or one. Accept or reject." The expressive gesture of his long fingers.

And she'd laughed. *Laughed.* "The only question?"

She hadn't even begun to understand the length and breadth of her idiocy, so enormous, its gravity field alone would crush anything for light-years around.

And so the zero had sprouted in their garden. Small and secret, it would bloom as this gaping cold absence where he'd torn himself away from the fabric of the world. Zero a red hole in his head. The number that lodged in his brain. He once told her that the Arabs invented zero, because they were a desert people, at home with absence. Now she knew why he'd come here to answer the question, this desert, this graveyard. This was his landscape, bitter cold, populated only by rocks and strange leafless trees, no softness or mercy, no touch of green. Her eyes cracked with the emptiness, the dry scoured ache in the pit of her heart. Why hadn't she argued, when he said *that was the only question?*

She waited for morning against the rough wall, humming softly to herself, *Tricks ain't walkin', tricks ain't walkin' no more* . . . Now she knew why he liked those old blues. Nothing had ever happened to man or woman that wasn't in the blues. If your life came apart, Lucille had been there before you, Louis, Bessie. You could learn how to keep on, you could count on them. A better guide to the labyrinth than anything she could offer, her pathetic ball of string. The blues had mapped the place inside and out.

The horizon began to lighten. White chalk marks appeared overhead in the colorless sky. Jet fighters from the marine base. Piloted by boys like Jeff McCann and Steve Coty, the football gods of Bakersfield High, nothing filling the domes of their skulls but thoughts of applause and their dicks and the crudest outlines of reality. Boys who wouldn't have appeared in public with Josie Tyrell, but if they gave her a ride, shared a joint or a forty ouncer, she could nurse the illusion she could be seen by a boy like Jeff McCann. And maybe, if she got him off right, he might talk to her, smile at her in the hall, call her up for a date on an off night, dance once with her at the prom. So eminently exploitable. *I hope you find someone* . . .

Michael had given her a dream better than any that Bakersfield could imagine. *He made you feel . . . worth.* That was his greatest gift, to see something more and believe it into being. But what happened when you were someone's idea, when the person thinking you up checked out? What happened to a dream without a dreamer? *I hope you find someone who can meet your needs . . .* Where did he think she would find that phantom? She had needs she hadn't even known about till she met him.

Someday, you'll be washing dishes in a trailer in Lancaster . . . Was that what she wanted? Even now, she could go with Meredith. But the labyrinth covered the world. The thing that had crippled the crippled boy, that had deafened the deaf-mute. The dark church of the mad monk. Michael wasn't in Europe, drivers and pony-skin coats, the Hotel Diplomat. That was the cross he had been nailed to.

The sun crawled up over the horizon as if risen from a bad night, dreading its passage over the landscape. It vomited on the wall of the motel and splashed the door where the *4* should be with unnecessary gold. Her nose was as cold as a coyote's dug in under a tumbleweed. She

gathered the quilt around her and gazed out at the motel yard and its pool — empty — the lone Joshua tree. Beyond that, no line of painted white rocks or ocotillo fence marked off the boundary between the motel and the desert, one bled right into the other.

The bubbling of birds filled the air. A line of quail burst from a shrub and dashed across the parking lot, their tiny hats bobbing. Like Jeanne's hat in the dream. The same question mark.

She stubbed out her cigarette against the motel wall and stood, wrapped the quilt around her like a stiff evening gown, and walked out past the pool onto the desert.

She found a faint trail in the dust, an old dune-buggy or jeep track, stretched toward the warming horizon, and she followed it. It didn't much matter where the path went, she wasn't the least bit curious, she just needed a direction. She followed it up and over a rise, then another, stopping every so often to gaze back at her shadow, Giacometti tall and thin, streaming back against the pale rocks and blond bleached grasses. *I am the long world's gentleman* . . . And every rock trailed its own blue pillar of shadow, each so clear it was almost alive. Blue and tan hills rolled in low lines on either side of the valley, their slopes sharp and distinct, each from the next, like a paint-by-numbers landscape.

She wandered from rise to rise in the bitter cold, the cheap motel bedspread snagging on cholla. Their fur of spines caught the early light in auras, like halos on saints. She'd never been much of a nature person. She liked the city, people close all around, crowds, the feel of something happening. Music, nightlife, being on the list, the girl everyone wanted to know — the possibility of more than dishes and diapers and the grocery store. But these days, she didn't much care to see people living their lives. It seemed pointless, like the swimming of a hit dog in the street. She could understand what people saw in the desert. What wasn't there, like Phil Baby always said. No people swarming over each other, everyone with a motive, everyone with a dream or a nightmare, so much wanting and longing, clutching, desiring, passion and hatred and terrible need. Even their kindness swarmed, like devils in the hair of Michael's self-portraits. Out here, death was suitable, there was room for it, the grip of life's relentless urges slackened, replaced by this icy simplicity.

She kept walking, turning, aimless, dragging

the quilt, even the jeep track had disappeared. Whatever you were, whoever you were, nothing distracted you from it here. The desert left you absolutely to yourself, it was zero embodied. It should have frightened her out of her wits to be lost in such emptiness, alone, like that dream with the coyote, but it was morning, and she wasn't afraid.

She turned to see if she could make out the Paradise, but it had vanished. The world had been reduced to its barest outlines, abstract — cactus and Joshua trees and rocks, the vast sky, the far blue mountains. Spaces for forgetting. She tried to remember her life before Michael, but it seemed like somebody else's. How busy she'd been, living at the Fuckhouse, days full of color and plans, nights feeling glamorous and part of it all. She never appreciated how much she'd had then. Maybe she shouldn't have let him wake her, learn something better, let him change her. For this is where his road led. This dead end.

Now it was just her. She didn't know where there was left to go. It didn't seem to matter, Europe or LA or nowhere at all. Death was bigger than anything. Bigger than love. Big as the universe. Death now or death later, that was the real question. So much like the Atomic Café, only everything on the menu was the same, there was only the question of how long you wanted to wait, how many quarters you had left for the juke-box. The pain of living another day, and another after that. How long did you want to lie on that rock with life's dirty bird chewing on your liver?

She oriented herself to a big square chunk of rock at the top of a rise that showed its pale gold side to the sun, keeping its blue face toward her, and made her way up to it. At least it didn't smell like swamp out here, not meat or moss or the sea. No surprise scents to wring you and twist you and make you cry out.

When she reached the crest, she paused, drawing the pure clean nothingness into her sad, tangled soul. She sat on the rock and no-ticed the square-shaped stones perched there. She sat staring at them, like listening to music in a far-off room.

It was a duck. Such an odd sensation. Some-one had been here before her. Way out here in the randomness of fucking nowhere. Someone had been here, and had bent over and picked up those rocks and placed them here. At the corner of a boulder at the edge of a rise. To mark the way for another human being, who might or might not ever happen by.

Or for himself.

Would a man getting ready to erase himself leave one last marker, a prayer?

The desert stood still as she gazed at those rocks, sitting on a boulder in the long-shadowed dawn. It could have been him. Or it could have just been a hiker, taken by impulse, leaning over and picking it up, setting it on end, capping it with another. *Kilroy was here.*

But that was the thing about zero. Its weakness. Even if zero had taken over the entire universe, the biggest fascist of all, one tiny gesture could deny it. One footprint, one atom. You didn't have to be a genius. You didn't even have to know that was what you were doing. You made a mark. You changed something. It said, "A human being passed here." And changed zero to one.

There it was.

Right there, on this waiting, breath-held desert. In a couple of ordinary rocks. It was here all the time. Shining in the first morning light. He'd lost faith in it, but there it still was. It hadn't died in room 12. It hadn't been eaten by zero, it hadn't been lost in the labyrinth. It wasn't back in the house in Los Feliz, it wasn't at the Hotel Diplomat. It was in this — what he had given her, Josie Tyrell, from South Union Avenue. Art model, student actress, and whatever else she was to become. This was his gift, marking his own passing.

She put another rock on the duck, and turned back to look at her own blue shadow stretching across the sand. In the distance, the dog zigzagged from cholla to cholla, stopping to piss on a tumbleweed. A roadrunner dashed across the gully. The curtain so thin after all.

Josie sat on the bed in number 4, smoking a ciggie. The sunlight shone bright and cold through the open door. She knew it was time to leave. There was nothing else to do but pack up and head home. And yet, how could she leave this place where he'd made his end? She sat up against the rickety headboard and picked cholla spines out of the bedspread, flicking them into the ashtray. Maybe she should take up knitting. Something quiet and productive. She didn't want to go back home, back to the empty house, as if Michael had fallen through a hole in the ice and just disappeared. But she couldn't drag his raw death through her days like this, like a giant bleeding moose head. Michael had made his choice. He wasn't dragging anything now. This wasn't her death. It was his. That was the sad and honest truth. Though it would stay with her, it

would be more like a black onyx heart on a silver chain, worn privately, under her clothes, close to her body, all her life. The guilt, the beauty, everything. It wasn't over, it had only begun.

From where she sat, leaning against the plywood headboard, she could see the manager's office through her open door. The girl was already up, working in the laundry room. That busy little form, bending in the darkened room at the elbow of the motel. How alone she was. This terrible place. Terrible yet mundane. Hell was perfectly simple. Just a few walls in the middle of nowhere. Just another part of the labyrinth.

Josie abandoned the bedspread, ground out her cigarette, and pulled her boots on. Feeling strangely thin and pure in the clear winter sunlight, she walked down to the laundry room. That dryer smell. How he loved that. The memory so clear it stunned her. She ducked into the warm darkness, dropped the key to number 12 on the neat stack of towels the girl had just finished folding. "I'm sorry you got mixed up in this. I wanted to thank you."

The girl snatched the key, dropped it into her sweater pocket, not looking at Josie. "He gets up soon. I must put back." She started for the door.

Josie put her hand on the girl's arm. "Listen, I

don't know what's going on here, but I'm leaving in a bit. Why don't you come back to LA with me?"

The German girl stared at Josie. "To LA?"

"Why not?"

Storms followed one another across the girl's face "I . . . I know no one. What would I do there?"

As if only movie stars lived in LA, as if nobody sewed sleeves onto dresses or fried chicken or cleaned rooms in cheesy motels in a town of eight million. "Sleep on my couch. We'll find you something."

Josie didn't think the German girl could get any whiter, but she'd been mistaken. "*Bitte.* Please. I cannot." She shrugged off Josie's hand and ran into the manager's office, shut the door.

Josie laid her face on the warm towels, pressed her nose there, waiting for the girl to return. When she didn't, Josie went back to her room. She washed her face, brushed her teeth, tried to do something about her matted hair, spit on some toilet paper and wiped at the raccooned mascara under her eyes. No wonder the girl didn't want to go with her. She looked like she'd slept on Hollywood Boulevard.

She assembled her guitar and her schoolbag, smoothed down the bed and hung the towels in

the bathroom. She washed off her sunglasses in the bathroom sink. She opened the curtains to the morning light, pocketing the roach clip. She knew she couldn't control what happened with the German girl, any more than she could control Michael or Meredith or anyone else. All she could do was try moving a stone. She could feel the girl now, hiding from her, beyond the door of yellow panes, probably wishing to Christ this wild-haired girl had not offered her a way to leave, making her feel her own gutlessness and fear that much more.

Josie waited a few minutes longer, fooling with "Big Butter and Egg Man" on the child-sized guitar, but still the girl didn't come, and Josie was awake, hungry, ready to be on the road. She had done all she could do here now. It was time.

She carried her things over the gravel to the short end of the L and packed up the Falcon. The manager's door remained closed, hospitable as a barbed-wire fence. So she got in, started up the car, ran it for a minute, giving the ancient engine a chance to warm up, rattling and shaking in the cold. She had to admit to herself, the girl wasn't coming. She too had chosen her labyrinth.

She turned on the radio, Buck Owens, and put the car in gear, backed and then headed down the drive, past the gate of the Paradise Inn, signaled left, and pulled out onto the highway. The sun behind her. Heading west. She had no idea what time it was, before eight for sure, on a Sunday morning. Even if she stopped for breakfast in Banning, she'd be home by noon.

She was about a hundred yards down the highway when she saw the girl in her rearview mirror, running down the drive of the Paradise and out onto the highway, a pink bag over her shoulder, her braids flopping in the early morning light. She waved her arms in the air as if Josie were in a plane, waving her down. Josie reversed down the empty two-lane, and the girl threw her bag in the back and hopped in, that mousy thing glowing bright as a lightbulb. She watched out the rear window as the Paradise grew smaller.

Turning front again, she threw a green book on the dashboard, about the size of a funeral prayer book. Josie picked it up. *Reisepass. Republik Osterreich.* She opened it on her thigh and spread it out in front of her on the wheel. A picture of the girl looking like a dog in headlights, just before the car hits it. *Wilma Rutger.* Wilma. Wilma and Josephine. Well, okay then. Okay.

Acknowledgments

I'd like to thank those who gave so generously of their care, love, and attention during the writing of *Paint It Black*. Muchos abrazos to the Three Musketeers, writers David Francis, Julianne Ortale, and Rita Williams, for their unceasing insight and encouragement, that willingness to read a scene just one more time. Many thanks to my wonderful readers Trudie Arguelles, Charmaine Craig, and Gus Reininger, who helped me see the forest again, when I could only see leaves and twigs.

Grateful thanks to my generous informants: Brazil-based concert pianist Ilan Reichtman and Peter Stumpf, principal cellist for the LA Philharmonic; artists Enrique Martinez Celaya, Greg Colson, and Lucas Reiner; art models Nancy Keystone and Melinda Ring; Warren and Leroy at

Diamond Towing; Lia Brody; the Skirball Museum, for their remarkable exhibition *Driven into Paradise,* which gave me a rare look into the world of the European exiles in Los Angeles in the Thirties and Forties; Anthony Hernandez, Director, Los Angeles County Department of Coroner; and the many websites supporting survivors after suicide, particularly 1000 Deaths.

I want to thank William Reiss, my agent, and Asya Muchnick and Michael Pietsch, my editors at Little, Brown, who stuck with this book through its long hard journey. No words suffice. And most of all, I thank my daughter, Allison, who has had to deal with such an awkward and demanding sibling on a daily basis — thank you for putting up with me.

About the Author

Janet Fitch, a Los Angeles native, is the author of *White Oleander,* an Oprah Book Club selection. Now translated into 24 languages, the novel was the basis of a movie by the same name. Her short stories have appeared in journals such as *Black Warrior Review, Room of One's Own, Rain City Review,* and *Speakeasy.* She received the Moseley Fellowship in Creative Writing at Pomona College in 2001 and currently teaches fiction writing in the Master's of Professional Writing program at the University of Southern California. She lives in Los Angeles.